Caught within the fire does a human heart grow cold.

Forsaken by the power that once gave it life to hold.

But life persists and mankind finds new purpose in the storm.

Nature shows no mercy; beneath ashes rage is born.

Field of Ashes

By

Nicoline Evans

Author: Nicoline Evans – www.nicolineevans.com
Editor: Kiezha Ferrell – www.librumartis.com
Cover Design: Dan Elijah Fajardo –
                       www.behance.net/dandingeroz

And a big thank you to everyone who has offered me support (in all ways, shapes, and sizes) during this entire process.

An ode to new beginnings

Chapter 1

Cedar City, Iron County, Utah

Through the ash he rose. Cellar doors unlocked and opened for the first time in six months, Sergei Lamorte stepped into the world above. He was greeted by ash and shadows. The world was not as he remembered it—everything was covered in layers of volcanic residue. It was a harsh, new environment that felt foreign, and when his head hit the open air, ash filled his lungs. He returned to the cellar's safety with a cough.

"The air is impossible to breathe."

"We need to get to the garage," Dante said with frustration. Brother to Sergei and co-owner of Lamorte Welding, he was sure their work gear would help them survive the harsh elements above.

"Suck it up and make the walk," their father, Oskar, urged. "Your mother and I are tired of living in this dungeon."

"The garage isn't far. We can use our shirts to guard our mouths and noses," Dante suggested.

"Alright, let's do it," Sergei conceded.

The men lifted the collars of their t-shirts to cover the bottom halves of their faces and embarked upon the ashy wasteland. After closing the cellar door behind them, they trudged through the new terrain. The air was thick, visibility was poor, and the world reeked of sulfur and death. Neither could see, but they made it to the garage from memory. They raised the large door, stepped inside, and closed themselves in. The air wasn't as clean as the cellar, but it was better than outside.

"Grab everything," Sergei said as he caught his breath. "Goggles, masks, bandanas, jackets, gloves. It's all flame retardant. There's no fire, but this is obviously volcanic ash."

"You think it was Yellowstone?"

"Had to be."

"Look," Dante said, pointing out the window. Three of the five houses across the street were demolished. The weight of the ash caused the roofs to collapse. The brothers immediately glanced toward their parents' home, relieved to see the roof was still intact.

"We'll need to clear the roof first," Sergei noted. "We survived this far, don't want something careless to be our end."

"And once we get settled, we can reinforce it to make sure it's safe," Dante added.

The brothers gathered enough protective gear for everyone hiding in their shelter. In addition to their parents, they each had their wives and children waiting out the destruction with them below ground. Also housed in the small cellar were both Palladon brothers and their families. A total of twenty-one people were cramped together underground for six months and it was time to change the scenery. Neither Lamorte brother knew what they'd encounter as they ventured off their parents' property on Pinecone Drive and into Cedar City, but anything was better than the dingy, damp crypt.

When they returned to the others, they handed out gear and everyone suited up.

"Women and children, make your way into the house to see if it's livable. If we can clean it up, we'll stay. The sky will clear and when it does it's better that we are near our main welding garage. We might need to rebuild." Sergei led this initiative. "Men, we are going into town to assess the damage and collect food. Most perishables will be ruined, but there should be plenty of packaged goods that are still edible."

"I'm headed to the roof with the antenna for my HAM HF SSB repeater," Oskar told his sons with pride. "I'll get the rest of the equipment moved from the basement and into the kitchen. See if you can get the packs at the warehouse to work. You know my QSO. It's been a while since they've been used, but it's worth a shot."

"You got it," Dante replied.

The group parted ways and the men walked to town on foot.

"We should stop at our office while we're in town. See how it held up," Gerald Palladon suggested. He and his younger brother Kelso owned KGP Metals, which was the only company that mined for iron ore in Utah. The Lamortes and Palladons were family friends with a working relationship spanning more than fifty years. The Palladons mined and the Lamortes welded their product. Oskar Lamorte was friends with the Palladon patriarch, Paul Palladon, who passed away a year ago. The family bond was strong and the moment the earth started shaking, the Lamortes eagerly welcomed the Palladons into their shelter.

Main Street of Cedar City was littered with dead bodies.

"Why were they out here?" Benny, the youngest son of Kelso, asked as he cleared the dust that collected on his goggles.

"Looks like they tried to outrun it," commented Gino, the oldest of the three brothers.

"They were buried alive." Benny's eyes were wide with fright.

"Probably choked on the ash."

"Volcanic ash turns into liquid cement when caught in the lungs and mixed with moisture," Vincent, the middle brother in

3

this clan, informed the others. He had been a sophomore at Southern Utah University and was studying to be a meteorologist before the world ended.

"I wonder if it hurt," Benny speculated as he tightened the knot of the bandana covering his mouth and nose.

"What are all the sores on their faces and arms?" Gino asked.

"Looks like their skin was trying to eat them," 17-year-old Benny added with a shiver.

"Acid rain often accompanies a volcanic eruption," Vincent speculated, "but the pH levels are so low in acid rain that this effect doesn't make sense. It might make holes in their clothes, but it wouldn't eat away at their flesh."

"Nothing about what we just survived is textbook," Gino responded. "This wasn't nature, this was something else. Look at the damage! Every inch of the earth was revolting before this hit us. That acid rain was probably pure poison."

"But that breaks all the rules of science," Vincent protested.

"I don't think this storm played by any rules. It's freaking supernatural."

"The smell is gonna make me barf," Benny added with a heave.

"Fried flesh and death: the aroma of the new world. Get used to it, buddy," Gino said with a punch to Benny's arm.

"That's enough," Kelso interjected, silencing his sons. Their morbid conversation was making everyone uncomfortable. It was bad enough that they had to see the dead with every step they took; no one wanted to think about the nature of their deaths as well.

"Just be grateful it ain't you," Sergei said with authority. He took lead of the group and directed them toward the welding garage his father established as a young man. Oskar ran the

4

company for three decades before he and Dante took over. Sergei found the right key among the many attached to his key ring and opened the door. The inside of the garage was dusty, but breathable. The offices attached to the side were even cleaner. They entered the main office and regrouped.

"I want to convert the garage at my parents' house into a mini-version of what we have here. It might be a while before traveling will be safe and I want to avoid making more trips than necessary," Sergei explained. "Grab all the tools you can fit into these duffel bags. We can use the hand trucks and wheelbarrows to move the bigger items."

"Should we take the Bessemer Converter?" Dante asked.

"Not yet. Once the air clears we can start making new steel. For now, we can't mine for iron ore, so it's useless."

The men grabbed all the items deemed critical at this moment, keeping their focus on tools that would help them clean up and seal their new residence from the outside air. Benny and Vincent grabbed brooms and shovels and filled two bags each of supplies. Gino filled his duffle bag with tubes of caulk, a caulking gun, a putty knife, dust masks, tarps, drop cloths, various types of tape, and an assortment of hand tools. He also grabbed a large ladder he planned to carry over his shoulder. Kelso had a wheelbarrow full of extra welding outfits and goggles, while his brother Gerald lugged two trunks of industrial sized cleaning supplies. Sergei retrieved the HFPacks from the attic where Oskar stored all his old Navy gear and began fiddling with the dials. After a few minutes he was able to catch his father's QSO channel.

"Dad?"

"Serg! You did it."

"We haven't talked over this radio since I was a kid. I didn't realize you still had it stored away."

"I studied hard to pass the Extra exam and get my ticket. Just because you boys got older and didn't want to mess around on the walkies with me anymore didn't mean I was just going to toss it. I spent twenty years in the Navy, twenty years attached to these radios saving lives. You don't throw that away."

"Thank God you didn't, this radio will be a huge help."

"You guys getting everything you need out there?"

"Yeah, I think so. How's Marlaina and the kids?"

"Good. Everyone is doing just fine."

"We'll be back soon."

"Over and out."

Sergei smiled, absorbing a little of his father's nostalgia, and then threw the four radio packs over his shoulder and returned his attention to the other men. They worked hard to scour the garage and offices for all necessary items. Though the return trip wasn't long, it was emotionally taxing. The streets reeked of death and avoiding a trip back motivated everyone to gather as much as they could.

"Look who I found in the basement," Dante said as he ascended the cellar stairs, followed by three dirty and emaciated young adults.

"Killian?" Sergei asked.

"Sorry," Killian stammered, "We had to break the handle off the back door of the garage to get in, but we had no cellar at my parent's place and this was the only spot I could think of."

"Shut up and get over here," Sergei said, pulling the young man into a hug. "I'm glad you're alive." He released his young employee and scanned his companions. "Where are your parents?"

"They refused to come," Killian shrugged. Tears rolled down the face of the young female standing behind him. "You know how religious they were."

"Are these your siblings?" Sergei asked.

"Yes, Dominic and Brianne."

"Nice to meet you both." Sergei looked back to Killian. "You look awful. Is this your first time out of the cellar?"

"Yeah, we ran out of food a few days ago and were living off crumbs for a while prior to that. The cellar was stocked, thankfully."

"My dad's been prepping for the end of times since WWII. You were smart to hide here."

"Yeah, we had plans to leave today or tomorrow to look for food, we just got stuck in a rut down there. We were growing delirious from the lack of food."

"And the dark," Dominic added with a shudder.

"The oxygen was so thin we could barely breathe, let alone think," Brianne said. "When we heard your footsteps overhead, it took a minute to realize we weren't dreaming."

"Then we came at the right time," Sergei consoled the Halloran siblings with a smile.

"We almost died out there," Killian continued. "We were watching Yellowstone explode on the news with our parents, and when the power went out I knew we had to find better shelter. We begged our parents to come, but they believed this was judgment day. They insisted it was God's will and said they were content with whatever fate He chose for them. So we ran. By the time we reached the garage the ash was half an inch thick on the ground and the acid rain had begun. We broke in before the rain burned us too bad, retreated to the cellar, and tried to clear the ash from our throats. It's been months and I *still* feel like I have ash in my mouth."

"You're lucky to be alive. When you follow us back you'll see the devastation it caused. It's an atrocity out there."

"I have no doubt."

"Let's get out of here. We still need to get food before we can head back," Sergei instructed.

Everyone was already loaded with supplies, so each of the Halloran siblings grabbed an empty wheelbarrow for the food haul.

They left the Lamorte warehouse and reentered the ash-covered landscape. Dante led the march toward Lin's Marketplace. The automatic glass doors were stuck open, so the entire grocery store was covered in ash.

"Cans and packaged food only," Dante shouted as everyone dispersed. The three wheelbarrows were left at the entrance and the men traveled back and forth through the aisles to fill them.

"This is awful," Gino shouted for all to hear, "but it's probably a good thing most people died. If they hadn't, there probably wouldn't be any packaged food left."

Sergei went straight for the pharmacy, where there were two pharmacists, an old woman and a college-aged male, huddled together lifelessly in a back corner. Their embrace was rigid post-mortem and topped with inches of ash. The sight enraged Sergei—every corner he turned revealed more death. It was cruel, unjust, and he couldn't control the fury it stirred within him. He tried to contain his anger, tried to focus on the task at hand, but the seed of resentment was planted, despite his efforts to remain rational. He collected all the antibiotics and medicines he recognized, as well as every inhaler available for his asthmatic daughter, then left the pharmacy and rejoined the others. The raid was successful, so they headed back to the Lamorte family home.

Sergei seethed inside, unable to pluck the roots of his growing animosity. There was no plausible justification for this tragedy and all the lives it took. There was no one to blame or punish for the fallout. But Sergei desperately sought retribution for the countless lives wasted. He wasn't sure how, or when, but he'd make this world right again, for those who survived and in honor of the fallen.

Chapter 2

The White Room

Cross-legged and focused on the forest floor, Juniper traveled through her mind to the designated spot where she and her Champion sisters met. It took a few tries to make the trip without Aria's guidance, but she was better at the mental journey now. Over her many visits in the past month, she managed to dig a path in her mind and keep it clear so the trip back and forth wasn't nearly as messy or hard to navigate. The process of retreating into herself and meeting the physical forms of her sisters inside her mind never ceased to amaze. The power hidden in the human brain was astounding and Juniper was grateful to be tapped into a small part she never knew existed before.

"You did it!" Aria exclaimed and gave Juniper a hug. Her long white hair was curled and she wore a short, feather-covered cocktail dress. Juniper looked down at herself to see she was wearing a ball gown made of olive silk and tulle. The bodice was covered in green amethysts and the heart-shaped neckline was lined with emeralds. Her long brown hair was wrapped in a bun and she wore a platinum tiara molded to look like small deer antlers. Every time she entered the White Room she found herself in brand new attire, as did the other Champions. Sometimes it reflected their moods, other times it indicated more. She took off the tiara to examine it and wondered what it meant.

Sofyla surfaced from a mound of sand. Her eyelashes were tipped with gold and her gown was made of gilded lace. The armband she wore was designed in the image of a rattlesnake.

Eshe arrived, right behind Sofyla, accompanied by a blast of smoke. Her dress resembled the coloring of a leopard and her hair was tied into tight, long braids. She looked around with regal authority as she assessed the state of the meeting.

"Why is everyone always late?" she asked.

"I'm here, I'm here," Coral announced as she materialized. She spat out water as she spoke. She wore a long, lavender satin skirt and a bra top covered in pearls. *"Zander and I were testing how long we could hold our breath under water. I'm at four minutes now."*

"That's incredible," Aria commented in awe.

"Where's Marisabel?" Eshe asked.

Coral shrugged. *"I assumed she'd be here already."*

"What about Sahira?" Eshe asked Aria.

"They are still making the trip to Nepal. The path the air spirits cleared for them is long and winding, but I suspect we will be united within the forthcoming week."

Dust accompanied Sahira's abrupt arrival. *"Sorry I'm late, I had to stop the progression to meditate. None of my followers understand this place, or how I meet you all here."*

"They don't need to understand it, they just need to respect your need to come here," Coral replied.

"They do. It's just been a long and cold journey. The air spirits cleared a trail through the lingering polluted smog, but the snow and remnants from the arctic freeze remain. It's frigid and tiring." Sahira took a few deep breaths and then finally relaxed. *"It'll be over soon."*

"Imagine being me or Marisabel," Coral commented. *"We are forced to remain in Antarctica until the air everywhere else clears. It's a frozen hell."*

"When do you think the spirits will let you relocate?" Juniper asked.

"I'm not sure, but hopefully soon. Thankfully we have solar panels heating the Davis Station, but those only generate minimal warmth. My people and I are doing okay, but Marisabel is struggling. She hates it there."

"I really do." Marisabel appeared wearing a simple blue dress and a headband made of scaled sequins. *"The cold has frozen the hope in me. I can hear the river calling to me, but I cannot respond. It's too far away."*

"Your aura is so sad," Aria commented, tears brimming her eyes for Marisabel. *"I will talk to the air to see if they can help in any way."*

"They can't," Marisabel responded monotonously. *"But thank you."*

"Maybe you just need Zaire by your side," Eshe offered. *"Those united with their Second seem to be much better off. If the core spirits tell me it's safe, I will lead him to Cape Town and help him and his followers find a boat for safe passage."*

"Don't." Marisabel shook her head. *"He is better off with you in the tunnels of Africa. I don't want to subject him to this sorrow. This place will tear the life from him too."*

"You need support," Juniper insisted. *"Let him help you."*

"I'd be lost without Riad," Sofyla said. *"He's helped me in ways I never dreamed I'd need."*

"I can handle it on my own," Marisabel objected. *"I will not subject another to my pain just so I can feel a little better. I will unite with him the moment we are freed from Antarctica."*

The space hushed as the Champions silently conceded to Marisabel's stubborn sadness.

"Onto the purpose of this meeting," Eshe announced. "As we are all aware, none of nature's spirits were able to recruit enough human souls after the purge. They will not be able to rebirth the environment magically. This means large areas of the planet are still smothered in ash and buried beneath igneous rock. I can attest that the majority of land in Africa is rock-covered, and most of it hasn't even hardened yet, which means there are large pools of magma still swirling beneath."

"The air spirits are trying to clean as much of the volcanic residue from Earth's air as possible, but they don't have nearly enough spirits to help as they thought they would. They can only do so much at a time," Aria added.

"The trees can't grow organically until the sun returns," Juniper advised. "And without a little magic, I don't imagine they'll be able to burst through the ash or hardened magma."

"Why can't Gaia intervene?" Sofyla questioned. "Surely, She has the power needed to fix our environments."

"Hasn't the soil told you?" Coral asked. "Gaia is gone. We are on our own now."

"The soil spirits haven't talked to me much since I went underground."

"Gaia only steps in when the fate of Earth is critically threatened," Coral continued.

"Gaia won't let us fail," Aria informed the others.

"And if we do fail, that's when She'll intervene again. For now, it's up to us to make things right," Eshe added.

"And if we fail, are we spared in the next global cleanse?" Sofyla's mistrust radiated. "Or will we be written off and replaced with a new solution?"

"It doesn't matter because we aren't going to fail," Aria reassured her.

"How can you be so sure?" the soil Champion questioned. *"It feels like we are being set up for disaster. We cannot make the trees grow or cleanse the air on our own, and the spirits of nature are so sparse they cannot tackle enough square footage at a time. My people will not survive if we are forced to live out the remainder of our lives underground."*

"Enough," Eshe said to stop Sofyla's spiral of paranoia from infecting the others. *"We just need to be patient and obey the orders given to us. Sahira is the only one granted permission to abandon her original post and join another in a new location. Everyone else must stay in their safe zones."*

"Why is she allowed to leave but the rest of us aren't?" Marisabel asked.

"The mountains told me it has to do with our evolution," Sahira explained. *"The mountain disciples need to progress at the same speed as Aria and those who are with her at the top of Mount Everest."*

Marisabel huffed in annoyance, but said no more.

"Has anyone else been testing out their new, gifted skills?" Coral asked.

"I've been toying with the dusty soil in these caves," Sofyla responded. *"We are out of our element, but I've managed to move loose fragments of the ground without using my hands. While traveling to meet Eshe, during a moment of intense fear, I created sand geysers that saved the lives of my people. I haven't experienced anything quite that strong since, but I know it's in me."*

"I'm on the verge of touching lava," Eshe contributed. *"My hands grew calloused on their own and when I noticed the change, I gave it a try and got really close. I can hover my hand millimeters above it for a full minute, but I'm training myself to withstand more."*

Juniper listened in awe and disappointment; she hadn't experienced any evolution in her capabilities.

"I'm not sure if mine is a gift or in my head," Aria jumped in, *"but whenever it gets too windy up here I focus on shifting the wind away from us and within a half hour or so, it usually ceases."*

"I've noticed no changes except sorrow," Marisabel said with harsh bluntness.

It caught the others off-guard, but resonated with Juniper.

"Don't feel bad. I haven't experienced anything new either."

Marisabel glanced over at Juniper with a half-smile of gratitude before her newly adopted expression of grave unhappiness consumed her face once more.

"They will come," Aria reassured them both.

"I need to get back to my people," Sahira expressed. *"They are stopped in the snow while I am here."*

"Return to them," Eshe said in understanding. *"In fact, we all should depart. This was a good check-in. I feel as though we are all on the same page. Let's meet again in a month."*

The Champions all mumbled in agreement and began disappearing. Juniper watched as their element accompanied their departures. Eshe left in flames, Sahira in dust, and Sofyla in sand. Aria was swept away like a breeze and both Coral and Marisabel dissolved like water. Juniper stood in the White Room, alone. The Hall of Mosses had morphed from a safe haven to a prison of volatile energy and she wasn't excited to return. Though the majority of her people supported her, there were many who questioned her leadership and were now vocal about their discontent.

She took a deep breath, inhaled the serenity of the White Room one last time, and then slipped from the recesses of her mind back to reality.

Chapter 3

Hall of Mosses, Olympic National Park, WA

Juniper opened her eyes to lush verdure. The bright green landscape of the Hall of Mosses was vibrant as ever. Though the sight gave her peace, those residing alongside her did not. Roscoe, Clark, Jeb, and Irene were her only solace among the wavering loyalty. She trusted Carine, Misty, Teek, and Brett to stay by her side, but often found them entertaining the polluted conversations. They became her best friends during their time working together at The Dipper Dive and she prayed they never abandoned her. Watching them listen to the propaganda Phineas Devereaux spewed made her nervous, so she kept her distance, aware that when the time came they'd need to pick a side on their own.

She stood and took a deep breath. The aroma of the forest lingered in her mouth and set her mind at ease. She was safe, regardless of the doubts presented to her daily. She would be okay.

Confidence restored, she left her private quarters and entered the shared living space of the large group.

Her friends and their families were huddled together over a campfire. After Roscoe's reemergence, she finally found the time and energy to get to know all the families better. Teek's parents, Paul and Tess Devron, were rebels just like their son. Both were covered in tattoos and wore the vests and patches of the motorcycle club they were part of before nature attacked. They were also hunters, so when the animals returned, they'd be helpful in procuring food.

Brett was enduring the end with his three younger sisters. Similar to Juniper's situation, their parents died when they were young. A boating accident took their lives when Brett was eighteen and he had taken care of his sisters ever since. Chloe, Kallie, and Brynn were in their early twenties, very sweet, and extremely helpful around camp. They adored their older brother and it warmed Juniper's heart to watch how protective they were over him. Anytime he went on an expedition, they swarmed and smothered him with motherly concern. Brett feigned annoyance, but his love always shone through.

Juniper learned that Carine's mother was an immigrant from Austria. Though she and her older sister, Lara, didn't speak Austrian, Marisse had a wonderful time sharing stories with the Böhme family in their similar native tongues. The Eberles and Böhmes grew tight and often stuck together.

Misty rarely left her family's side. Her parents, Kurt and Olivia Courtland, owned a commercial fishing boat, so they had lots to talk about with Jeb and his wife, Alice. Her brothers were also a nice addition to the group. Cole and Ian were in their early thirties and had started an architect and lumberjack company together. They were tall, sturdy, and invaluable to the prolonged survival of the group. While it was ironic that their profession was killing trees, they did not do so with malice. They valued nature, more than most, and their livelihood was eco-friendly. They never stripped a forest naked, or cut down trees that weren't needed. Juniper initially worried that the trees would be angry with their presence, but after getting to know them she imagined their auras glowed a brighter green than most. Misty's younger brother, Luke, stayed in the family business of fishing and was already plotting ways to acquire protein through the ocean. Aquatic life hadn't returned to the rivers yet, so he was eager to get a crew over to the Pacific to try and fish there.

Juniper prayed they all stayed by her side after the clouds cleared, but the more time that passed, the more she suspected the Devereaux family had turned them against her.

The Devereauxes were foul and she regretted bringing them into the forest more and more each day. Their disapproval of her started quietly, but now they expressed their distaste openly.

"Are we expected to live out the rest of our lives like wild animals?"

Juniper took a seat next to Luke Courtland and tuned into the latest gripes from Claudia Devereaux. Though Juniper was now present, Claudia continued unabashed.

"There are ways to rebuild. Sources of energy to tap into. We can make our lives easier and recreate some semblance of normalcy."

"You're missing the point," Juniper responded. "The reason we are stuck in this predicament is *because* of the way we lived in our old lives. If we go back to our old ways we are only repeating the damage and setting ourselves up for another purge. And if we prove ourselves incapable of growth, I suspect we won't be so lucky the next time nature attacks."

"It's absurd that you think trees are capable of intelligence," her husband Phineas chimed in. "They are inanimate. They do not make choices. You telling us that they, along with the oceans, soil, air, and whatever else, decided to eradicate us only proves you're unfit to lead."

"Then how do you explain what happened?"

"Science and bad luck."

"Believe what you want. I've already proved to the lot of you that I'm not crazy." She looked at her friends and their families as she spoke. "I am trying to keep you alive. I led you to the only safe spot in the area and I've never suggested any ideas that would harm you or your loved ones. I don't know why you're so quick to listen to their negative contributions, but it's insulting."

"Juni, it's not that we aren't grateful for what you've done, but it's been six months and it's hard to understand why you wouldn't want to rebuild," Brett said.

"I want to rebuild, I just don't want it to be anything like what we lost. We can use nature to make shelter, and when the sun comes back we can use it for energy. I do not want to return to dirty energy sources just to make our lives comfy. Not at the expense of nature."

"We are such small numbers though," Carine protested. "I can't imagine our minimal usage of resources would cause any significant dents. The planet is enormous and we are a mere blink in the big picture."

"That type of thinking landed us here today. Small doses of pollution eventually turn into large doses as we multiply and the masses get cozy in their luxuries. There is no controlling the damage once it spreads. No stopping people once they gain power from dispensing destruction. We cannot repeat old patterns."

"That's a little dramatic. We are only talking about small ways to make surviving a little easier," Misty tried to explain.

"They've been talking about coal, oil, and natural gas energy for weeks, which are the filthiest options available. They are only thinking about their own comfort, not the practicality of anyone's safety or surviving long-term. You trust these people?"

She threw an arm at the Devereauxes. "They will be the first to abuse the luxuries if they are granted that option. And they'll convince others to indulge and expand the moment they get comfortable. Mark my words, if we go that route it will backfire."

Her friends went quiet, so Phineas defended himself.

"You assume the worst of us, which is a shame. We only want to better the lives of everyone. I fear we will never see eye to eye on this matter and that you will find yourself terribly alone when this lot wakes up and realizes you aren't a messiah. Their lives will be plagued by misery under your lead."

"You might trick them to follow you, but I promise it will only lead to their demise. Maybe not in their lifetime, but in their children's and grandchildren's. You cannot see far enough ahead to realize how your actions will shape the fate of future generations. And the most appalling part is that you want to make the same exact mistakes as our ancestors. We already saw how this plays out."

"We'd regulate," Claudia insisted.

"You'll lose control, just as humans have before." Juniper shook her head in disgust. "I'm done with this argument."

She walked away and no one followed. She wasn't sure if anything she said sunk in or if her words were wasted.

As she walked down the main trail of the Hall of Mosses she noticed her outburst had caught the attention of many. She still had to become better acquainted with the people Roscoe brought back with him and worried this was a terrible way to start. Though maybe they were more likely to understand her reasoning—they were the ones who heard her message through the trees.

Roscoe was with a group a few campfires south. She took a seat next to him, rested her head on his shoulder, and listened as Bernard and Martha Landry discussed how they met fifty years ago.

"She was the prettiest girl at the dance," Bernard explained. "So I got up the courage to ask her out and she said yes. I picked her up in my father's Pontiac Chieftain and took her to the movie theater to see Doris Day in *Lullaby of Broadway*."

"That's when he became a habit with me," Martha said with a smile.

"Oh, I can't break away, I must have you every day. You're getting to be a habit with me," Gerald sang.

"It's true," Martha said, squeezing his hand with affection.

"Those were simpler times," Gerald said with a sigh.

Everyone around the campfire nodded and reveled in their loving nostalgia. Love stories of the future would look much different.

Juniper glanced up at Roscoe with a tender smile. She was grateful to have him by her side.

The Wolfe family approached with food and joined their gathering.

"Phineas is infuriating," Birk, patriarch of the Wolfe family said as he opened a can of hot dogs and handed them out.

"I had to leave that group a few minutes ago," Juniper agreed. "He's spreading poison."

"Same old? Or something new?" Roscoe asked.

"Same old nonsense," Laurel, matriarch of the Wolfe family answered as she combed the knots out of Noah's hair with her fingers. "They'll end up repeating tried and true mistakes if they leave us to recreate the world as Phineas desires."

Noah waved his mom off his hair and moved to sit next to his oldest brother. Dedrik handed Noah a stick with a speared hotdog before speaking.

"I don't trust that family and I'm having trouble understanding how others do. They know nothing about the forest, nothing about surviving. They'll die out there before they ever get a chance to build whatever warped empire he's dreaming of."

"What bothers me the most is that my friends and their families have been listening to him," Juniper said.

"Don't read too much into that," Roscoe advised. "I doubt they are buying it. They're probably just listening for something to do. It's boring out here and his crazy talk is entertaining."

"I hope you're right."

"I am." He kissed the top of her head then pulled her closer.

"Is it cool if we go for a walk?" Baxley asked. He was the second eldest son of the Wolfe clan. Dedrik was 24, he was 21, Wes was 18, and Noah was 16. They were very close and even though the forest had morphed since the attack, they remained skilled at navigating the new trails.

"It's fine by us," Laurel spoke on behalf of herself and Birk.

They looked to Juniper for final approval.

"Just don't go far," Juniper requested.

The boys stood and departed. They stopped asking if they could ride the dirt bikes weeks ago, aware that the conservation of gasoline was imperative for when the sun returned.

Juniper hadn't heard from the trees in a while and suspected she wouldn't hear much moving forward. The Champions knew their mission and no longer needed consistent guidance from their elements. The job was to survive, in a simpler manner, and give humanity a second chance on Earth. All she waited on now was word that the world beyond the Hall of Mosses was safe to traverse. She'd like to hear it from the trees, but was willing to take the news however it arrived. Tensions in camp were electric and she wasn't sure how much longer she'd be able to keep everyone happy. If they didn't make a move soon, she feared their loyalty might shift to those willing to risk the dangers of the outside world.

Chapter 4

Cedar City, Iron County, UT

The thick layers of ash covering the interior of the Lamorte home were cleared and the small group was able to seal all windows and doors to prevent more from entering. Sergei took extra bed sheets from his parents' linen closet and made signs that he hoped would attract other survivors. Over the front door he hung the largest.

WE SURVIVED.

He, Killian, and the Palladon boys hung the remaining signs around town, which instructed all other survivors to find them at the Lamorte's home address. The larger their group became, the better their chances of survival would be. More hands to build and gather food, more minds to help brainstorm the best ways to endure. In time, Sergei hoped they'd attract many survivors and repopulate Cedar City. He was ready to lead; all he needed was a populace.

While he and the younger guys scoured the town for survivors, his brother Dante led the initiative on the home front. After cleaning, clearing, and sealing their parents' home, they began work on the neighbors' homes. Any house with a standing roof was fair game. After scouting the neighborhood and finding multiple families dead within the safety of their homes, they realized the air was more toxic than they initially thought. These people should have survived, yet they perished with relatively clean air and food left in their pantries. No one knew if the air was most poisonous during the initial ashfall, or if the toxins still lingered, but they planned to treat the air as a threat until it could be proven otherwise.

With a thoroughly sealed home, it was safe to move about without protective gear. Once they got the other homes up to their safety standard, new survivors found would be able to live there. Vincent warned the group that all water was likely poisoned by the acid rain and ash, so the group survived off bottled water, which was plentiful since their area appeared vacant of survivors. And when they eventually ran out, meteorologist Vincent and dooms-day prepper Oskar were both prepared to teach the group how to filter, bleach, and boil the polluted water outdoors.

There was no electricity or running tap water, but the gas lines to the house were still connected and they were able to use the gas stove. With fuel siphoned from abandoned cars, they filled their generator with gasoline. This gave them moments of light and warmth in the dark of night.

Sergei and the boys returned from their second trip into Cedar City with no new recruits.

"No one?" his wife Marlaina asked.

"None yet, but our signs are up," Sergei answered. "I think we need to break into houses in case people are still hiding and afraid to surface."

"We better do that soon," Killian advised. "I imagine most people did not have fully-stocked doomsday cellars like Oskar's. If they haven't surfaced since the volcano blew, they've surely died from starvation by now."

"Maybe they're still hiding in their cellars, but have gone in and out to grab food from the local stores," Renita, Dante's wife, suggested.

"The only footprints on Main Street are ours," Sergei responded.

"And there weren't any when we trekked to the warehouse a few days ago," Dante added. "Ours were the first."

"There are other streets in town," Marlaina said with a scoff. She pulled her young children in close. "Main Street isn't the only way to get places."

"Of course not," Sergei said to soothe his wife's annoyance. Their children were young, but old enough to understand what was going on. Xavier was eight and Lucine was six. They absorbed every word the adults said and it showed through the fear on their faces.

"Are we the only people left on the planet?" Xavier asked.

"Absolutely not." Sergei knelt down to address his son. "We found Killian, Dominic, and Brianne after we came out of grandpa's cellar. We will find more, don't worry." He kissed Xavier's forehead before continuing. "No more talk about this in the house," he instructed the other adults.

Both Palladon families had older children who were able to process their grim situation without it altering who they were fundamentality. Dante's children were all under the age of four and it would be an issue eventually, but not yet. Sergei was the only one currently faced with this dilemma and he did not want this frightening reality to shape who his children grew to be. He wanted them to be strong and unafraid; he wanted them to see the world as a place where anything was possible. Death and mortality were not issues he wanted them worrying about, and he would do everything in his power to craft them a childhood full of wonder and joy.

The other adults respected his wishes and all conversations about their progress in finding survivors took place away from the little ones. Sergei had to remind the young Palladon boys a few times to keep their voices down or take their conversations

26

elsewhere, but it wasn't long before Gino and Vincent started to remember on their own. Whenever they didn't, 13-year-old Rebecca Palladon, daughter to Gerald and Peggy, was fierce in reminding them. She had grown very close to the little Lamorte children and always scolded her older brothers and cousins whenever they forgot to talk quietly about topics that were scary to the kids.

"I swear," she huffed to Sergei on a particularly boring afternoon. "You'd think they lost their brains. Just the other day, Lucine and Callista were playing with their dolls and Dennis and Oliver barged into the room talking about what it would feel like to choke on ash!" Rebecca crossed her skinny arms. "I smacked Dennis on the head."

Sergei smiled at her young assertiveness. "I appreciate that. They will learn. How old are your brothers again?"

"The twins are 15, though they act younger than me."

"Keep up the good work. The little ones are already forced to grow up in a world much scarier than anything we were ever faced with. I think it's best we let them enjoy their innocence for as long as possible."

"I agree." Rebecca spoke like an adult trapped in a pre-teen's body.

"You're a good kid," he patted her on the shoulder and she smiled with pride. A compliment from Sergei was a big deal. Before she could say thank you, Dennis and Oliver stampeded into the room, chasing each other over antique baseball cards they found in the attic.

"They're mine! I found them," Oliver shouted.

"You shouldn't have put them down," Dennis provoked as he ran around the couch.

"Whoa," Sergei said, stepping in and grabbing Oliver by the collar.

"That asshole took them from me!" he protested.

"Watch your mouth."

Oliver looked to the left to see Dante's kids on the floor, playing with toys.

"Sorry. But he did."

"I don't care who took what. Those cards belong to my father. Give them to me." Dennis obliged begrudgingly. "You're too old to behave so childishly. I'd expect this sort of behavior from the kids, not two 15-year-olds."

"He's just been so annoying lately," Oliver expressed.

"You're so freaking sensitive," Dennis said as he rolled his eyes.

"These are tough times and emotions are high," Sergei said, letting go of Oliver. "I can completely sympathize with that. But it's time to grow up and deal with your issues like men. I imagine half the things you're fighting over are petty and ridiculous, considering the current state of the world."

"They are," Rebecca chimed in. "I heard them fighting over a dead girl this morning."

"That's a horrible thing to say," Oliver snapped at his little sister.

"Well, she probably is."

"Enough," Sergei demanded, then focused back on the twins. "Being a teenager is hard, I've been there, but the world has changed and neither of you get the luxury of a hall pass. By all means, find fun during these dark times if you can, but the fighting needs to stop."

Being chastised by Sergei was just as devastating as a compliment from him was uplifting.

"Sorry," the twins said in unison.

"I'll talk to your dad. I'm certain he will agree."

The boys departed, giving each other slight shoves as they left.

"Boys," Rebecca huffed, with a disapproving headshake before she sat on the floor and resumed babysitting Dante's little ones: Callista, Freya, and Gideon.

Sergei hoped they could clear up some of the neighbors' homes soon so the families could spread out. Living under one roof was growing tiresome.

Lucine ran into the room, frazzled.

"Daddy," she wailed, "I lost Dewdrop! He's missing!" Her big blue eyes were filled with tears. Her stuffed bunny had been by her side every night since she was born.

"Calm down," Sergei said, lifting his tiny daughter into his arms. "We will find him."

"What if he's hurt," she sobbed.

"I will find him for you. I promise." He kissed her forehead and put her down.

"You *promise*?"

"Yes."

She looked up at her dad with serious concentration before wiping the tears off her face with her sleeve. She took a deep breath through her inhaler, then silently accepted her father's promise and went to play with her younger cousins and Rebecca.

He left the living room and could hear Dennis and Oliver still arguing in the distance.

"Those twins are something else," Killian said after rounding the corner and bumping into Sergei.

"Dante and I were like that too. I can't remember how old we were when we finally grew out of it."

"Dominic and I still have moments, and we're in our late twenties," he laughed.

"Gino, Vincent, and Benny don't seem to have that tension."

"Every family is different," Killian shrugged.

"I hope my kids get along with each other and their cousins as they get older. Living in this new world will be tough enough; constant bickering will only make it worse. They need each other, especially once I'm no longer around."

"Don't worry about those things yet. You're doing a great job. And by the time they are old, I imagine all the plans you've been talking about will be in motion and they won't have it nearly as hard as we do right now. You're doing the best you can for them."

"I'm trying."

Killian was young, but insightful. "While the state of the world makes me happy I don't have any kids, seeing you with yours makes me wonder if I'm missing out. I don't have your unyielding motivation or determination to survive. I'm just trying to live day to day while you're thinking fifty years from now. It's inspiring to watch and it makes me really glad I'm with you during these times."

"That means a lot, Killian. Thank you." Sergei grabbed his shoulder with sincere gratitude.

"No problem. You're a good leader. We are lucky to have you."

"That sentiment goes both ways." Sergei changed the topic. "How's the neighborhood cleanup going?"

"Good. We're almost done with the house next door."

"Fantastic." Sergei began planning how he'd present Gerald and Peggy with the option to move there, he didn't want them to be offended. Perhaps he'd just ask if the twins could relocate. Sergei smiled to himself—it was possible Gerald and Peggy would love that idea too.

Sergei made his way to the kitchen and found Marlaina and Renita carving into the surface of a large dining room table.

"Your father had this extra table in the basement," his wife explained. "It's big enough to put in the middle of the road and we thought that might stop others in their tracks better than the sign on the door. Think about it: Most people are going to have their faces wrapped to stay safe from the ash. With heads down, they're just trying to find where the ash ends. How often do you think they are looking up?"

"Not much," Renita answered the question for him. "So this may help."

Sergei was impressed. "It's a good idea. I think you should put it at the intersection rather than in the street in front of the house. Write your message on both sides; you can probably use a marker on the bottom side since the wood isn't as dark. Were there any other unused items down there that we could write similar messages on?"

"Probably. It's like a thrift store down there," Marlaina answered with a laugh.

"We can always take extra furniture from the neighbors' houses too," Renita added.

"Okay. Good work. I want to add these pieces throughout town. Let me know when you're done with this table and I'll work on acquiring more to mark up."

The Lamorte women recruited others to help craft messages onto furniture. The table and two old mattresses were done by early afternoon and their husbands took them out and placed them at the surrounding intersections. On each item they also drew arrows pointing toward the Lamorte house.

"It would be hard to miss us," Kelso said through his facemask.

"The roads were free of footprints till we made ours," Gerald commented as he readjusted his goggles. "I don't think anyone has been out here."

"We've been inside two of the neighbors' houses so far and each had its dead residents inside," Dante added with defeat. "Dad refused to listen when I tried to tell him."

"There wasn't even room for another small child in that cellar, let alone a grown adult," Sergei insisted.

"That's why he didn't want to hear about it. He wanted to save everyone, but couldn't. He feels guilty."

"He shouldn't."

"I would," Dante objected. "Actually, I *do*. How is it fair that we are alive and they are all dead?"

"It's not fair, it's just the fact of the matter." Sergei was growing aggravated and began the trek back to the house. He shouted through his facemask and the men followed. "I feel awful that so many people died, but guess what? We are going to keep finding bodies and there is nothing we can do about it. Best way to deal is to grow calloused to the sight. They aren't going away. This is our new reality. We didn't kill them, and I refuse to feel survivor's remorse. There's too much work to be done and I will not let useless guilt slow me down."

The men stayed quiet as they reentered the house. Sergei did not follow. He crossed the ash-covered yard and entered the neighbor's house. Gino was in the living room, sweeping up the last remnants of ash with a broom.

"Hey, Mr. Lamorte," he said in greeting.

"I told you to call me Sergei."

"Sorry."

"Where are your brothers?"

"Vinny is upstairs sealing the windows and Benny is in the basement. My Aunt Peggy came by before and said you guys were looking for furniture to mark up. Benny has been down there ever since."

Sergei headed for the basement and found Benny on the floor, carving a message into a wooden desk.

You are not alone. Join us: 15 Pinecone Drive.

"How many have you made?"

Benny jumped in shock.

"Holy crap, I didn't realize you were there."

"Didn't mean to startle you."

Benny caught his breath, then answered. "I've made four; two desks down here and two coffee tables upstairs. I figure we can draw arrows on them once we place them."

"Good idea. Are you up for a trip?"

"Right now?"

"Yes. I want to get these placed as soon as possible."

"Sure." He stood and helped Sergei transport the desks to the first floor. They filled Gino and Vincent in on the task and the boys prepared to exit the shelter of the home. With bandanas and goggles in place, they left the neighbor's house and retrieved hand trucks from Oskar's garage. It wasn't easy to maneuver through the thick ash, but they made their way.

Main Street used to be a busy highway with four lanes of traffic traveling in both directions, but now it was abandoned. Empty cars were left stranded and sat scattered and useless, covered in ash.

"We should take the time to clear this road," Vincent suggested as they struggled to push the hand trucks north. "It would be nice to have a section of town we could walk through without getting all this crap in our boots."

"You want to broom all of Route 130?" Gino asked with amusement. "You realize how long that would take?"

"What else do we have going on?"

"The house clean ups," Benny answered.

"I'd rather be out here, grooming the routes we use for food."

"It's not an awful idea," Sergei said in contemplation. "Spending that time out here would give us a better chance of finding others. Vincent, you'll lead the street cleanup. Gino, you keep up the good work on the neighborhood homes."

The boys accepted the delegation of responsibility and returned to silence. Pushing the hand trucks was a chore and it took most of their energy not to drop the furniture.

"Can we stop in the Ranch Store?" Gino asked. "I need to restock supplies for the cleanup."

"Yes. And let's leave your coffee table in the highway in front of the store," Sergei instructed. "You run in with Vincent, and Benny and I will take care of the placement."

The older brothers entered the store, while Benny used his switchblade to carve an arrow into the coffee table. It pointed in the direction of Pinecone Drive.

"Do you really think others survived this?" Benny asked once his arrow was complete.

"Yes. Maybe not in this town, but elsewhere. I'm sure of it."

"Do you think we should leave some signs on Veterans Memorial Highway in case out-of-towners take the big roads to pass through?"

"Absolutely. As you start clearing the roads, make an obvious path from the highway to Route 130. If travelers see a manmade path, they'll know others survived."

"Good idea."

"Once that path is done, let me know and we can place a sign out there."

Benny nodded in understanding and his brothers returned with a wheelbarrow of supplies. They wore expressions of deep grief.

"There was a pile of bodies in there," Gino explained.

"A pile?" Sergei asked. "How is that possible?"

"It was more of a huddle," Vincent explained. "Looked like they were gathered close as the ash hit. They died sprawled all over each other."

"Smelt rancid," Gino shuddered.

"First time I smelt anything more powerful than this smoky, burnt debris."

Sergei dropped his hand truck and marched toward the Ranch Store. The boys followed, unsure what he was doing. Upon entering the store, the sight of corpses was immediately visible. Sergei took a deep, aggravated breath, then grabbed matches and lighter fuel from the camping section and headed for the bodies.

Without speaking, he doused the pile, struck a match, and let the flame land on the nearest body. The crowd of bodies caught fire and burst into an inferno. Sergei and the boys took a step back as the flames grew. The ground was concrete and the ceilings were three stories high, so there was nothing for the fire to latch on to as the bodies burned. The increasing smoke billowed out the large front doors, which were left ajar.

Sergei was done feeling guilty every time he saw an innocent life ravished by nature. He was done pretending that it didn't bother him. If the bodies weren't there to see, the discomfort he felt would stop.

The Palladon boys stood at a distance and watched in horror as the human flesh bubbled and decomposed with speed. The smell intensified as the top layers of skin vanished and the yellow fat underneath started to drip out. The sight was nightmarish.

The bodies weren't burning fast enough, so Sergei dumped the entire canister of lighter fuel onto the burning corpses. He shook the can with fury, spreading the liquid everywhere. The flames rose in height and the bodies began to burn faster.

"Can we leave?" Benny asked, but no one heard him. The smell crept beneath his facemask and he ran out of the building, heaving. Gino took notice of his youngest brother darting from the scene and followed him out. Vincent tried to get Sergei's attention, but failed.

Sergei could not take his attention away from the blaze of carnage. The flames reflected in his eyes and the world around him disappeared. He was numb. The traumatic sight paralyzed his senses—all noise vanished and he was unable to smell the ripe, volatile odor of burning flesh. He developed tunnel vision around the smoldering bodies and could see nothing else.

"Sergei!" Vincent shouted for the fifth time, but received no response. Sergei was in a daze. Disgust, sorrow, and confusion lined his heart, but the most potent emotion he felt was that of newfound power. Watching these people burn gave him a sense of accomplishment, and he wasn't sure why. Each time he realized he was enjoying this cremation his senses grew duller.

He could not rationalize this unnatural reaction and could only stop those thoughts by shutting down.

Vincent's words weren't working, so he punched Sergei in the arm. The impact knocked him back to reality and he looked at Vincent with confusion.

"What the hell?" Vincent asked, perplexed.

"This is awful." Sergei wore a look of revulsion, for what he had done and how it made him feel.

"I know, let's go."

Sergei finally broke free of his debilitating stupor, but could not lose the perverse feeling of glee. Something foreign lived inside him; a dark seed inside his heart had finally received water and was beginning to bloom. He tried to ignore the feeling, tried to shake it off so the boys would not see, but in the quiet of his heart, rage continued to grow.

"Let's get these signs into town," he said, unwilling to address what he had done.

No one talked as they spaced their furniture from Main Street to Thunderbird Way. On the walk back, their hand trucks were easier to drag through the ash and Gino finally broke the silence.

"You could've warned us, you know."

"Yeah, a heads up would've been nice," Benny added.

"Sorry," Sergei apologized. "It just seemed like the right thing to do and if I didn't take action immediately I might've lost my nerve."

"Makes sense," Vincent said, still shaken.

"We need to start burning all the bodies. Not only in memoriam, but because the smell is only going to get worse as the ash clears and the bodies rot. We need this town to be clean and livable again. I want the women and children of our families to enter Cedar City and feel at home." The boys said nothing in response. Sergei went on. "I know it's a gruesome task, so I'll lead this initiative."

Gino, Vincent, and Benny nodded in agreement and followed Sergei. As they went by the Ranch Store again, smoke billowed out of the adjacent front doors.

"We should make sure the fire is out," Sergei suggested and detoured toward the store. The boys begrudgingly followed. As he and the boys entered, the sight was different, but just as awful. There were no more flames, only small patches still smoldering, and the bodies were melted. Some were burnt to the bones and the dust of their carcasses merged with the ash that killed them months ago, others still had simmering skin attached.

"We will need to make sure they burn longer so all the flesh is gone," Sergei thought aloud with peculiar ease.

"Why can't we just bury them?" Benny asked.

"You want to dig hundreds of graves?" Sergei asked. "This is faster and much more respectful than digging one giant hole for a mass burial."

No one argued with him.

"The fire is out. Let's head back," Vincent suggested, afraid Sergei would linger too long again.

The smell of scorched flesh followed them for miles. Benny kept lifting his mask to spit in hopes the odor would leave his throat, but it continued to linger. Tears welled in his eyes as the taste of death sat at the back of his tongue.

"It's stuck in my mouth," he finally exclaimed in panic. He ripped off his mask and began scraping his tongue.

"Put your mask back on," Vincent demanded. He picked up his younger brother's mask, shook off the ash, and forced it back onto his face.

"It's terrible," Benny sobbed.

"I know. I can still smell it too."

"It will go away," Sergei consoled.

"What if it doesn't?"

"It will. Man up." The boys were not used to this side of Sergei. "And don't talk about this at the house. It's too gruesome to share with the group. I will get your father and Gerald on board, and we will take care of the rest."

The boys nodded in understanding, and Vincent led the return journey back to the house. He wanted to get away from the smell, the memory, and Sergei. His brothers followed close behind.

Sergei was adapting to their harsh, new reality the best he knew how. If the others were not capable of performing the cruel tasks needed to handle these situations, then he had no problem stepping up and being the bad guy. His end goal was normalcy, for his wife and children, and he would do whatever was necessary to bring back the world he once knew.

Chapter 5

Hall of Mosses, Olympic National Park, WA

Days in the forest passed slowly. The children of the group found ways to stay entertained, but they weren't allowed to travel far to do so and their rambunctious behavior intensified the tension amongst the adults.

"Beatrix!" Hanke Böhme shouted in his thick German accent. He and his family assimilated well since being saved in Maple Grove. "Stop riling up the little ones. Learn to behave more like Liesel." Beatrix shot a perturbed look at her older sister who sat quietly under a far-off tree with a book. Liesel was thirteen, two years older than Beatrix.

"But Vati, she's so boring. I want to play with the other kids."

"It's driving the adults mad. Come sit with me, and bring your sisters."

Beatrix obeyed, dragging her younger sisters along and leaving the other kids behind. She sat cross-legged next to her father and plopped her head into her hands. Odette and Emeline sat next to her, but continued to play by drawing pictures in the dirt with sticks. After a few moments of quiet defiance, Beatrix found herself helping her younger sisters perfect their crude sketches.

"What is that supposed to be?" she asked Emeline, who was five.

"You."

"I have five fingers on each hand, not four." She grabbed Emeline's stick and fixed the hands. "And you made my hair look like spaghetti."

Emeline grabbed her stick back, hastily destroyed the picture, and then threw a tantrum.

"Did you really need to do that?" her mother, Felicie, asked as she picked up Emeline to hold her on her lap.

"It looked nothing like me!" Beatrix argued.

"She's little. You know better," Hanke chastised.

Beatrix rolled her eyes and surrendered. She watched the older kids continue their game of freeze tag without her. Noah was "it" and was chasing Valerie and Cade Culver. The boys had bonded over their near death experience while traveling to the Hall of Mosses and they'd been good friends ever since. The teens darted over and around the adults who were scattered through the wide trail. Everyone expressed outward aggravation when the adolescents leaped over where they sat, but the game did not stop and Beatrix looked on with longing.

Noah was on Cade's tail when Zaedon Devereaux extended his leg and tripped him. Cade flew forward and smacked his face on a nearby tree trunk. When he sat up, his face was covered in blood.

"What's wrong with you?" Noah hollered as he ran to Cade's side.

"I was over it," Zaedon said, disinterested in the pain he caused.

"You really hurt him." Noah helped Cade stand and instructed he tilt his head to stop the blood flow.

Roscoe and Juniper were making their regular rounds along the long trail when they came across the scene.

"Whoa. What happened here?" she asked.

"Zaedon tripped him," Noah answered.

"It's true," Beatrix shouted from her spot next to Hanke. "I saw it."

41

Zaedon groaned. "They were running around like wild animals. In and out of the trail, jumping over us. Sometimes stepping *on* us. I had enough."

"We really need to move out of here," Juniper said to Roscoe, exasperated. "They should be allowed to have fun and act their age, and there just isn't enough space here."

"Have you heard from the trees?" he asked under his breath. She shook her head in response.

"Let's get you to the medical kit," Juniper said, addressing Cade. "And next time, find a nicer way to ask them to stop." She shot a disapproving look at Zaedon, who was twenty-two and knew better than to trip an eleven-year-old. The young man shrugged, unconcerned by his own cruelty.

Valerie and Noah followed as she led Cade down the trail to where she kept the medical supplies. Irene, Mallory, and Zoe were there, keeping Irene's little ones entertained with picture books they had grabbed from town.

"What happened?" Irene asked as they approached.

"Cade fell. We need to clean him up."

Irene helped Juniper tend to the boy's wounds as Noah and Valerie watched.

"I wish my brothers would play," Noah said during the silence. "If we got the older guys in on it, it would turn into an epic game of manhunt."

"They know better," Juniper replied. "There isn't enough space for a game like that, and though I trust you and your brothers in the woods, I can't allow the others to wander off for a game. When we relocate, everything will be better," Juniper reassured him.

"I like it here, I just wish everyone was allowed to spread out more."

"So do I. I'm hoping to get some good news soon." She smiled down at Noah, who was sixteen and on the verge of becoming a young man. She was happy he still held onto some of his youthful nature and did not want her rules to rush him into adulthood. She wanted the younger generation to hold onto their playful spirits for as long as possible; their youthful energy was a critical counter-balance to the pessimism of the adults.

After Cade's face was tended to, they all separated. Irene returned to her children, Valerie and Cade went back to the spot where their parents were set up, and Noah whistled an old show tune Bernard taught him as he searched for the older couple. He had taken an interest in them since things settled in the woods, and if he wasn't off gallivanting with his brothers, or playing games with the younger kids, he was often with Martha and Bernard.

The air spun around Juniper's head, tossing her long curls in every direction.

Juniper, Aria said. *There are issues in Antarctica.*

What do you mean?

Coral just reached out to me and said that Marisabel is in trouble. She isn't eating and has completely lost touch with her connection to the water spirits.

How does she know? I haven't heard from the trees in a while. I'd consider myself out of touch too.

No. She is out of touch as in she no longer cares; no longer feels bonded. She has expressed that she feels abandoned and it's beginning to show as resentment toward the spirits.

Why on earth did they have to send her to such a cold place? Juniper asked.

I'm not sure. I haven't heard anything from the air regarding whether or not we can leave. Neither has Sahira.

Did Sahira get to you okay?

Yes, they lost a few along the way. Some were dear friends of mine from home. There was a deep sadness in Aria's voice. *But we are together now, and Sahira is overjoyed to be reconnected with her sisters. It will be okay.*

I'm sorry for your loss.

Our lives will never be easy. I've come to terms with that. We are going to watch a lot of people we love die.

Juniper had not thought of that. With their gift of eternal life, many would come and go as they lived on. It was a foreign concept; one she imagined she'd never get used to.

Still, Juniper went on. *It happened much sooner than it needed to.*

I'm just happy to finally have Erion by my side. It really helps to have my Second here. I'm strong on my own, but having another person absorb some of this responsibility is life saving. I feel so much lighter now that he is here.

Marisabel really needs her Second. Is she the only one without one at this point?

Her and Eshe, but Eshe is currently finding a route to her Second beneath the earth.

How is Sofyla doing down there?

Okay, but she is ready to leave. She is running the show since Eshe is often nowhere to be found.

I can't believe Eshe is trying to get all the way to Hawaii underground. Juniper stated in amazement. *Is it even possible?*

I imagine she is getting guidance from the core.

And the spirits haven't told her when they think it'll be safe for the rest of us to leave our current locations?

If they have, she hasn't mentioned it. She isn't easy to reach. She's so hell-bent on reaching Keahi that I think she's ignoring my attempts to reach out.

I hope she would tell us if they said anything. She must know that Marisabel is suffering.

I think she would. After hearing about Sahira's struggle to reach us in Nepal, I honestly believe it just isn't safe enough to leave. The only reason they got to us without perishing is because the air cleared a path for them. If they hadn't, they would've died the moment they descended Mont Rose.

This is awful, Juniper said, thinking of her unhappy followers.

And I have a feeling it will be some time before we are allowed to leave, Aria added. *Sahira and I are beginning to suspect we won't ever be allowed to leave the mountain. Every time I hear from the air they instruct me to climb higher.*

Higher?

Yes. I think that's how we will evolve. When we first got here, it was almost impossible to breathe. We've been here for half a year and the altitude isn't nearly as crushing as it used to be. The cold has become easier to bear as well. It's weird. I don't know why they'd want us to evolve in this manner. A human living up here is impractical.

Maybe they don't know how this will all pan out, so they are just preparing you for a long stay up there.

I hope you're wrong, Aria groaned.

So do I. 'Cause that means the rest of us will be stuck in one place too.

Marisabel won't last much longer. Aria sounded distressed.

Let's hope for a miracle.

Aria wished her goodbye and then disappeared. When Juniper tuned back into the world around her she was greeted by chaos. Down the trail, Brett was throwing a fit. She raced to her friend's side to see what was wrong. As she reached him, his angry rant was redirected to her.

"You said we were safe here!"

"You are. What happened?"

He grabbed his youngest sister's arm and brought it into Juniper's view.

"Look at Brynn's arm."

A rash bubbled with gooey pus from her wrist to her elbow. The skin was raw and appeared to be disintegrating.

"When did you get that?"

"A few days ago," Brynn answered. "It started off as a small cut on my wrist and it grew to this." She was holding back tears. "It hurts so bad."

Juniper did not know what to do. Brett was inconsolable and she was not a doctor. She'd never seen an infection so severe, nor did she know what could've caused it.

"Let's try some antibiotic. We have a ton stocked up from our raid of the pharmacy."

"This forest is not safe," Phineas Devereaux declared. "We must leave before it begins to eat the rest of us alive."

"Stop your nonsense," Clark retorted. "It's just an extreme case of poison ivy. No need to scare everyone."

"I've never seen poison ivy look like that before," Hanke Böhme said with skepticism. "And I was an avid outdoorsman as a young man in Germany."

"Nether have we," Cole Courtland said on behalf of himself and his brother Ian. "We are lumberjacks. Wood and plant borne rashes are our specialty. Whatever Brynn has is new to us."

"Everyone, calm down. I'm sure a round of antibiotics will help." Juniper had no idea if what she said was true, but desperately hoped so. She called out to the trees inside her mind, hoping they'd tell her what the infection was and how to heal it, but she received no help.

Days passed and the antibiotic did nothing. Brett's rage was now uncontrollable and the Devereauxes were gaining increased leverage over Juniper. With each day that Brynn's arm got worse, the others became more inclined to believe that the forest was no longer safe. Brynn's visible and undeniable pain only enhanced the issue. By the end of the week, the group was discussing how to leave, with or without Juniper. Carine pulled her aside to warn her.

"It's not good," she advised her longtime friend.

"What do I need to do to change your minds?"

"Present us with a better plan."

"I don't have one yet. I just need a little more time."

Carine sighed. "There's no one stopping you and the others from joining us."

"I can't do that."

"And we can't stay here," Carine insisted. "Not while there's no progress being made. Living out the same day over and over while waiting for a sign that might never come feels wrong. There has to be more we can do. We need to take the initiative."

"The trees haven't abandoned us, I promise."

"I believe you, I just need to move on." Though Carine's voice was filled with remorse, her conviction was final. "I hope we can stay friends."

"I doubt we will ever meet again," Juniper replied harshly, her defenses up.

"Well, you'll remain my friend despite the distance."

Tears filled Juniper's eyes, but she did not break. Carine did not know how to ease her act of betrayal. Nothing she said made her friend feel better. "Just so you know, this has nothing to do with Phineas. None of us are buying what he's selling; it's just that he's offering a plan that involves leaving this claustrophobic forest. We don't want to leave you, but there's no other option. I'll stay loyal to you till the day I die."

"Not a tough promise to keep. It's dangerous out there." Juniper maintained her stoic façade through wet eyes.

"I wish you'd wish us well," Carine pleaded. "I don't want to leave you like this."

"Then don't leave."

Carine forced a hug on Juniper, burying her in an embrace, hoping that one day she'd be forgiven.

They parted without saying anything more.

Juniper marched through the forest, looking for the others.

"Please don't go," Juniper begged Misty in private.

"Juni, living here isn't practical. We know it's ashy out there, and we plan to stay protected from the air, but there has to be something better, something more suitable."

"I promise you, this is the safest place in the vicinity. The only other safe spots are in the mountains of Nepal, the caves of Africa, and Antarctica."

"I don't believe that. This world is too large for those to be the only remaining spots fit for human life."

"Please don't go."

"We don't blame you. In fact, we are incredibly grateful that you even got us to this point. But it is time to move on." Misty's expression was distraught. "We wish you would come with us."

Juniper tried to remind herself that they never experienced the power of the trees inside their heads; that they did not fully comprehend all she went through to save them. They did not hear from the other Champions, they did not have access to anything beyond the Hall of Mosses. She thought she had done enough to make them believe, but their faith in her leadership was not strong enough. They were determined to survive without Juniper's aide.

"I am so afraid you will die out there. What if I can't find you once we are allowed to leave this place?"

Misty shrugged, unable to answer without confirming Juniper's fears.

"We will miss you," Misty stated.

Juniper experienced a surge of rage. She stormed down the path to find the Devereaux family.

"How do you expect to keep all these people safe? It's on you if they die out there."

"Anything is better than here," Claudia scoffed.

"We have family in Arizona," Phineas added. "I highly doubt the ash reached that far south. We will follow the major highways to get there."

"You are fools."

Roscoe stepped in. "She saved your lives, and this is how you thank her? By convincing the majority of people she saved to abandon her?" His face was red with fury.

"I'm so sorry, Juni. We do appreciate what you've done, but it doesn't make sense to stay," Carine said apologetically.

"It isn't safe here," Brett added. "We need to find land that isn't surrounded by death. We are trapped here. Everything around this forest is ruined."

"There has to be civilization beyond this little spot that is still functioning," his sister Chloe added. "I don't believe everyone died. I don't believe every inch of land is uninhabitable. We just need to be proactive and search for those areas of sanctuary."

"How do you plan to heal Brynn's arm while you're out there, trying to survive the elements?" Juniper asked, her anger trembling. "You'll be too focused on staying alive to tend to her wound."

"It is something we will deal with day by day," Phineas answered with confidence.

"You will die out there!" she demanded.

"No, we won't," Phineas insisted. "You are overdramatizing the conditions. The only danger we will encounter is ash."

"You saw the attack of the trees. How could you possibly believe it will be so simple to survive? There is no telling what you'll face out there."

"You are living in fear, and that's no way to carry on," Claudia scowled.

"I am living by the order of the trees. We have not been given permission to leave, which means it isn't safe. They are protecting us. We must heed their advice."

"There she goes with the trees again," Zaedon scoffed.

"You've lost your mind," Genevieve added.

Juniper was tired of defending her sanity.

"Who is going?" she asked the entire crowd.

The Devereaux family raised their hands first. Brett and his sisters were next. As the hands slowly rose into the air, Juniper took note: Carine and Misty both planned to leave with their families, along with the Böhmes and Culvers.

"What about you, Teek?" Juniper asked, trying to mask the betrayal she felt.

"My parents and I are staying."

She nodded in appreciation, then turned to the others. "As for the rest of you, if you don't want to be here, then please leave. You're no longer welcome." She glared at Carine, Brett, and Misty as she spoke.

"Now you're kicking us out?" Claudia asked with a laugh. "How rude. After all the patience we've shown, to tell us to leave without giving us proper time."

"These are her friends you're taking away," Roscoe snapped. "People she loves and cares about. Why linger? Why drag it out? You've been talking about leaving for weeks, so do it already."

He stormed away, taking Juniper with him. The rest of the group remained, shell-shocked by this development. Their group was about to be cut in half.

When Juniper woke up the next day, those who planned to leave were gone. Only Roscoe, the Wolfe family, Clark, Roscoe's father Aldon, Jeb and Alice McLeer, Teek and his parents, Cindy and her husband, and the ten people Roscoe brought back with him from Gold Bar remained. The group was small and the sight of the significant loss hit Juniper hard.

Juniper's fear outweighed their betrayal. She imagined all those who left would die within the month. It was heartbreaking and she couldn't help but feel like their doomed fate was her fault. She worked so hard to save and convince them to trust her, and now they were gone.

She leaned heavily on Roscoe during the days following their departure, and his sturdy presence temporarily helped fill the void. The journey moving forward would be tough, but she was grateful for those who remained by her side.

Chapter 6

Eshe Ahikiwe, Champion of the Core, made swift progress through the underground tunnels of Africa. When she reached the coast of Senegal, she was forced to move slower and more carefully as the depths were greater and the walls much thinner. The spirits led her toward the volcanic islands of Cape Verde where she would be able to rest for the first time in weeks. Navigating the tunnels beneath Africa was easy compared to the non-existing ones beneath the Atlantic. One wrong move and she'd break the wall separating her from the ocean, flooding her entire underground tunnel system. The spirits guided her every move, instructing her where to carve as she widened certain passageways with her pickaxe. She was safe under their supervision.

When she reached the archipelago of Cape Verde, she climbed upward and took a break in a cave beneath the Pico da Cruz Mountain. Her body relaxed as it readjusted to a more comfortable altitude. She was evolving with rapid speed; she could already descend to unimaginable depths, withstand extreme heat, and move at incredible speeds.

Keahi, she called telepathically to her Second. *Are you there?*

I am here. His response came in less than a minute. *Where are you?*

Right off the coast of Senegal, in a cave beneath the island of Santo Antão. I'll be out of African territory by tomorrow.

You ought to rest. You haven't stopped moving since you left the others.

I feel fine.

That's not the point. You are pushing yourself too hard. I'm not going anywhere. Stop racing.

Marisabel and I are the only two Champions without their Second. She is deteriorating while the others are thriving. I think you can understand why I want you by my side.

Gee, I thought you were just eager to meet me.

Of course that is part of it, but I do not want to face a similar fate as Marisabel. I was starting to feel like she does when I made the decision to take this matter into my own hands. I have to take action. It's the only thing that makes me feel better. I do not know when the world above will be safe for you to get to me, and I'm not risking my mental stability while waiting. There is no time to fall apart. You are the only other human connected to the core. I need a partner as I lead my people.

You realize I cannot travel back with you. I tried to descend to the deeper tunnels of Mount Loa and couldn't. My head felt like it might explode in that air pressure.

I already told you I'd travel back and forth.

That's unfair to you.

It's good practice and more time spent immersed in my element. This trip is speeding up my evolution. Did I tell you that I found a pocket of lava before I left Senegal and was able to touch it for a second? Her voice was filled with excitement.

No, you hadn't mentioned that.

It was amazing. Once we are together I think these abilities will begin to show in you too.

A piercing pain shot down her forearms and into her fingers. She raised her hands to inspect them, but saw no sign of injury. She ignored it.

How are your people? she asked. Before he could answer the pain returned, much worse than before, and caused her to howl in agony.

What's wrong? Are you okay? Keahi asked, but Eshe was too engulfed in the excruciating sensation to answer. The pain was so intense that the dim underground world went black.

Answer me! Keahi demanded, but she couldn't. The best she could do was breathe. If she tried to talk she feared she might choke.

Through the pain she stood and tried to climb higher where the air wasn't so thick and sparse. She stumbled and fell many times, but eventually made it to higher ground. Light from the world above came through some of the cracks and made it easier to see. Her hands were covered in blood.

She caught her breath and managed a few words.

My fingernails. They're gone.

Gone? How?

I'm not sure.

There was a long pause.

You need to get back to the others, Keahi demanded. *Sofyla can help you.*

Eshe said nothing. All she could focus on was swallowing the severe pain. But he was right; moving forward was not an option until her nails grew back. The pain was too severe and the exertion of adrenaline would only make them bleed more.

Eshe? Please tell me you are going to head back to Kilimanjaro.

Yes. I will go back. But as soon as I am healed I am continuing my journey to you.

Fine. For now, focus on healing. Reaching me isn't worth sacrificing your health.

I'll check in from time to time.

Eshe broke the connection and stumbled backward. She caught herself on a nearby wall, intensifying the pain the moment her hand touched rock. Tears fell, the first she had shed in months. She wiped them off with the back of her wrist and began the long trek back to where she left the others.

I'm coming back, Eshe said to Sofyla.

It took a few minutes for Sofyla to tune in.

Is everything okay? Have you run out of food again?

I'm injured.

What happened?

My fingernails fell off. I'm not sure how, but I can barely breathe it hurts so bad.

Take your time, don't overexert yourself.

Eshe broke the connection without responding.

She could manage no more than a slow walk for the first week. She had moved so fast on her trip out that she still had enough water to sip slowly from her water pack. She couldn't eat because it hurt too much to touch anything, so her energy depleted fast. By the start of the second week, her fingers stopped bleeding and were coated with thick scabs. This lessened the pain and she was able to pick up her pace. She began eating again, but found her stash was thin. She only allotted enough food to correspond with her previous pace. Now that she was moving at half-speed, her supplies weren't lasting.

On her way toward Hawaii, she had stopped in Bamako, Mali to replenish and hoped she could get that far again before her body broke down completely.

The spirits of the core guided her in the right direction. Though she was able to reach great depths, she still did not have the proper internal compass to navigate these tunnels on her own.

She made it to Mali and ascended into the dark, ash-covered world above. She pulled the scarf out of her small knapsack and wrapped it around her face before leaving the safety of the cave and entering the city of Bamako.

In town, she was not only able to find food, but also a pharmacy where she gathered some supplies to help her aching fingertips. Once back in the cave, she lathered her scabbed fingernails in antibiotic cream, wrapped her hands in gauze, then carried on.

It took another three weeks before she reached Kilimanjaro. The trip back took double the time. When she trudged, exhausted back up the narrow trail toward where the others waited, she felt a sense of relief. She wasn't alone anymore.

Sofyla waited by the cave entrance.

"Eshe! I'm so happy you are back. We've missed you."

"I missed all of you too. How is everyone?"

"Everyone is fine. How are *you*?" She gently picked up one of Eshe's hands and examined the gauze, which was blood-drenched.

"As good as I can be."

"Did you fall?"

"No. There's no logical explanation. I was just sitting down, talking with Keahi, when this killer pain shot down my arms. When I looked down, my fingernails were gone."

"That's strange."

"No kidding."

"Let's change your bandages and get you fed. Some of your followers have been traveling back and forth into Arusha to get us food. I think they've depleted the town's small supply though, so they might need to start heading in a new direction."

"Nairobi isn't a terrible walk. A few days, tops. I grew up there and I am positive it will have plenty of non-perishable goods."

"I'll let them know." Sofyla sat Eshe down and began unwrapping her hands. As the gauze came off, the damage was revealed. Her hands were covered in dry blood, the scabs were torn off and stuck to the gauze, and in their place were newly forming nails.

"Your nails are growing back weird," Sofyla noted. "Why are they so dark?"

"I'm not sure." Eshe raised her hand and examined her new fingernails. They were dark brown and a texture she did not recognize. Their regrowth came with pain, but she assumed it was the scabs tearing off.

Her thumb nail was almost fully grown. Though it was still tender, Eshe took the risk and touched it. It was rock hard. She looked up at Sofyla with wide eyes.

"It's not a regular fingernail."

"What do you mean?"

Eshe turned to face the rock wall and dragged her sharp-edged thumb nail down its surface. She pressed hard and made a long, indented mark in the rock surface.

"Whoa," Sofyla gasped.

"Feel how hard it is."

Sofyla gently touched the surface of Eshe's nail in awe. "What is it made of?"

"It looks like granite." Eshe raised her hand so it caught some of the natural light that filtered into their cave. The moment the light touched her fingertips, a metallic shine bounced off them. "Maybe iron as well."

"That's incredible. Once they heal you won't need that pickaxe anymore."

The thought hadn't crossed Eshe's mind yet, but Sofyla was right. This was another evolutionary gift.

"This will help me get to Keahi faster."

"And wherever else you want to go. It's too bad the rest of your followers haven't been given the same abilities as you; they could help you carve paths all over the globe."

"In time," Eshe said softly with wonder. This was only the start of even greater possibilities than she ever imagined. She had eternal life, she'd live through multiple generations of core-born humans. They'd evolve in her image and one day, she'd rule the underground.

Chapter 7

The stench of burning bodies decorated the city. Sergei, Dante, Kelso, and Gerald continued to cleanse the town of the deceased, but with so many cadavers to eliminate, the emotionally exhausting afternoons seemed never-ending.

After seeing how people died huddled together in public places like The Ranch, Sergei realized there would be similar scenes all over town. He wasn't wrong. In the span of one week they eradicated five bodies at Taco Time, fifteen at the department store, and fifty at the Days Inn Cedar City.

Today they planned to tackle the local Baptist church.

The pews were filled with lifeless bodies and Sergei led the men down the aisle, counting as he walked.

"I got eighty."

"Same," Kelso confirmed through the bandana wrapped tightly around his face.

"The odor is seeping through my face mask," Gerald noted.

"Let's get to work," Sergei said, also hoping to escape the pungent odor.

"We can't burn them in here, it'll take the whole building down," Dante observed. "We ought to drag them out back."

"All eighty of them?" Kelso asked.

"You want to burn the church down?"

"No, but that's a lot of dead weight. No pun intended."

"All the other places we've gone had tile or concrete floors. This place is all wood. I'm not trying to have the wrath of God on me for burning down one of his holy establishments," Dante said with stubborn conviction. "I've been through enough."

59

"We'll bring them outside," Sergei concluded, walking to the nearest body and maneuvering it to the ground. He then grabbed the dead man's ankle and lugged him outside. Dante, Kelso, and Gerald followed his lead.

Two hours later, they had a large pile of bodies in the backyard of the church. Sergei circled the heap, emptying two full canisters of lighter fluid, then tossed a match onto the pile. The bodies ignited immediately and the smell intensified.

Kelso gagged and walked away, while the other three watched the bodies burn. Gerald and Dante wore expressions of compassion, while Sergei's stare was concentrated. Most days he felt an eerie sensation of power during the burnings, but today, all he felt was rage. Being forced to do this, over and over, was maddening. He was angry that his fate had been reduced to something so morbid and he felt himself growing hardened to the atrocious sight.

"There's nothing more to do here," Sergei announced. "There's no wind, no weather; the flames have nowhere to spread and will extinguish on their own."

The men returned to 15 Pinecone Drive without speaking. Upon entering the Lamorte family home, they separated to be with their families.

Sergei found Marlaina reading a book to Xavier in one of the spare bedrooms. He stood at the doorway, watching for a moment, before his wife caught sight of him in her peripheral.

She stood, leaving Xavier to read the next paragraph on his own. She wiped the dusty residue off Sergei's head and then gave him a kiss.

"We are reading Harry Potter. He's doing pretty good reading it on his own," Marlaina said with pride.

"Where is Lucine?"

"She went to the bathroom. She'll be back."

Sergei nodded. "I'll let you get back to your story."

He kissed her forehead and left the room.

He hadn't eaten since breakfast, which was almost eight hours ago, so he went to the kitchen to refuel. He turned the gas stove on with a match, opened a can of soup, and poured it into a pot. As he stirred the contents, his gaze shifted out the window.

The backyard was filled with mountain mahogany shrubs and two large Utah juniper trees. They were dead beneath the ash. Sergei squinted to take a closer look and noticed there were toys hanging from the branches of the trees. An even closer look and he spotted a small heap on the ground—a little body dressed in a purple nightgown. His heart stopped.

Soup still boiling, he ran out the back door without any shoes or protective face gear. The ash entered his airways immediately, causing him to cough and almost choke. He pulled the collar of his shirt over his mouth and took the smallest breaths possible while running.

He reached the little mound of purple to find Lucine, unconscious and not breathing. As he picked her up he noticed her stuffed animal, Dewdrop, hanging from one of the branches.

With his baby girl nuzzled in his arms, he ran back into the house.

"Marlaina!" he shouted, coughing out more ash. The desperation made his voice crack. He didn't know what to do; he didn't know how to help his little girl.

Marlaina rounded the corner and at the sight of her daughter lying unresponsive on the kitchen table, she burst into sobs. She raced to their side and tried to determine what to do next.

"Why is she like this?"

"She was outside!"

Oskar and Edith raced upstairs from the basement. Edith pulled her daughter-in-law away from Lucine's side as Oskar stepped in and began using the CPR training he learned in the Navy. He worked hard to resuscitate his granddaughter, and after a few, frightful minutes, succeeded. Lucine awoke with a gasp and as the oxygen reentered her lungs, tears of shock fell down her cheeks.

Marlaina and Edith ran to Oskar's side and embraced Lucine. Sergei stood in horrified astonishment and did all he could to stop his hands from trembling.

Edith handed Lucine a new inhaler cartridge to help her catch her breath and Oskar rubbed the back of her head. Marlaina kissed her face every chance she got, holding back tears as she did so.

After the terror subsided, Sergei transitioned into disciplinary mode. "Why did you go outside?" he demanded.

"Dewdrop! He was out there." She arched her neck to look over her grandmother and out the window. "Did you get him?"

"You can't just run outside without an adult," Sergei scolded. His tone was harsh and Lucine shrunk where she sat beneath his anger. "It's dangerous out there. You know better."

"I'm sorry, I just –"

"No excuses. You disobeyed me."

"Be easy on her," Marlaina insisted.

"No. I will not lose any of you to something stupid and reckless."

"She's a six-year-old," Edith said, trying to console her son, but he was too enraged to think rationally.

"And she's already got asthma! We could've lost her just now. How are you all so calm?"

"We are grateful that we *didn't* lose her," Oskar said, pointing out the obvious. Sergei wasn't sure why he was the only one who felt rage.

"Why was the rabbit outside?" he demanded. The rest of the house was standing outside the double-door entry to the kitchen, tuned in to the unexpected drama. Sergei focused his attention on them. "Who did it?"

His gaze landed on the twins. They held their breath as he stepped closer.

"You little punks thought it was funny to string her toys from the trees?" Sergei interrogated.

"We found a BB gun in the garage and were just practicing our aim," Dennis stammered.

"But we didn't hang the rabbit. I swear," Oliver insisted.

"You really expect me to believe that?"

"We didn't!" Dennis glanced over at Xavier, who hid behind the shadow of his Uncle Dante. The young boy shook his head slowly, warning the older boys not to tattle on him.

"She almost died because of your foolishness," Sergei continued his rampage.

"We were trying to be more responsible, like you said," Oliver continued, "and we thought learning to shoot might help one day."

Sergei grabbed the young boy's face and pulled him closer, "Is that what you thought? If anything happened to her I'd have strung *you* from the trees for target practice."

"That's enough!" Peggy declared, pushing Sergei off her son.

"What's wrong with you?" Gerald demanded. "It was a goddamn accident."

"Your sons have been a nightmare to live with."

"They are teenaged boys, what do you expect?"

"Make them grow up!"

"You've lost your mind," Gerald said with disgust before sheltering his family with an extended arm and leading them away from Sergei's rage. Dennis and Oliver glared at Xavier with hateful betrayal as they were carted away, but no one else noticed the exchange.

Kelso and Renee followed close behind.

"You're being irrational," Dante stepped in. "Dennis and Oliver are young, rambunctious boys. They're doing the best they can. This situation was an accident. Just be grateful you got to Lucine in time."

Sergei responded by punching Dante in the face.

Blood poured from his nose and everyone rushed to his side.

"What the hell is wrong with you?" Renita asked as she held her husband's head and Edith wiped the blood from his mouth.

"My daughter almost died!"

"I get it, but this is outrageous. You better check yourself, and fast," Dante said, spitting out blood as he spoke.

Sergei's extended family left the kitchen to take care of Dante, leaving him alone with Marlaina, Lucine, and Xavier, who still lurked in the doorway.

"Why did you hit Uncle Dante?" his daughter asked.

"I'm sorry you had to see that, baby. Daddy was just so scared of losing you. I was so mad and frightened; I should not have hit him."

"I'm sorry I went outside."

"It's okay. I love you and I am just happy you're not hurt."

He buried Lucine in a tight embrace. Marlaina watched, worried about her husband's mental state. He was supposed to be leading the others toward happiness and prosperity, not losing his temper and acting irrationally. She looked at her husband with grave concern.

"I will apologize," he said, still holding Lucine.

Marlaina nodded, then exited the kitchen, guiding Xavier to follow.

"Way to make a bad situation worse," Oskar said as he returned. "I was going to lighten the mood with some good news, but you ruined it."

"What news?"

"I made contact with other survivors."

"With the radio?"

"Yeah. Come see for yourself."

Oskar led his son into the sealed back porch where he had his large radio set up. The porch screens were replaced with plastic tarp and the air was stagnant. Oskar fussed with the frequency until it was back on the setting he had scribbled into his notebook.

"Hopefully they'll respond."

"Where are they?"

"Cameron, Louisiana. They are former military brats like me." Oskar put the receiver to his lips. "Clovis, do you copy?"

There was a moment of static before a voice came through the other side.

"Oskuh! Ya back. What happenin' now?" His Cajun accent was thick and hard to understand.

"Just wanted to introduce you to my son, Sergei. He's leading the brigade here in Utah."

"Hey Clovis. Happy to make contact," Sergei offered.

"Good on you, too. Been lonesome here in Cameron thinkin' we be the only survivors. Got my family and some neighbors

65

wit me. Only fifteen. This radio caught a crew in New Orleens, dou, so wer tryin' to link with dem soon."

"That's fantastic," Sergei replied. "We haven't found any other survivors in our area yet, but our groups should connect in the near future. We'll be stronger with numbers."

"Ahlors. We'd pass a good time joinin' crews."

"What are the conditions where you are?"

"We got ash, but da mud pits wrecked us good. Dey came from nothing, no big rain or storms, and swallowed up people whole. Got most of us."

"No rain at all?"

"Mais, we got the acid rain too. Stung like a swarm of angry wasps. But it wassint whatchu'd think ta make waters rise. Our marshy lands sucked people to their deaths. Dem swamps turned on us."

"Have the soils returned to normal?"

"Weh, dey be actin' right again."

"Good to hear. We are still struggling to clean the air. Not sure how we are going to manage, but we are starting with a town clean up."

"Seems right."

"We are welders, and we are stationed here with miners. You ought to join us in Utah. We have the skills and tools to rebuild."

"Be it warm? Us Cajuns don like no cold."

"There's no weather at all. You'd be fine."

"Lemme think on it. We got proper housing here too, an' clean air."

"Your soil situation puts me on edge."

"I said it be right now."

"Still, I think being safely landlocked is a better option. Who knows what's brewing in the oceans now." Sergei was answered with silence. "Just think it over."

"I will. Till tomorrow. Adyeu." Clovis was gone.

"Don't let his accent fool you," Oskar said addressing Sergei's concerned expression. "I served with many a Cajun and they may sound simple, but most are quick as a whip. They know how to survive and they ain't no fools."

"Good, we can't afford any deadweight tag-a-longs."

"He sounds like a workhorse, says he already cleaned up most of Cameron. He's the kind of guy we want by our side."

"Alright. Let's hope he agrees to make the trek to Utah." Sergei turned for the door, but stopped before exiting. "Great work with this. This is just the kind of hope the others need."

Oskar gave his son a curt nod of appreciation and Sergei left.

He knew Dante would forgive him—he still owed Dante a punch or two from their younger years. So he directed his attention to the Palladons, who would require a more immediate apology.

Contact with other survivors over a thousand miles away was huge and he was sure it would counter-balance his actions. He was sorry for grabbing Oliver's face, but still felt that his rage was justified. He needed everyone to start acting right; he needed them to live up to his standards. Their behavior had to match his long-term goals for the group, and accidents resulting from tomfoolery were unacceptable. If they planned to endure under his lead, they'd need to behave accordingly. With slick manipulation masked with compassion, he'd groom his family and friends into the perfect following and build a world worth fighting for.

Chapter 8

Hall of Mosses, Olympic National Park, WA

The forest felt empty with the absence of so many. Juniper did her best not to let the void change her resolve, but it was hard to pretend that their departure wasn't devastating.

"I still can't believe Brett, Misty, and Carine followed them," she confided in Roscoe a week after they left. "They were my friends."

"Try to let it go. We can't change it now."

"I know, but if they aren't dead yet, they probably will be soon, and that's on me."

"No, it's not. You warned them, begged them to stay. At the end of the day, humans still have free will. You can't force anyone to do anything." Roscoe kissed the side of her head. "I worry for them too, but it's out of our control."

Juniper understood, but struggled to shake the guilt. The trees were quiet and made no comment on the mass exodus, so she wondered how this affected her long-term goals. She could rebuild with those who remained, but it would be hard. She and Roscoe and the young couple from Gold Bar were the only pairs capable of repopulating. The others were too old and those who were young enough were all male. The only young females were two of Irene's kids, who were babies. There was no one for Teek, the Wolfe brothers, or the Hazedelle brothers from Gold Bar to pair up with and this dilemma greatly concerned Juniper.

Everyone was aware of this issue, but no one talked about it. Harping on the problem would not make young female survivors magically appear, so it was better for everyone to keep moving forward. Juniper prayed for a miracle every night.

"Do you think we should start upgrading our shelter here?" Clark asked the next day as the small group sat around the bonfire.

"I just don't want to have everyone expend all their energy, only to be told that we need to relocate," Juniper replied. "I don't know what the next move is, or when it will happen. I'd feel awful if you all worked hard to build homes and had to leave them behind."

"Does that mean no word on the weather or animals yet either?" Paul Devron asked. Teek sat beside his father, eager for this news as well.

"No, not yet. It's fortunate that the weather is still missing though. I imagine it's almost November and we'd have died from the cold if it reappeared."

"It's the end of November. We should all be celebrating Thanksgiving with our families right now," Tess Devron informed the group. Paul and Teek both put an arm around her. The group went quiet in mourning.

"Why don't we celebrate together?" Roscoe suggested after a long, quiet minute, hoping to lift the sullen mood. "We're family now, after all."

"And have a Thanksgiving dinner consisting of canned hotdogs and potato chips?" Cindy asked. For a park ranger, Cindy's poor adjustment to life outdoors still surprised Juniper. "Sounds awful."

Her husband Carl nodded in agreement.

"These pity parties need to stop," Juniper said, reclaiming authority of the conversation. "I think having our first Thanksgiving in this new world is a wonderful idea. It may not be anything like what we are used to, but with the right attitude it can be lovely."

"Agreed," Laurel and Birk said simultaneously.

"I need something nice to look forward to," Jeb added. "We all need a distraction."

"Tess and I were chefs in our past life," Paul said. "We can find a way to make the canned and packaged food taste like fine dining."

Clark led the trip to and from the abandoned grocery store in Maple Grove. They had already cleaned out most of the food that was still edible, but Tess and Paul were able to snag some sealed spices that were previously overlooked.

When they returned to the Hall of Mosses, a long stretch of the path was cleared and small boulders were maneuvered to line its edges.

Tess, Paul, and Alice began cooking, while Juniper and Roscoe showed everyone to their seats. After everyone was situated, Juniper took her boulder-seat at the end of the row near the bonfire where their meal was being prepared. Her iPod was in the knapsack she brought and she hadn't used it since the attack, so she hooked it up to her portable speaker and put on her Motown playlist. "Cruisin'" by Smokey Robinson came on first and the mood was noticeably soothed.

Dedrik, Baxley, and Wes told Martha and Bernard about their young love lives before the purge, and the older couple gave them wise advice for when love came their way again. Laurel and Birk pretended not to listen, but couldn't help but overhear their older sons' gripes about girls their age.

"They're impossible to figure out," Baxley concluded after they each gave specific examples.

"That's the fun of it!" Bernard advised. "Because then, when she realizes she loves you back, well, there is no greater feeling in the world."

"And when she doesn't?" Dedrik asked.

"You move on and become a better man for it. Rejection builds character. The hardest part is remembering that you must treat the next girl with the exact same enthusiasm as the one who turned you down. Can't make a person suffer for another's mistake."

"It's so tiring," Wesley griped. "Part of me is happy there are no girls our age around."

"Really?" Dedrik asked, bewildered. "Sure, it can be a headache, but I don't want to be alone the rest of my life. I really hope we *do* find other survivors that are our age."

"I hope we do too, for each of you," Bernard jumped in. "Giving love and having it returned is worth every heartache along the way."

They continued their conversation while Noah entertained Cindy, Carl, and Jeb with wild stories of the antics he and his friends used to get away with at school.

"We used to skateboard on the roof of the high school during lunch. We got away with it for a whole month before someone ratted us out. We heard the vice principal was onto us, so we started wearing Halloween masks. On the day she finally confronted us, we were already on the roof and she screamed at us from the ground to climb down. She threatened detention, suspension, expulsion. She even threatened to call the cops. She made such a scene that the whole grade came out to watch as she yelled. The school security guards tried to anticipate where we'd climb down. There were eight of us, so we ran in opposite directions. My buddy John and Howie got down by jumping onto the top of a school bus." Noah laughed as he recalled the memory. "They ran straight to my house, because it was closest. My mom freaked out."

Laurel tuned in at the mention, and added, "I didn't know what they had done, but I knew it was trouble and that Noah was involved. They both wore the silliest smirks as they ran through my front door."

"My buddy Joey and I used a walkway canopy to get down and landed right next to the Vice Principal and one of the guards. I thought we were done for, but we darted past them and all the kids who had come out for lunch crowded the space and gave us time to get away. It was amazing."

"I remember those days," Cindy laughed.

"We weren't hurting anyone, just having a little fun," Noah said with a shrug.

"I miss my youth," Jeb said with a chuckle.

"The whole grade rallied so we didn't get in trouble. It was so cool. We had to go back in the middle of the night to get our skateboards off the roof."

The song switched to "Lean on Me" by Bill Withers as dinner was served.

"I love this song," Aldon said, speaking for the first time all night. Roscoe looked over at his father, happy to see him smiling for a change.

Tess, Paul, and Alice walked around with trays of the best looking food they'd seen in months. Tess passed out the sides, which were artichoke hearts over crostini topped with marinara and a tuna cannellini bean salad. Paul carried a large pot of tomato Velveeta soup, and Alice brought the main courses, which were skillet stroganoff and tuna tacos with mango salsa. It wasn't a conventional Thanksgiving dinner, but the trio certainly delivered the best food anyone had eaten in a while.

The mood was jovial as everyone filled their bellies. The conversation was light and happy, the music was good, and the food delicious. By the end, everyone was stuffed. The Wolfe boys departed first to surrender to their food comas near their sleeping bags. Martha and Bernard left next. Since they were older, they got one of the three mattresses that were lugged into the forest. The other two were in rotation so that everyone got a comfortable sleep every few days.

"As" by Stevie Wonder came on and Juniper looked to Roscoe as the song played.

"This is us."

They left their boulder-seats and sat on the ground next to the speaker. The song played and the lyrics depicted a love that happened as naturally as the changing seasons; a love that would endure the end of time.

"*And I'll be loving you always,*" Roscoe sang along with Stevie as he held Juniper in his arms.

Though the song wasn't written for them, the lyrics managed to capture their exact feelings for one another, and some of the lines even depicted their current situation with eerie accuracy. It was a moment of magic. They shared seven minutes musically transported away from their current hardship; seven minutes of blissful escape. The song ended and "Dancing in the Street" by Martha and the Vandellas came on. Her iPod died halfway through the first verse.

"I wish I had a way to charge this thing," she said in frustration as she unplugged the speaker. "Music would make everything better."

Roscoe kissed the side of her face, "We'll just have to make our own."

"You do *not* want to hear me sing," Juniper laughed.

They relocated to their corner of the forest and fell asleep. A few minutes into her slumber, a voice arrived.

Meeting in the White Room.

Juniper sat up and tried to determine the source. She was getting better at differentiating the voices of her Champion sisters, and though it was brief, she was sure she heard Coral's Indonesian accent.

She crossed her legs and focused on the spot in her mind where the White Room was located. It only took a few moments before she was hurdling through her subconscious depths and into the meeting. All her sisters were already there, wearing their elegant and lavish aura gowns. Marisabel still looked sad in her plain blue dress made of cotton.

"The soil spirits talked to me, finally," Sofyla announced in her thick Ukrainian accent. Though the Champions all spoke different languages in the real world, in the White Room, they all spoke the same. It was interesting how their accents remained though, and Juniper wondered how she sounded to the others.

"What did they say?" Juniper asked.

"That it was time to move. I was instructed to relocate and meet you in Brazil."

"Me?" Juniper asked, puzzled. *"The trees haven't told me I could leave yet."*

"Well, I guess you'll be hearing from them soon because this involves both of us."

"What about me? Brazil is my home! I want to meet you there too," Marisabel declared.

"They didn't mention you," Sofyla said with sympathy. *"I'm sorry."*

"This isn't fair." Marisabel departed without warning. Her disappearance came with a splash and the icy water of her

image passed through Juniper and Aria. The sensation was chilling.

"*Did they say why she can't join us?*" Juniper asked.

"*No. Only that it would be me and you. We are the last set that needs to unite.*"

"*So I guess Gaia is pairing us up,*" Coral observed.

"*Not me,*" Eshe said. "*I'll be alone once Sofyla leaves.*"

"*Probably because you're evolving so fast on your own,*" Sofyla speculated. "*Plus, we aren't meant to stay in that heat with you. My terrain is the soil horizon; yours is everything beneath.*"

"*Valid point.*"

"*I'll take care of Marisabel,*" Coral offered, her tone much softer than usual. All the Champions sympathized with Marisabel's distress, but Coral was the only one who could offer real life support.

The Champions parted ways and once Juniper mentally returned to the Hall of Mosses, she fell asleep next to Roscoe with South America on her mind.

Chapter 9

Cedar City, Iron County, Utah

One month had passed since the scare with Lucine, and Sergei smoothed everything over with a round of apologies. The men understood his fear of almost losing his daughter and suspected that they too might have reacted irrationally in the heat of the moment. Sergei remained on his best behavior as he earned back their trust and reestablished their loyalty. Christmastime was upon them and everyone was in jolly spirits. It was almost like the incident never happened.

The children of the group helped their mothers make a Christmas tree out of an old porch umbrella. It was enormous and bright red, but the best they could find in Oskar's basement. They crafted paper snowflakes and hung those alongside tin spirals cut from soda cans. The ornaments dangled at all different lengths from the edges of the umbrella to the pole. It looked nothing like a traditional Christmas tree, but in the candlelight it was quite pretty. Having it in the main living space reminded everyone of the passing holiday and managed to lift their spirits.

Despite the jovial mood in the Lamorte house, there was still gruesome work to be done. Sergei, Dante, Kelso, and Gerald burnt most of the cadavers scattered through the public establishments of Cedar City, but they hadn't yet tackled the homes and weren't sure if it was worth the effort. There would be so many bodies in the vacant houses, and they had other, more pressing issues to handle. Sergei wanted to begin repurposing the roofs in the neighborhood and start making steel with their Bessemer converter. The faster he set solid roots here, the more inclined survivors from other parts of the country would be to leave their homes and join him in Utah.

Gino, Vincent, and Benny were making solid progress clearing the ash from the roads and sidewalks. They went out every day from morning till noon, then again after lunch until dinner. A week after Lucine's incident they began to bring their twin cousins along, per the request of their father and uncle. Gerald thought it wise to give his sons some responsibility to keep them occupied. The addition of Oliver and Dennis sped their progress and they were almost done clearing most of Main Street.

Gino led the way as the crew headed into town for another round. The road to their next spot was already clear, so the walk was easy.

"It's a shame the air is still toxic," Killian commented as he and Dominic carried the large ladder at the back of the group. "We've done all this work and we still aren't safe."

"The clouds have to clear at some point. Once they do, the weather will come back and the wind will take this dust up and away," Vincent said optimistically.

"Or our bodies will adapt and we will become creatures of ash," Dennis fantasized.

"Or we won't adapt and we will all die," Oliver countered.

"The skies will clear and nature will take care of it naturally," Vincent retorted with an exaggerated eye roll. "I studied this at school."

The twins mocked their older cousin behind his back, but said no more.

As they reached the line of ash where they stopped yesterday, the Palladon cousins got their brooms ready and the Halloran siblings set up their ladder at Main Street Grill. Killian,

Dominic, and Brianne did their best to sweep the ash off the tops of the buildings that hadn't collapsed yet.

"I'll climb first today," Brianne offered as her brothers adjusted the ladder. She ascended with one hand on the rungs and the other holding her broom. When she reached the roof of the Grill, she kept one foot on the ladder and stomped the other through the ash. The moment her foot made contact, the entire roof caved in. Dominic and Killian held the ladder, ready to hold their sister up in case the wall fell too. The ladder shook violently as the roof fell, but the wall remained intact.

"Holy crap," Benny shouted in reaction from across the street.

"I think this one's a no-go," Brianne called out sarcastically. She climbed down and they moved on.

"This Best Western is attached to the Grill. If this one fell, I imagine that one will too," Killian said. "Let's skip it. We can climb the Sizzler."

They set up the ladder and Brianne made her way up. When she got to the top, she tested the roof the same way she tested the others. The impact of her foot did not cause it to collapse, so she stepped onto it carefully. Killian and Dominic climbed up after her and together they swept the perimeter of the roof and worked their way toward the center.

Benny worked on the street below, pushing his brothers' piles of ash into the main pile for the day. Dennis and Oliver helped relocate the pile to the front of the collapsed Grill since the lot was now useless.

Ash cascaded over the side of the Sizzler as the Halloran's cleared the roof. Brianne observed the younger boys sweeping the street and was happy to be on roof duty.

"I hope Vincent is right about the weather. Look at that pile they are making. And all the other piles left along Main Street." She pointed down the road and five massive ash dumps were visible.

"I think weather will make it worse," Killian responded. "The moment wind becomes a factor, all this hard work we've done will be ruined. Areas we already cleaned will get covered again. The air will be way more dangerous to breathe."

"So there will just be massive ash piles forever?" Dominic asked.

"I don't know. I think we should take a day to lightly dampen the piles. You've seen how hard it is to break through the layer that got wet from the acid rain. It turned into putty-like cement. If we dampen the piles they should stay intact when the weather returns."

"But won't that make the pile impossible to move?" Dominic asked.

"I think it would make them easier to move. It if hardens we might be able to relocate it as one unit," Killian speculated.

"Once we reach Veteran's Memorial Highway there will be less roofs to clean. Maybe we can take a day or two to backtrack and water the ash piles," Brianne suggested.

"Sergei won't let us waste water on that," Killian said.

"We can use public water that hasn't been filtered," Brianne suggested.

"No, that's still potential drinking water that will keep us alive."

"I'm not coming out here anymore to waste my energy on this clean-up if we can't guarantee that all this work we've done won't be for nothing with the slightest breeze," Brianne expressed.

"There are tons of spray bottles with liquids inside them at the auto body shop and the grocery store. It's not water, but it'll get the ash wet so it doesn't move," Dominic suggested.

"It's an option," Killian said as he thought it over. "We will discuss it with the others."

They were done sweeping the roof of the Sizzler. They carefully walked from their meeting point in the center back toward the edges. Killian and Dominic kept their brooms up, while Brianne continued sweeping up residue.

"Looks like the Palladon boys are about done with this section of the street," she announced.

"Already?" Killian asked in shock, keeping his eyes glued to each step he took.

Brianne answered with a quick scream that was followed by silence. Killian and Dominic snapped their heads around to see that their sister was missing. Killian's heart raced as he reached his edge and hurried along the perimeter to her former location. When he got there he saw the small section of roof that collapsed beneath Brianne.

"Gino," Killian shouted over the side of the building. "Brianne fell through!"

Gino dropped his broom and raced inside while Killian and Dominic carefully climbed down. Gino found her lying in a heap of roof rubble, barely conscious. He knelt by her side and assessed her injuries.

"Looks like a broken ankle and wrist for sure," Gino announced as her brothers ran inside. "I imagine there's some head trauma too. She's not very responsive."

"Bri," Dominic said, trying to get her to respond. "It's Dom and Killian. We're here. Come back to us." He stroked her hair and Killian held her hand.

She moaned and it was clear she was trying to fight through the pain.

"Take your time," Killian said in a soothing tone.

There was a loud creak overhead.

"I don't think we have much time," Gino noted as part of the ceiling cracked and dust fell. The loud snap echoed through the empty restaurant and they took this as their warning to vacate. With care, they lifted Brianne and carried her out. She groaned in pain as they moved her broken bones, but did not resist. When they reached the street the roof collapsed, sending a billowing cloud of ash toward them. The force sent Gino to his knees, causing him to drop Brianne's legs. When it cleared, they were coated in ash and Brianne was lucid. Quiet tears rolled down her cheeks and her brothers gently placed her body down.

"Where does it hurt?" Killian asked.

"Everywhere."

Vincent raced to them with a wheelbarrow, which Killian used to cart Brianne back toward Pinecone Drive.

"Don't fall asleep," he advised. "You might have a concussion."

She nodded and did her best to keep her eyes open. Her goggles were filthy and the lack of vision made it hard to stay awake.

"I'm going back with you," Dominic stated. "I'll make sure she stays awake." He began flicking her shoulder repeatedly.

"Ow," she mumbled and Dominic laughed—she was going to be okay.

"We are going to stay behind. There's a lot left to do," Vincent said.

Killian nodded and left with his siblings. The Palladons got back to sweeping. A few hours later they reached the intersection of Main Street and UT-56.

"Want to walk the remainder?" Vincent asked his brothers and cousins. "Might give us an idea of how much we have left to clean."

Gino and Benny nodded their heads, while Oliver and Dennis moaned, but obliged. They trekked down UT-56, which was covered in a few inches of ash.

"The air is extra dirty here," Oliver commented.

"Yeah. I hadn't realized till now, but it seems the areas we cleaned also have better visibility. I guess we're making more progress than we realized," Vincent observed. "Once we clear this road, this air should improve."

"Maybe just being in those spots, moving around, has made all the dust disperse," Gino suggested.

"It's possible. We are disrupting the inactivity and stillness." Vincent wasn't sure how to explain any of it. He recalled all that he learned in his science courses, but the more he thought about it, the more it didn't add up. He kept trying, though, and hoped if they were able to connect with other survivors and travel beyond Cedar City, the pieces would come together and it would start to make sense.

They reached the intersection of UT-56 and Veteran's Memorial, and turned left onto the large highway. It was long, filthy, and scattered with cars. Some were abandoned and some had the lifeless bodies of its passengers still strapped in their seats. Those who left their vehicles in an attempt to flee were dispersed throughout the ash. Every few feet the boys had to step over a dead body.

"This is a nightmare," Dennis commented.

"Feels like a scene from an apocalyptic movie," Oliver added.

"It's no worse than what we came across in town," Gino stated. "You two missed Sergei burning a pile of corpses at the Ranch Store. The smell was brutal."

"So was the visual," Vincent recalled. "The flesh bubbled as it burned."

"I'd rather not relive it, thanks," Benny said, hoping to put a stop to the returning memory.

"Didn't seem to faze Sergei at all. That was weird, right?" Vincent asked.

"Yeah," Gino answered, "but he is in survival mode. I think he's operating with as little emotion as possible in order to keep the group productive. He's become our unofficial leader. He's got the master plan in motion. If he breaks down, the rest of us might splinter and crack."

"Doesn't his meltdown last month count?" Oliver asked.

"His daughter almost died. He had to watch his father resuscitate her back to life."

"All because you assholes used her favorite toy as a target in your shooting practice," Benny added.

"Imagine how terrified he was," Gino said.

"And how useless he must have felt having to watch someone else save Lucine," Vincent added. "He couldn't save her himself."

"It wasn't us, it was Xavier," Dennis finally confessed. "We were outside shooting when that little brat came out with the stupid rabbit. He wanted to shoot with us, so we let him hang his target and practice."

"Damn," Benny said in shock. "He really let you guys take the fall."

"He's an evil little monster. I glanced back at him while Sergei was yelling at me and he shook his head so I wouldn't rat him out. He was willing to sacrifice me to save himself." Oliver shook his head with disbelief.

"It's not cool, but he is only eight-years-old. He was probably afraid," Gino tried to rationalize.

"The kid needs to learn about accountability," Dennis retorted.

"Regardless, the whole thing was screwed up. I'm pretty sure Dante's punch would've been mine if my parents hadn't stepped in," Oliver retorted with certainty.

"No way. Sergei wouldn't hit a kid," Gino insisted.

"I think he's losing it," Dennis said in agreement with his twin.

The older boys shrugged, unsure how to defend Sergei any further. They admired him, but Dennis and Oliver were family. All they could hope for was time to heal this wound.

The boys continued down Veteran's Memorial Highway toward exit 57 where they'd turn onto Cross Hollow Road.

"Sergei wanted us to mark up this area in case other survivors use this highway as a means to travel," Gino recalled. They hadn't received much instruction from Sergei since the start of this task, and realized they had forgotten the most important part.

"I didn't see any footprints," Vincent said, sensing his brother's dismay.

"The least we can do is write a message in the ash. Tomorrow we can start clearing this area and bring a piece of furniture with a clearer message carved into it."

"And if anyone comes through, they'll see the tracks we left," Dennis added, motioning toward the footprints they left behind. Gino nodded and began writing in the ash.

SURVIVORS IN CEDAR CITY

He drew a large arrow beneath the words.

"Drag your brooms and shovels as we walk back to the house," Gino instructed the others. "The message and trail should be good enough for now."

Goggles fastened and bandanas in place, the boys moved forward, marking their path as they walked. The world was dark and their fate was uncertain. This new life was not easy or comfortable, and each day came with hard work and continued struggle. As time passed and they continued to be the only survivors in the area, the long-term picture seemed grim. The outlook was not promising, but Sergei maintained confidence, and under his lead they held onto hope.

Chapter 10

Hall of Mosses, Olympic National Park, WA

Juniper and Roscoe informed the group of their mission to relocate to South America. While they were skeptical about the long journey, everyone could agree that they were happy to make a move.

"We will be meeting Sofyla there and combining groups."

"Who is Sofyla?" Laurel asked. Juniper forgot that she had only ever mentioned her Champion sisters by name to Roscoe, Clark, Irene, and her Dipper Dive co-workers.

"She is one of my Champion sisters. Her element is soil."

"Makes sense to link you up with her," Jeb commented. "Trees and soil are a perfect pair."

"Yes," Juniper agreed. "I've never met her, but she seems lovely. Her aura glows bright yellow every time I meet her in my mind."

The group smiled at this, not fully understanding what she meant, but happy to imagine the beautiful image.

"I've purposefully limited use on our vehicles for this moment," she continued. "We can travel some of the way via dirt bike, quad, and Jeep. If we cannot find gasoline during our travels, we will ditch the vehicles and continue by foot."

The Wolfe brothers recruited the Hazedelle brothers to help them ready the vehicles. The brothers from Gold Bar were older, in their young thirties, and strong. As they prepped the transportation, Juniper led the group and helped everyone determine what items to pack and what to leave behind. As she was advising Bernard and Martha to take the figurines out of their duffle bag, a voice arrived. The sound started by her feet and circled up her body till it reached her ears.

Can you hear me? Sofyla's thick Ukrainian accent rang loud and clear through her mind.

Yes. It took a moment, but I can hear you.

We are beginning our travels today. Eshe is guiding us to the coast of Senegal and from there we will find a boat and take it to Brazil. Where should we plan to meet?

I'm not sure. I don't know much about the Amazon.

Give me a second. I will summon Marisabel.

Juniper felt the connection widen and a chilly sensation ran down her spine.

Who called? Marisabel asked.

It's me, Sofyla. Juniper and I are trying to determine a safe and easily accessible spot to meet in the Amazon.

You realize the Amazon is an enormous rainforest, right?

Of course we do.

Well, there is no easy place to meet, but I can offer a few options. Where are each of you coming from?

Juniper answered. *I am coming from Washington in the United States. Sofyla is coming from the coast of Senegal.*

Best way to guarantee you meet is to follow the north shore of the Amazon River. Sofyla, you ought to start in the coast town of Amapá, and Juniper, your trip is more complicated. You'll need to enter Colombia and follow Ruta Nacional 75 till its end. It will drop you in the city of Calamar. From there, walk southwest until you reach the Rio Uapés. You should come across the river before the town of Queramiki. If you don't, you walked too far south. Follow the river through Colombia, into Brazil, and stay along its north shore. When you reach the first fork in the river, travel south. The river turns into the Rio Negros at that point, and you must follow that until the city of

Manaus. *After that point, it becomes the Rio Amazonas and you'll be on course to meet up with Sofyla.*

Got it. Juniper said, taking note of her instructions. *Thank you. I wish I could join you there.*

We wish you could too, but you cannot leave Coral on her own in Antarctica. Sofyla sympathized. *We must obey the direction of nature's spirits. Gaia knows best, and through them we are guided by Her.*

I know. It's just miserable here. Coral is evolving and I feel like I'm dying.

You cannot die from sadness, Sofyla reminded her. *Our lives are eternal.*

That notion has lost its charm. I can't live this way forever.

You won't have to. Juniper tried to ease her sister's fear. *I bet you'll be allowed to join us sooner than you think.*

I hope so.

Hang in there, Sofyla said. Her encouraging smile radiated with warmth through their connection. *And call out to us anytime you need a friend.*

Thank you. Please let me know how my home looks once you arrive. I miss it terribly.

We will.

They said their goodbyes and Marisabel left the conversation.

Seems like a good plan, Sofyla said.

You will likely reach your side of the river long before we reach ours. Don't travel beyond the city of Manaus. Stay on the Amazonian side. We will find you there.

Okay. Sofyla agreed.

It is going to take a very long time for us to connect.

Luckily, we have the power of telepathic communication on our side, as well as the gift of eternal life.

Just remember that we aren't invincible. Juniper warned. *Everyone keeps mentioning our eternal life like we are immortal.*

It's almost like being immortal. Immune to all disease, able to heal most wounds. There's no reason we all shouldn't live forever.

If we treat it like it's immortality we will certainly grow careless and push its limits. As far as I'm concerned, I never got the gift. I am not invincible, nor would I wish to be.

Once everyone around you gets old and gray, then starts dying while you stay the same, you'll have no choice but to realize the power of Gaia's gift.

Until then, I'm holding onto normalcy.

Boring.

If boring equates to cautious, then fine. I'm boring. We have a lot of work to do and I want to be around to make sure it gets done. When do you plan to head to Senegal?

Tomorrow. Eshe will lead us there.

Fantastic. We are beginning our journey this evening. We will be in touch.

Of course, Sofyla said as she departed. *Safe travels, Sister.*

Their connection separated and the voices of those around her returned to their normal volume. Roscoe was crouched in front of her, packing his knapsack.

"Who was it?"

"Sofyla. And Marisabel, briefly. We were just determining how best to go about this."

"And?"

"It's going to be a long journey. There's no easy place to meet, so we are going to follow the river until we run into each other. She'll likely get there before us, so she knows to wait where the river changes."

"We will get there, don't worry." Roscoe stood and kissed her forehead. He sensed her worry and was able to soothe it with his confidence in her. He had no doubt in her lead and she was grateful for his trust every day. All she could hope was that the others maintained similar faith as she led them on what was sure to feel like a never-ending quest.

With so many people gone, they had plenty of vehicles to transport those who remained. Everyone put on their protective gear before loading up; goggles and facemasks were critical once they left the safety of the forest. The Wolfe brothers paired up on the two remaining dirt bikes, while Juniper rode the Jaden Jaunt and Roscoe and Teek took command of the quads. Birk drove Juniper's old Jeep that rescued those from Maple Grove, Jeb drove his own Jeep that he brought, and Russ Hazedelle drove the third Jeep. Once all the engines were on and running, the Wolfe brothers led the way.

The forest was devoid of navigable trails and the Jeeps had trouble following, so they headed west in order to reach Hoh Valley Road. The road was mostly in tact with the occasional tree sprouted in their path. They moved slowly so the Jeeps could keep up. The further away from the Hall of Mosses they traveled, the worse the conditions got. The air became dusty, the visibility grew worse, and the road began to disappear beneath the overgrowth of nature. When it turned into Upper Hoh Road, the setting became dangerous. Juniper and Roscoe took the lead and led a slow progression toward US Route 101 in Forks. Though it was the longer route, it was also safer than going off road.

The ground was covered in a small layer of ash, which made the tire traction awful. The dirt bikes kept sliding, causing near wipeouts, and they were forced to slow down even more.

Juniper stopped as she reached the highway. Once everyone was parked behind her, she shouted through the bandana wrapped around the lower half of her face and addressed the group.

"These roads are terrible. We need to be careful."

"What's the plan?" Clark hollered from the Jeep at the back of the group.

"I want to follow the major highways. I think they are our safest bet. I'm sure there will be spots of destruction along them, but at least we will know we are heading in the right direction."

"Do you know the way?" Irene shouted from the backseat of Jeb's Jeep.

"No, but once we get to Olympia we will find a map."

"Let's keep moving," Aldon said with a cough from the front seat of Jeb's Jeep before rolling the window up. It was the only Jeep with its roof intact. The others were topless and exposed to the worsening air. He, Martha, Bernard, and Irene's four small kids rode in the sealed Jeep since they were the oldest and youngest of the group.

Juniper listened to Aldon's request and led the group forward. At the pace they moved, it took four hours to reach the city of Olympia. There was a gas station that had not exploded during the purge, so the group loaded up canisters into the back of the Jeeps and filled their tanks.

Juniper climbed through the rubble of the collapsed convenience store to search for a world map. She found the rack of maps beneath a piece of roofing and dug through the collection of county and state maps before finding a national map. It had all the roadways of each state, and though it wouldn't help her cross into Mexico, it would help them get to the border.

Roscoe, Clark, and Irene approached.

"Interstate 5 south into Portland, then Interstate 84 east into Idaho," Juniper said as she followed her trajectory along the map with her finger. The others paid attention. "From there we take Interstate 15 through Utah and into Las Vegas, where we can catch US Route 93 into Arizona. There's a lot of small roadways to switch between there, but if we can reach Interstate 19 in Tucson, we have a clear path into Mexico."

"None of these highways are a linear shot across the border," Irene noted. "We are going to waste so much time zig-zagging along these highways."

"You've already seen the state of the smaller roads around here. They are ruined. Though the highways are ash-covered and broken in some spots, and likely to be littered with abandoned cars in more crowded areas, they are mostly intact. They are the clearest paths we have," Juniper rationalized. "If we go off course and try to make paths of our own, or follow non-existent roads of the past, I fear we will get lost."

"Getting lost would waste far more time than a few roundabout roadways," Clark added.

"And there won't be any gas stations or food stores on the smaller roads," Roscoe reminded them. "Going the long way might provide us more opportunities to find salvageable gas from pumps and abandoned cars."

Everyone nodded in agreement.

They joined the others where they nibbled on snacks around the Jeeps. Once the collective energy of the group was restored, they returned to their vehicles and carried onward. The trip was going to be long, but their attitude remained positive. With their optimism intact, Juniper felt confident moving forward. They would make it to Brazil, they would unite with Sofyla, and they would make a new home in the Amazon.

Chapter 11

Cedar City, Iron County, Utah

Oskar set Brianne's broken bones and strapped them to planks of wood. Time would determine how they healed. Despite the set-back from her injury, the town was looking better and Sergei kept pushing for continued improvement. Another month passed and his determination and leadership helped push the group into the new year with productivity. The younger men continued sweeping the roads and roofs, while he, Dante, Kelso, and Gerald discarded all evidence of death in the city. Oskar stayed in frequent contact with Clovis. The more time that passed, the more likely it seemed that Clovis would lead his people from Louisiana to Utah. Sergei worked hard to convince him that Cedar City was best for all. He had the materials to rebuild, as well as years of welding experience. There was no better place to start than home.

Sergei was in the back room with his father when shouts echoed through the empty town. They both tied bandanas around their mouths and put on goggles before stepping outside to determine the source of the noise.

The voices were muffled beneath protective gear, but sounded familiar.

"Sounds like Benny," Oskar speculated.

"It has to be one of the Palladon boys." Sergei walked to the front of the house and onto the street, Oskar followed close behind.

Benny came running toward them and collapsed his hands to his knees once he reached them.

"What's going on? Is everyone okay?" Oskar asked, alarmed.

"Yes," Benny answered between heavy breaths, "We found other people. Other survivors."

"Where?" Sergei asked with stern authority.

"They were traveling south on Veteran's Highway. Gino is leading them here now."

"Where did they come from?"

"North, I guess." Sergei was visibly perturbed by this obvious answer, so Benny explained himself. "I didn't stick around to chat. I wanted to tell you the news."

"I want to meet these newcomers."

"Yeah, they shouldn't be too far behind."

"Catch your breath inside where the air is cleaner," Sergei advised and Benny obeyed.

After a moment, Oskar spoke.

"This is fantastic news. More people to help rebuild and an outside viewpoint on this whole catastrophe. Maybe they'll know more than we do."

"I'm not anticipating anything productive until we meet. They will have their own leaders with their own goals, and if they conflict with ours we cannot take them in. Best we don't get our hopes up till we talk to them."

"Fine, but even if the least they do is provide us with better intel, then it was a positive encounter."

"Let's wait and see." Sergei refused to let his guard down; he feared the potential rival of leadership with this new group. He liked his role of power and did not wish to share it with an outsider. If it seemed that might be the case, he'd encourage the newcomers to carry on with their travels.

There was no sign of Gino, so he and Oskar went inside to inform the others. Marlaina was particularly excited. She retrieved Xavier and Lucine from the room where they played with their little cousins to tell them the news. Giving them this sliver of hope made her feel better; it made her feel like she was doing her job as their mother, and relaying good news was the best she could currently do for them.

Lucine was elated to know other people were alive and nearby, while Xavier remained unfazed.

"Isn't that great?" Marlaina asked, hoping to get a joyous reaction from Xavier. "Others survived."

"Sure, but in the end it doesn't matter. We're all going to die eventually." Xavier turned his back to his mother and returned his attention to the city he was building with his Legos. His rapid decline into a jaded young man frightened Marlaina. Though he was only eight, his demeanor was that of a weathered forty-year-old and the toll of what they were enduring showed in his lack of spirit. He did not like to play with the other kids and he often made dreary comments about death.

"Look at me, young man," Marlaina demanded. Xavier turned back around to face her. "You will snap out of this gloomy attitude and welcome these newcomers with the rest of us."

He didn't argue, just obeyed with sullenness. She picked up her infant niece and nephew, Freya and Gideon, and Lucine led four-year-old Callista by the hand. Dante and Renita were still being told the news in the kitchen with the others. When they joined the rest of the group, she handed one-year-old Gideon to Renita and stood next to her to listen. Sergei explained the forthcoming arrival to an intent audience. When he finished, Renita replied first.

"I hope you aren't planning to squeeze them into this house with us."

"Absolutely not. One of the structurally sound homes still remaining on this street will become their new home if they choose to stay."

"Glad to know all that cleanup won't be for nothing," Killian said. Brianne sat next to him with her leg wrapped in bandages and strapped straight to a piece of plywood. She nodded in agreement.

"I just hope they don't come in here and try to take over," Renita continued. "It would only take one bad apple to spoil everything we've built."

"I have that in mind as well," Sergei assured her. "I won't let that happen."

"This is *good* news," Oskar reminded everyone. "Let's not jump to negativity before they even arrive."

"Just keeping it honest," she replied with blunt conviction.

Marlaina looked over at her sister-in-law with disbelief. Renita was an acquired taste. She was brash and opinionated, but well intended. It took years for Marlaina to dig through Renita's spiky layers, but they eventually grew to love each other. They were the only two women on the planet, besides Edith, that understood what it was like to be in love with a Lamorte. Oskar, Sergei, and Dante were a different breed of man, often hard-headed with tempers that were impossible to contain. It took a very confident, patient, and docile woman to endure the wrath of their unpredictable moods. The women often had to put their egos aside in order to maintain peace in their homes. Marlaina and Renita were both poised and independent in their own ways, so swallowing their pride in order to sooth their husbands' egos wasn't always easy. Having another strong woman to confide in often eased the brunt of their personal sacrifices, knowing another worthy woman was doing the same.

Marlaina was happy to have Renita as part of her family, even though they often proved to be total opposites in personality.

"I am excited to meet the newcomers," Marlaina announced. "I believe their arrival will be a positive contribution to the group."

Many others nodded and mumbled in agreement with Marlaina's sentiment. They left the kitchen as a group, put on their protective gear, went outside, and stood in the middle of the street with anticipation. They waited outside for fifteen minutes in tense silence before Gino, Vincent, Dennis, and Oliver could be seen in the distance leading a large group toward them.

"That's way more than I expected," Dante said.

"We are outnumbered," Sergei said to himself, but Dante heard.

"They are on our turf. They'll need to abide by our ways. If they can't, or won't, they'll need to go."

Both Lamorte brothers were on the same page; neither wanted to lose control of what they were working so hard to build.

Sergei worked on forcing a genuine smile as the group approached. It wasn't that he was unhappy they were here, he just struggled to silence his pessimism. As soon as he felt secure in their allegiance to *his* lead, his worry would subside.

He took a step forward once the newcomers were within earshot.

"Greetings," he shouted through his facemask. His arms were extended and raised. "I am Sergei Lamorte. This is my family, some by blood and some by choice. We are happy to welcome you to our city."

Though the facemasks and bandanas hid the expressions of the new arrivals, the warmth of their smiles was felt. It was a joyous occasion and the moment Sergei shook the first outstretched hand his guard lifted—these people were just happy to come across other survivors.

"You've done a lot of great work here," the man who led the group expressed. "Gino took us on a detour through town. It was the cleanest area we've seen in months."

"We work hard here and hope to get our beloved home back to normal soon. We have the tools and skillset to rebuild the moment the cleanup is complete."

"That's what we were hoping to find," the man replied. "Others as motivated as us to rebuild and get our lives back to normal. What's your plan?"

"My father, brother, and I are welders. The Palladons are miners. Together we can rebuild every inch of this city. There's an iron mine a few miles west, so there's really no better place to start."

"How about energy? What are your plans for that?"

"There's a coal mine here, too. Can't expect to reestablish electricity anytime soon, so we'll have to revert to old methods."

"We are kindred spirits, you and I."

"Where were you headed?" Sergei asked.

"Arizona. We had family down there and figured the ash might not have reached that far, though we aren't sure if they survived."

"Well, you're welcome to stay here with us. We have plenty of amenities and the living conditions are comfortable, considering the state of things. And of course, we'd be grateful for the extra hands in our rebuild." Sergei scanned the group, greedily elated to see many large men.

The masked man looked at his wife and after a moment of unspoken communication, he turned back to Sergei with smiling eyes.

"I think we will. Thank you." He extended his hand once more. "My name is Phineas Devereaux and I am delighted to join your cause."

Chapter 12

Coast of Senegal, Africa

Sofyla and her followers followed Eshe across the country from the caves of Kilimanjaro to the coast of Senegal. They had to surface many times as she and her people could not descend to the same depths or withstand the same levels of heat as Eshe, but they made the trip without any injuries.

"Why am I changing so much faster than you?" Eshe asked as Sofyla's people boarded the working boat they found at a nearby port. Her irises grew a deeper shade of red every day.

"I suppose it's because you are immersed in your element. I've been living beneath mine since the purge and haven't had its power filtering through me every day like you have. At least I hope that's the case. I want to discover my own evolution, too."

"You're probably right. You'll start changing the moment you reach the Amazon."

"It's a shame I can't go back to the Ukraine. There is no better soil on Earth than the Chernozem belt. I am sure I would evolve if I were stationed amongst the black soil."

"The soil of the Amazon will be fertile too. Do not fret. Gaia would not lead us astray."

"I am going to miss you," Sofyla confessed.

"I will miss you too. It will be strange only talking to you telepathically from now on. Not only are you one of my Champion sisters, but you've also grown to be one of my best friends."

"I feel the same way." She threw her arms around Eshe and they shared a hug before she had to join the others on the boat.

"Keep me updated on your progress," Eshe requested as Sofyla boarded.

"Of course."

Sofyla's father, Yure, took the helm and led them out to sea. He was a skilled sailor and had confidence he could guide them to Amapá. With his nautical charts, his bearing and magnetic compasses, and the marine chart plotter set to the correct latitude and longitude, Yure set forth. The water was dark and choppy. The air was warm from the heat of the sun beyond the ash clouds, but there was no sunlight or moonlight to control the ocean currents. The water was volatile as it tried to regulate conflicting tides on its own.

"We have an issue," Yure shouted from the captain's cabin.

"Already?" Sofyla asked. They were barely at sea for an hour.

"I cannot control our course. The water is too unstable. We've been heading southwest for one hour, but the waves have taken us northwest. I've been adjusting our course throughout, trying to maintain the correct heading, but no amount of toggling with the helm seems to be helping."

"But are we still headed southwest?"

"South. We are off course and have to back track."

"Are we aimed at Brazil's coast?"

"Yes. Until the waves take us elsewhere again."

"I will send up others to help. If staying on course means we need to have hands on the wheel at all times, then that's what we'll do."

Riad was her Second and had rapidly morphed into the love of her life. She never expected to find such a companion after learning about her responsibilities as a Champion, but was grateful the soil spirits selected him for her. He was a great help and stayed with her father in the captain's cabin at all times.

While she was taking care of everyone else on the boat, he would speak to her through their telepathic connection and give her updates. The outlook was grim.

A week passed and their fight against the currents was never-ending. They barely made any progress due to the fact that they were constantly trying to cover the distance they lost. She was grateful to have Riad and her parents during this struggle because the faith of everyone else on board was wavering. They were running out of food and water, and there was no land in sight. A few of the men began fishing, hoping there was still wildlife beneath the ocean but their lines came up empty every time.

Sofyla leaned over the boat's railing and let the mist coat her face. Covered in seawater, she called out to Coral telepathically.

We've been adrift for almost two weeks. Our food supply has diminished to crumbs and we are almost out of drinking water. A few of my followers have been trying to catch fish to eat, but there is no ocean life to be found.

The sea creatures are hibernating in the depths. You won't catch anything until the clouds part, Coral explained.

We will die out here!

I will talk to the ocean spirits to see if they can guide you to land.

Thank you. This is a disaster. I never realized the ocean would be so volatile.

Yes, the ocean spirits are struggling. The lack of light from the sun and moon has greatly altered their tides and ecosystem.

I still don't understand why the clouds remain, Sofyla expressed.

Neither do I, but there must be a good reason.

You have sunlight, right? Sofyla asked, reconfirming a fact Coral told them in the White Room a while ago. It wasn't discussed often as it caused tension amongst the Champions.

Yes, we always have. The clouds never reached Antarctica. I suppose it wasn't necessary since there weren't any people here except our followers and us. Though I'd bet the cold we face is just as unbearable as your darkness.

Probably, Sofyla confessed.

Both issues are beginning to interfere with our *survival and* our *chances of success in the new world. The whole point was for us to rebuild a better society, and none of us can do that without warmth and sunlight.*

Yeah, there must be a justifiable reason. I just wish we knew what it was because this is awful.

Hang in there. I'm going to get you help.

Coral departed and Sofyla's attention returned to the dark, rough sea. The water was a murky shade of gray, which blended into the color of the sky. The horizon was barely visible due to the matching shades of gloom. She stood outside the captain's cabin and could hear her parents arguing over whose turn it was to steer.

"I can do it," Yeva said with exasperation.

"The currents are too strong," Yure insisted. "I'm not saying you are weak, but I don't want you to hurt yourself. I am left in a sweat after each shift. So is Riad and he is young and fit. I would never forgive myself if you got hurt doing my job."

Yeva looked at him with stubborn resolve, but understood his concern. She underwent open heart surgery a few months before the purge and he and Sofyla had been coddling her ever since.

"I understand you think I'm fragile, but I promise you I'm not. You and Riad need a good night's rest and I am perfectly capable of helping."

"You're not getting your way this time. I won't bend."

Yeva was used to getting her way, so she marched out of the room, determined to try again when Yure was a bit more tired. Riad followed her out of the cabin, but remained with Sofyla on the deck. He wrapped his arms around her and they watched the waves crash against the side of the boat. He kissed her neck and she relaxed in the safety of his embrace. Finding love in the end of times was the last thing she expected, and having it delivered by nature still amazed her. She felt extremely lucky and eternally grateful to have him. He was solid and steadfast. His presence eased her nerves and restored her confidence whenever it wavered. She was strong on her own, but having him there meant she did not have to carry the burden on her own. His love was a comfort for which she felt blessed.

She let herself melt in his arms. As she drifted away in happy thoughts that did not involve their current predicament, the sky seemed to brighten. Her heart fluttered as she imagined the clouds parting for the sun.

"Do you see that?" she asked.

"See what?"

"The clouds! They are moving." Sofyla stood up straight, releasing herself from his hold, and focused on the spot in the sky where the light seemed brighter. But as her concentration became fixed on the small spot, the light disappeared. "I swear I saw the clouds parting." Her voice quickly deflated from the letdown.

"I'm sure it will happen soon," he reassured her.

Sofyla swallowed her disappointment and resumed her normal bravado.

"I have to check on the others." She gave him a kiss. "I'll be back soon."

She left the top deck and descended the stairs to check on her followers residing amongst the lower levels. The day was dark but her energy radiated. She attended to her responsibilities with the fleeting hope of the sun's return lingering in her heart.

Chapter 13

Cedar City, Iron County, Utah

The day was filled with laughter and merriment as the groups merged. Marlaina and Renita took Claudia Devereaux, Felicie Böhme, and Jolene Culver on a tour of the neighborhood homes. Together they decided which families would stay where. Carine, Misty, and Brett already made it clear that they wanted their families to live together and were not as picky as the older women as to which house they got. Once the homes were assigned, 21 Pinecone Drive was chosen as the entire group's shared home. It had an enormous, open layout on the first floor, which was perfect for large gatherings.

After a good night's sleep, everyone gathered at 21 Pinecone to celebrate. Edith Lamorte and Felicie Böhme prepared the meal while the other women did their best to keep the influx of young children rallied and entertained.

Genevieve and Zaedon Devereaux quickly bonded with the older Palladon boys and Halloran siblings. All in their twenties, they formed a fast friendship. Though Carine, Misty and Brett weren't much older, they kept to themselves and their immediate families. The trek to Utah had been emotionally draining and they had become even less fond of the Devereaux family since departing the Hall of Mosses. The trio sat on dusty couches in the corner of the large living room while everyone else bustled around them.

"I'm still not sure we made the right choice," Misty said with a sigh. Her older brothers were in the backyard talking strategy for rebuilding. The moment Sergei learned that Cole and Ian were lumberjacks with degrees in architecture he recruited them. They were swept away and welcomed as part of the Lamorte's elite and confidential team of leaders. Luke was included in the group, but Sergei did not view him with the same regard or value as he did her older brothers.

"You need to let it go," Carine said, exasperated. They had already hashed this dilemma out multiple times on the walk south. "They will be fine, and so will we. We did what we thought was best for our families. They can't be mad at us for that."

"They've probably already forgiven us," Brett added.

"Teek, maybe. I doubt Juniper has," Misty responded. "Did you see the look on her face as we walked away? Absolute betrayal. I don't think there's anything worse we could have done to her."

"She will forgive us." Carine insisted. "We have to let it go."

Misty dropped the topic and folded her arms over her stomach, unable to erase the remorse she felt.

Brett's sisters were doing a better job of fitting in than he and his co-workers. Brynn sat on the floor and played with Dante's small children. Her infection healed a week after they left— turned out they just needed to give the antibiotic more time to work.

Chloe and Kallie kept Lucine entertained. They sat in a line and braided each other's hair. The moment the Böhme girls saw the hair-braiding train, they left the game of tag they were playing with the other children to join.

"Thank you," Marlaina mouthed to Chloe, grateful that they got four of the children to stop running around in a space that was already cramped.

Sergei reentered with his crew of men at his back: Dante, Kelso, Gerald, Phineas Devereaux, and the Courtland brothers.

Divisions of leadership were formed and the lines were clear. Sergei was at the top, with Dante close behind. Gerald and Kelso Palladon ranked third and fourth, while Cole, Ian, and Luke Courtland filled out the rear. Phineas offered no useful skillset or survival knowledge, but his zest for progress kept him among them. His ambition worried Sergei, so he kept a close eye on him. Sergei already sensed his desire to weasel his way to the top, and he would not allow that under his watch. The Lamortes would always rule this roost.

Oskar Lamorte was part of the leaders, but remained stuck to his radio. He was hell-bent on finding more survivors across the nation. It was a noble mission and kept him spared from the manual labor.

Sergei had plans to transform the younger men into secondary leaders, but for now, Killian, Dominic, Gino, Vincent, and Benny were doing well as helping hands. When Xavier reached adolescence, he'd begin molding him as well. He also had high hopes for Gerald's daughter, Rebecca, who was strong-willed, loyal, and becoming a fierce young woman.

Everyone else was steadily morphing into faithful followers. They helped wherever and whenever they were needed, but offered no original plans or ideas. Without special skillsets, their primary function was support. Sergei tried to see their helping hands as vital, but he often found the crowded rooms and excessive noise bothersome. They were essential to his plan and if he wanted to lead this group as the successors of the human race, he needed as many numbers as he could get, so he battled the negative feelings that often arrived when he thought of what they contributed. It was minimal and infuriating, but he bit his tongue and hid his condescending thoughts.

"Are we ready to eat?" Sergei asked with grandeur as he tore off his facemask and entered the room.

Everyone stopped what they were doing and took their places at the long row of mismatched tables. Edith and Felicie brought out the large dishes of prepared food and placed them along the table. Working with canned items only, the options were a bit strange, but the group was happy to sit down and share a meal.

Sergei sat at the head of the table with Dante on his right and Marlaina on his left. Everyone else filled in the open seats, with the newcomers staying closer to Sergei so he could talk to them.

"I'd like to know more about where you all came from," Sergei began as he filled his plate with food. "Phineas mentioned Washington, but we got caught up in talks of strategy and never finished that part of our conversation."

"My family and I lived in Seattle," Phineas answered. "When the attacks happened, we were returning from visiting family on the coast."

"Attacks?" Dante asked.

"The trees," Phineas answered. "Didn't the same happen here?"

"I don't understand what you mean by attacks."

"The trees attacked," Claudia explained. "They started sprouting to enormous sizes at exponential speeds. They tore apart buildings, destroyed the highways, and killed everyone in their way."

"All we experienced was the eruption, ash, and acidic rainfall," Marlaina chimed in.

"I suppose it's because we live in the desert," Sergei added. "What I don't understand is how that is possible. Volcanoes erupt, sure, but trees killing thousands of people? That's impossible."

"I would've said the same if I hadn't seen it with my own eyes," Phineas responded. "We barely survived."

"But how?"

"The explanation is strange and I doubt you will believe it."

"Try me."

Phineas released a heavy sigh before continuing. "As the trees were attacking, my family and a few others were trapped in the middle of a circle of large trees. The branches moved like whips and the vines were strangling anyone within reach. A young woman in a Jeep called out to us, claiming she could save us. Having no other option, we gave her our trust and followed her lead. She took us into the forest, which seemed like the worst place to hide, but the further we went, the safer the terrain became. It turned out she knew the only safe haven in the area," he begrudgingly admitted.

"How did she know where to find safety?" Sergei asked.

"She called herself the Champion of the Trees. She insisted she was chosen by Gaia, Mother Nature, to help a few select humans survive the purge."

"So you're telling me the state of our ash-covered world was not the result of an inevitable eruption? That it was part of a planned attack?"

"Correct. According to Juniper, Gaia chose seven 'Champions' across the globe who were responsible for keeping small groups of humans alive. Once the dust of the attacks settled, these small groups would emerge from their safe havens and begin again. They'd live simpler, cleaner lives on Earth, and create a society that respected nature."

"Why were they worthy of survival but the rest of us weren't?" Renita blurted, appalled at the injustice.

"We aren't sure," Phineas answered. "We weren't supposed to survive, we just happened to be at the right place at the right time."

"I'm not buying any of this," Oskar said. "It all sounds like a load of horse crap."

"We felt the same," Phineas said, "That's why we left. She refused to leave the forest and we wanted to start anew. She said the trees would tell her when it was safe to leave, but we'd had enough of her asinine claims. She thought she was some kind of messiah."

"I won't lie," Jolene Culver interjected. "I believed her at first. She saved us, I was grateful, and her actions seemed to prove that her claims were valid. But as time went on and we struggled to find comfort in the forest, my family and I grew weary. She stubbornly insisted we stay put, but had no valid reason why."

"I still believe her," Misty said. "I think she is chosen by nature, or whatever gods there are, and that she only meant well. I've been friends with her for years, and she predicted all of nature's attacks before they happened: The tsunamis in the South Pacific, the avalanches, arctic freeze, and toxic fog across Asia and Europe, the mudslides and quicksand in Canada and the Middle East. She knew about the severe flooding in South America and the super volcanoes. She had insight no one else was privy to. I only left because I couldn't stay in that claustrophobic forest any longer."

"You say she predicted all those tragedies before they happened," Sergei countered. "Why didn't she warn anyone?"

"Would you have believed her?" Brett asked.

"But did she even try? Millions of innocent lives were lost and she could have saved them."

"I don't think she had any power to stop the catastrophes," Carine said in defense of her friend, "and she did send emails to the mainstream media, but no one responded. It all happened so fast, her emails were probably never seen."

"If I worked for a media outlet and received that email, I wouldn't have taken it seriously," Brett added. "Even if I saw the world collapsing around me, I would've assumed she was just another crazy person looking for a moment in the limelight before she died."

"I still want to know what made *her* worthy above everyone else," Renita insisted.

"She's not," Phineas answered.

Sergei's pleasant mood shifted from calm to volatile. He wasn't sure what he believed—the story was wild and delusional, but the facts appeared solid. If it was true, there were women on this planet who knew of the devastation headed toward humanity and did nothing to prevent it. They let the masses die. They emerged unharmed on the other side of this tragedy as murderers. The blood was on their hands.

"Rebecca, please take the children out of the room," he insisted. She obeyed and escorted all the little ones upstairs with help from Valerie and Cade Culver.

"They don't deserve to be alive," Sergei continued once the kids were out of earshot. "These 'Champions' are demons among men." He spat as his rage did the talking. "Whether there is a god behind their knowledge or not, to claim to be 'chosen' and then let so many die is a travesty. From what I gather, they were not only chosen to champion nature, but also to assist in the slaughter of millions."

Misty jumped in, attempting to defend her friend. "According to Juniper, she was instructed to save a small group. Not everyone. The masses were *supposed* to die," she explained, cringing as she did so. The words felt raw as they left her mouth.

"Millions of innocent children were supposed to die?" Sergei challenged. "Her loyalty should have been to her species, not to some false god bent on destroying mankind. All the Champions are at fault and I feel obliged to settle that score on behalf of the millions who perished."

"You want to pursue a vendetta against the Champions?" Hanke asked, taken aback. "I truly believe they did all they could, given the situation."

"They could've done more. They should have let themselves look like lunatics if it meant a few more lives would be saved."

"I think there are bigger issues to tackle," Brett said, hoping to stop this vendetta from taking shape. "If we focus on killing *them* rather than making *our* remaining lives better, we will *all* lose in the end."

Sergei shook his head. "On principle alone, these Champions need to die. Mother Nature chose them? They are Her 'solution'? Well, I am not on board with *Her* plans. I will not bow and accept this unjust cruelty. How can we sit back and let Her carry on without any resistance? She ought to be stopped and eliminating Her Champions is the first step."

"We are talking about a divine entity here," Carine reminded him. "Not some living, breathing woman we can access."

"Which is why we deliver revenge through Her favorite mortals. Through them we send a message to Her. She may have had plans to kill us all, but She failed, and we will not go down without a fight."

114

The room became quiet as everyone's thoughts stirred around varying concerns. Were the Champions innocent? Were they guilty? Would Sergei's unexpected crusade be their eventual downfall? If gods were at play, did they stand any chance against them? Or would these gods strike them down the moment they fought back? They managed to survive, and so far, no action was taken to eradicate them. Was this fight worth the risk?

The veins in Sergei's neck bulged and everyone kept their thoughts to themselves. It was clear he was set on this new mission and there would be little anyone could do to stop him. Half the group seemed to match his conviction the more they let his words settle into their hearts, while the other half wondered if more death would only lead them further astray. The group was split, but no one vocalized their concerns. Sergei was too heated, too impassioned to reason with.

"I need names and locations of the other Champions," he demanded of the newcomers.

"She never talked about them in much detail," Misty responded first before anyone else said too much. It was a lie. Juniper had confided in her, Carine, and Brett. They knew the names and locations of quite a few Champions, but she hoped to spare them from Sergei's rage.

"I don't believe that. Rack your brains. I am positive she threw their names and locations around in passing. We will continue our efforts here, but the moment we have access to these Champions, be ready. Evil has no home in our new world."

"Honey, please calm down," Marlaina begged, but her request only angered him further.

"Calm down? If this news does not enrage you as much as it does me, you may not have a home here. That goes for all of you. We are all victims to the same tragedy and I can only hope this revelation sets a fire beneath your bones. We are alive, we have survived, and we will avenge the fallen. If you have half a heart, my conviction will resonate." He pushed his plate and stood. "There will be war."

Chapter 14

Lost at Sea, Sofyla Yurchenko, Champion of Soil

An enormous wave crashed against the side of the boat, causing it to tip and sway. Sofyla and Riad held onto the railing as the water splashed and covered the deck. Riad's embrace kept them secure and after a moment, the tides returned to normal.

"I don't know what will happen," he whispered, "but I know I'll be okay as long as I have you."

She turned her head to give him a kiss. As they shared a tender moment, the boat's trajectory shifted.

"There's nothing I can do!" Yure hollered from the helm. Riad and Sofyla ran into the cabin to help, but the wheel was spinning out of control. Riad tried to grab it, but it smacked his hand, causing an immediate bruise, and continued spinning. Sofyla held his wounded hand in hers and after a moment, the bruise disappeared. The sight of their small injuries healing before her eyes still left her in awe.

When the wheel finally stopped, they were headed northwest. Yure took the wheel and tried to turn the boat south, but it wouldn't budge. Riad took a turn, yielding the same result.

"It must be the ocean spirits," Sofyla finally concluded.

"What do you mean?" Riad asked.

"I told Coral about our situation and asked if she could help us. She offered to ask the ocean spirits if they could guide us to land."

"Did you specify where? Because they are not leading us to Brazil."

"No, I assumed the spirits would know."

"Currently, we are heading toward the Gulf of Mexico," Yure said as he examined his maps.

"Can you talk to Coral again?" Riad asked.

"I'll try, but at this rate any land is better than this ocean," Sofyla responded. "Juniper is making a very long journey on foot to the Amazon, and if we cannot redirect this ship to reach Brazil, we will have to do the same from wherever we land."

"I'll keep trying to redirect our course, but it doesn't look promising. We are at the mercy of the sea." Yure took a seat near the wheel.

A week passed and they were still off course. Sofyla spoke to Coral, but there was nothing she could do to help. The ocean spirits were engaged with her ship and not answering Coral's calls pleading that they guide the boat toward the coast of Brazil. Coral apologized and Sofyla prepared for the worst. They weren't sure where they'd dock, or how, so she and Riad prepared the group for the imminent uncertainty they sailed toward.

The ocean spirits guided them safely through the tight cluster of islands in the Caribbean Sea. There was no apparent life on any of them, just destruction. From what she could see during their slow glide past each island, the flooding killed everything. The water levels were back to normal and the damage caused to the shorelines, vegetation, and housing along the coasts was horrific. There was still debris from cars and buildings floating in the water between islands. Bloated bodies drifted at the discretion of the waves, slamming into larger pieces of wreckage and getting tangled within the smaller clusters. This somber reminder of their reality hit Sofyla hard as they sailed through the watery graveyard.

It took three days before they were far enough into the Gulf to see the coast of North America. Sofyla recognized the shape of Florida's coastline as they soared past. There was no controlling the speed of their boat and as they traveled closer to the shore, they prepared for a crash landing.

By sunset, the spot of their inevitable collision was visible. The group braced themselves for the hit, holding onto the railings and sturdy structures throughout the boat, though this did not prevent the majority from flying across the deck and getting minor injuries upon impact. After a quick round and determining that everyone as relatively okay, Sofyla lowered the damaged walkway to the sand and everyone departed. Sofyla exited last after ensuring all her people were safely off the broken vessel.

"Where are we?" Yeva asked. The sand was white and led to grass covered dunes. Sofyla walked toward the spot where the sand met grass.

"I'm not sure," she replied before continuing her exploration. She saw a large abandoned building in the distance and walked toward it. At its entrance was a sign that read Fort Pickens.

"Anyone know where Fort Pickens is?" she asked.

The group of native Ukrainians and Saudi Arabians shrugged, never having heard of it before.

"My guess is Florida or Alabama. Or maybe Mississippi is next to Florida," Sofyla attempted to answer her own question, trying to recall the layout of a US map in her head. "We were pretty close to the Floridian shoreline before we crashed. I'm not sure where the state lines are, but it's one of those."

They continued walking along the road and found a sign that read: Pensacola Beach, 5 miles.

"I think we're in Florida," Yeva offered.

"I think so too," Sofyla agreed. "We obviously can't get to Brazil through the Gulf. The water is too dangerous. We are going to have to take the long way."

"Which way is that?" a young man asked.

"Along the coast. We will take our time, don't worry. Perhaps we can even meet up with Juniper and her people sooner than anticipated. They are coming from the northwest and will have to travel through Mexico to reach Brazil. If timing is on our side, we can connect and make the trip into the Amazon together."

The group liked the notion of this—the more people they had, the better their likelihood of survival. More able bodies, more hands to gather food, more brains to strategize.

They began to walk west and eventually came across large signs that marked the state borders. Everything was covered in muddy residue and it quickly became clear that this area suffered from severe flooding. Between occasional stops to eat and rest, it took three days to reach Mobile, Alabama, and another four to reach Gulfport, Mississippi.

Sofyla did her best to stay strong for her people. They were making great time, but everyone was hungry and unhappy. She stopped the entire group every time someone expressed they were in pain or tired, and did her best to stock as much food amongst the groups' packs as possible.

Riad and her parents were a great source of support, but she did not like to lean on them too much. Her parents were old and fragile, even though they pretended they weren't, and Riad had enough on his plate with his extremely dissatisfied followers. They were far more outspoken about their unhappiness than those who followed her from Ukraine. She reminded everyone daily that they'd find comfort in a few months once they reached Brazil, but the further they traveled along the coast, the worse the conditions became. By the time they reached Mississippi, the ash that was previously at a safe distance in the clouds now plagued each breath they took. Many still had the scarves they used to stay protected from the sandstorm during the purge in the Rub' al Khali desert. Those who lost their scarves went into town with Sofyla to search for suitable replacements. Not only were they able to find good handkerchiefs to guard their mouths and noses, but also an entire rack of sunglasses. The additions to their wardrobe offered new comfort to the group and helped ease the tension.

Juniper, are you there? Sofyla called out through her mind. It took a few minutes before she received a reply.

Sofyla, how are you?

We are okay. I meant to reach out sooner, but it's been a crazy week.

Have you reached Amapá yet?

Funny story. We are actually in Mississippi right now.

Mississippi? Why?

The ocean is unstable without sunlight or moonlight to control its currents. We were having trouble navigating, so I spoke to Coral and she had the ocean spirits help guide us to land, except I forgot to mention our destination. I assumed the soil spirits and ocean spirits were on the same page, but apparently not.

That's so out of the way. Are you walking the coast to get to South America?

Yes. I don't want to be lost at sea again. I'd rather have my feet on the ground. It will take much longer, but at least we are safe. No risk of drowning on land.

Good point. My people and I are about to cross into Utah. If you're up for it, you can wait for us in Mexico and we can make the

121

remainder of the journey together. I imagine you'll be waiting a while because you're much closer than we are, but it might be nice to tackle the harder part of the trek as one unit.

I completely agree. We will be traveling along the eastern coast of Texas and once we reach the Mexican border, we will wait for you there.

Great. I'm sorry you were taken off course, but maybe it will end up working out better this way.

It's possible. We might have never found each other along the Amazon River.

Exactly. Talk to you soon.

Juniper disconnected and Sofyla returned her attention to the group, who rested on the sidewalk of a gas station. They ate snacks that were sealed and protected from the harmful chemicals in the air and chatted amongst themselves. It made Sofyla happy to see the two groups within her following bonding. They had refused to interact with each other the first few weeks they were together beneath the volcanoes of Africa. They often opted for the company of Eshe's followers over those they joined beneath Sofyla's lead. The trip to Senegal was a little better and brought forth more intermingling, but it wasn't until their fate became unsure on the boat to Brazil that they started to trust one another. Sofyla wasn't sure why that moment took so long to come, but she was grateful it had. Now, as they traveled and embarked upon the hardest part of their journey, the group felt harmonious. They helped one another, took time to teach each other their native languages, and developed friendships. Though there was still an underlying sense of dissatisfaction, Sofyla was happy to see tiny battles being won.

They continued toward Louisiana, refueled and eager to put more miles behind them. To avoid the swamplands south of

New Orleans, they followed US Route 90 through the city, which was deserted. The ground was still soggy from the flooding that occurred prior to the volcanic ash dusting. Most of the buildings had crumbled and those that hadn't now stood on weak foundations. The ash on the ground was hard to walk through as the moisture from the flooding turned it into a thick putty. Its consistency was cement-like and it caked onto their shoes.

They followed the highway until they reached New Iberia. From there, they continued west onto LA 14 and switched between highways until they were back at the coast. They were not free of the swamplands, but avoiding them by way of the main roads was easier here. LA 82 took them through Vermilion Parish and when they reached the town of Grand Chenier, the group was brought to a shocking halt.

In the middle of the road was an old beige couch with words spray painted onto its cushions.

Sofyla walked closer to the couch and did her best to translate the inscription. She was able to figure out half of what it said, but struggled with the rest.

"Who can read English?" Sofyla asked her Ukrainian and Saudi Arabian followers. Many could speak a little English, some could write a few words, but none were fluent. She tried again, reading all the words out loud, but only understanding the meaning of a few.

"*Survivors in Cameron! Come see! Follow neutral ground n take your rodier to 27 riverside. We be waitin', ready to welcome ya mama and dem!*" She looked at her followers with wide eyes. "Fellow survivors, surely, but none that are part of a Champion's following."

"Other people survived?" Yeva asked. "I thought only the Champions were granted safe havens."

"Correct, but the spirits promised to save worthy souls who were unable to reach the Champion of their aura's reigning element. Perhaps these people are bound to nature and were spared."

"They must be," Riad contributed. "The only survivors of this purge are those Gaia chose, right?"

"Right," Sofyla said, certain this must be the case. "I don't understand the full message here, but they seem to be telling us they are in Cameron, which is probably a town, and to follow the roadway marked 27. I suspect there will be a river to indicate the direction to go."

"Is it worth the detour?" Riad asked.

"Of course. This is my purpose. I am here to help others endure these times. And for all we know, it won't be a detour. Maybe it's on the way."

"I understand, still, something about this doesn't feel right."

Sofyla took a step closer to her Second. "It is my responsibility to find and guide these people. They are likely scared and confused. This is my calling, it's what I was chosen to do. I suspect they will be happy to learn the truth behind their survival and will follow us to the Amazon."

"I hope you're right."

"I am," she said with a smirk. She gave him a small kiss before turning and leading the group onward.

It wasn't long before they encountered the turn-off for LA 27. It continued west and was on course for where they were headed. It followed the coastline and led them through the ruins of a town that appeared destroyed long prior to the purge. The deterioration was old and though the aftereffects of nature's attacks were apparent, the damage ran much deeper.

The further they traveled, the more handmade signs they saw. The other survivors drew arrows on everything they could find so that newcomers would find them. Random pieces of furniture littered the sides of the highway, leading Sofyla and her crew in the right direction. When they reached Cameron Elementary School a small boy greeted them. He stood in the middle of the road wearing nothing but jeans and a facemask. He was skinny, dark-skinned, and silent. The street remained quiet as they walked closer.

"Hello," Sofyla said in English. Her thick Ukrainian accent caused the boy's head to tilt with wonder. "We saw your signs and hoped to meet other survivors. Are there adults nearby?"

The boy nodded and then took off in a sprint. There was no way Sofyla or her people had the energy to chase after him, so they waited. When he came back, he was followed by an older gentleman, who looked much like him, and a few other adults.

"Dis ma paw-paw," the boy declared as the older gentleman stepped forward.

"Pleasure ta welcome ya'll."

"Thank you," Sofyla replied, trying to keep up with all they said, but having trouble understanding.

"Cho! Co! Yer voice! Where ya'll coming from?"

"Ukraine and Saudi Arabia. Found shelter in Africa for a while, then made our way across the Atlantic, but the ocean was too rough to navigate and we crashed in Pensacola, Florida. Been walking ever since."

"F'True? Dats a long journey."

"Very long."

"Wus here dats so important ta make dat trip?"

"Our new home."

"Dis could be yur home. We binlookin' fer more people, more survivors."

"The air is cleaner south of here. You should join us."

"How're you so certain dats da right spot ta be?"

"I can explain once we get to know each other a little better. The truth is large and hard to believe. For now, I think it's best we skip it."

Clovis' eyes narrowed in on Sofyla, but he did not press for more. He unclipped his walkie-talkie from his belt and spoke rapidly to a person on the other side. Sofyla could not decipher what he said. After the brief message was relayed, he turned to her wearing a large smile and beckoned her to follow.

"We'll feed ya," he offered, then led the way. He took them through backyards on a direct path to a road off the main strip. Not even a mile down Amaco Road, the ruins of the old town center were replaced by vacant marshlands. Sofyla suddenly felt unsure about these new friends. She glanced over at Riad, who appeared to share her uncertainty.

"Where are you taking us?" she asked Clovis.

"Homebase. Roof is secure and all our food 'n water is stored dere."

Sofyla nodded and dropped her line of questioning. She did not want to offend their attempts at hospitality. After seeing how they lived and grasping their full situation, she'd be able to customize her approach when convincing them to follow. Based off the dreary conditions she was already experiencing, her hunch suspected it wouldn't be hard to sway their resolve. Fifteen minutes later an enormous manor appeared in the distance. It was the only house on this lonely stretch of road, but the sight of it gave her comfort. Soon they'd eat, enjoy good company, and she could begin the process of recruiting the Creoles.

Clovis led them up the front porch and opened the door, allowing each guest to enter before him. Yure and Yeva entered last and Clovis fastened the deadbolt, locking them all inside. The loud click caused Sofyla's heart to jump and her mistrust returned. The foyer was dark and all she could see were the silhouetted shadows of Clovis' people.

He walked the perimeter of the room, lighting candles as he went. Once he made a full circle, the room was outlined by a faint glow. He then walked to a table that was placed at the center and ignited the wick of a lantern. This light burned bright and illuminated the harrowing scene.

Men strapped with various forms of firearms encircled the group, blocking them from all exits. Sofyla examined the development with outrage, then glared up at Clovis in question.

"What is this?"

"Tell me your truth," he demanded.

Sofyla stood taller and shook her head.

"Now!" His shout was accompanied by a hard backhand to her face. Riad and the other men stepped forward to defend her, but the moment they did, the rifles were raised and engaged. Sofyla was hunched over, but managed to raise a hand to stop her people from initiating a bloodbath. She opened and closed her mouth a few times to get the feeling back in her jaw, then stood with confidence again.

"I don't understand why you are doing this."

"I'm doin' this cuz there're devils out dere and you might be one of dem." He took a pistol out from his waistband and placed the barrel against the side of her forehead.

"I don't know what devils you speak of, but I promise you. I'm not one of them. I was protected in order to assist people like you. I am here to help."

"Tell me how you know about safe spots."

"I know because I was chosen."

"Chosen?"

"Yes. By Gaia, Mother Nature. I am the Champion of Soil. If you follow me you will be safe."

He cocked the hammer of the gun. "This is sounding mighty grim for ya."

"It's okay if you don't believe me. I can show you!"

"Oh, I believe ya. But that's da *problem*."

"Why?"

"Cuz only devils let millions die while hidin' in safe spots." His eyes were wild with hatred as they shifted from Sofyla to his men. "Kill 'em."

The men opened fire, killing everyone in their immediate vicinity. Those trapped in the middle scrambled and tried to fight back.

Sofyla was caught in Clovis' sturdy grip. Riad charged toward them, but Sofyla stopped him.

Save the others, she pleaded with him telepathically.

I must save you.

No. Get them out of here. Run as far as you can. I'll find you.

Riad hesitated, but obeyed. The large Ukrainian men of the group were doing a good job overtaking the scrawny Creoles. While they fought, others escaped through broken windows. Sofyla watched as Riad helped the survivors climb out. Once the Creoles realized what was happening, they unlocked the front door and gave chase. Gunshots fired as her people ran for their lives.

I'll be waiting for you, Riad said with a look of defeat before running after the others. The few remaining Ukrainian men attempted to help Sofyla, but the moment Clovis raised his gun, she screamed and insisted they leave. When they refused, Clovis fired, killing the largest among them, motivating the others to flee. He continued firing at them as they scrambled toward safety.

It was only Clovis and Sofyla left in the foyer. Everyone else who remained was dead. She couldn't bear to examine the faces of those lost. There were too many.

Clovis wrapped an arm around her neck and dragged her toward the table that held a large radio. He fiddled with the dials until the static stopped.

"Oskah? Sergei? You dere?"

It took a few moments before he received a reply.

"Oskar, here. How's it going?"

"We caught one."

Chapter 15

Interstate 84, Oneida County, Idaho

The journey was long and indirect, but following the major highways was their safest bet. Juniper wished they could forge a direct path to the Mexican border, but the damage caused by the trees and super volcano was too severe. There was no telling what they would encounter in the newly formed wilderness, so they stuck to the abandoned highways.

While the roadways were safer than off-roading, they were still cracked and damaged from nature's attack. There were many times Juniper's caravan of dirt bikes, quads, and Jeeps had to slow to a stop so they could maneuver around large fissures and broken roadway. The further south they traveled, the worse the ash became. It was a few inches thick and made riding very dangerous.

Finding fuel had become a non-issue—there were plenty of abandoned cars to siphon gas from on the highways. The sight of so many deserted vehicles was tough to get used to, but as the days passed and the sight of the dead passengers trapped inside their cars grew familiar, the group became numb to their sorrow. Not in lack of empathy, but for the sake of their sanity. All they could do was accept the facts surrounding their survival with compassion and gratitude, and keep moving forward. The sight was a constant reminder that they were lucky to be alive. It also reminded the group that they had Juniper to thank for their survival. No one spoke of it, they were too focused on the daily toll of their voyage, but their loyalty to her grew stronger as they witnessed the destruction they narrowly avoided.

Juniper and crew crossed the state line and entered Utah. These roads presented a lot more of the same: ash, darkness, damaged roadway, and abandoned cars. The air was beginning to cool and Juniper wasn't sure if that was due to their departure from the Hall of Mosses, which was a safe haven engineered by Gaia, or if the ash cloud was finally creating a volcanic winter. It felt like there was a greenhouse effect occurring initially, but months passed and all the warmth trapped beneath the cloud was replaced with a slight chill. The drastic change in temperature was great motivation to move at a swift and steady pace. She had hope that the Amazon was magically protected like the Hall of Mosses. If they reached the jungle, perhaps the conditions would change for the better.

A few miles from Honeyville, UT, Bernard fell ill. He had suffered a heart attack a few months before the purge and ran out of his medication in Idaho. They stopped at every pharmacy they came across, but could not find the prescription he needed. Despite the lack of medicine, he seemed to be doing okay until he had a seizure unexpectedly and his dormant heart issues were triggered. He died the following day.

They buried Bernard and began heading toward Honeyville, when Martha's intense grief induced a massive heart attack. She never had heart issues previously, but the loss of her love broke her heart.

The entire group mourned their loss—this was the first set of deaths among them. They all loved Bernard and Martha and struggled to let them go. Juniper's mortality was put in check as she realized she'd outlive them all. In time, she'd be forced to watch the deaths of everyone she cared about and this reality did not sit easy.

They carried on with heavy hearts and reached the town of Honeyville.

"Look," Dedrik shouted from the front of the group and pointed at a standing gas station—most had exploded in the attacks. The Jeeps were running low on gas and their extra canisters were almost empty.

Juniper led the caravan into the lot and everyone parked their vehicles. Jeb, Clark, and Roscoe began assessing the pumps to make sure they were safe, and once deemed clear, began pumping gasoline into the canisters.

"I bet Gaia hates that we are still relying on gasoline to survive," Roscoe said as he placed a cap on his canister and began filling a second.

"It's a means to an end," Juniper replied in a shout from across the lot. She was trying to break the lock on the door to the adjacent auto body shop. "As soon as we reach the Amazon we won't need gasoline ever again."

"But wouldn't it be fun to race around the jungle on dirt bikes?" Wes asked.

"Not at the expense of the land. The emissions would kill the vegetation."

"What if there was a clean way to ride?"

"I'm not a chemist and have no clue how to make an engine run without gasoline."

"Neither am I, but I've got a lot of time to think this over."

"Come up with a clean alternative and you can ride as much as you want."

Wes nodded and walked away, determined to figure out a way to make the bikes work without fuel. He walked directly to Dedrik, who was a proficient mechanic, and they began discussing the matter in an intense whisper. Juniper didn't suspect they'd find a solution, but encouraged the discussion.

When she finally broke the lock of the auto body shop she was greeted by a welcomed sight. Three large pickup trucks sat behind the garage doors, each with plows attached. With the thickness of the ash increasing, they'd been searching for these parts since they left Washington. The Jeeps were already equipped to handle such additions, all they needed were the plows.

"We've got snow plows," she exclaimed as she pushed each garage door open.

"Yes!" Noah shouted and ran toward the trucks to examine the wiring.

"This will make riding so much easier," Bax said, following his younger brother.

Dedrik was able to remove the plows from each truck and fasten them to the Jeeps. Paul, Aldon, and Jeb helped. It only took a few hours before they were in working order and ready to go.

All the vehicles were refueled and the canisters of extra gas were fastened onto a trailer they acquired in Burley, Idaho. Coolers filled with non-perishable food and cases of sealed water were also placed on the trailer. They continued their journey, this time with the three plows leading the way. They pushed inches of ash to the side and made paths for those on the dirt bikes and quads behind them.

I-84 transitioned into I-15 as they traveled south and a large peak to the east of Honeyville became visible. It was enormous, beautiful, and untouched by the purge, and it crossed Juniper's mind that those types of spots would have been unintended safe zones for others. As the thought of finding survivors swelled inside her heart, she realized the grave reality of this possibility: it was unlikely any one would have thought to run to nature for shelter, not while nature was the predator they wished to escape.

She let the notion go.

As they approached Salt Lake City, the scenery changed from damaged countryside to annihilated city. Though the mountain ranges surrounding the area were lovely and standing tall in their glory, the city they sheltered had crumbled. The trees' attack left the smaller sections torn apart, and the volcanic eruption shredded the city with fissures. The skyscrapers collapsed, destroying everything nearby, and the ash smothered all that remained.

The group moved slower to prevent any mistakes. With no wind to disperse the dust and debris from the fallen buildings, it remained stagnant and caused poor visibility. When they came upon the large fissures, they often weren't visible until the last moment. They had to reroute twice to avoid large cracks in the earth.

Jeb led them through the ruined city, plow down and headlights on. Juniper followed his lead with the others, her mind wandering as she trailed at the back. Something felt wrong. She wasn't sure what it was, but her heart ached. A sudden wave of melancholia washed over her and she couldn't define the source. After a moment of contemplation she determined the sight of the wreckage around her wasn't the cause of her undefined sadness. It felt much deeper. It came from someplace else, somewhere she couldn't reach. It did not stem from her surroundings or from her own mind. She thought of her sisters.

Sofyla, Aria, she called out telepathically. *Marisabel, Eshe.* No response. *Coral? Sahira? Someone respond, please.*

Are you okay?

Juniper was relieved to hear the thick Icelandic accent after a few minutes of silence.

Aria! I got a feeling something was wrong. Everything is fine on my end, so I assumed it was one of you.

We are okay. Sahira is telling the children stories about ancient India before they fall asleep and I am with Erion and Monte talking about our next food run. Aria paused. *Though I have been feeling quite sad today. I wasn't sure why, but I've been rather gloomy.*

Yes, me too. A surge of melancholy slammed me in the chest. Out of nowhere. Have you spoken to the others recently?

No. You're the first person I've heard from since our group meeting a few months ago. I've been caught up in ascending.

Ascending?

The air spirits instructed us to climb higher. It will take centuries before our bodies acclimate to the air density and temperature, but the goal is to thrive at great heights.

Wow. I wonder why.

We aren't sure either, we're just obeying. Have you heard from the others?

I spoke with Sofyla a week or two ago. Marisabel not too long before that.

The only two in transit are you and Sofyla. The others should all be safe in their assigned locations. Though I heard Eshe has been trying to dig tunnels to Hawaii. Maybe it's her.

Maybe. I'll try to contact her and Coral.

Okay. Let me know what you find.

They disconnected and Juniper focused on her current situation. She was still riding the Jaden Jaunt behind three Jeep

Wranglers, the Wolfe brothers were paired up on two dirt bikes, and Roscoe and Teek were on the quads. Everything was fine, so she tuned out and called Eshe.

She tried for 15 minutes with no response. Her heart began to race, nervous that something had happened to her. She switched to Coral and had to wait ten minutes for a response.

Hey, Juniper. Sorry I didn't answer earlier. I was underwater with Zander. Still haven't figured out how to multitask down there.

It's okay. Have you heard from Eshe recently? I'm worried something has happened to her.

I just talked to her a moment ago.

So she's okay?

Seemed it. Definitely nothing worth reporting except some painful evolutionary changes she's going through. She said she heard you calling her while we were speaking and that she'd reach out to you later tonight.

If it's not her, then who?

What do you mean?

Did you feel strangely sad today at any point? Like a wave of sorrow washed over you for no apparent reason?

Yeah, actually. It happened to you too?

And Aria. Something is wrong and I can't figure out who it's coming from.

I see Marisabel every day. She's still miserable and sulking. Maybe her depression is starting to seep into us.

No, I don't think that's it.

The only people I did not speak to today were Aria, Sahira, and Sofyla.

Then it has to be Sofyla. Juniper's heart raced. She hadn't checked in with her in a few days. *I have to go.*

Juniper disconnected and began searching for Sofyla. She called out with persistence, but received no reply. The other end felt empty; the weight of her presence was gone. It reminded her of when she thought she lost Roscoe, but Juniper did not suspect any of the elements were blocking the signal between herself and Sofyla. There was no justifiable reason to break their connection. They needed to be in touch frequently so they could find each other once they both reached Mexico.

Sofyla, she tried again. *Are you okay? Please answer me. I am worried.*

No response.

The group stopped in Provo, Utah, which was just as devastated at Salt Lake City. They scoured the rubble for food and water to add to their growing collection while Juniper grabbed Roscoe, Clark, and Irene to share her latest concern.

"Something has happened to one of my Champion sisters."

"What do you mean?" Irene asked.

"I got an overwhelming sense of grief as we traveled through Salt Lake City. At first I thought it was due to the massive amount of destruction we were seeing, but it felt deeper than that, and came from further away. It's hard to explain. So I reached out to the other Champions and by process of elimination, Sofyla is the only one who hasn't been in contact with the rest of us in a few days. I fear she is in trouble."

"Isn't she the one we are supposed to meet up with in the Amazon?" Clark asked as he chewed on beef jerky.

"Yes. Last I heard she crashed into the coast of Florida and was leading her group along the shoreline of the gulf and into Mexico. I don't know how far she got, or where she is now. She isn't answering my calls."

"That's concerning, not only for her sake but also for ours," Roscoe said. "If there is greater danger out there, we ought to know about it before we lead our people into it. God forbid there's some element of nature that is still actively destroying life. We don't want to fall into its trap."

"It can't be nature. I'm thinking she is hurt."

Roscoe looked at her with a confused expression, but did not verbalize his concern. They still hadn't told the others about their gift of eternal life. Juniper sensed his confusion and tried to clarify without saying too much.

"It feels grave. Like she won't survive."

Roscoe understood and the others listened in contemplation.

"How can we help her if she can't even answer you to let you know what's going on?" Irene asked.

"I'm not sure. I will keep trying, though. I'd like to hurry, if possible. The sooner we get down there the faster we can give her aid."

"I don't think that's wise," Roscoe warned. "What if it was done by an outside source? We'd be driving right into a similar fate."

"Like I said, I'll keep trying to find answers, but we need to help her if we can. I won't let her die alone."

"She has her people," Clark reminded her.

"I'm not so sure about that. I sense she's alone and in pain."

"Riad wouldn't abandon her," Roscoe said.

"We don't know the circumstances."

"Keep calling her," Clark said, swallowing his last bite. "We can hurry, but confirm that we aren't heading into trouble."

"Okay. We can stop at the southern border of Arizona. At least we will be closer and can get to her faster once we determine what's going on."

They all agreed that this was the best plan and joined the rest of the group for lunch. Juniper studied the map as the others ate. I-15 would take them through the towns of Cedar City and St. George, then out of the way and into Las Vegas. From there they had multiple options to redirect their route south into Arizona. She worried it would take too long and that Sofyla would die before they could get to her.

She folded the map and tried to reach her sister again.

No response.

Chapter 16

Cameron, Louisiana

The room was dark and Sofyla was alone with her injuries. Clovis performed a violent round of questioning, to no avail, and left her to suffer with her wounds, hoping the pain would motivate her to say more during the next round. She could feel Juniper reaching out to her, but did not have the strength to respond. The cuts were deep and stung as they healed.

It was the first time she cursed the gift Gaia had bequeathed—she feared the rage Clovis would bestow upon her once he realized she did not possess the expected human fragility. All she could hope for was that the blood smeared across her face remained and he would not notice the missing wounds.

He left her to rot alone for half the day, thinking the silence would amplify her pain and provoke her to speak. But by the time he returned, the pain was long gone. He sensed her renewed strength and greeted it with bewildered fury.

"You should be broken," he hollered. He grabbed her chin and directed her eyes to meet his. She averted her gaze to avoid making eye contact. "Look at me!" he demanded.

She refused. With his free hand he pried her eyelids open and turned her head.

"You can't be lucid." His face constricted with confusion. "I gave you a proper whoopin'." Then his eyes widened. "Where dem bobos go?"

He jerked her face in all directions as he searched for the missing wounds.

"No." The word came out as a breath. He ran to the radio. "Come in, come in." he demanded. A few moments later, a man's voice replied.

"Dante, here. What's going on?"

"She healed!"

"What do you mean?"

"She wouldn' answer me so I whooped her, left her ta fester, came back round n' all da bruisins are gone. Not a cut left on her."

"That's not possible."

"But it happened!"

The radio went silent for a moment. When Dante came back, he sounded as if he had consulted others.

"Can you bring her here?"

"Naw. We can't move now. Who knows what else she can do."

"We need names and locations. If you can't get them out of her, you have to let us try."

"I ain't dragging my kin ta Cedah City so ya'll can crash n' burn like I been. I can do this myself. I don' need ya ta do my job."

"That's not what we were implying. If you come to Utah, we can all work together. I thought that was the plan all along."

"Yeah, but dis changes things. A Champion showed up in my town, not yours. Maybe we ain't supposed ta be out west. Plus, we got those new contacts in New Yahk n' da Capitol. We ought ta be figuring one spot with dem."

"Fine. Worry about your current task. Sergei will figure out the rest."

Dante ended the transmission and a slight static emanated from Clovis' radio.

"Ya heard 'im, tataille." He took a step closer with his blade raised. "I gotta do what I gotta do." He placed the knife against the side of her cheek. "Tell me names."

"Never."

"Awrite."

He plunged the knife into the side of her cheek and tore the skin apart. A gaping gash went from her cheekbone to the side of her mouth. She wailed in agony.

"Dat'll take a while ta heal, am I right?"

Sofyla answered his violence with stubborn silence.

"If you wanted me to talk," she muttered through the pain, moving her lips as little as possible, "you probably shouldn't have mutilated my mouth."

"Hm, true dat. Guess I gotta just hurt ya in other ways till it heals. Cause it will, won't it?"

She shook her head.

"Don' lie ta me!" He stabbed her in the left collarbone.

Tears fell down her face. The pain took over her senses as Clovis continued shouting and spearing her with his knife in non-lethal locations.

Juniper, Sofyla tried to escape the brutal situation through her mind. *Juniper.*

Sofyla! Juniper's voice cracked with relief. *I am so relieved to hear from you.*

I'm not okay.

What's wrong?

I am going to die.

Juniper could sense that Sofyla's thoughts were frail and hard to send.

Where are you? We will come to help.

No! No. You cannot come here. They will kill you too.

They?

Other people survived. They aren't part of our mission. They are outliers. Rebels. They want the Champions dead.

How do they know about us?

I don't know. But the moment I mentioned I was chosen, their friendly welcoming morphed into a slaughtering. They attacked before I ever got a chance to explain. Clovis captured me and I begged the others to flee. Riad is with them now, I hope. I hope they made it. Men with guns chased them out of the house, so I can't be sure. She took a deep breath to restore her energy, then continued. *My parents are dead.*

Juniper felt Sofyla weeping on the other end. Her thoughts were coated in grief and hopelessness.

What can I do? Tell me how to save you and I will.

It's not worth it. They can't see your face. They can't know who you are. All they want from me are the names and locations of the other Champions. I won't give them what they want. I won't let them hunt you.

We can find a way.

No. You need to stay far away from Louisiana. They are in Utah, New York, and Washington, D.C. too.

We are in Utah now.

Reroute. Go the long way. Whatever you have to do to avoid these monsters.

We can't let them get away with this!

It's not worth the fight. You will live forever, they won't. Just stay safe and you can outlast them. Sofyla coughed; it was wet with blood. *I have names. Clovis leads the rebels in Louisiana. He's torturing me now and will likely kill me. Sergei, Dante, and Oskar run the rebellion in Utah. Cedar City, I think. They are a family. Their last* name is Lamorte. I get the impression they currently run the show. Clovis does almost anything they tell him to.

What about New York and D.C.?

I don't have those names. I just overheard the Lamortes and Clovis talking about how they made contact with others in those states.

I can't let you die alone.

You have to. If I can find a way to escape, I will, but he's already discovered that I can heal, and since I'm not talking, I figure it won't be long before they cut their losses and rid the world of one Champion.

We need to figure out how they learned about us. You said he knew before you explained.

Yeah, and his opinion of us was spoiled. Someone poisoned his mind. I didn't even get a chance to explain our entire ordeal before he ordered his men to kill. Whoever relayed our mission did us no service in the telling. Clovis believes we are devils. He says our hearts are blackened by the ghosts of every dead soul we carry.

What would he have done in our position?

Doesn't matter because he's not. He's on his own and he believes we ought to die for our sins. These survivors are righteous. They believe they are the Champions of the human race.

That's our job, Juniper insisted.

No, technically it's not. We are Champions of nature, tasked to protect our chosen few. They want vengeance on behalf of mankind. They act for every human, living and dead. We are their enemy.

We did nothing wrong.

I don't think we did either. I believe we all did the best we could. Problem is, they don't see it that way and they refuse to listen. Juniper. You have to steer clear of these people. They are delusional and bitter. Nothing we say will change their opinions on what we had to do to survive.

Juniper did not know what to say. She had been battling her own guilt for months, needing constant reminders from herself and those around her that she did her best under awful circumstances. Now, she was being faced with the reality that others in this world blamed her for the death of millions.

Check in with me as often as you can, Juniper requested. *I will let the others know what is happening.*

I will gather as much information as I can before he kills me.

Don't talk like that. You will find a way to survive.

I will certainly try. Sofyla quieted for a moment to assess her current situation. *I think he's done with me for the moment. I need to focus on healing.*

Stay strong. We will talk again soon.

The light weight of Sofyla's presence vanished and was replaced by nothingness. The normal pull she felt from each of her sisters, even when they weren't speaking, was lessened by one.

Sofyla returned to the dark room and was greeted by a close-up of Clovis. He was leaning in close, examining the damage he'd done.

"Oh, ya back with me?"

Sofyla gritted her teeth and took deep breaths through her nose. It took all her might to ignore the pain that coursed through her body.

"Got anythin' new ta share?" he asked.

She answered with heavy breaths and a fierce stare. Clovis did not appreciate her defiance.

"Guess ya ought ta sleep on it." Then he knocked her out with a punch.

Chapter 17

Cedar City, Iron County, Utah

The effort to rebuild was in motion. Gerald and Kelso Palladon reopened KGP Metals and began training everyone eighteen years and older the art of mining iron ore. They started slow, never going too deep or too fast for fear their existing mine shafts were unstable after the supervolcanic eruption. After a week of moving through the underground tunnels with care, it was determined that their routes were safe. Gino, Vincent, and Benny already knew how to mine; they were in line to take over the company once Kelso retired, so they helped teach the others proper mining techniques. Oliver and Dennis were also future owners of KGP Metals, but were too young to enter the mines. Gerald didn't trust that his sons were mature enough yet to handle the dangerous responsibility.

While those of age were taught how to mine for iron ore, Sergei, Dante, and Oskar prepped the Bessemer converter. With it, they'd be able to turn the iron ore into steel and rebuild their city. Sergei had plans to make it bigger and better than before. He was angry with nature, angry with his fate, and intended to cover every inch of earth with steel. It was spiteful, he knew that, but it was the only retaliation he had any control over. Once mankind reclaimed the planet, he'd have the power and ability to hunt down the Champions and seek true vengeance.

The others did not know of his plans to drape the landscape in metal, and he did not plan to tell them. They'd call him insane and drown him in logic. He knew his desire to snuff all life out of nature was an impulsive reaction to the truths he learned a few days ago, but this mission kept him sane. His rage was all-consuming, and without an outlet he feared it would eat him alive, so he kept his plans a secret.

They were in contact with high-profile survivors in NYC and DC. Though these new contacts used to hold seats of power, the world had changed and their former titles meant nothing. Sergei and his following were the largest and the most adept at enduring these new conditions. Their NYC and DC recruits still had not left their bunkers and did not know how to survive the harsh environment above, so they looked to Sergei for leadership.

Those who survived in the safe rooms of the Pentagon had access to massive weaponry buried deep beneath the earth and once they established themselves beneath Sergei's lead, access to such power would make him unstoppable. He'd reclaim the earth for mankind and rid the world of traitors. It wouldn't be long before the so-called Champions were at his mercy.

Clovis already caught one, and with the right tactics, he'd get her to reveal the whereabouts of the others. So far he was coming up short, but there was no time frame and she was sure to break eventually. Clovis claimed she was able to heal at unnatural speeds, which only intensified Sergei's hatred. Not only were these women granted immunity from the apocalypse, but also gifted with some sort of regenerative magic. It was maddening. The more he learned about the Champions, the more he abhorred them. He dreamt of taking Clovis' spot and killing the Champion himself. The image gave him relief. Her death would be retribution for every soul she let die.

"Darling," Marlaina said as she entered the room where he stewed in his thoughts. "Cole and Ian have the blueprints ready."

"Fantastic, send them in."

The men walked in and placed their charts beside Sergei on the bed. They were lumberjacks, not miners or welders, but the company they owned before the purge specialized in architecture using wood. Though the material being used was different, their expertise in building solid structures was invaluable.

"Best way to go about this is building similar structures throughout the town. Less variation means less work. Once the guys get the hang of layout on the first few buildings, the rest will come easy," Cole explained.

"I agree," Sergei said. "What about the excess material from all the buildings still standing?"

"We did a walk-through and it would be possible to build around what still stands," Ian said while pointing to the chart. "Everything in Cedar City was built with decent distance between walls. It's not like New York City where everything is on top of each other. Granted, after we start it will begin to look crowded. The old will be sandwiched between new."

"I'm okay with that."

"We figure we can clean up the old once we're more established. The ash is the killer right now. We need the skies to open up so the weather returns. Without wind, the ash will sit here forever."

"Our new contacts in DC have planes and tanks. We've already bartered with them; we will rebuild their cities if they give us full access to their arsenal. They also know the locations of every military bunker across the country. Though I didn't dive into this topic with them yet, I plan to get the codes to them all, specifically those closest to us so we are in control of the weaponry and equipment. I don't want our cleanup and safety to be at their mercy."

"Bigger machinery would help a lot," Cole expressed. "Maybe we can find a location to dump the ash, cause right now it's stagnant and in our way."

"I will work on that. I want you two to focus on the rebuild. Killian is a skilled welder. Teach him the blue prints first. He will be in charge of the process when Dante and I are not around."

"Will do," Ian said as he folded the charts.

"How are things progressing with the captured Champion?" Cole asked. Only those in positions of leadership within the group knew of their faraway prisoner. The few men who knew had varying opinions on the subject. Sergei and Phineas were most eager to see the Champion perish, while Dante, Kelso, Gerald, and Oskar urged them to show more compassion. Cole, Ian, and their younger brother Luke hated everything about the imprisonment. They still did not believe the Champions were ill-intended and wished for the others to see things their way.

"I know how you feel about the matter and I do not think it's wise I divulge too much. We have other important matters to focus on."

"We just want an update."

"Clovis hasn't gotten the information we need from her yet. She won't talk."

"I doubt she ever will," Ian said, thinking of Juniper.

"Then she will die."

"You do realize they are only human, right? They were chosen, not by their own fault, and they are doing the best they can. I don't think it's fair that we punish them for the burden they were forced to carry," Cole insisted.

"The problem is that they did not do more," Sergei tried to explain for the hundredth time. "I heard no reports of crazy women across the planet predicting the apocalypse."

"Why would a credible media outlet air what they believed to be nonsense?" Ian asked.

"They used to do it all the time. It would have been an amusing story, if nothing else, yet I never caught wind of it. These women did *nothing* to save the human race."

"I honestly believe the Champions did the best they could with what they had," Cole tried again. "They didn't orchestrate nature's attack."

"But they knew it was coming and stayed silent. They stood by and let millions of people die. Their lack of action makes them guilty."

"All I can say is that the Champion that saved us was kind and well-intended. She meant no harm to anyone and was doing the best she could."

"Well, it wasn't enough and one day, we will catch her too."

Sergei's tone was definitive and sure, which silenced the brothers. They did not want to be part of his insane quest for vengeance and they suspected Misty would be greatly disturbed by Sergei's determination to kill Juniper. There was no reasoning with him now, so they dropped the subject and left, hoping progress in the forthcoming weeks would silence Sergei's wrath against the Champions.

Chapter 18

Cameron, Louisiana

The torture and questioning continued. Sofyla was weak and struggling to heal. The more Clovis caused her harm, the harder it was to mend her wounds.

She had no desire to give up; she wanted to escape, find Riad, and continue living, but the prospect of that was looking grim. Clovis was ruthless and full of unwarranted hatred and she suspected he'd kill her before he ever let her walk free.

Clovis emerged from the shadows with a hammer in hand. He emptied a bag of nails onto the table, retrieved one, and glided toward Sofyla.

"Awrite, tataille. What ya got ta say today?"

Sofyla glared up at him and shook her head.

Furious that she still defied him, he placed the tip of the nail against her bound hand and pierced it with a single blow. The nail went through her skin and into the wooden armrest. The bones in her hand were crushed and she squealed with pain. Her teeth clenched as she tried to mute her agony, but it was impossible to remain silent.

"Talk!" he demanded.

She answered with a delirious moan. The world around her was going dark as her blood gushed to the floor. Pain shot up her arm and into her brain, causing the room to disappear.

Sofyla, a voice whispered.

She couldn't answer.

Sofyla, it's Juniper. Can you meet us in the White Room?

She sobbed in understanding, then did her best to mentally transport herself away from the unrelenting persecution.

It took a few minutes to gather enough strength to leave, but when she finally made it, all her Champion sisters were there. They stood in their places in the circle as she appeared before them on her knees. Her yellow glow was muted and she wore nothing but dirt and blood.

The moment she made eye contact with Eshe, she began to cry. The tears fell, leaving streaks across her filthy face. Her sisters ran to her side, kneeling beside her and encasing her in a loving embrace. They shielded her naked body and offered her warmth and comfort. Sofyla lifted her hand to see that she carried the wound from the nail into this sanctuary. Though the injuries were painless here, their marks remained. There was no escaping her aggressor.

"How did this happen?" Eshe demanded. Her orange aura now had flickers of fiery red.

"We crashed on the wrong shore."

"I am so sorry," Coral said with tears in her eyes.

"It's not your fault. I never told you where we needed to go. You also didn't know about these rebels. It was a trap. They lured us in."

"I will make them pay," Eshe spat, her tone lined with venom.

"No, you must stay far away from them. They will die on their own. Don't start a war."

"They started this war!"

"Eshe, please."

"I'm with Eshe," Sahira exclaimed. *"We've done nothing to them, yet they capture and torture one of our own. We would have welcomed them with open arms! Instead they call us devils and declare that they plan to hunt and kill us."*

"They will perish in due time; they don't know the safe zones. Sahira, you and Aria are safe atop Mount Everest. Eshe is untouchable beneath the earth. Coral and Marisabel couldn't have a more remote

location than Antarctica, and Juniper will be safe once she reaches the Amazon. Stay where you are." She looked at each of her sisters as she pleaded.

"We need vengeance," Coral insisted.

Sofyla shook her head. "Don't be like them."

They absorbed her words before Aria eventually broke the silence.

"She's right. If we seek them out, it could backfire. We could all die."

"This gift of eternal life isn't working out quite like Gaia planned, huh?" Coral asked with sarcasm.

"I doubt She anticipated troupes of blood-thirsty rebels whose driving purpose in the new world is to hunt down Her Champions and kill them," Marisabel replied.

"They still don't know your names or locations," Sofyla reminded them. "But they do know that we can heal. He's been using it against me. The things he is doing to me would've killed me days ago if I was normal. The gift has become a curse."

"Don't say that," Aria insisted. "It's the only thing keeping you alive."

"You better keep fighting," Eshe commanded. "You can survive this."

"I'm trying."

"Lie," Coral suggested. "Tell him false names and locations."

"No." Sahira objected. "Maintain your silence. The moment you talk, he'll think he has no further use for you."

"Why haven't the soil spirits come to your aid?" Aria asked.

"Yes, I hear from the core all the time. They guide me every day." Eshe stated. Aria, Sahira, and Coral all nodded, indicating that they frequently heard from their chosen elements too.

"The trees haven't talked to me in ages," Juniper countered, baffled that the others were still in contact with their elements.

"I haven't heard from the soil in months. I think it's because the trees and soil are still trying to break through the ruins caused by the super volcanoes."

"But you are in dire need! They should find a way," Aria insisted.

"Louisiana is one giant swamp and there is no soil for them to contact me through. There is nothing they can do."

They all became quiet in understanding.

Sofyla's eyes widened in horror.

"Something is wrong."

"What do you mean?" Juniper asked.

"I'm not sure, but he's acting different. I have to go. I love you all."

Before they could respond Sofyla was gone. The further she traveled through her mind, the more she could feel the discomfort of her reality. Each wound throbbed again and by the time she was back in her constraints, the pain was blinding.

"Welcome back." Clovis wore a wicked grin. "Did ya know ya talk in your sleep?"

Sofyla's heart rate quickened; she was unsure what she said out loud.

Clovis sauntered to the radio and dialed his cohorts. Sergei answered his call after a few minutes.

"She talked. Was in her sleep, but I got names and places."

"That's fantastic. What are they?"

Clovis picked up a notepad he had been scribbling on while Sofyla was far away in her mind.

"Let's see. Dere's a Juniper."

"I know that one. Phineas and his people left her safe haven in Washington."

"Kay. Marisabel, who might be in Antarctica. Is dere a coral sea down dere? That mighta been a place or a name. Not sure."

Sofyla squirmed in her chair, appalled that he had gathered accurate information.

He continued, "She said da name Aria a few times. I think that one goes with Sahira. And I know she said Mount Everest near those names. It was a lot of mumbling."

"I was having a dream! Those are people from my past life, before the purge," Sofyla insisted. "They are all dead now."

"Don't lie ta me. You'd've saved dem if you loved 'em."

"They wouldn't follow me. I tried, but they thought I was crazy."

"Ask her how she knew the name Juniper then," Sergei said over the radio.

Clovis looked at her with a raised eyebrow. Sofyla hesitated.

"There was a Juniper tree in my backyard. We often had picnics beneath it." She prayed they believed her lies.

"I don't buy it," Sergei said after a moment of contemplation. "Any other info?"

"Something about the underground. That part I didn't catch well."

"Okay. That's five out of the six names we need. Even got a few areas to look in to."

"Maybe she'll say more next time she passes out."

"No need to wait and see. We have enough. Kill her."

Sofyla squirmed in her chair.

They know! She cried out inside her mind, hoping any of her sisters might catch her warning. Caught in a panic, her thoughts were scrambled and she couldn't think of anything else to say. *They know!*

"Let's see if you can survive a bullet to the brain."

Clovis placed the barrel of his pistol against her forehead and pulled the trigger. The bullet cut through her brain and cleared the backside of her skull. The kill was instant and left her no time to heal.

The soil deep beneath the concrete foundation of the manor shook and Clovis crouched, afraid it was an earthquake. The rumble was strong but subtle as the earth wept for its Champion.

Chapter 19

The White Room

"She's gone," Eshe said the moment the weight of Sofyla's presence vanished from their hearts. Aria, Marisabel, and Juniper fought back tears, while the others battled their anger.

"Where is Gaia?" Coral demanded. *"How could She let this happen?"*

"Haven't the ocean spirits told you?" Aria said as she wiped a tear off her cheek. *"Gaia is faraway in a different galaxy. She is the mother of many ecosystems throughout the universe. After orchestrating the purge, She left with the assumption that all was in order and the world would rebirth naturally on its own. We knew our tasks and the spirits of nature were slowly regenerating."*

"Well, She was wrong to leave," Juniper stated. *"Though I haven't heard from them, I know the trees aren't doing well. The entire continent is smothered in ash and I imagine the areas directly near Yellowstone are pure pumice and obsidian rock. I thought the trees would've grown back by now. The earth should be flourishing, instead we're still living in a wasteland."*

"The trees have it hardest of all," Aria replied. *"They never recruited the number of souls they needed to repopulate the land. Now that Gaia has left, they are forced to do it naturally. There is no magic to help the forests spread. The only spots sealed by Gaia's magic are our safe zones."*

"I guess that's why I haven't heard from them much," Juniper speculated.

"Who told you all of this?" Eshe asked Aria.

"The air. Gaia did not anticipate any backlash; She thought we'd be alone and safe."

"Well, we're not. Does She know that?" Coral asked.

"I'm not sure," Aria replied.

"Why haven't the spirits of the core informed me of Her absence? Eshe wondered aloud. "How are you the only one of us who knows this information?"

"I would have told you all sooner, I just assumed you knew. Maybe each of your elements are focused on other matters."

"I can only think of Sofyla," Marisabel said, her depressed aura was even gloomier than usual.

"We must seek vengeance." Eshe's fierce determination returned.

"She said not to," Marisabel reminded her. "I think we ought to listen."

"I don't care what she said. We have to honor and defend her, even if it's just her memory."

"Did you hear her parting words?" Juniper asked. She was answered with blank and confused faces from the group. "No one else heard her? She said 'They know'."

"They know?" Aria repeated. "What does that mean?"

"I can't imagine the monster got her to talk in the few minutes between her departure from here and her death," Sahira speculated.

"I assume we have to figure he did, otherwise she wouldn't have sent that warning. We need to be careful. That could mean they know our names and/or our locations. In either case, I really think we ought to keep our distance," Juniper advised. She could sense Eshe's dissatisfaction. "We will honor Sofyla's life by respecting her wishes."

No one argued with Juniper.

"What about Riad?" Coral asked, reminding them that there was a whole group of people out there without their Champion.

"Sofyla insisted that he and the others run. He wanted to stay to help, but she convinced him otherwise. Without him, her people had no connection to nature."

"Can he speak with the soil now that Sofyla is gone?" Sahira wondered, but no one knew how this worked; it was foreign territory.

"I'm not sure," Juniper replied. "We should try to reach out to him telepathically in case he's now directly connected to us like Sofyla was, though I suspect he won't be. I'm holding onto hope that I'll find him at our meeting spot in Mexico. I imagine he intends to continue Sofyla's work."

"Let us know if you do," Coral insisted.

"We need to hold meetings more often. We go too long without checking in," Sahira stated.

"Yeah. I want updates every time the air tells you anything about Gaia," Eshe requested of Aria. "I'll be asking the core about it, but we all need to stay on the same page. As I take it now, Gaia is gone and we are on our own with minimal ethereal assistance."

"Yes," Aria replied. "Nature's spirits are still here, just not as powerful as before. Gaia can't come back anytime soon because the matters She is tending to out there are too grave to abandon. Just like She couldn't leave us during the purge, She cannot leave Her other children during their darkest days."

"I sense we are encroaching upon another set of dark days if we don't handle the upsurge of rebels," Coral speculated.

"Let's just keep our distance," Juniper said. "What can they do to us if we are out of reach?"

"If we don't stop them while they're weak, who knows what they'll eventually gain access to," Eshe warned. "Right now, distance is safety, but in a few years that could change. If the world ever returns to the way it used to be, distance will not protect us."

"*The ash cloud is supposed to clear next month,*" Aria informed them.

"*It is?*" Marisabel asked with hope. Though she already had sunlight in the arctic, its return to other areas meant her chance to leave was approaching.

"*Yes, but I will talk to the air spirits and see if there's any way to make it stay a while longer. The rebels will run out of food eventually and if we can keep them in the dark, they'll eventually die from thirst or starvation.*"

"*It's depressing that we have to take such measures,*" Juniper said with distress. "*We shouldn't be sabotaging their survival, they should be joining ours.*"

"*They drew this line, not us,*" Eshe reminded her. "*Sofyla offered them friendship and in return they killed her.*"

"*They also expressed their desire to hunt and kill the rest of us,*" Coral added.

"*I know. It's just a shame.*"

"*It seems as though the flaws of humanity have followed us into the new world,*" Aria said with a heavy heart.

Marisabel sighed, "*I suppose Antarctica is better than any mainland now. We get sun, even if it's miserably cold.*"

"*And you're more out of reach from the rebels than the rest of us,*" Juniper added to Marisabel's fleeting glimpse of optimism.

She nodded in agreement. "*I still wish I could meet you in the Amazon.*"

"*I do too, but the conditions are too unstable. We saw what happened to Sofyla at sea. Even with the ocean spirits as guides, the risk is too great. When the sun returns, things will change. For now, you're better off in Antarctica.*"

Everyone sympathized with Marisabel's desire to relocate. No one truly enjoyed their designated hideouts, but it was all they had and they needed to learn to adapt.

They took a moment to embrace as a group and remember Sofyla in their connected silence. The space was dense with heaviness as they began to depart. They lost one of their own and her sudden absence left a hole no one knew how to fill.

Chapter 20

Veteran's Memorial Highway, Enoch, Utah

Roscoe led the group while Juniper dealt with the loss of Sofyla. The group stopped in the town of Enoch so that Juniper could focus all her attention on Sofyla and her Champion sisters.

They spent two days relaxing and bonding while Roscoe, Clark, and Irene stayed close to Juniper as she dealt with the fallout of Sofyla's kidnapping. It was hard for Roscoe to watch Juniper helplessly struggle to save her sister from afar, but he never left her side. When the end arrived, Roscoe felt it before she told him. Her grief was overflowing and the excess flooded the telepathic space they shared.

She's dead, Juniper said an hour after it happened. *Please tell Clark and Irene.* She didn't have the courage to say the words out loud.

I will. Are you okay? He looked into her eyes with loving concern.

No. I lost one of my own. Not to an accident or something unavoidable, but to humans. A man filled with ignorant hate took her life. Worst part is that he is not alone in his hatred, he is one of many survivors who have a bounty on the Champions.

I won't let anyone harm you.

We are only human. If we ever get ambushed like Sofyla and Riad did, you'd have no control over the matter.

I'd never run.

If it meant the survival of everyone else in our group, you'd need to. Roscoe wasn't trying to belittle Riad's choice to flee and leave Sofyla behind, but he certainly did not agree with it. Juniper could sense his hesitation. *And if I begged you to run and you refused, I'd never forgive you. In the end, it's not about you and me, it's about the survival of the human race. These rebels cannot be all that lives on. They've taken their stance and they clearly represent all that Gaia intended to wash clean. We must remain steadfast and create a better world for mankind.*

Roscoe did not want to argue with her. *I love you.*

I know. She was overcome with emotion; for Sofyla, for herself, and because of Roscoe's stubbornness. *I love you, too.*

Should we continue forward?

Yes, we've stalled here too long.

Roscoe gave her a kiss before leaving their nook in the rubble and returned to where the bulk of the group waited.

"Time to hit the road again," he announced.

The Wolfe brothers prepped the bikes and quads, making sure they were filled with fuel. Mallory and Zoe helped Irene get the kids situated in their Jeep, while everyone else gathered everything they had unpacked during the short stay and readied to leave.

Jeb led the pack in his Jeep, plowing the ash and clearing a path for those behind him as he moved forward. As they traveled south, the ash became significantly less thick than it had been in Idaho and northern Utah. It gave Juniper hope that they'd reach clean air and land again soon. Multiple super volcanoes erupted across the globe, as well as many smaller volcanoes in Africa, which meant most of the earth was smothered in varying severities of ash. She just hoped they'd be in the clear once they reached the edge of Yellowstone's aftermath.

She called out to the trees often, but they remained silent. Her faith did not waver; she knew her mission and understood that they had much work to do that didn't involve her. They needed her to be independent and strong; reliable and determined. She would not fail them.

Juniper rode at the back of the group and kept an eye on those riding ahead.

Signs for Cedar City appeared on the side of the highway and fear flashed through Juniper's heart. This was one of the places Sofyla warned her about.

Rebels live here, she advised Roscoe, who rode his quad toward the front of the group. *This is one of the places Sofyla mentioned.*

Should we veer off and take an alternate route?

I'm not sure, she answered. The road appeared abandoned and the cars and ash were untouched. *Try to get a view of the road ahead. If at any point you see signs of life, like tracks in the ash or anything of that nature, tell me. Perhaps they are far into the town and never come out this way.*

Got it.

Instead of repositioning himself behind Jeb's Jeep for a better view, he shifted into fourth gear, darted ahead. Noah rode on the back of his quad and had to readjust his grip to stay on as they raced forward. Dedrik's Jeep swerved as the sight of his younger brother flew past. He waved his arm and yelled profanities at Roscoe, but to no avail. Roscoe was now in the lead and acting as a scout for the rest of the group.

"Sorry," Roscoe shouted to Noah as he shifted into second gear and slowed the entire progression. The engines were now quieter and their presence less audible. "We need to be on the lookout for survivors."

"Survivors?" Noah asked, unaware of all that went on behind the scenes of their trip to the Amazon.

"Yeah. We caught word they might be here and if they are, we need to avoid them."

"Why wouldn't we invite them to join us?"

"Because they want to kill us."

"Why?" he asked, confused.

"It's complicated, just trust me. If you see signs of life, tell me."

Noah wasn't sure what to make of this strange development, but agreed to assist.

A few miles down the highway and still no sign of life. Roscoe's tire tracks were the first on a long blanket of ash. Another mile down the road and everything changed. The smooth blanket was suddenly broken by hundreds of footprints that trailed off the highway at the exit they were approaching. Roscoe's eyes followed the path of the tracks and saw manmade signs on old couches and tables propped along the sides of the highway. The messages written on them were an attempt to lure other survivors in.

He held up his fist as he came to a stop.

They're here, he said.

Before Juniper could answer, two cloaked bodies emerged from the highway's exit. They stopped in their tracks the moment they saw the large caravan of vehicles paused outside their home.

A moment of tense hesitation passed as both parties contemplated their next move. Roscoe turned and quietly instructed Jeb, Dedrik, and Clark not to say or do anything until he made the call. They relayed the message to those riding in the Jeeps with them. Juniper inched her bike forward and relayed the same message to those on the quads and dirt bikes.

The figures approached, shovels over their shoulders and faces masked by bandanas and goggles.

Roscoe's heart raced as he readied to tell his group to flee. He was on the verge of making the call when one of the strangers called out his name. The shock of being addressed directly distracted him from making any decisions and the strangers turned their approach into a brisk jog.

"Roscoe!" the man said as he neared. Roscoe kept his guard up. "It's me, Brett."

"And Misty," the female said, removing her protective gear momentarily to show her face.

"What are you guys doing here? Why aren't you still in Washington?" Brett asked, more worried than curious.

"We are relocating," Roscoe answered.

"Why?" Misty's voice also indicated concern.

"We were instructed to. It was time."

What's going on? Juniper asked Roscoe from the back of the caravan.

It's Brett and Misty.

Juniper shifted into first gear and maneuvered to the front of the group.

"You survived?" Juniper asked, stunned. Her expression was filled with relief. She kicked the stand of her bike so she could dismount to hug them, but they both stopped her. She looked around, panicked as she noticed one of her best friends was missing. "Where is Carine?"

"No, stop. You have to leave," Misty demanded, her voice frantic.

"We plan to."

"You have to leave *now*," Brett clarified.

Juniper was so elated to see her friends that she missed the obvious fact in their reunion; they were in alliance with the rebels.

"You're with *them*?" she asked.

"No, we aren't. Not like that. This whole witch hunt for Champions happened after they welcomed us into their homes," Misty tried to explain.

"Then explain," Juniper insisted. "We already know some of it, like the fact that the rebels you're bunking with have a bounty on my head. Sofyla relayed what was happening before she was murdered," her voice was drenched with accusation.

"I told you she wasn't lying. This should be news to them, but it's not," Misty hissed at Brett.

"I knew she was the real deal, stop acting like this is my fault."

"Who told them?" Roscoe demanded. "It was obviously someone from the group that left the Hall of Mosses with you."

"It was Phineas," Brett said.

"Figures," Juniper huffed.

"He told them everything he knows."

"Everything, with a lot of exaggerated details," Misty clarified. "We tried to tell the story and speak the truth, but it was too late. He riled up the leaders of this group enough to set their opinions in stone."

"Didn't help that Sergei was a hot head *before* we got here," Brett continued. "Phineas just gave him a new target to direct his rage at. He and the others blame the Champions for all of this." He raised his arms, implying the disastrous state of the world.

"This is *not* my fault," Juniper insisted.

"*We* know that, but they are too angry to listen, too angry to care. You have to leave," Misty begged.

"We've already screwed you over enough. Please go so that we don't cause you anymore trouble," Brett pleaded.

"Come with us," Juniper insisted.

"Our families are back in town. We can't leave them."

"Go get them." Juniper refused to back down; this was a test of their loyalty.

"There's no time."

"Do you *want* to stay?" Roscoe asked with accusation. "Because if so, just tell us so we stop wasting time, energy, and emotion on you. Juniper beat herself up for weeks worrying whether or not you survived. If you're done with us, just say it, so we can be done with you too."

"No, it's not like that," Misty swore. "As soon as we saw Sergei's true colors, we wanted out. But my brothers got roped into his plans because they are architects and we haven't figured out a safe way to leave yet."

"Your way out is with us," Juniper said with stern conviction.

"I adore you Juniper, but I will not leave my family behind. And if you wait for us to retrieve them, the others will find you. We aren't leaving with you now for *your* sake, not ours."

"Sergei has a very loyal following here and most of them are down that ramp, cleaning up. It won't be long till one of them ventures up here," Brett warned again. "This clan of survivors grows more cult-like every day. Sergei in an unstable leader and he has the group focused on all the wrong things. I'm not really in the loop, but the snippets I catch lead me to believe he'll make this world far worse than it was before nature tried to take it back."

Far off voices became audible.

"Please leave!" Tears of desperation began to form in Misty's eyes. It was clear their loyalty remained with Juniper.

"Fine," Juniper conceded. "But if you mean all that you say about these people, find a way to leave and head into the Amazon Rainforest."

Juniper's bike stalled during the conversation, so she jumped on the kick start to rev the engine.

"Okay, but *where* in the Amazon?" Brett asked.

"Just follow the river. You'll find us there."

Chapter 21

Cedar City, Iron County, Utah

Brett and Misty watched Juniper lead her people forward, leaving obvious tracks in their wake.

"How are we going to explain this?" Misty asked, wishing she had realized this huge dilemma beforehand.

"We aren't going to. Whenever they find the tracks, we play dumb."

"But this will make it easy for Sergei to find them. There's a clear path leading directly to Juniper."

"Right, but he doesn't know this trail leads to *her*. It could be any set of survivors. Let's rejoin the others before they realize we were up here."

They ran into Dominic and Killian near the exit to the highway.

"Where were you two?" Dominic asked as he tossed a shovel full of ash over his shoulder and onto the pile he created.

"Bathroom break," Brett lied.

"Bathroom break? Okay, sure." Killian winked at Brett as he assumed this answer was code for recreational play.

Brett continued. "Dante told us to come get you. They are trying to teach the others how to forge steel from iron ore and want you there to help."

Killian used to work for the Lamorte's, so the lie was believable. The brothers followed them back to the Lamorte welding warehouse.

"Hallorans, get over here," Dante shouted the moment he saw them. Brett was relieved that his lie played out well.

Killian and Dominic joined Dante, Sergei, and Oskar in the demonstration of how the Bessemer Converter operated. The entire group of survivors looked on as they created their sixth round of steel.

Killian blasted the inside of the converter with air and flames blew from the top of the machine. Sergei explained that the color of the sparks indicated the quality of the batch, while Dante drove home the importance of safety. After thirty minutes of air blast and instructional tips, the mixture was ready. Together, the Lamorte brothers tilted the converter and poured the molten material into the ladles for holding. Once the converter was emptied, they transported the material from the ladles into rectangular molds, where the steel would harden into pieces they could build with.

The group watched in awe. Xavier and Lucine stood at the front of the crowd. Their admiration for their father shined bright as the sparks of fire reflected in their eyes.

They were four hours into the lesson when they completed the eighth batch and let everyone depart for a lunch break.

"When do I get to help?" Xavier asked his father.

"In a few years." Sergei knelt as he addressed his growing son.

"Why not now?"

"You're only eight years old."

"I'm turning nine soon."

"That's too young. Once you grow a little more and pack on some muscle we can let you help."

Xavier rolled his eyes and folded his arms. "I hate this place. I hate my life."

"Don't say that," Marlaina said, interjecting herself into their conversation. "You are lucky to be alive."

"I am angry!" Tears of frustration welled in his big blue eyes.

"So am I, son," Sergei maintained his calm. "But we must focus our anger and use it for good. One day you will take over my role as leader. You have great purpose in this new world. Don't let your emotions get the best of you."

"I don't want your job. I don't care about any of these people."

Marlaina and Sergei huddled around their young son to try and shield his tantrum from those who hadn't left the warehouse yet. Xavier sobbed. "I want my old life back."

"I am working hard to make it as close to what you remember as possible," Sergei promised, struggling to maintain his patience.

"It won't ever be the same," Xavier complained. His venomous energy was abnormally potent for someone his age.

Sergei lost his temper and clamped his hand around the small of his son's neck. He then pushed the young boy out the back door and slammed it behind them. They were alone.

"What is wrong with you? Are you stupid? Or just ungrateful?" he demanded as he let go of Xavier's neck.

"What are we fighting for?" Xavier asked, rattled but conviction unwavering. Tears poured down his face. "All this hard work and stress, why? I heard what Phineas told you about the Champions. No one wants us alive! Not even God!"

"Don't speak like that."

"But it's true. God protected them, not us. We were supposed to die with everyone else."

"If we were supposed to die, then we would have. But we didn't, so obviously there is more to the grand plan than anyone knows. We have a greater purpose. We were meant to survive. If God wanted us dead, he'd strike us down right now."

"But why didn't we get shelter from nature like the Champions did?"

"I'm not sure, but I suspect foul play. The Champions didn't even *try* to save people outside their immediate locations. We should have been with one of them, I'm sure of it, yet we never received the message. Why? Because the Champions failed. The wrong people were chosen for the job. So what do we do now?"

"I don't know."

"We take those jobs from them and do them ourselves. We aren't quitters, we are workers. We do not stop and we do not bow to anyone. We are the Champions of the human race, do you understand me?"

"Yes, Dad."

"I better never hear you say you hate your life again. Your life is a blessing and you need to treat it as such. As of tomorrow you're on the streets with Benny, Oliver, and Dennis. That will give you purpose."

Xavier did not want to help with the manual labor, he wanted his luxuries back: video games, after school playdates, his favorite TV shows. He was not cut from the same cloth as his father. It wasn't in his nature to work until the loss of sweat caused dehydration or until his hands were calloused, bloody, and shaking. But he did not argue with Sergei. He would obey because he loved him, because he had no other choice, but not because he agreed.

"Good. It's settled. You'll grow to understand." Sergei ruffled the hair atop his son's head before reentering the warehouse.

Xavier was left standing outside alone. The tears had stopped but their tracks stained the grime on his face. He wasn't wearing his facemask, nor did he feel inclined to put one on. Instead, his adrenaline returned as a rush of rebellion. He inhaled deeply and swallowed as much dusty air as he could. The coarse particles caused him to cough, but they did not stop him. He was human; he was bigger than the tiny, unseen terrors in the air. Mind over matter, he felt invincible.

Another deep gulp and hacking cough later, all his rage was validated. He'd been battling the notion of mortality since they emerged from his grandfather's bunker into an unrecognizable world. When he pushed the limits of his rage, he was always left feeling remorse, but not anymore. He finally understood that nothing truly mattered. Not his life or those around him, not the Champions or those they saved—they were all pieces in a game he didn't want to play. But his hand was forced; he was alive and had no choice but to participate. So he would, but he'd do it his way. He would test this world's boundaries and in time, grow comfortable living with his demons.

Moments of clarity tried to claw through his sociopathic spiral, but to no avail. All he felt was the desire to destroy. He could not be the boy he was before entering the cellar while embracing the boy who exited. They weren't the same; there was no room for both inside his head. It was time to make a choice and the winner was clear. He used his sleeve to smudge the trails of tears from his cheeks and adopted an empty smile. He had a long life ahead of him and the boy who exited the cellar was more equipped to survive the ruthless days ahead.

He reentered the warehouse.

"Are you okay?" his mother asked.

"I'm fine." He looked up at her with his new smile, which she was hesitant to accept.

"Are you sure?"

"Yes, Mom. I get it now."

"Alright." She wasn't exactly sure what he meant, but trusted Sergei gave him good advice. "I love you, you know that, right?"

"Yup." He couldn't say it back. The words meant nothing now. "I'm going to head back to the house to eat. Want me to bring Lucine?"

"Yes, thank you."

He took the hand of his six-year-old sister and left through the large garage door.

"What are you going to eat for lunch?" Lucine asked her older brother.

"Nothing. I'm not hungry."

"But you told mom you were."

"I lied. Want to go on a walk before we head home?"

"To where?"

"Anywhere."

"Okay." Her asthmatic breathing was shallow, but she managed to keep up with her big brother.

They walked all the way down Main Street until they reached Cross Hollow Road.

"Want to check out the highway?" Xavier asked.

"Will we get in trouble?"

"Of course not."

"What about Mom and Dad's rules?"

"Those only matter if you care. Let's go."

He pulled her forward and they walked around the shoveled jug handle till they reached the main road.

The sight was traumatic. A van filled with dead bodies was pushed next to the entrance. The back door was ajar and the bodies of children who had choked on the air sat in their seatbelts with eyes wide and mouths open. Multiple vehicles were abandoned along the highway, turning it into a sizeable graveyard. Xavier tilted his head as he counted the motorized tombstones in his mind.

Lucine began to hyperventilate.

"I knew her," she said between heavy breaths, pointing at a girl in the back of the van. "She was in my class."

"Small world," he replied sarcastically.

"I don't want to go any farther," Lucine sobbed, unable to control her emotions.

"Stop crying."

"Do you have my inhaler?" she asked through the tears.

"You don't need that. It's all in your mind." He ripped off Lucine's facemask and threw it. Her eyes widened with fear and betrayal as she tried to hold her breath. "Stop fighting, just breathe."

Her tears poured faster.

"If you can't beat it, I'll give you my face mask. Just relax." Xavier knelt down so they were eye to eye. A flicker of wickedness gleamed through his stare. "Trust me."

She was hesitant to believe that she could breathe without her facemask. After her near death experience and her father's resulting anger, she never planned to go outside without one again.

"I'm not strong enough," she mumbled, still trying to hold her breath.

"Yes, you are. Think of all that has happened. Death only comes when it's meant to. If you die right now, then that's how it was supposed to be. But if you live, then you'll see that your asthma doesn't control you."

Lucine had no choice but to try; she couldn't hold her breath any longer. She took a few small, panicked breaths.

"Stop freaking out," he insisted. She listened, because she had no other choice, and was able to get her breathing back to normal.

"Give me your mask," she demanded, angry with her brother.

"You don't need it," he said as he handed it over.

"That was mean," she pouted, her eyes still wet with tears.

"I just wanted you to see how strong you are."

"What if I died?"

"I knew you wouldn't," he lied—this was a test to learn the limits of his apathy. Not once did his heart flutter with emotion.

"I'm telling Mom."

"You want me to get in trouble? They'll never let me hang out with you again."

"I don't care."

"That would make me sad. You're my little sister and I love you. I wasn't trying to hurt you, just trying to help. Think about it, now you know you can survive without the mask."

Lucine eyed him suspiciously. "Just don't do that again."

"I promise I won't."

She looked back out at the highway and was reminded of the death that surrounded them.

"I don't want to be here anymore."

Gino and Vincent emerged onto the highway.

"What on Earth are you two doing here?" Vincent asked.

"What are *you* doing here?" Xavier retorted defiantly.

"Okay, little prince." Vincent's reply reeked of sarcasm.

"Where is your facemask?" Gino asked Xavier.

"Over there."

"It should be on your face."

"I don't need it."

Vincent retrieved the tossed facemask and handed it to Xavier.

"Put it back on."

Xavier obeyed, only because he did not have the energy to argue.

"Do you see that?" Gino asked the others.

"What?" Xavier asked.

"Those thick plow tracks."

"Whoa," Vincent commented as he noticed the marks.

"People passed through without stopping? They had to see our signs," Gino expressed, distraught that they missed a chance to add numbers to their group.

"Maybe they had someplace better to go," Xavier retorted with indifference.

"Still, to drive by without making contact? There's no one left in the world! Why wouldn't they at least stop to see what we were up to, or to invite us to join them?"

"My dad won't ever leave this place. It's good they didn't waste their time."

"You're a real downer," Vincent scoffed. "Let's head back and let Sergei know what we found."

The older boys led the young Lamorte children back to 15 Pinecone Drive.

"Tracks on the highway?" Sergei asked.

"Yeah. Looks like they came through with a plow," Gino answered.

"How many people?"

"The plow tracks got wider in certain spots, so maybe there was more than one truck with a plow attached. And there also appeared to be various tire marks in the light dusting the plow didn't clear," Vincent answered. "It would be hard to guess a number, but I suspect it was a large group."

"They should have stopped. We have signs all over the highway," Sergei muttered to himself, shocked that these travelers would forsake the chance to connect with other survivors. "It doesn't make sense."

"I wonder where they were going," Oskar pondered aloud.

"We only have to follow their tracks if we want to find out," Gino pointed out.

"No, it's their loss," Sergei said after battling his confusion. "They chose to ignore our signs of welcome. We will not waste our time chasing dead men. They had their chance."

Brett and Misty heard the commotion and were relieved to catch Sergei's dismissive opinions of Juniper's pass through. He, of course, was unaware that a Champion just gave him the slip, and they intended to keep it that way.

Chapter 22

Manaus, State of Amazonas, Brazil

Weeks passed before Juniper and company found Riad and those remaining of Sofyla's following at the border of Mexico. They were shaken and scared, but grateful to join Juniper's crew. The disciples of the trees provided strength for those of the soil as they traveled onward, still grieving. Riad was inconsolable and Juniper hoped he was able to find some peace in his unfortunate reality by the time they reached the jungle.

When they crossed the border of Panama into Colombia, it became clear they had entered the western edge of the Amazon Rainforest.

<<*Welcome home,*>> the trees greeted Juniper. It had been a while since they talked to her and it was nice to be reminded that on a greater scale, she wasn't alone. Their welcoming was all she received, but she suspected she'd be hearing from them more often now that she was in the jungle.

When they reached the ruined city of Manaus two months later, Riad was still distraught. After many attempts by various people to console him, it was decided that it was best that he be left alone. In time, he would heal, and the others needed to focus on making a home in the ruins.

Manaus was overtaken by trees. Nothing remained of the city except painted rubble scattered along the forest floor and throughout the lush canopy. As they settled in, artifacts from a former life were found hidden among the trees. It was disturbing to find the clothes and belongings of the dead at every turn, but the group grew accustomed to these grim discoveries. Part of their job here was to clean that which the trees could not, so they did their best.

The Amazon was their new home; their new sanctuary. It was large and sprawling, giving them plenty of room to grow, and Juniper suspected once their cleanup in Manaus was done they might relocate to an area less haunted.

The months passed and the group made small homes in the area. The sky still hadn't cleared, which meant the air spirits were successfully holding off the return of the sun. She missed the sunshine and wished to feel it on her skin again, but she also had no problem enduring the dark a little longer if it helped them outlast the rebels.

The groups were intermingling and making a home together in the jungle. There were more females in Riad's group than males, which meshed perfectly with Juniper's male-dominated crew, and a year into their cohabitation, three babies were on their way. The news brought joy to the entire group and hope for the future was restored.

She and Roscoe were trying to have a child of their own, but struggled to conceive as quickly as the others. The inability to create a family frustrated Juniper. Subsequently, she spent a lot of time wandering the jungle alone, deep in thought.

<<*The animals will return,*>> the trees said to her as she walked alone one afternoon. When she questioned their proclamation, a large bird flew overhead.

Amazed by the sight, which felt foreign after so long, she chased the bird on foot, hoping to see where it was headed. The bird led her into a clearing along the Amazon River where thousands of animals marched in a herd toward an unknown location. The sight was incredible and caused her to halt her pursuit of the bird.

Animals of every classification were a mere fifty feet away. She observed in awe, astounded that so many were kept safe during nature's apocalypse. What astounded her most was that most of these animals did not belong in the jungle. Lions from Africa walked beside bears from Canada, both of which ignored the smaller species of mammals from all over the globe. Under the guidance of Earth's spirits, their appetites were put aside in order to get wherever they needed to be.

How will they get home? Juniper asked, hoping the trees were still listening.

<<*This is their home now. In time, different areas of the Amazon will adapt to fit each species' needs.*>>

How did they get here? she asked. *Most belong on faraway continents.*

<<*Those that could not walk to this landmass were transported by the ocean spirits. Per the guidance of Gaia, the animals were harbored in the western section of the Amazon during the purge. Every species alive before the purge is alive today and has the chance to endure in the new world.*>>

I have to tell the others.

Juniper ran with renewed excitement back to camp. Upon receiving the news, the others shared in her joy.

"While it's great, it also means we have to be more careful," Clark pointed out the obvious to rationalize their excitement. "We don't want to turn into dinner."

"It's so bizarre that animals from all over the globe ended up here," Dedrik commented.

"Just another bout of nature's magic," Roscoe replied. "Nothing surprises me anymore."

"There were hippopotamuses and giraffes," Juniper continued, unfazed by Clark's warning. "Antelope, crocodiles, and rhinoceroses. The sight was incredible."

"Can we go see for ourselves?" Wes asked.

"Yes, but be careful. Follow the river west and you'll come across them. I think it's best the animals don't see us yet, so stay in the shelter of the trees and out of sight."

"Will do," Wes replied. The Wolfe brothers led a small group toward the location, leaving Juniper behind with a few others. Roscoe walked to her side and buried her in a hug.

"How are you doing?"

"I'm still sad we haven't had any luck getting pregnant, but seeing animals again certainly brightened my mood."

"It's a sign of good things to come."

She gave him a loving kiss, then departed to her private corner of the jungle where she often went to speak with her sisters. It was quiet and gave her the space she needed to reach them without distraction.

She sat on the forest floor and dug her fingers into the soil. She called out to her sisters telepathically, waiting for any to respond, but received nothing. This was unusual and old fears began to resurface as she worried if they were okay. She kept her eyes closed and tried again. The sound of a bird chirping came from overhead; the animals' march had spread to this area.

Eshe? Aria? Marisabel? she tried again.

::Hi there, Miss Juniper.::

She did not recognize the voice; it wasn't the trees and it wasn't a fellow Champion.

A slight shift occurred in her mind's voice.

::*Who is this?*:: Juniper asked with alarm, unaware that she now spoke on a different telepathic wavelength. She kept her eyes closed so she did not lose focus on this new connection.

::*I don't have a name,*:: the voice replied.

::*You must have a name.*::

::*But I don't. Can you give me one?*::

::*Where are you?*::

::*Right in front of you.*::

Juniper opened her eyes and her fear was replaced with confusion.

A small, red fox sat a few feet away, staring at her with curious admiration.

::*The trees told us about you. We are family,*:: the voice continued.

It wasn't possible. Juniper buried her face into the palms of her hands, erasing the sight from view, then looked up again to see the fox still staring at her with patient intent.

::*Are you okay?*:: it asked.

"Are you talking to me?" Juniper said out loud to the fox.

::*Can't we be friends?*::

::*Did I accidentally eat a hallucinogenic plant? Or am I just trapped in a strange children's movie?*::

::*If you don't want to be friends I can go.*:: The fox's head tilted down in rejection. It turned to walk away, bushy tail dragging as it left.

"No!" she objected. ::*Come back.*::

The fox turned with joyful anticipation and ran much closer to Juniper this time. It stared up at her with love.

::*Can I have a name?*:: it asked.

She held out her hand and the fox walked closer to catch her scent.

::How about Rooney?:: she replied telepathically.

He licked her hand in response and walked beneath her hand so that she rubbed his back. He then plopped his body next to her thigh.

::We have a lot in common. I like to be alone, too. There are so many creatures out there right now and I don't know where I fit in, so I thought it might be nice to be alone with a friend.::

::I'll be your friend.:: Juniper couldn't believe she was engaging with a fox. Logically, it was crazy, but something felt right about her connection to the animal. *::Why can I hear you?::*

::Because you're our Champion.::

::I'm your *Champion?::*

::Yes. You are Champion to all creatures of land.::

::So I can speak to all animals.::

::Maybe not to fish.::

::But anything that can live on land?::

::I suspect so,:: Rooney answered.

She finally received an evolutionary gift from the trees. Rooney sensed her delight.

::I bet there are a lot of other special things you can do, now that you're home.::

::You might be right.::

::It's awfully dark here.::

::It's dark everywhere.::

::Not where I came from. The sun still shines there.::

::Really?::

::I could show you.::

Juniper felt a sudden burst of motivation. Relocating would be a hassle, but it was worth it if it meant having sunlight again.

She returned to the group, Rooney tailing her, and told them the news.

"One spot just happens to have sun? How is that possible?" Jeb asked.

"Gaia, I suppose," Juniper answered. "The animals needed the sun to survive."

"Then why didn't She spare our safe spots from the clouds?" her Aunt Mallory asked with accusation. "Humans need sunlight too."

"They were supposed to clear by now, but the air spirits are halting the sun's return in hopes it will help us outlast the rebels."

"I say we go where the sun is," Noah said, joining the conversation with the adults.

"The *fox* told you this?" Zoe asked with doubt. "I've been buying what you've been selling for a while now, but this one seems like a stretch." Her cousin's expression constricted with disbelief.

"If we get there and the sun is out, then you'll know I'm not lying."

They found the rest of the group near the garden and told them the plan. Everyone was excited about the prospect of returned sunlight, but wary about relocating.

"It's a long walk and we have a few pregnant women in the mix now, how do you suggest we go about this?" Russ Hazedelle asked. He wrapped an arm around his Ukrainian girlfriend, who was one of the women expecting.

"We'll go slow," Juniper replied. "There's no rush. I just think it's a better place for us to be."

The group nodded, agreeing with the plan.

After a year of stationary living, the group prepared for another round of travel. Rooney led the way, maintaining a slow pace so the humans could keep up. The jungle was filled with life again—insects buzzed all around them and they often caught sight of different animal species creating new lives in their private corners of the forest. It seemed to Juniper that there was a grace period amongst the animal kingdom for each species to repopulate and flourish before predators and prey reclaimed their roles in the food chain. Many of the animals greeted Juniper as she passed, wishing her well and praising her as their Champion. It was peculiar, but Juniper accepted the influx of love with gratitude and hoped she was able to live up to their praise.

Due to the birth of two children and the death of a soil disciple, the trip, which should have taken a month, took six months to complete. They lost one, but gained two. The longest pause in the journey was for the death of Riad's uncle. He was old and weak from the journey through the purge and all that happened since. When he passed, it was peaceful, but Riad took it hard. He already lost so much and adding another tally to the death count of those he loved didn't sit well. Juniper worried it wouldn't be long before they lost him too.

::One mile to go,:: Rooney advised Juniper. *::Look up.::*

Juniper obeyed and saw a sight in the distance that she sorely missed. There was a break in the ash cloud and sunshine poured through. It was still out of reach, but visible.

"Everyone, look up into the distance," Juniper instructed the group. Many had their heads down, focused on the forest floor and watching their every step. Her words broke them of their concentration and the view ahead rejuvenated the group. Everyone began murmuring with excitement and the pace of their trek increased. Within the hour they crossed out of the shadows and into the light. The large group broke off into smaller groups, and everyone searched for the corner of the jungle they'd call home.

Juniper grabbed Roscoe's hand and walked toward the coast. They could hear the ocean lapping against the shore as they got closer and Juniper inhaled a large breath of the salt-water air. The smell and taste brought back fond memories and the nostalgia was soothing.

"This is home," she said with confidence.

Roscoe pulled her into a tight embrace. "We couldn't have made it without you."

"Goes both ways," she said with a smile. "I need to tell my sisters the news."

Roscoe took off his sneakers and walked into the water, letting the crashing waves wet his feet. Juniper retreated to the tree line and knelt next to a half-eaten Heliconia flower. The bright red blossom was slowly dying because small rodents had nibbled on the roots. Juniper scanned the area and saw many jungle flowers suffered similar fates. It was a sad sight, but nothing she had the power to remedy.

She closed her eyes and dug her fingers into the soil.

Aria? Coral?

No response. She did not understand why no one was receiving her messages. She opened her eyes to a stunning discovery. The Heliconia flower was blooming with speed. She lifted her hands to gently touch the blossom, but the moment her fingers left the soil, the flowers rebirth paused. Juniper placed her fingers back into the soil and the flower's growth resumed. With hesitance, she lifted her fingers once more and as she suspected, the flower stopped again.

"No way," she muttered to herself.

<<You are ready now.>>

Though the trees did not specify *what* she was ready for, in her heart she knew. The sun was out, the animals had returned, and Juniper's bond with nature was stronger than ever. Her gifts were finally appearing and weaving themselves into her genetics. She turned to look at Roscoe, who was enjoying the blissful serenity of the ocean.

It was time to bring new, evolved life into the world.

Chapter 23

Davis Station, Antarctica

Coral emerged from the icy water, her dark hair slicked against her scalp. The sudden slap of cold air against her skin still came as a shock and she hoped an adjustment in her evolution addressed this issue soon. It had only been a year since the purge, but Coral trained every day and was already able to hold her breath for eleven minutes. Zander was at five minutes. She was also able to withstand the freezing temperatures of the ocean surrounding Antarctica for thirty minutes at a time. Her maximum depth thus far was twenty feet and the more time that passed, the deeper she was able to dive.

While her evolution was progressing fast like Eshe's, Marisabel wasn't changing at all. She often stayed cooped up in her room at the Davis Station, talking to Zaire telepathically. He didn't make the trip from South Africa to Antarctica before the super volcanoes erupted and for many reasons, wasn't able to try again since. The oceans remained unnavigable, the new threat of rebels made the idea of traveling dangerous, and most importantly, Marisabel insisted he stay in Africa. She was miserable on the cold continent and did not want him to suffer alongside her. He would have tackled any obstacle to reach her, but not if she didn't want him. So he stayed put, waiting for the day things changed.

Instead, she found peace in the warmth of her bed with Zaire's voice in her head. Her people had grown angry with her and felt abandoned, so Coral took on the responsibility of leading them. They grew to trust her like they once trusted Marisabel and shifted their loyalty to the ocean.

Once Coral felt comfortable with her own gifts, she began training both followings in the water. First, she helped them learn to adjust to freezing temperatures. After a few weeks of them entering the water every day, their tolerance began to shift and the temperatures weren't as traumatic. Next, they practiced the art of expanding their lung capacity. Three times a day she and her following went out to the water and practiced holding their breath. Though she was at seven minutes when they first began training together, everyone else could not last more than two minutes with her underwater. But they kept trying. They witnessed Coral's perseverance and success, and remained inspired to keep trying. By the time Coral reached ten minutes, most of the others were at three.

She talked to Aria often, who was doing similar training atop Mount Everest. They still hadn't reached the summit, but were climbing closer each month. Both groups were slowly learning to acclimatize to oxygen deprivation, and both were finding gradual success. When Coral struggled to help her people at first, Aria suggested they meditate before going underwater. Being from South Kalimantan, Indonesia, where her Chinese ancestry was legally shunned and her identity was smothered by racial hatred and violence, Coral struggled to believe that calm techniques could inspire progress, but she suggested her people try anyway and then watched in awe as their success underwater increased. Achieving a level of zen before submerging relaxed their muscles and minds, and helped them go further in their practice. Seeing their newfound triumphs over what had previously been a huge struggle, Coral adjusted her own mindset and began meditating with them daily. She released the stubborn, calloused outlook she held from years of being allowed to embrace only half of her identity and found tranquility when she let the anger go. The moment she let mind overtake matter, her abilities increased.

Six months later, her mindset was fully in tune with her desires. She led the group toward the inlet of water positioned southeast of Davis Station. The sun was bright and blinding against the white snow and ice covered plains. When they reached the water, everyone prepared for the day's practice.

They stripped down to their underwear and eased into the water. Toes first, then ankles, shins, knees, and thighs. It took an hour before the group joined Coral and Zander at neck level.

"Let's begin," she instructed. She closed her eyes and began to hum. The others followed suit, closing their eyes and humming their own rhythms. The air filled with the buzz of their meditation and once each person reached a state of zen, their humming stopped and they waiting patiently for the others to join. One by one the noise decreased until it was silent again. With one hand in the air, Coral used her fingers to count down from three and when her final finger dropped, the group submerged.

Coral dove deep and maneuvered so that she was stationed under the rest of the group. She liked to watch their progress and felt better knowing that she was keeping them safe from below. Zander swam a slow circle around the perimeter of the group, keeping an eye on his underwater watch as he did so. At two minutes he held up his fingers to let the others know the time count. So far no one had surfaced for air.

At the three-minute count, many in the group began fidgeting. Thirty seconds later, half the group surfaced for air. The other half stayed where they were, focused on their zen. Not only were they training their lungs to expand, but slowly, they would evolve their biological makeup. Coral was certain the changes were happening on a genetic level and it was her hope that all the work they were doing would be passed down through future generations, making this process easier for those to come.

At the four-minute count, the majority of those remaining surfaced, leaving only five people underwater with her and Zander. This was considerable progress. Within the next thirty seconds, each person surfaced at different times. Coral could've stayed under much longer, but rose to the surface alongside the last person.

"That was great," she exclaimed, not out of breath like the rest of them. "Maximum time was four minutes and thirty-two seconds."

"Why are we doing this again?" her older brother Gus asked, speaking on behalf of the group.

"It's what the ocean wants. We may not see the reason for change in our lifetimes, but we are prepping future generations for survival and greatness."

"Feels like you're trying to turn us into amphibians," her father commented with a grunt.

"We are becoming one with our element. The element, need I remind you, that saved our lives. We might be here for a while and it is essential that we train our bodies to adapt to this environment."

"Adapting to the cold, I understand, but why must we learn to hold our breath for so long?" Gus questioned.

"For the future, for our survival. I am not sure what is to come, but I do know that you all are meant to evolve alongside me."

The group murmured in appreciation. The notion of turning into super humans was often discussed in private, and everyone was grateful that Coral wanted others to join her in greatness.

"On a more practical level," she continued, "we are currently living on a large iceberg that's surrounded by miles of ocean. Our boats are out of fuel. When the time is right, how do you suspect we are going to leave here?"

"You want us to swim to land?" her father asked, stunned and in disbelief.

"Possibly. Time will tell. For now, I want us to prep for all possibilities."

The group's questioning ceased. They trusted Coral, they trusted the ocean, and though there was some doubt, the overall feeling was excitement. Their potential future was a thrilling prospect.

Coral was elated to see their progress and remained hopeful. She did not know what was in store, but she was successfully evolving and helping her people make the change alongside her. Though the advancement was very slow, she was flourishing in the tasks the spirits had assigned. The future was bright and on track.

Chapter 24

Coast of Macapá, State of Amapá, Brazil

Juniper relayed the hope she received from the trees to Roscoe and their quest to conceive continued. Two months passed without any results.

"I don't understand," she confessed. Her confusion and disappointment affected everyone around her.

"It will happen when it's meant to," Roscoe assured her.

Juniper gave him a smile of appreciation before departing to be alone. She walked to the coast and sat beneath an enormous Brazil nut tree. Rooney met her there and curled up with his back touching her thigh. He had become a dear friend in the past few months and Juniper often forgot she was finding comfort in an animal. He felt human to her; their souls were on the same frequency and his outer form no longer mattered. To others, it still seemed strange, but to Juniper it was like they'd been friends for years.

::You seem sad.::

::I am.::

::Gaia knows what She's doing.::

::Am I not meant to bring life into the world?::

::If not, there is probably a good reason.::

Juniper sighed, aggravated that she had no control over the situation.

::The trees told me it was my time.::

Rooney said nothing more, but provided love and comfort telepathically through his silence. He wanted her to be happy.

Roscoe found her hiding place and sat on the jungle floor next to her. He wrapped his arm into hers and gently reminded her that he loved her without saying a word.

The trio sat beneath the tree for hours in quiet contemplation. Juniper turned her thoughts off after those running through her head continually increased her anxiety.

::*What?*:: Rooney asked as the sun began to set behind the distant ash clouds.

::*I didn't say anything.*::

::*Yes you did.*::

::*No, I didn't.*::

::*The voice came from you.*::

::*I didn't say anything,*:: she insisted.

Rooney dropped his questioning and fell back asleep. An hour later, a voice mumbling gibberish emerged. It was soft and the words were hard to decipher. She looked down at Rooney, who breathed heavily in slumber. Maybe she was hearing fragments from his animal dreams.

But then the voice spoke again and it sounded similar to her own.

"Do you hear that?" she asked Roscoe, who looked over at her with drowsy eyes.

"What?"

"They aren't talking to you too?"

"Nope."

"Great, more voices inside my head."

She shook Rooney awake and hoped to find he was the unintentional source, but the voice continued after he was awake.

::*Do you still hear it?*::

::*Yes, and it's coming from you.*::

"But I'm not talking," Juniper said out loud.

"He says it's coming from you?" Roscoe asked, his curiosity piqued.

"Yeah," Juniper scoffed, but Roscoe took Rooney's words to heart. He bent over and placed his ear to Juniper's stomach.

"Listen closer," he urged her.

Understanding what his suspicions were, her heart began to race with excitement. She put her previous frustration aside and opened her mind to the possibility.

I am listening, she thought, hoping to coax the voice to talk again.

The voice spoke again and this time she felt the source. It came from the small life growing inside her. Tears filled her eyes as she looked down at Roscoe with a smile and nodded.

"We are going to have a baby."

The nine months of pregnancy passed quickly and Juniper spoke to her baby throughout it all. The child could not speak English yet, so they communicated through emotion. Not only was her child gifted with the ability to telecommunicate with Juniper, but also with the animals, and she was excited to see if her baby was born with any additional evolutionary gifts.

When the day of birth arrived, it was late-summer and the midwives of the group were skilled through practice. Four babies joined the group since the purge and Juniper's would be the fifth.

Jasper Tiernan-Boswald was born in the early hours of morning. His arrival synced with the rising sun, which Juniper did not see as a coincidence. The moment was magical and her bond to the earth never felt stronger. Roscoe sat beside her with tears of joy in his eyes as she held Jasper close to her heart.

Jasper grew up with the entire group as his extended family. The love they felt for this small boy was overflowing and Juniper was exceedingly grateful that the others accepted him as their own.

Four years and three months passed since the purge and everyone was finally finding happiness again. The clouds cleared over the Champions' safe havens and sunlight spread across the entirety of the Amazon. Each family had their own piece of earth to call home amidst the treetops and forestry, but remained steadfast to Juniper. Life was finally good, finally safe, and everyone was thriving. There was plenty of natural food to eat, clean water to drink, and companionship. This was what Juniper had been waiting for, and now that they were done relocating, everything was falling into place.

"It's my birfday," Jasper shouted up to his Aunt Zoe, who was absorbing the early sun on a branch next to the tree home she shared with her mom and sister.

"I don't believe you," she teased. She had more love for the boy than Juniper ever dreamed possible. He stripped her hardened outer shell and brought out her best. He had the same effect on her Aunt Mallory, who he referred to as Nana. She never expected her relationships with these female relatives to improve, but was grateful they had.

"It *is*!" he laughed and Zoe made the climb down the ladder. She picked up her tiny nephew and gave him a huge kiss on the cheek. Though he was only turning two, he was able to speak and walk like a four-year-old.

"Do you want to play with your cousins?"

"Yes!"

"When they wake up I'll send them down. I love you, Monkey, and happy birthday."

Clark emerged from his area of the jungle and Zoe climbed back to her resting spot.

"I'll eat you, boy," Clark greeted in his monster voice.

"But it's my birfday!" Jasper replied, ready to play.

"Then I imagine you'll taste extra sweet today!"

Clark raised his arms overhead, growled, and chased the birthday boy. Jasper screeched with delight as he raced away from slow-moving Clark. Behind a tree hid Jeb, who jumped into sight the moment Jasper was about to pass by. He scooped the small boy into his arms and spun in a fast circle, causing Jasper to giggle. When he stopped spinning he pretended to eat Jasper, which only increased the boy's laughter.

His joy filled the air and when he was placed back onto the jungle floor, the emotion radiated into the soil. Jasper stumbled with dizziness to the nearest tree and plopped to the ground to recuperate, still laughing. To the shock of both men, the moment he touched the tree, a batch of small, bluish-violet Ageratum flowers sprouted around him.

"Did he just do that?" Clark asked in a murmur.

"I think so," Jeb replied in awe.

The boy sat in his patch of vibrant flowers, staring up at the older men with his large, crystal green eyes. He wore a smile that indicated he knew what he had done. When he began to laugh again, the flowers growth spread. Unlike the average two-year-old who would have ripped the flowers from the soil or crushed the blossoms beneath their rough touch, Jasper handled the flowers with gentle precision, careful not to harm their delicate petals.

"We have to tell Juni and Roscoe," Clark said. "Stay here with him, I'll be back."

Clark returned with Juniper and Roscoe shortly.

"He did that," Jeb said, pointing to the flowers Jasper sat in as they approached.

"Really?" Roscoe said, his eyes wide with amazement.

"Oh, I'm so happy," Juniper cried. "I wasn't sure how many of my gifts would transfer to him, but now he has them all."

"You can do that too?" Clark asked. Juniper forgot she hadn't told anyone of this gift.

She knelt down, placed three fingers into the soil, closed her eyes, and focused. Within a minute, Wild Ginger plants began sprouting along the jungle floor, popping up among the foliage already there.

"Holy smokes," Clark said with a gasp.

"When'd you learn you could do that?" Jeb asked.

"A few months before I got pregnant with Jasper."

"Why didn't you tell us?" Clark asked, offended.

"Sorry! There's just been so much going on with all the babies and the building of our community. Don't be mad," she pleaded with a smile.

"I am mad," Clark huffed.

"I can make it up to you."

"How?"

"You two are the first we are revealing our latest news to."

"Oh yeah?" Clark's eyebrow raised with intrigue.

"We are having another baby."

"What?" Clark and Jeb exclaimed simultaneously.

"That's wonderful," Jeb said as he buried Juniper and Roscoe in a bear hug.

"Another jungle child to smother with love," Clark said as he joined the embrace. "I feel like a proud grandpa."

"You both are like family to us and to our children. I'm not sure what we'd do without you," Roscoe confessed, validating

Clark's declaration. Juniper nodded in agreement. Family surrounded them here and there was no place she'd rather bring a child into the world.

Chapter 25

Cedar City, Iron County, Utah

The seasons returned two years after Yellowstone erupted. Though the ash cloud remained, the temperatures began to fluctuate drastically. In Utah, the summers were chilly and the winters were unbearable. They barely survived their first arctic winter. When it arrived unexpectedly, the entire group stayed huddled together for three months in the living room of 21 Pinecone Drive with just enough fuel to power the generator and heat the house. They ran out of fuel two weeks before the chill broke and barely hung on through the freeze. After that, they quickly adapted and learned that they needed to prep for winter months in advance. They gathered food and fuel for the generator throughout the year so that they could hunker down and hibernate through the worst of the cold.

Sergei spent their first frigid spring clearing a path through the ash on US Route 50. He learned that this stretch of America suffered the same temperature changes as Utah, but the cold was far worse in the northern states. It took six months to complete the clearing of the highway and he found countless distraught survivors along the way. He told them how he transformed Cedar City and promised he would do the same for them. Desperate, they latched onto his words of hope and let him take charge. Within the year, every survivor along US Highway 50 looked to Sergei for leadership and trusted he'd save them from their dire conditions.

While his promises for luxurious comfort and grandeur construction were aplenty, he truly believed he could deliver. Cedar City was a pristine example of his capabilities and now that the rebuild was finished there, he began to move east. His work crew tripled since the start and they could move much faster now. There was no true way to get rid of the ash, not without air currents, so they did their best to build around the heaping piles that were swept and plowed into collection areas.

Four years into the rebuild of America, Sergei had firmly established himself as the leader of the new world. Not only did he have the skillset to produce, but also the charisma to convince every new survivor he found that they'd be safest with him. He showed them his vision of the future, one that appeared better than what was destroyed, and most were so desperate for hope that they latched onto his confidence without question.

A trip to DC proved fruitful in his campaign to lead. Not only did he eventually meet those who granted him access to his current arsenal of vehicles, but it also expanded his following.

With everything going smoothly, Sergei found himself returning his thoughts to the slaughtering of the Champions. He had put the mission aside for a while, but with no dire or immediate tasks to distract him, and everything running like a well-oiled machine, he found himself dreaming of their murders at night. When his dormant hatred resurfaced, it was stronger than ever.

"Xavier," he shouted down the hall. His 12-year-old son emerged a few moments later with bedhead and a confused expression.

"It's too early," he complained, pulling the blanket still wrapped around him tighter.

"This is a test," Sergei stated, holding a fire-lit lantern close to his son's face. "I want to make sure you remember who our enemy is."

"The Champions," his son answered without hesitation.

Sergei sighed with relief, happy to know the time away from that mission hadn't lessened its importance.

"Good. We must continue the work we are doing now, but the quest for vengeance must never be forgotten. There is no telling when the time to strike will arise; it may not be in my lifetime, but in yours, and I need to ensure that you value how important it is to avenge the fallen."

"I know, Dad. I haven't forgotten."

"They think they are better than us because nature spared them, but *no one* is better than us. The Lamortes reign supreme. Look what we've built. We've made progress while they've stayed in hiding, doing nothing. They were chosen as saviors? Chosen to rule mankind in the new world? Well, the gods chose wrong. I may be gone when an opportunity to attack arrives, but you must carry out the deed and ensure our family has no opposing force of power on this planet."

"I will." Xavier didn't need any convincing. Though he was young, his opinions were solidly formed. "I won't allow devils to live among us."

"Good. You've got your sister to protect, forever and always, and one day you'll have a family of your own."

Appeased that he was training his son correctly, he let Xavier go back to bed and prepared for his trip down US 50. Batches of his freshly recruited were congregated in towns along the highway, learning to survive together and waiting for him to show them the way to a better future. This tour would consist of ten stops in small towns on his way to retrieve a set of access codes in DC.

The new world needed a leader and Sergei was deemed the man for the job. Government officials from the old world who survived the fallout in underground bunkers were thoroughly impressed with Sergei and trusted him to lead mankind into a new day. He did not need their approval, but he did need their codes. Once he had them, he'd have unlimited access to every military bunker, armory, depot, hangar, and vehicle shed in the country. With control of these resources the Champions didn't stand a chance. Mankind would reclaim all that it lost with Sergei in charge.

He sat in bed with a flashlight aimed at his notebook while Marlaina slept beside him. His light kept her awake and when he began mumbling his speech under his breath, she turned over and stared up at him with bloodshot eyes.

"Sorry, hun," he apologized half-heartedly. "This is really important."

"I know, but do you have to do that in here?" she asked, her voice creaky with exhaustion.

"I'll be gone for a while and I want to be near you tonight. I promise I'll be done in a few minutes." He leaned over and kissed the side of her head. "Since you're awake, let me ask you something. How do you feel about me taking Xavier on this trip with me?"

Marlaina sat up with sudden alertness. "Absolutely not."

"I've made this trip a few times now. There is nothing dangerous out there except the same stuff we deal with here. The ash is all you have to fear. I am doing away with democracy, replacing it with a new-age monarchy, and one day he will take my place as leader. It's not only important for him to see the work I'm doing, but also for all the people out there to see him by my side. They need to know him, need to trust him. When the time comes for him to take my place, they need to support the transition."

Marlaina groaned in objection, "He's only twelve. There may not be any danger, but I don't think he's mature enough to handle seeing so many desolate people. It's heartbreaking, you said it yourself, and I think he's fragile right now. He's been acting peculiar the past few years, like he has no emotion and is numb to the world. I am afraid seeing such suffering would send him into a tailspin."

"It might be *exactly* what he needs. He is sheltered here. Everything in his world is safe and comfy. I've noticed his lack of caring, lack of enthusiasm too, and a quick heartbreak may be exactly what he needs to snap out of this phase."

Marlaina contemplated the idea. Nothing she tried had been working and every day he slipped further away into a state of utter apathy.

"Maybe you're right," she finally conceded. "But if I agree, I want updates every day."

"Of course. US Route 50 is cleared and safe for travel. Our first stop is Grand Junction, Colorado. The people there are happy and hopeful now that I've entered their lives. They will welcome us with open arms."

"I trust you."

He gave her a kiss, closed his notebook, and turned off the flashlight. There would be time to study his speech on the ride out. Right now, it was more important to give his wife all the affection he had for her. They would be apart for a long time, so he loved her like he might never see her again.

The next morning, Sergei told Xavier the news.

"Are you excited?" he asked his disenchanted son.

"To be stuck in a car with you, Uncle Dante, and whoever else you're bringing for weeks on end? That sounds miserable."

"You get to see the world outside of Cedar City, you'll meet other survivors, you'll get to see what we are fighting for."

Xavier shrugged. "I guess seeing what it's like out there might be cool."

"I promise—this will be a good experience."

His son sighed, packed a bag, and joined the men by the Humvee an hour later. Killian and Dominic were stocking the truck with supplies while Gino checked to make sure each gun was loaded. These men would take turns driving, and together would act as guards for the Lamorte men during each stop. Xavier couldn't dull the feeling of superiority as he watched these men prep for the trip.

"Ready for an adventure?" Killian asked when he noticed Xavier standing on the side of the driveway in observation. He was 31-years-old and maintained his former role as a loyal employee to Sergei and Dante. He was handsome, as was his brother Dominic, and Xavier took notes as they flirted and captured the hearts of the young women in the group. One day, he'd obtain a similar charm and woo the women his age, but for now, he just observed with fascinated curiosity.

"Hope it's not boring."

"It won't be." Killian heaved a full case of water into the trunk. Brett's sister Chloe stormed across the street, passed Xavier without acknowledging him, and zoned in on Killian. She ripped off her facemask and shouted at her lover.

"Were you going to tell me that you were leaving?"

"I didn't want to make you upset," he stammered, lifting his own facemask so it rested upon his forehead.

"So leaving without saying goodbye was the better option? Are you dense?"

"I'm sorry."

"You plan to be with others out there?"

"I don't *plan* to—"

She slapped him across the face.

"Don't come back to me when you return."

Chloe turned and stormed off. Xavier watched with his jaw agape—she was even more gorgeous than usual as she sauntered away in fury.

"You're an idiot," he said to Killian.

"She'll take me back, just watch."

Xavier was intrigued by the notion. It would be a move of calculated genius and he was eager to see the outcome. It if worked, it meant that no didn't always mean no—a highlighted footnote in his mental documentation of the Halloran brothers' escapades.

He was astute enough to observe that such cunning games of the heart, while brilliant, were wasted on love. They could be using their manipulative skills on greater matters, but chose to focus their energy on females. It occurred then to Xavier that this was what separated them from his father and uncle. Though Killian and Dominic were smart and capable, they were easily distracted—another critical observation to highlight in his notes.

Once the Humvee was loaded, they said their goodbyes. Dante embraced his wife Renita and three children. Xavier did not think much of his younger cousins and avoided them whenever possible. To his dismay, they raced to him in this moment of farewells. Callista was eight and gave him a hug filled with eager admiration. Freya was seven and followed her older sister's lead. Gideon was five and Xavier hoped to one day transform this little boy into someone he could tolerate. For now, the child was too loud and silly for him to take seriously.

Gino gave long goodbyes to his brothers, Vincent and Benny. They were extremely close and this was the first time they'd be separated for a long period of time since they survived the apocalypse. His parents, Kelso and Renee Palladon, gave tearful goodbyes to their eldest son, happy he was chosen for such a great responsibility, but sad to see him go.

With the help of Oskar Lamorte, Kelso and Gerald Palladon would take charge of Cedar City while Sergei and Dante were away. They were the only people the Lamorte brother's trusted with their empire.

Killian and Dominic had no family except for their younger sister Brianne. Their goodbye was quiet, but impactful. They relied heavily upon each other and Brianne struggled to let them go.

"We'll be back soon," they promised before taking their spots in the Humvee.

Killian sat in the driver's seat while Dominic and Gino sat in the open back of the pickup. They wore extra safety gear on their faces and held their rifles across their chests.

Xavier walked to his mother and sister to say goodbye. Marlaina had tears in her eyes, but Lucine was hesitant to show any emotion.

After giving his mother a long hug, he turned to his little sister.

"Won't you miss me?" he asked.

"I'm not sure," she replied. He antagonized her a lot, pushing her limits when she did not want to be pushed. He did it as a form of control, a way to instill her with fear. He was aware that she'd love him unconditionally and he toyed with that fact, bending and breaking her so that she not only loved him, but was also submissive to him. Often times it worked, but occasionally she pushed back.

"You will."

"I might be happier with you gone."

"That hurts my feelings."

"You don't have any feelings," she reminded him. He smirked, aware that she was correct. She knew him better than he realized.

"Well, I will miss you."

"You'll just miss torturing me."

"Everything I do is to help you. One day you'll see that."

She rolled her eyes, uninterested in the battle he presented. She could point out numerous occasions where he almost killed her, but she didn't. Instead she gave him a hug.

"I hope this trip is what you need."

He pushed out of the hug and stared down at her quizzically. He wasn't sure what she meant by that, but the implication felt deep, like it touched upon a topic buried at a depth he wasn't willing to dive.

He hopped into the back seat of the Humvee and forgot her parting words.

Phineas raced out of the house before they could leave.

"Shouldn't I go with you?" he panted with desperation as he reached the truck.

"Why on earth would I want you there with me?" Sergei sneered.

"To help," Phineas replied, accosted.

"You've done nothing but get in the way these past four years, what makes you think you're important enough to go on a mission like this?"

Phineas shrunk with embarrassment. "I thought I was part of the group," he said in a hushed tone, hoping to prevent the others from hearing his eager pleas for validation.

"You're part of the group, of course," Sergei said, loud enough for the others to hear, then transitioned to a whisper, "but to assume you are on equal footing as me?" He shook his head condescendingly. "If I let you lead this group with me you'd send us into ruins. You are feeble minded; you have a heart made of putty. You break too easily." Sergei hissed. "Look at how you quiver," he said, pointing at his trembling hands. "You are a weak man."

"I've done my best for you," Phineas stuttered. Their conversation returned to a volume that the rest of the group could hear.

"Of course you have, and I am grateful. It just isn't enough. You aren't enough of a man for a role like this. I'm sorry if that comes as a letdown, but it's the truth. You are valued and I'll never be less than honest with you."

There was an awkward tension amongst the group as they watched their beloved leader belittle a grown man.

Phineas was used to this treatment. Ever since he arrived with the others four years ago, Sergei took digs at him whenever possible. It started as small jabs and morphed into an assault on his character. The change was slow and by the time it became evident, Phineas was too broken down to notice. He overvalued Sergei's opinion and deteriorated beneath its harshness. As Sergei made it clear he did not value who Phineas was as a man, Phineas started to devalue himself as well. He became a shadow of the man who left the Hall of Mosses. All his purpose was washed away and replaced by Sergei's criticism. He now lived to please their adopted leader and nothing else mattered.

"Sorry," Phineas stammered. "You're right. I am out of line."

"I forgive you."

"Thank you."

Phineas retreated to the back of the crowd and everyone waved as Killian drove the large vehicle away.

Chapter 26

The Humvee had plenty of gasoline. With most of the world's population dead, and plenty of gas stations still standing to raid, they were able to stock up and replenish when needed. On the rare occasion that they were running low without any gas station in the vicinity, they siphoned fuel from the vehicles abandoned on the highway.

The trip to Grand Junction was a straight shot without any detours. They reached the town in five hours and pulled into the deserted parking lot of Colorado Mesa University. While there were no cars in the lot, there were plenty of people. The survivors in this location were huddled in a crowd, awaiting Sergei's arrival. They cheered as he exited the Humvee, arms wide, and approached them. When he reached the crowd he began shaking hands and offering kind words to those who fawned over him.

The moment he exited the vehicle, his entire demeanor morphed. The grumpy mood and foul scowl he donned throughout the entire car ride vanished and he now wore a smile Xavier did not recognize. Though the expression was foreign, the young boy understood the charade; he'd been crafting his own for the past few years. A new respect for his father swelled inside his hardened heart; they were the same after all, both faking at similar games.

The survivors were dirty and skinny. They could not grow produce, so they lived off whatever packaged, uncontaminated food they could find. There were about fifty of them here and Xavier kept his distance as he observed. Sergei was the main attraction, but many were excited to see his Uncle Dante too. Together, the Lamorte brothers had become a symbol of hope.

Sergei waved Xavier over. The boy obeyed reluctantly, but the crowd was too cheerful to notice his disdain. They embraced his presence next to his father with open hearts and Xavier finally understood why his father dragged him along. By the end of this trip, he would join his father and uncle in their position of power. He too would become a symbol of hope—a power he had not anticipated, and one he suspected was unwise to place in his hands. He was twisted inside, warped and toxic, and though he hid it well, he was very aware of the darkness that grew inside him. He looked up at his father, who concealed similar deformities. They never spoke of their shared demons, but Xavier saw the change in his father the moment he stepped out of the shelter and into the ash. He reentered the underground cellar with a monster on his back, one that slithered through his ear and sunk its claws into his brain. Xavier's monster was also birthed from the ash and arrived the moment he emerged from the cellar. Though the dark presence he and his father lived with was similar, he doubted they'd ever discuss the matter. The demons preferred secrecy.

Xavier faked a smile and played along, standing next to his dad with feigned pride. When the group settled down, Sergei climbed onto the hood of the Humvee and addressed the crowd with a loud, commanding voice.

"I am grateful to see all your smiling faces. We have big plans for the future, and your continued hope and optimism is playing a huge part in our shared success. Without all of you here, the effort to rebuild would feel pointless. Somehow, we survived what was meant to kill us. We were blessed with a second chance. We stand here today with our heads held high and our spirits intact. We will *not* let this misfortune tear us down, we will *not* bow to an unfair fate. We *will* prosper and rebuild a world we can be proud of; a world we can say we built together, a world worth fighting for. It will take a lot of hard work, but it's for the greater good. When we finish, there will be safety and comfort again. Remnants of our old lives will be returned to us. We will thrive despite the odds." The crowd cheered.

Dante took the stage. "The effort to rebuild is rapidly moving east. We hope to rebuild every inch of the land bordering US Route 50 within the next few years. Doing so will connect all the survivors to one another and allow us an opportunity to rebuild our society. Our journey to DC is long, so we can only stay the night, but we look forward to stopping by again on our trip back to Utah."

The crowd led the men into one of the main buildings of Colorado Mesa University. The survivors had turned the campus into their own little town and made it as comfortable as possible. They showed the men to a vacant lecture hall and left them to get situated.

"The leader here told me they've orchestrated a bonfire feast in our honor," Sergei explained as he collapsed into a red-velvet theater chair.

"When does that start?" Dante asked, also visibly exhausted.

"Whenever we reemerge."

"I'm down for a feast," Killian shrugged, unsure why everyone else seemed aggravated by the kindness.

"Canned garbage and plastic wrapped sugar. Living the dream," Gino said with spiteful sarcasm.

"Sure, it'll be the same crap we've been eating at home, but it sounds like they went to some effort to make it better than usual. Plus, we'll get to meet the locals and see who else is alive."

"You just want to get laid," Gino declared with accuracy. Killian shrugged, donning a devious smirk.

"Don't you?"

"Obviously." Gino was now 25 and hadn't had intimate contact with a female since his last girlfriend five years ago. "But there's no guarantee we won't be out there, wasting energy on boring conversations and choking down bad food for nothing."

"No pain, no gain," Dominic joined the conversation.

"Forget all of that," Sergei said. "We have to go regardless of whether or not you idiots get lucky. The point of this trip is to build trust in our fellow survivors. If they continue to back me as their chosen leader, then we will be sitting pretty once the world is rebuilt and returned to normal. This little feast is an important part of the process. Clean up and prepare to be on your best behavior."

"Does that mean no women?" Killian asked.

"Do what you want, but be respectful. I don't need rumors flying around that the men by my side are horny savages."

"Understood. Come on, Gino. It's time we found you a lady friend," Dominic teased.

Killian threw an arm around his younger counterpart as they headed for the bathroom. "God, you smell. No wonder women run from you."

"Shut up," Gino pushed Killian off him.

"Just trying to help a young buck out."

The door slammed behind them.

"They are tiring," Sergei said with exasperation.

"They're young," Dante replied. "We were the same at that age."

"Killian is 31. I was married by then."

"So was I, but you know what I mean. It's a different time."

Xavier listened to the continued banter and wondered where he fit in with this group. The more he realized he was out of place among the older men, the more he realized he was just here so his dad could show him off. He didn't contribute anything to the journey, he couldn't even join in on the conversations. He was just a little kid along for the ride.

He stood up and tried to leave without saying anything.

"Where are you going?" Sergei asked before he could escape.

"To get some food. I'm hungry."

"Okay, interact with the people out there. Make them like you."

Xavier sighed and departed. He hated this game.

Autumn months were upon them and the cold air of yesteryears was even more frigid beneath the ash cloud. Since it was too cold to gather outside, the Colorado survivors assembled a large bonfire on the University's basketball court. It was an enormous flame, but the ceilings were high and far from reach. The smoke filtered out through the high, open windows of the gymnasium.

Xavier entered the fray without anyone noticing; the majority of the crowd was drunk and too caught up in their own revelry. He was the only kid in attendance, which felt strange since he thought this was a group feast. A middle-aged woman approached him first.

"The Lamorte boy!" she exclaimed as she marched over.

"My name is Xavier," he corrected her.

"Welcome to the feast, Xavier." Her genuine smile never wavered. "There are a lot of kids your age here, they are in the gymnasium next door. Where is your father and uncle?"

"On their way."

"Fantastic. The feast will begin once they arrive. Go meet the other children and enjoy yourself." She pointed him toward the adjoining gym. Before he could reach it he bumped into Killian, Dominic, and Gino. A group of girls accompanied them.

"They look a little young for you geezers," Xavier commented.

"Don't be jealous, little man," Dominic teased as he ruffled the top of Xavier's brown hair. "You'll get your turn one day." He took a swig from the bottle of rum he carried, then passed it to one of the girls, who followed suit.

"Kids' room is over there," Killian said with a slur.

"Where's the food they promised?" Gino asked.

"I want Twinkies and refried beans," Dominic proclaimed as he took a step closer to the large bonfire and began to dance. "Gods above, make it rain food!" He pounded on his chest and stomped his feet, doing a sloppy imitation of a tribal dance. The girls giggled and the other men joined Dominic's tomfoolery.

"Twinkies and refried beans," Killian chanted at the fire repeatedly as he twirled and looked more like a ballerina than a warrior.

"Lord, we pray!" Gino cried.

"You look like idiots," Xavier chastised as he watched, mortified, but all the other survivors appeared to find humor in their antics.

"Don't you want to *eat*?" Dominic slid to his knees in front of Xavier and grabbed him by the collar of his jacket. "Aren't you *starved* for factory food?" he asked in the most overdramatic, earnest voice he could fake.

"Bye." Xavier pushed him off and walked away from their loud debauchery. He was certain his father would disapprove of their behavior.

218

After reaching the other side of the gym, he turned around to see that Killian, Dominic, and Gino had won the favor of the crowd. Perhaps Sergei wouldn't be mad after all.

Xavier found an empty row at the top of the bleachers and watched the embarrassing scene from afar. Everyone but him seemed to be having fun, though he was the only sober attendant. He was the only one who was truly present, therefore he was the only one witnessing the scene as it truly was. He made a note to avoid alcohol—losing control and acting like a fool was not a look he aspired to wear.

Sergei entered the room and stood in the shadows watching the foolish escapades in private. His face twisted with rage, but Dante kept a hand on his shoulder and made him wait. The more he observed, the more he realized this was what the people wanted: fun. They were desperate for a good time and his men were providing that. He took a deep breath and stepped out of the shadows. Killian, Dominic, and Gino froze in fear the moment they saw him; Xavier could feel their terror from across the gymnasium. While they anxiously awaited Sergei's reaction, the other survivors turned their attention to Sergei but never lost their joyful smiles.

"I can't believe I am missing all the fun!" Sergei shouted. Those who knew him well knew his happy reaction was fake, but accepted it with relief. The survivors shouted with glee and invited their new leader to join the merriment. The humorous ritual stopped and the feast began.

The food was terrible, but the people of Colorado put a lot of effort into making it taste fresh, so they pretended it was delicious. Sergei made great progress earning the trust of these survivors and everyone went to bed happy. After a decent night's rest, they left in the morning with full stomachs.

Next on the tour was Pueblo, Colorado. The little city was utterly destroyed by the trees and ash, but the people living there found shelter under the rubble of the old courthouse. It was grandiose in its time, neoclassical in its architecture, but the roof collapsed and the golden dome that once sat at the top of the structure was now the entrance. They had to maneuver through a specific path of crushed marble and fallen columns to get inside, but once they were in, the sight was breathtaking.

The roof and walls fell in such a way that it created the perfect sanctuary. Much of the beauty of the old architecture endured in the building's broken remains. The survivors made a home there and welcomed Sergei and his men with open arms. Taking shelter beneath the rubble felt peculiar to Xavier—the paradox of destruction paired with beauty was surreal and felt impossible, yet there he was. This was his life. The hardship was extreme and he understood why so many people clung to Sergei's promises—he was their only hope.

Newton, Kansas; Jefferson City, Missouri; St. Louis, Missouri; Bedford, Indiana and Cincinnati, Ohio were next on the list and each brought forth more frightened, but determined survivors. Each found innovative ways to endure while they waited for Sergei's expansion to reach their area. The people of Newton and Jefferson City sealed up their respective hospitals and took refuge there, while those in Bedford did something similar with their local Walmart. In St. Louis, they made their shelter at the large, castle-like train terminal. Though a few of Union Station's red-roofed peaks were destroyed, they managed to patch and seal off all openings to the outside world. There was a fire going in the opulent, main lobby and the heat remained indoors. The people of Cincinnati also used their metro station for shelter, but went underground. They took over a stretch of underground railways, sealed the exits to the world above, and made their homes inside the dingy station stops and abandoned metro cars. The sewers were used for ventilation.

They stopped in Clarksburg and Winchester, West Virginia before reaching the wasteland of Washington, DC. Everything had crumbled. Though the survivors met them at the Washington Monument, which had cracked in half, they were actually stationed at the Greenbrier Resort and bunkered beneath the hills of the Blue Ridge Mountains of West Virginia.

Sergei made nice with the former leaders of the nation, told them of his journey east, and confirmed that the people had spoken. They wanted him as their leader. These former officials had done their own research, traveling up and down US 50 to gather a consensus from the survivors, so they were aware of the shift in power. It was a new age that required a new type of leadership, and they handed Sergei the keys and maps to most of the government facilities across the country. Though he now had access to most of the bunkers, the old world leaders insisted that they maintain possession of the codes to the larger weapons. Though Sergei wanted missiles and bombs most of all, he did not fight them. Those weapons would come in due time. He expressed his gratitude and they departed with a month to go before winter arrived.

On the journey back, Xavier did some deep reflection. Each stop on the way to DC reminded him how grim mankind's situation had become. Though he'd been living a similar reality in the ash of Cedar City, this was the first time he truly understood the lengths people were going to survive. He saw their pain and suffering, saw their hope and perseverance, and the reality of mankind's fate began to sink in. He always understood that the situation was dire, but never grasped the extent to which that was true. Desperation and despair blanketed the nation, as did the grit to survive. He and his family were at the helm of this new frontier and for the first time, he felt excited about the future because it belonged to him.

Chapter 27

Coast of Macapá, State of Amapá, Brazil

Nine months after Jasper's second birthday, Juniper gave birth to another healthy baby boy. Landon Tiernan-Boswald joined her jungle family and proved to be even more rambunctious than Jasper. By age two he was not only running around, but also climbing trees. He could reach the top of almost any tree and he often chose the tallest ones to scale. Juniper had the entire group on alert, and if anyone saw him climbing, they were instructed to stop him. But even with every eye on him, Landon found ways to climb. He had yet to fall, and though she appreciated his skill, and luck, it still terrified her and the other parents.

Once the other children caught wind of his rebellious activity, they all wanted to participate. When Russ's five-year-old fell from a low hanging branch and broke his wrist, Roscoe had to intervene. There was no stopping Landon from his quest to climb, so Roscoe took him on long trips into the uninhabited forest where Landon could climb in private, without the other children looking on in admiration. His abilities were astounding and after a few months of watching his son scale great heights, Roscoe found himself attempting these feats too. He'd never been much of a climber, but he wasn't terrible. The more he practiced alongside his incredible toddler, the better he got. After a few weeks, he finally succumbed to Jasper's begging and let his oldest son tag along. There was no surprise when Jasper turned out to be a natural as well.

"You've got to try," he insisted of Juniper one night before they fell asleep. "I think it's another gift. The boys and I are way too good at it."

"I will, but not for a while."

"Why not?"

"We've got another little one on the way," she answered with a smile.

Elodie Tiernan-Boswald was born a few days after Landon's third birthday. She entered the world without a single cry, and her happy demeanor remained as she grew.

On her first birthday she sat in front of a mud pie her brothers made for her. The entire group huddled around her and sang "Happy Birthday." Elodie's eyes widened as the disjointed chorus of singers crooned with happiness on her behalf. As soon as the group finished, Elodie mumbled the song again, but by herself. While the words were garbled, her pitch was perfect. Everyone listened with amazement. As she continued singing, a feeling of bliss overtook the group. The tone of her voice sent everyone to a place of inner happiness.

When she finished, she slapped her hands into the mud pie, flinging wet sludge onto her brothers. The group laughed, unaware of the trance they underwent at the will of a one-year-old. While they did not recognize what had happened, Juniper and Roscoe did. She looked at her husband with alarm and he nodded in understanding.

No way, Juniper thought, completely stunned.

Yep. Our baby girl just hypnotized us. Roscoe shook his head, half smiling and half concerned. *This is gonna be a tough one to control.*

And to replicate. I sing all the time and I've never had that effect on anyone.

Looks like she got one of the gifts before us. We better learn how it's done before she gets older, otherwise she'll rule the roost.

No kidding.

None of the other newborns arrived with special gifts, only Juniper's children, but she suspected future generations would be born with similar abilities. As her children grew, they did their best to teach their young friends their skills. Jasper left trails of vegetation and flora everywhere he went and Roscoe sectioned off a large piece of the jungle just for him and his plants. Roscoe taught the others how to grow and tend to their own plants the old fashioned way, while his kids popped in from time to time to add their own magical touch to the garden. Jasper made things grow with his joy, Landon used his adrenaline, and Elodie used her singing voice.

Once Landon turned five, he was allowed to teach his young friends how to climb under parental supervision. No one was able to scale trees as fast as him, but they tried. Jasper was the only one who could keep up. When Elodie turned two, she could already run and began attempting to climb alongside her brothers. Though Roscoe never let her ascend too high, there was no denying her innate ability to climb. Juniper had faith that the practice of scaling trees would become engrained into the genetic makeup of these children and that future generations would reap the benefits. They'd be living in the jungle for the rest of time and it was imperative that they adapted. Eventually, the spell over the animals would break and the food chain would return to normal. Humans needed to evolve before that happened.

Elodie was the only one of her children who was tasked to hide her talent. Roscoe and Juniper insisted that she tell no one of her abilities, and so far, she had maintained her secret. They both feared it would frighten the others, and they took great care in grooming Elodie to be kind-hearted and well-intentioned. They hoped that if she was gentle and empathetic in nature, she would never use her gift to harm another. To their great relief, they didn't have to try hard. She was the most benevolent person among the lot. Compassion coursed through her veins and spilled out with every melody she hummed. When she began speaking at the age of two, Roscoe and Juniper realized there would be no struggle to keep her kind. All her questions came from a genuine place, as did her actions toward others.

<<*The transition has begun.*>> The trees informed Juniper as she watched Landon teach the other children of the group how to scale. Elodie sat in her lap, mumbling a melody to Rooney, who was curled up next to them.

Our evolution? she asked.

<<*Yes. In a few generations, all will be granted the gifts your children possess. Continue the teaching, continue nurturing their bond with nature, and all will unfold as it should. You've made us proud, dear Champion.*>>

Juniper smiled, grateful and honored. Her relationship with the trees had felt strained since the purge, but upon arriving in the Amazon and making a home here, their bond had returned to normal. Their connection was stronger than ever.

::*I'm happy I found you,*:: Rooney communicated as he nuzzled his furry red head against her thigh.

::*As am I. We are family.*:: She looked down at the small fox, who she loved as if he was one of her children.

::*Thank you for letting me into your world.*::

::*Our world,*:: she corrected him. Though she was chosen as Champion of the Trees, she did not see herself as ruler of the land. Her people had freewill, as did the animals and trees. She treated each living creature and organism with deep respect, aware that each had their own journey and purpose on this planet. They were not here to serve her, but to honor themselves and Gaia. Leading with such gentle serenity created an environment of mutual reverence and shared positivity.

Juniper and her people were nine years into their lives in the new world and all was right. She had built a family, not only with Roscoe, but with the entire community, and nothing could break their bond. They were blessed and their gratitude was alive and electric among the jungle.

Chapter 28

Cedar City, Iron County, Utah

"Touch it," Xavier demanded in the most docile tone he could fake.

"Do you even like me?" Odette Böhme asked.

"Yeah," he lied.

"Odette," Liesel shouted from the other side of the fence. "Where are you?"

Xavier put a finger to her lips to keep her quiet.

"Wo bist du?" Liesel tried again in German. No reply.

Xavier kept his gaze locked on Odette's, willing her to disobey.

"Father is looking for you! He will not be happy if I return alone," Liesel warned.

"I have to go," Odette insisted in a whisper.

"No, stay with me." He leaned in and kissed her tenderly, working his way from her lips down the side of her neck. She enjoyed it for a brief moment before shaking him off.

"I can't." She stood up and began to climb the dead tree they sat beneath.

"I'll never kiss you again," he threatened. Odette shrugged and scaled the branch that hung over the fence. "Coming, Lissy," she called out to her older sister, who was walking away.

Odette jumped off the rotted tree branch to the other side of the fence.

"What were you doing over there?" Liesel asked.

"Nothing important," Odette replied.

Xavier listened to their conversation as they walked away. The rage living inside him boiled beneath the layer of numb cynicism he'd crafted over the years. He wanted to evolve as a man, but the experience thwarted him every time. He was turning seventeen soon and if the world were as it once was, he'd have had plenty of girls to choose from. But as things were, his selection was few and most were older and uninterested. The frustration this caused him was immense.

He left his meager attempt at a picnic date and returned home. The streets of Cedar City were lined with tall, steel buildings. The establishments that had not fallen from the ash were reinforced with beams and patches of steel. It wasn't pretty to look at, but it was functional. The new towers were built around and over top of what stood there before. They did their best to clear the ash, but most of it remained jammed between buildings, out of the way, but not gone.

His father's expansion to the east felt never-ending. The anticipated completion of the rebuild came and went two years ago, and three years later they still hadn't reached Cincinnati. Though the progression was slow, the survivors along US 50 were loyal to Sergei's initiative and heard of the progress already made. They were eager to have access to Sergei's steel making factory. They wanted him to reconstruct their cities and were willing to pay any price for his services. And for now, Sergei was willing to accept payment in the form of unwavering loyalty. The people were at his mercy and he used that to his advantage. His slow pace was intentional; it solidified the devotion these people felt toward him. Forcing them to wait was imperative, time set their allegiance in stone, and he was confident he'd be elected president once the last building was erect.

Xavier hadn't been allowed to go on another cross-country trip with his father. Marlaina still thought he was too young to be trekking across the wasteland of America with Sergei. Though he couldn't be there, knowing that the new world would one day belong to him was a comforting notion. It sent a tingle of joy through his jaded heart.

He took the long way home, hoping to calm the anger brewing in his chest. Rejection stung. He turned the corner onto West Harding Ave and saw Lucine crouched next to one of their new, half-built structures.

"What are you doing?" he asked, announcing his presence. She shushed him then waved him over. He knelt next to his younger sister, confused.

"Look," she said, moving away from the crack in the structure so Xavier could see.

Inside, a group was convened. Brett, Misty, and Carine led the meeting.

"How'd you find out about this?" Xavier asked.

"Phineas told me to keep an eye on them. He didn't know what they were up to, but suspected something. So I started following them and discovered he was right."

"Why are they holding private meetings?" he asked in a whisper.

"Just listen."

To his dismay, the discussion revolved around a plan to leave Cedar City and abandon Sergei's lead. A fury fueled by betrayal boiled inside Xavier and prevented him from hearing their reasons.

"We've sheltered them, fed them, adopted them as extended family," he seethed. "How could they do this to us?"

Lucine shrugged. "I still have yet to learn why they are doing this in secret and what they are hiding from us, but it will come out in time. Maybe they just think their choice to leave will make us mad."

"There has to be more."

"I think so too. I always knew they were trouble." Lucine's eyes narrowed with hatred as she spoke. "We have to tell father."

"Absolutely. Let's go."

The Lamorte teenagers marched home, fueled with purpose. As soon as they entered their home, they sought out Oskar.

"We need your radio to contact Dad," Xavier demanded.

"What for?"

"We have disturbing news," Lucine replied to her grandfather.

Oskar sighed. "Will it send him into a fit of rage?"

"Most likely," Xavier responded, unconcerned that he'd be fueling his father's unstable emotions.

"I don't think it's wise we test his patience. He's doing a good job with the expansion and focusing on noble pursuits. He dropped the hunt for Champions years ago and is focusing on the greater good."

"He never dropped the hunt, it's merely paused. Those devils will pay," Xavier corrected Oskar with confidence.

"Regardless, he's onto something good. Let's not distract him."

"I think he ought to be informed that there are traitors in our midst," Lucine insisted.

"Traitors? In what way?"

"A crew of people are planning to leave."

"Then let them leave, who cares."

"You're missing the point, Grandpa. It's the principle of the matter. They're ungrateful," Lucine explained.

"Leave it be," Oskar insisted. "Your father doesn't need more reason to be angry. The answer is no."

Oskar walked away from his grandchildren, resolute in his answer.

"What do we do?" Lucine asked once he was out of earshot.

"We wait till he's asleep."

Later that night, Lucine tip-toed into the bedroom where her grandparents slept. Oskar snored loudly and Edith tossed and turned. He kept the key ring in the top drawer of his bed stand and she was able to retrieve it without any trouble.

She and Xavier crept through the sleeping house, careful not to wake anyone. When they reached the porch they went through all the keys until they found a fit. They approached the large radio with caution, unsure how it worked.

"What buttons do we push?" Lucine asked.

"I'll figure it out."

It took Xavier five minutes to turn the radio on. He left the dial on the frequency it was set to in hopes that the last person contacted was Sergei.

"Shut the door," he demanded. Lucine obeyed and Xavier attempted to make contact.

"Calling Sergei," he said into the receiver. There was no reply. Lucine flipped through the pages of her grandfather's notebook while Xavier tried and failed again.

"Look," she said, pointing at a list of frequencies attached to different names. "Dad is on 1.843."

Xavier adjusted the dial and tried again.

"Dad?"

Sergei replied a few moments later.

"How'd you get access to the radio?"

"We have to tell you something."

"I hope it's important."

"We have traitors," Xavier explained.

"How so?"

"Lucine caught a group of people planning to leave."

"Who?"

"A whole bunch. Brett, Misty, and Carine are in charge. Their families are part of it, plus the Böhmes and Culvers. They've been holding secret meetings. If they want to leave, they should just say it, not sneak around behind our backs. They are up to something."

"Ungrateful rats," Sergei spat, validating Xavier's insistence to relay the information. "They're probably trying to undermine my leadership and take over in some capacity. Do they know that you saw them?"

"No."

"Good. Keep spying," Sergei ordered. "Find out where they plan to go."

"Should we stop them if they try to leave before you get back?"

"No. If they leave, follow them. Don't let them know you're tailing them. We need to know what they're up to. We are claiming this world in our family's name, we are building a kingdom; I must be aware of all that happens."

"Understood."

Sergei ended the transmission and the Lamorte teenagers looked at each other, prepared to tackle their new mission. No one would get away with betraying their family.

Chapter 29

Cedar City, Iron County, Utah

Lucine continued spying while Xavier prepped the Palladon cousins on the situation. As he expected, Gino, Vincent, Benny, Dennis, and Oliver were just as furious as he was.

"After all this time, and everything we've done for them," Gino seethed. He was now 31-years-old and had a family of his own, but the young man he was when the outsiders joined them reared to the surface. "I'll kill them myself if I have to."

"Let's not be hasty," Xavier interjected, unable to hide the satisfaction he got out of Gino's irrational loyalty. "Let's see how they behave in the next few days."

"They probably would've died if we hadn't taken them in," Benny added, reinforcing the validity of Gino's outrage.

"We welcomed them into our extended family," Vincent added.

"Why didn't they just tell us they had other plans for their future?" Oliver asked, "It's not like we wouldn't have listened, or let them leave if their plans didn't align with ours."

"Because they are hiding something," Xavier replied. "If they want to leave, let them leave, but I will not let them hurt us in the process. We need to discover what they are keeping secret."

"You think they are planning a sabotage?" Dennis asked.

"I'm not sure. What I do know is that they don't agree with my father's approach to leadership and may try to overthrow him."

"They'd never succeed. He has too many people on his side. Too many people are dependent on what he provides," Vincent rationalized.

"Correct, but it doesn't change the fact that they might still try. And if they do, they need to be eliminated. Ideas are a disease when they fester, and we don't want ideas of this nature spreading to others. It's an act of treason that we cannot tolerate." Though Xavier was significantly younger than the men who gathered around him, through his father he'd obtained their devout respect.

"What if we find out there is no secret? That they just want to leave and separate from us?" Vincent asked.

"I guarantee there will be more," Xavier said with confidence. "I can sense it."

"How will we discover the truth?" Benny asked.

"Lucine is stationed outside the old BBQ Hut where they've been holding their meetings."

"Why there?" Benny asked.

"The rebuild there was abandoned mid-project," Xavier replied.

"Yeah, the foundation was too unstable," Gino recalled.

"Hence the privacy. No reason for any of us to return there: it's condemned." Xavier shook his head in feigned disappointment. He didn't truly care; he merely craved the anticipated violence. It brought him to life; it jump-started his stalled heart. "I am going to check-in with Lucine. I'll update you soon. Be ready for anything."

The Palladon men nodded and Xavier departed. He found Lucine crouched in her usual spot, eavesdropping on the conversation inside. He found a crack in the building's siding and placed an ear to it, hoping to hear something useful.

"I'm worried we'll get lost," Felicie Böhme expressed in her thick German accent.

"We can't get lost if we follow the river," Carine replied with impatience, as if she'd reminded them of this fact many times before.

"But how can you guarantee we won't get lost, or hurt, *before* we reach the river?" Hanke asked, backing his wife's concern.

"We can't guarantee anything other than our lives will be far better there than they are here," Brett answered with solid assurance.

Xavier glanced over at Lucine, who shook her head in disbelief.

"We ought to tell them we are leaving," Cade Culver, the youngest at the meeting requested. "They've sheltered us for nine years. I grew up here. It would be rude to leave without saying goodbye."

"You cannot tell a soul that we are leaving," Misty insisted. Cade opened his mouth to object, but she cut him off. "We've already explained why."

"Sergei is intense, there's no denying that, but he's not a lunatic," Cade insisted. "They will appreciate a proper farewell."

"And when they press you for info, what will you say?" Brett interrogated the twenty-year-old. "Because you know they won't let us leave without learning every detail of our plans."

"We lie. We come up with something clever together, so that we all have the same story, and that's what we tell them."

"And when they follow us to see if it's the truth, what then? I suspect it'll end with our deaths," Brett countered.

"They won't follow," Cade insisted. "They have so much going on here—they are preoccupied."

"No one says a word," Carine ended the argument with finality. "We've caused Juniper enough pain, we will not risk bringing her more."

Lucine kicked her brother's shin, eyes wide with forbidden knowledge. She opened her mouth to talk, but Xavier put a finger to his lips and hushed her before she could say anything. He needed to focus on every word the traitors let slip.

"Could you imagine if we led these psychopaths right to her?" Misty shuddered as she spoke. "I'd never forgive myself."

The group became quiet and they seemed to silently come to the same conclusion: It wasn't worth the risk.

"We leave tonight, before dawn. It's ten o'clock now, so you each have a few hours to pack what you need and get some rest. Meet near the highway's entrance at 4 a.m."

The group broke, dispersing out of the abandoned building, and Xavier and Lucine held their breath as they hid behind a steep pile of ash. No one saw them.

"The secret is the Champion. They are leaving us to be with her," Lucine gasped with enthusiasm once they were alone.

"How on Earth are they in touch with her?" Xavier wondered aloud. "How do they know where she is?"

"Who knows, but Dad is going to freak. This betrayal is way worse than if they had tried to overthrow him. They know how much he hates the Champions, and how long it took Grandpa to convince him to put that pursuit aside to focus on more immediate projects," Lucine ranted.

"I know, I know. This is going to send him into a tailspin," Xavier conceded.

"I can't believe the Courtland brothers are with them. Dad trusted them," Lucine was filled with anger, disappointment, and uncertainty. "What do we do?"

"We tell him, of course."

They raced back to the house and waited for Oskar to fall asleep before borrowing his keys to the radio room again.

When they finally connected with their father, the mood was tense.

"It's all for a Champion," Lucine explained. "They are leaving us to join one of them."

They could feel Sergei's rage radiate through the receiver, though he did his best to maintain his composure.

"Which one?"

"Juniper."

"How do they know where to find her?"

"We aren't sure."

"You'd think they'd have told me her location when I was vocal about my desire to find the devils. They let me carry on like a fool with no clear direction, when all along they had the answers I sought."

"It is a true betrayal," Xavier said to justify his father's returning anger.

"They leave tonight," Lucine continued. "What should we do?"

Sergei paused for a long moment before responding.

"Nothing."

"What do you mean, *nothing*?" Xavier retorted, appalled. "They are committing treachery."

"Leave it be."

"Don't you want to seek vengeance on the Champions?"

"Of course I do. That's what I want more than anything, but I will not send my children to fight in my place. Wait till I get home. We will find another way to track down the Champions."

"No," Xavier objected. "This is our only chance!"

"There will be others."

"But you said we should follow them."

"I have changed my mind. I have to focus on the greater good."

"I've already prepped some of our most loyal men," Xavier insisted. "They are ready for whatever commands we give them."

"I said no." The anger in his tone was lethal. Xavier knew better than to continue this argument.

"Fine."

Sergei disconnected and Xavier looked to his sister.

"He's not thinking straight. We have to do this for him. I'll bring a radio pack and he can catch up with us once he's back in town."

"Good idea."

"You'll be staying here," he informed his fifteen-year-old sister.

"No way."

"Yes way. You'll slow us down."

"How so?" she asked, outraged. "I'm young and healthy."

"You have crippling asthma," he retorted.

"I am *not* crippled by it. I am perfectly capable."

"Dad is already going to be mad that I disobeyed him. If he finds out I let you tag along, I'm done for. He's too protective over you."

"This is unfair."

"Deal with it," Xavier concluded as he searched for an extra radio pack.

"I want to help," Lucine begged.

"Then go tell Gino the news. He knows who to prep for the journey."

Lucine stormed out of the room, annoyed but willing to obey. Xavier found a spare radio pack on the top of a large filing cabinet and checked to make sure it was working. Once he determined that is was, he scribbled a list of essentials they'd need to bring. It was midnight and he only had four hours before the traitors planned to disembark. He had to hurry.

"Knock, knock," a tired old voice came from the doorway. Xavier's hand froze and his head snapped in shock. He was caught. "What do you think you're doing?" Oskar asked.

"I'm doing what's right."

"No, you're stirring up trouble."

"You don't know what I know."

"Then tell me. We are on the same team," Oskar reminded his grandson. "We should want the same things."

"The traitors are leaving to join a Champion."

"Okay." Oskar showed no sign of outrage, just calm and infuriating wisdom. "And why is that our problem?"

"Has your brain gone soft?" Xavier spat.

"No, it's quite sharp, actually. Seems I'm one of the few left who can still see reason."

"We need to eliminate those devils. Why can't you understand that? I'm going to track their journey. They'll lead us right to her."

"Your father approves of this?"

"Yes," Xavier lied. "Looks like we're *not* on the same team. You've sided with the devils."

"I don't agree that they are 'devils'. The purge happened, there's no changing that. Fast forward to here and now; why are we so hell-bent on hunting down and murdering the few humans left on this planet?"

"If they had any humanity in them they wouldn't have let millions die."

"Having witnessed the aftermath, do you truly believe they had any say in the matter?" Oskar tried to reason, but Xavier had been conditioned to blindly hate the Champions.

"They could have done more. Even now, they avoid us. I bet they are living like kings in spared corners of the world while we are left to rot in the ash."

"Those are assumptions. I imagine they are struggling, too."

"You're a delusional geezer. Get out of my way." Xavier swung the radio pack over his shoulder and marched toward his stubborn grandfather who blocked the doorway. "I said move!"

Xavier used his shoulder to shove his grandfather. The force knocked the old man to the floor.

"You're making a mistake," Oskar insisted from where he fell. "Dante and Marlaina won't let you leave. I'll see to it."

"Is that so?" Xavier seethed. He stormed back to his grandfather who lay helpless and injured on the ground. He would not let anyone stand in his way. As his rage bubbled over, rendering him temporarily blind, he placed the sole of his boot on his grandfather's neck. "Promise you won't say a word."

"No," Oskar protested.

"If you don't, I'll see to it that you never say another word again."

"You've turned rotten."

"It's a new world and we have devils to conquer. Pick a side."

"The only devil here is *you*."

Xavier pressed his foot down harder and Oskar gasped for air.

"Don't force me," he threatened. The moment was a blur and all he could focus on were the insults and his hatred. Everything in between was lost.

A light turned on down the hall and the sudden illumination snapped Xavier back to his senses. He lifted his boot and looked down at his unconscious grandfather.

"Who's down there?" Marlaina called from upstairs.

"I was wondering the same thing," Dante yelled from his downstairs bedroom.

Xavier bent to shake Oskar awake, but his grandfather was unconscious. He slapped the old man across the face, but yielded no result. Footsteps approached. Dante would ring his neck if he knew what he'd done. He placed a finger under his grandfather's nostril and felt air; he wasn't dead. Only half of him experienced relief, while the other half felt dread. When Oskar woke up he'd tell them what he'd done and nothing would ever be the same. They'd see through the normal façade Xavier wore, they'd finally see him as the unstable sociopath he'd become. He could not let this happen, he had a long life of leadership ahead of him and it was critical that the group trusted him. The thuds of Dante's footsteps grew closer. Did he sacrifice his future or his grandfather? This moment was pivotal and there wasn't much time to decide.

Kill him. The voice he heard belonged to Sergei.

Per the imaginary advice from his father, Xavier pinched Oskar's nose close and covered his mouth with a rag he grabbed off the stove. But when Oskar's body began to convulse from the lack of oxygen, Xavier let go. He couldn't do it. A tear rolled down Oskar's cheek as the oxygen returned. He'd be in deep trouble the moment his grandfather woke up.

Dante faced the dark kitchen and searched for the light switch. Xavier used this moment to crawl into the radio room and flee through the back door. Though he ran as fast as he could, he still heard Dante's bereaved bellow the moment the lights went on.

Xavier wasn't as strong or ruthless as he once believed. He was soft and still had love in his heart. His anger doubled as he doubted his final decision to let his grandfather live. Was it the wrong choice? In the long run, would it ruin him? Did his mercy make him weak? He suddenly doubted who he was and what he stood for. He was not the puppet master, just another pathetic puppet. Xavier scoffed at his own faint heartedness. The threat of all that could follow in the wake of his mistake made him sick, still he ran despite the nausea.

When he arrived at the back of the BBQ Hut, Lucine was already there with the others. Xavier was skilled at swallowing his emotions and did his best to forget what just happened.

"Orders are in," he announced as he approached. "We follow the traitors until they lead us to the Champion. My father will catch up with us." He patted the radio pack he wore.

"Got it, boss," Gino said on behalf of himself and his cousins. Though they were all a lot older, it was understood that Xavier was in charge.

"Everyone kept their mouths shut?" Xavier asked.

"Didn't tell a soul," Vincent replied and the others nodded in agreement.

"Good. They only would've tried to stop us."

When the group of traitors arrived at the BBQ Hut, Xavier and his soldiers watched from the shadows of a large ash pile.

"Lucine, it's time you went home. Keep me updated via radio."

"I will," she replied begrudgingly. She still wanted to go, but knew better than to fight with her brother. She'd never win.

Lucine left and within the hour, the traitors were making their departure. Xavier and his men stayed a safe distance behind to keep their presence concealed and followed the traitors into the night.

Chapter 30

En route to the Amazon

Brett, Misty, and Carine led the group through the back roads until they reached US 89. They were the first to make footprints in its sleek ash covering.

"This route should make it hard for anyone to follow," Brett explained as the group murmured in complaint. "They stick to Veteran's Highway, so using alternate roadways should help."

"If they ever come this way they'll see our tracks," Hanke said in warning.

"We just have to hope they won't," Misty replied.

"Sergei will personally murder us for this if he ever finds us," Ian stated.

"With pleasure," Luke added.

"He's going to feel blindsided," Cole agreed.

"I told you not to get so close to him," Misty reprimanded her brothers.

"What were we supposed to do? Refuse? Once he found out what we could do we had no choice. He's a maniac. I had no problem drawing out blueprints if it meant I was spared from his savagery," Ian said in defense.

"He has a temper, no doubt, but I never saw him hurt anyone," she retorted.

"You didn't see what he did to Phineas behind closed doors to keep him in check," Cole replied and shook his head.

"It was brutal," Luke confirmed.

"What did he do?" Brett asked.

"It's hard to explain, but it started with small, hard to detect moments of intimidation. He took every opportunity that was presented to shut Phineas down. Every idea, every attempt to help; I guess Sergei saw his desire to lead as a threat," Ian explained.

"He *did* lead us to Sergei, so I guess I see where his fear stemmed from, but he certainly wasted no time putting Phineas in his place," Cole added.

"He didn't just put him in his place, he minimized him to a shadow," Luke objected. "For the past few months, I caught Phineas talking to himself more times than I was comfortable to count."

"So did I," Carine said. "Such an extreme shift from who he used to be. How'd Sergei manage this?"

Cole explained. "Well, it went from sly passive aggressiveness, to blatant mockery, then it became physical. Sergei would go on bouts, making Phineas look incompetent and dumb. His mockery often sent the group into fits of laughter at Phineas's expense, making his pride grow a little smaller each time. Every time Phineas tried to speak up and defend himself, Sergei narrowed in. He'd get real close, scream in his face, slam him against walls, and choke him till he conceded. It didn't take long to break him. I'd say it happened five times before Phineas stopped fighting back. He was demoralized. He was changed into a weaker man; a man Sergei could trust."

"The way he did it was an art," Luke contributed. "As horrified as I was, and as grateful as I was that it was Phineas and not me, it was still impressive. I somehow felt honored to witness such malicious finesse. Sergei is a sick, sadistic lunatic, but man is he good at what he does. The moment I caught myself in awe of his vicious flare, I knew we had to get out."

"I don't understand how you found that impressive," Brett objected.

"Me either. That's just the effect he has on people. Maybe it's the confidence with which he does terrible things, or maybe it's the unyielding influence he has over so many. Either way, the power he has is dangerous."

"The whole thing was messed up and unnerving." Cole felt the same way as Luke, but could tell the group was unable to understand what they'd been through as close confidents of Sergei. "The moment Phineas broke was when we started taking your plans to leave seriously," he told Misty.

"We fear he's having similar effects on the people he has connected with while traveling to and from the east coast. If he is wrangling them and whipping them into faithful soldiers, that's really bad news for the rest of us. It won't be long before he expands his reign over the entire continent and we find ourselves as his unwilling subjects," Ian predicted.

"But that's not how it's supposed to be," Misty protested. "It's supposed to be Juniper and the other Champions in charge of the new world."

"Then they better start making moves because time is running out. Sergei is moving fast and the bigger his expansion grows, the harder it will be to stop him," Cole advised.

"It's good we are reconnecting with Juni," Brett said. "They can't possibly know what lurks outside their safe haven."

"They knew about Clovis," Misty reminded him.

"Well, in case they don't know about Sergei's rise in power, it's good that we are on our way to warn them."

"He's right. Everything happens for a reason." Carine smiled at Misty, who nodded in return. She was finally putting aside her guilt for abandoning Juniper and realizing that their detour in Cedar City was the best thing they could have done for her.

The group continued toward the border of Mexico. They weren't sure where they were going exactly, only that they had to reach the Amazon River and follow it until they found Juniper. A lot of time had passed since she told them to find her this way, but they had faith she was still there. Brett, Ian, and Cole led the group with maps and compasses they found at a collapsed gas station market in Page, Arizona. The first few days after leaving were filled with paranoia and fear, but the more distance they put between themselves and Sergei's growing empire, the better they collectively felt. Though everyone began to relax, Misty found it hard to feel safe.

The group finally reached Route 66 and set up camp in Winona, Arizona.

Everyone grew used to sleeping outdoors and though the ash cloud remained, keeping everything dark, the dust wasn't nearly as bad. They continued to wear their protective gear, but imagined the facemasks and goggles would be unnecessary soon. The pop up tents they acquired at a Walmart outside Cedar City proved invaluable as they set up their sleeping quarters like pros.

"Do you hear that?" Misty asked her brother Luke. She pointed at the darkness behind them and he paused to listen.

"No. I can't hear anything over the chatter and crackling fire."

She grabbed his arm and pulled him away from the group.

"I think we are being followed."

"Stop worrying," he held his older sister's shoulders as he spoke. "If they were following us, they would've stopped us by now."

"Not if they are waiting to see where we are heading."

Luke sighed, then shouted into the darkness of the night. "If you're waiting to see our end game, you've got a long road ahead of you! *We* aren't even sure where we're going!" There was no reply. He looked back at Misty. "Better?"

"No," Misty rolled her eyes. "That won't stop them."

"I really don't think we are being followed. I understand your concern—you're worried about leading them to Juniper— but I think you're making yourself sick over nothing."

"I hope you're right."

"I am." He kissed her forehead. "Get some rest."

They walked back toward the rest of the group and separated. Misty found Brett's tent and Luke sat next to Brett's sisters near the campfire. The group was small but solid. They spent years bonding over their departure and debatable betrayal of Juniper, then over whether they belonged in Sergei's growing empire. It took a long time for the group to agree to leave the Lamorte camp, but they all felt better now that they had. They were on the road to something better and the shared hope kept them moving forward.

Chapter 31

Xavier kept his men at a safe distance from the traitors on the trip down Route 66. During the daytime, when the earth beneath the ash cloud was illuminated, they stayed far away and out of sight. At night, when the world shifted to blackness, Xavier and his crew got closer. They needed to hear what the traitors spoke about, where they were going, and any inside information that would help them defeat the Champion when the time came. As the traitors settled for the night in Winona, Xavier hid in the shadows around their campsite. Each man of Xavier's crew of rebels hid alongside him to eavesdrop.

For a while, the conversation was a bore and they spoke of things that did not matter—this was how most nights went. Brett, Misty, Carine, Ian, Cole, and Luke, who were the main leaders in the group, went to sleep and the others stayed up around the bonfire talking about frivolous topics. On this night, Luke and Carine stayed up with the others and Xavier hoped they would drink too much and develop loose lips.

Brynn took the bottle of whiskey from her sister and took a swig. Kallie grabbed it back and hiccupped.

"I can't believe we aren't out of the states yet," Chloe, the oldest of the Marose sisters commented with a slur. "I don't know why we are walking east instead of south."

"It's easier to follow the coast than to trek through the middle of Mexico," Luke explained. "We don't have a map of Mexico, don't know if we'll ever find one, so the shoreline is our best bet."

No one argued. Luke was handed the bottle and he took a sip.

"I just wish the sun would come back," Lara, Carine's older sister, complained as she took a sip from her personal flask. "The lack of light has made me permanently depressed."

"Me too," Kallie agreed. "Everything feels pointless."

"It's not, though," Carine objected. "We finally got the courage to leave Utah. We are off to find a safe home with Juniper. Good things are finally happening."

"I know," Lara sighed. "During the day, when the world is a little brighter, it's easier to stay optimistic. But at night, I just want to disappear. We are all together, I know, but I feel so alone."

Lara lost her husband when he refused to join her, Carine, and their mother at the Hall of Mosses. He was now dead and Lara's guilt for letting him stay behind haunted her daily. Everyone around the campfire knew her story and sympathized with her loneliness.

"We will be joining a brand new community within the next few months," Carine said. "Try to stay positive because things will get better."

"I'm trying," she promised.

Cade limped out of his tent and rubbed his eyes. He was twenty now, but never fully recovered from the accident in the forest the day the trees attacked.

"Can you guys shut up? It's really late and I can't sleep with all the talking."

"Sorry, bro," Valerie replied to her younger brother. "We'll keep it down." She let out a small burp then took another sip of whiskey.

"Forget it," he hobbled toward them and sat next to his sister, who passed him her paper cup.

"Don't tell mom," she urged.

"Obviously."

He finished what was left in the cup and cringed from the potency.

The group started talking about their first encounters with alcohol as young adults. They shared wild stories of their drunken younger years and remained in a state of constant laughter until Brett emerged an hour later to remind them that people were sleeping. This time, the group dispersed and went to bed.

Xavier was furious that he got no additional details on where they were heading. He continually missed the route planning discussions during the day because he couldn't get close enough to listen, and at night, all he heard were the drunken ramblings of whoever chose to stay up late.

"Let's relocate so we aren't spotted in the morning when they wake up," Xavier instructed his men after the traitors were in their tents.

They found a spot behind a collapsed McDonald's and laid out their sleeping bags. They did not sleep in tents. They took too long to dismantle and they always had to be ready to move at a moment's notice.

When early morning came and the sky shifted from black to gray, voices from the traitors' camp woke Xavier and his men. They were awake and preparing to depart. Xavier and his crew stayed quiet and followed at a safe distance once they started moving.

An hour into the walk, he received a call on his radio. It was the first time he had heard from his sister since he left a week ago.

"Where are you?" she asked.

"What a greeting," he stated sarcastically. "I'd have thought you'd want to know how I was doing, considering you've ignored my calls all week."

"I'm too busy worrying about how Grandpa is doing." Her tone was vicious.

"What's wrong with him?" he asked, feigning ignorance. He slowed and fell behind so the others couldn't hear.

"Don't act innocent," she spat. "I know what you did."

"I don't know what you're talking about."

"Quit playing dumb or I'll disconnect."

Xavier paused and contemplated his options.

"Did you tell anyone?" he asked, his voice low and threatening.

"Not yet. Everyone is a mess and I didn't want to make it worse. I don't think he's going to make it."

"So he hasn't gained consciousness since?"

"You're a heartless bastard. How could you do this to him?"

"It was an accident."

"Your footprint was imprinted on the skin of his neck when Uncle Dante found him! How is that an accident?"

"It was, I swear. You have to believe me."

"I don't."

"I wasn't myself. I was riled up and not thinking clearly. It was a mistake."

"For the sake of your soul, I hope he doesn't die."

"Me too." It wasn't a lie, but it wasn't the full truth either. Xavier wished the altercation never happened, but he also did not want Oskar to wake up. All he wanted was for his actions to remain a secret, at whatever cost.

"Where are you?" she asked again.

"Leaving Winona, Arizona."

"Dad is on his way home from Oklahoma. He found more survivors there. He's obviously racing back to check on Grandpa, but also because you and the others went missing. He is furious, so I didn't tell him where you went. I'm keeping my hands clean."

"Then how is he going to know where to meet us?"

"Radio in once he's back. Explain it to him yourself."

"Fine. When is he expected back?"

"In two days."

"Stay quiet until then and keep pretending like you know nothing. I'll take care of the story when I talk to him."

"I hope you know you're rotten."

"So I've been told," Xavier replied, unfazed. "You still love me, though."

"I wish I didn't."

"Love you, sis."

"You're the worst." She ended the call.

Xavier entered a light jog to catch up with the men ahead of him.

"Important call?" Vincent asked.

"Just my sister giving me an update. My dad will be back in Cedar City soon and I'll give him our location once he is. I suspect he'll use one of the Humvees to catch up to us."

The men mumbled in understanding and kept marching forward.

When two days passed and he still hadn't heard from his father, he began to wonder if Lucine told Sergei what he had done. If so, he could never return home. He fell back from his men and tried to call his sister. He spent an entire hour trying to make contact before she finally replied.

"What?" Her tone was filled with aggravation.

"Is Dad home?"

"Yes."

"Why hasn't he contacted me?"

"Because he's busy trying to save Grandpa."

"Who's with you right now?"

"No one."

"Did you tell him?"

"Tell him what? That *you're* the one who did this to Grandpa? I've never seen Dad so angry. He will take pleasure in killing Grandpa's attacker and I don't hate you *that* much."

"Once he gets out here, sees the mission we're on, and enacts the vengeance he's desired for so long, he'll understand why I couldn't let Grandpa stop me. Once he meets me here he will be reminded of all we lost because of the Champions and will be proud of me for seizing this opportunity."

"So you are going to tell him the truth?"

"I will, when the time is right. How's Grandpa doing?"

"Bad. I doubt Dad will leave his side until he starts to get better."

"Do you think he *will* get better?" Xavier had torn feelings about both potential outcomes.

"I'm not sure. You really made a mess."

"Does Dad know I'm out here?"

"No. No one knows where you are. Mom is distraught and thinks you ran off with the others."

"Tell Dad I took a radio. He has to meet us. He *has* to be the one to kill the Champion. It's all he's talked about for years.

Everything will be better once we rid the world of another Champion."

"That won't heal Grandpa."

"No, but it will remind everyone why I needed to do what I did for the greater good."

"I'll tell Dad to radio you on the condition that you stop calling me."

"Fine."

Lucine disconnected.

Xavier tried to swallow the discomfort her words gave him. He had no doubt that his father *would* kill him if he found out the truth at the wrong time or in the wrong way.

It was imperative to his survival that he maintained control.

Chapter 32

Juniper rolled over and kissed Roscoe awake. He smiled at her with sleepy eyes.

"Watch this," she said as she dug her fingers into the soil. A moment later, a batch of liana vines sprouted at the bases of the two trees they slept between. The woody vines climbed the tree trunks to the first set of low hanging branches, then dispersed overhead until they connected in the middle. Juniper stared up at the masterpiece she was weaving, eyes glowing greener than ever.

The lianas braided together until they formed a woven shelter over their mossy bed. Roscoe's mouth was agape in shock.

"When did you get so good at that?"

"I've been practicing," she said with a smirk.

"I wish I was given similar gifts." He rolled over and buried his face into her neck.

"We have a very long life ahead of us. You'll evolve with the others." She kissed the side of his head and sat up. "I've been trying to make a tree grow, but it's an enormous challenge."

"You'll figure it out."

"Yesterday, while the kids were napping and you were with the others at the gardens, I traveled north to be alone so I could focus on growing a kapok tree. I put so much energy into it that I fell asleep immediately after. If Rooney hadn't woken me up when everyone was gathering for dinner, I'd have slept there all night."

"I would have found you before that happened."

"I know you would have, I'm just saying it's draining."

"Well, kapok trees are gigantic. Try starting with something smaller."

They rose and walked a few feet to where their children slept cuddled next to each other. Jasper had his arms wrapped around tiny Elodie and Landon's toddler-sized body was sprawled over top of them. They breathed in unison.

"I've never felt a love as deep as what I feel for them," Juniper said in a whisper.

"Me either, which is impressive considering how much I love you."

Juniper nodded in agreement. It still amazed them that their children were born with special gifts, and that eventually, all of the people of the trees would evolve to have the same. The thought gave her great joy.

"I'm going to take Jasper with me today when I try to grow a tree. I think he might be able to help."

"He was born with the gift," Roscoe stated in agreement. "It can't hurt."

Momma, Elodie crooned telepathically. Juniper walked over to her and carefully removed her from beneath her brothers.

"Good morning, my love." She kissed her daughter on the forehead and Elodie returned the love with a sleepy smile. The absence of their little sister caused the sleeping boys to stir. Landon woke up first, grumpy as usual. He stared up at his parents with a tired scowl.

"What's wrong?" Roscoe asked his son with a smirk. Landon threw his body to the side so that his dad could not see his face. This startled Jasper awake and he accidentally punched Landon in the face. Landon immediately retaliated by shoving his older brother. Jasper wasn't much of a fighter, nor was he prepared for this sudden attack upon waking, so he curled into a ball while Landon pounded his small fists against his back. Roscoe swooped in and lifted Landon off Jasper, to which Landon began to sob.

"He hit me!"

"It was an accident."

"But it hurt," he cried.

"You'll be fine," Roscoe cradled his recently turned 4-year-old while Juniper helped Jasper up.

"You okay?" she asked her 8-year-old.

"Yeah. He's crazy." Jasper shook his head while observing the temper tantrum.

"He's still little. He'll grow out of it. Want to do something fun with me today?"

"Yes," Jasper answered, his green eyes shining bright.

"Great. Let's get Elodie to Grandpa Aldon, then we'll go on a hike."

Roscoe joined the Wolfe and Hazedelle families at the vegetable gardens and Aldon babysat their younger children with the help of Irene and Zoe. She took Jasper by the hand and led him to a remote location where they could practice.

"What are we doing here?"

"Have you ever grown a tree?"

Jasper took a moment before answering. "I don't think so. Maybe a small one, but I can't remember."

He was constantly running around the jungle, making flowers bloom and shrubberies grow, so his fuzzy memory wasn't a shock.

"Would you like to help me grow a tree?" she asked.

"Yes!"

"Fantastic," she said with a smile. "You know what a palmetto tree looks like. Focus on that." With their hands close, they dug their fingers into the soil and closed their eyes. Juniper could feel the wisteria climbing and blossoming all around them. She wasn't sure what Jasper was growing, but it felt wrong. She opened her eyes and saw an enormous red bromeliad at the base of a nearby tree. She shook Jasper and he opened his eyes.

"Whoops," he said, realizing what he made.

"It's okay, I didn't do any better," she said, pointing at the soft purple wisteria hanging on the branch above them.

"What did we do wrong?" he asked.

"I don't know," she answered, her fingers still firmly planted in the soil.

Let me help you.

The voice came as a shock and Juniper looked down at Jasper to see if he heard it too. He appeared unalarmed.

I can help you. The voice had a thick Ukrainian accent.

Sofyla? Juniper asked via thought. Her eyes welled with tears.

I never left.

But you died. We felt it happen.

Yes, but my spirit lives on in the soil.

Juniper's heart rate quickened.

Why did it take so long for you to find me?

My spirit lives in the soil now and it was very disorienting at first. I was lost in the swamps of Louisiana for a few years. Then once I got my bearings, I raced to find you. How is Riad?

He has withered away. He has barely spoken to anyone since you died.

How long ago did I pass?

About eight years.

Really? Feels like it happened yesterday, Sofyla sighed. *Time passes differently here.*

He will be thrilled to know you live on through the earth.

Let me speak to him.

Juniper nodded, then looked down at Jasper who stared up at her with great concern.

"Why are you crying?" he asked.

"I was just visited by a dear friend who I lost a long time ago. She spoke to me in my mind, just like we do within our family."

Jasper did not completely understand, but the sight of his mother crying caused him distress. He stood and hugged her where she knelt.

"Please don't cry," he pleaded as he rubbed the back of her long curly hair.

"They are happy tears."

He took a step back and stared into her eyes with curious intent.

"They don't feel happy."

"That's because they are lined with grief. My friend died in a terrible way, so I am happy to hear from her, but still very sad that I lost her."

Is this your son? Sofyla asked, sensing the boy's presence from where his bare toes touched the soil.

Yes. The pride and love she felt for Jasper filled her one-word reply.

He has a beautiful soul.

Rooney raced through the trees to where Juniper and Jasper were.

::*I sensed your sorrow. Is everything okay?*:: the red fox asked.

::*Yes, we are fine. Thank you. Would you do me a favor though?*::

::*Anything.*::

261

::Bring Riad here.::

::How? He can't hear me.::

::I will tell Roscoe that Sofyla's spirit has returned and you can lead them both here. I would do it myself, but I need to be here with Jasper and Sofyla. Roscoe will convince Riad to come.::

Rooney trotted back from where he came and she relayed the message to Roscoe with brevity. Juniper hoped one day others would also be able to speak telepathically to the animals, but for now, only she and her children had that gift.

Let's build a tree while we wait, Sofyla suggested.

What are we doing wrong? Juniper asked.

Imagining the tree you wish to build is good, but you also need to pull from the magic of the trees around you. Without their help, you won't have enough energy or stamina required to build something so powerful. It's beyond human capability, but you are bonded with the trees and can use their strength to enhance your own.

Juniper looked at Jasper, who watched her with engaged concern. She knew what Sofyla meant; she felt her connection to the trees in every breath she took, but she wondered if Jasper had that same bond.

"Do you feel the trees?" she asked him.

"What do you mean?"

"It's hard to explain."

"Well, when I grow things the space inside my chest swells." He held a hand over his heart. "And when I touch a tree, or put my fingers in the dirt, my mind goes quiet and I feel happy."

"Yes, that sounds right." He could not speak to the trees like she could, but he certainly was bonded to them in his own way. "When we try again, focus on the feeling the trees give you. Focus on the swelling of your chest and how happy the quietness makes you feel."

"What about your friend?" Jasper asked, confused at the topic change.

"She is still with us. Dad is coming with her Second soon. Until then, we ought to use this time productively."

Jasper shrugged in agreement and returned to his knees beside his mother. They dug their fingers into the soil and tried again. They did not agree on which tree they would try to grow, but focused on the feeling the trees gave instead.

An enormous surge radiated through Juniper's fingers. Normally, she would keep her eyes closed, but the sensation was so overwhelming that she opened them.

Instead of seeing what was happening in front of her, she saw everything from a different point of view: She was looking down on herself and Jasper. His head was bowed, his fingers clutching the soil, and her face was staring upward, green eyes bright as the sun. She didn't fully understand what was happening, but it felt right, so she let it continue.

As the surge in her fingers grew, so did the viewpoint from which she observed. She and Jasper grew smaller as her point of view grew taller. Branches covered in large, green leaves sprouted around her and she finally understood what was happening. She *was* the tree; she was seeing the world from its perspective.

When the surge stopped, Jasper lifted his head to see what they built. His expression filled with wonder and he looked over at Juniper to share the moment. But she wasn't inside her body; she was still seeing through the tree. Her eyes were fixed upward and her body vacant.

"Mom?" Jasper asked, his voice cracked with alarm. He stood in front of her and tried to force her to look at him. "Where are you?" he begged as he shook her shoulders.

As soon as his fingertips touched her bare shoulders, she returned to her body. She shook her head a few times to get her bearings and buried Jasper in a hug the moment she became aware of the fear she caused him.

"Where did you go?" he demanded between sobs.

"I was in the tree. I was looking down on us from above."

"It was scary. I thought you were dead."

"I'm sorry. That's never happened before."

"It's okay." Jasper calmed down and wiped the tears off his face. He took a step back and observed their creation again. "We did it."

"That's because we built it from the heart." She placed her hand on his chest. His breathing returned to normal and he smiled at his mother, proud of what they made.

<<*It is time,*>> the trees announced, though only Juniper heard.

For what?

<<*You must build habitats across the continent for all of Earth's creatures. There are many displaced animals in this jungle and they need proper living conditions if they are to survive.*>>

You want me *to do this?*

<<*You are capable.*>>

How will I know what to build for them?

<<*The animals will tell you what they need. They've already relocated to their designated spots on the continent. All you need to do now is go to them and create.*>>

This could take years.

<<*It will take years. More than the people around you will live to see. But sunlight has already returned to the entire continent and you must start the process of adapting the landscape so that the healing can begin. The animals have already spent too many years outside their*

natural habitats. They must repopulate and they cannot do so until you give them proper homes.>>

Where do I start? Which species needs the change the most?

<<The order will occur instinctively.>>

The voice of the trees departed and Juniper focused back on the situation at hand: She just unveiled a brand new evolutionary power, Jasper was entirely too stressed for an 8-year-old, Sofyla's spirit lingered underfoot, and Roscoe was on his way with the most broken man she'd ever known. On top of all of that, she was tasked to restructure the entire jungle so that every animal residing there could live comfortably. She never imagined it would get easier, but she certainly enjoyed the lull between large responsibilities. Nine years passed without much action, and though she enjoyed the time she was granted to relax, this moment of returned stress reminded her that her work as Champion was not done. There was much to accomplish and after spending a moment to recollect her wits, she greeted the challenge with a smile.

Chapter 33

Roscoe arrived with Riad, whose shoulders hung from the weight of his forever broken heart. Juniper stood with her arm around Jasper as they approached.

"Sofyla's spirit has returned," Juniper said with a smile.

Riad's sunken eyes peered up at her with skepticism.

"After so long?" His thick Arabian accent was filled with doubt.

"I know, I was confused at first too. Her soul lives in the soil. She was lost in the swamps for a while, but once she got her bearings she found her way back to us." Juniper knelt down and dug her fingers into the dirt. "Join me and you'll see for yourself."

Riad released a heavy sigh and knelt down with reluctance.

He placed the tips of his fingers into the soil and closed his eyes.

Riad? I am here! Sofyla cried.

Juniper looked over at Riad with an excited smile, but he showed no reaction. He hadn't heard her.

Riad? Speak to me, please. I miss you terribly.

I don't think he can hear you, Juniper replied to Sofyla, then spoke out loud to Riad. "She is calling to you."

"I don't hear her." His breathing intensified and his eyes filled with tears.

"Stop holding back. Let your heart believe."

"No," he shouted. He ripped his hands from the dirt and wiped them on his pants. "I refuse. I have suffered for so long. I cannot let hope live where it cannot exist."

"She is here! I promise. I would never lead you astray."

Riad's resistance continued, so she grabbed his hand and forced it back into the soil. She held it there beneath her own.

Talk, she instructed Sofyla.

Riad?

At the sound of her voice, Riad fell to the ground and pressed his cheek against the soil.

It's not possible, he sobbed.

But it is, she insisted. *I am here with you in spirit. I will never leave you again.*

"Let's give them a moment," Roscoe suggested to Juniper and Jasper.

Juniper lifted her hand from Riad's to exit their conversation, but the moment she did. Sofyla's voice disappeared from Riad's mind mid-sentence. He sat up with alarm and began digging at the soil frantically.

"What's wrong?" Juniper asked, alarmed.

"She's gone!"

Juniper touched the soil again and heard Sofyla's voice loud and clear. Her eyebrows creased in confusion. She took Riad's hand and placed it back onto the ground. His body relaxed again as Sofyla's voice returned to him. When Juniper lifted her hand from his, he looked up at her with confusion.

"Is she gone again?" Juniper asked.

"Yes," he replied.

Juniper sighed. "I think I know what's happening. You can only hear her through me."

The glimmer of hope Riad felt vanished and his expression returned to dire gloom.

"What if I want to talk to her in the middle of the night? What if I need to hear her voice when you are spending time with your family? I want to talk to her at all times; I cannot ask that of you."

"I will be here for you as much as I possibly can."

"It won't be enough. I know that sounds crazy and selfish, but it's the truth. I want to be with her at all times."

Roscoe stepped in. "Well, buddy, you're just going to have to take what you can get." He sympathized with Riad, but was by no means going to let him take advantage of Juniper's kindness. "Be happy that there is *any* option to reconnect with Sofyla."

Riad nodded, understanding his desires were irrational.

"I will do my best for you," Juniper reinforced. She placed her hand back over his so he could talk to Sofyla again, then looked to Roscoe and Jasper. "I'll meet you two at home."

Roscoe nodded and escorted Jasper back to camp. Juniper spent an hour with Riad and Sofyla, helping them rekindle after so many years. It was heartbreaking and reminded Juniper of her own eventual fate. Though she and Roscoe were granted eternal life like all the other Champions and their Seconds, one day they both would die and her spirit would live among the trees. She wondered what would happen to Roscoe after he passed over.

"Do you think I'll join her in death?" Riad asked, his thoughts circling around the same question as Juniper's.

"I was wondering that myself. I don't know what will happen."

Riad maintained his silence and entered a state of deep thought. Juniper could not read his mind, but got an eerie sense that he was contemplating dark matters.

"You know," she said to break his sullen concentration, "there's no guarantee you'll be together again in death."

"I wasn't thinking that."

"Okay, good," Juniper sensed he was lying, but did not press the issue. "Let's head back."

When they returned to where the majority of their group had built homes, Riad left to be alone and Juniper found Roscoe and her children with Clark and Aldon at the river.

Though Aldon was their true grandfather, Clark had become a second. The men got along well and shared a great love for the children.

For years, Aldon kept his distance from everyone, including his own son. Though Roscoe tried to integrate him into the group while they endured the dark days at the Hall of Mosses, he refused to open his heart. Juniper resigned to an estranged relationship with her father-in-law, but when she gave birth to Jasper, everything changed. When Aldon held his grandson in his arms for the first time, she saw him smile with genuine happiness for the first time since she'd met him. Her young son put life back into the old man. He was reinvigorated and able to find a reason to live again. For the first time in years, Aldon Boswald felt joy.

Clark had been a father figure to both Roscoe and Juniper for years, so it made sense that he adopted the role of grandfather to their children. He loved them with all his heart and they loved him back.

Juniper arrived to a chaotic scene of merriment and laughter. Clark was pretending to be a river monster and chasing her sons through the shallow depths of the river. Aldon sat on a large rock with Elodie, teaching her some of his favorite songs. Roscoe left the riverside to meet Juniper half way.

"How'd it go?" he asked.

"Eh, as well as expected. Riad has been carrying his grief for so long, he cannot see clearly without it. He makes me nervous."

"It will be okay."

"It got me thinking what will happen to us when our time comes. I'll live on, like Sofyla, through the trees, but what will happen to you?"

"The spirits of the dead get a choice, right? To live on through nature or to forsake this world and embark a life free from humanity in space. Well, I'd choose the trees. I'd always choose you."

"Yes, but from my experience, talking to her spirit through the soil is very different than when I talk to the spirits of the trees. She is a solitary entity. She still has the memories from her life and is very much human. The trees are a collective entity. It's all the souls of humans combined into the trees as one. They don't feel human, nor are they able to recall their human lives. You might not remember me."

"Impossible."

"I never considered any of this until today."

"All the more reason to take advantage of our gift of eternal life."

"And what about our children? What happens to them? Did the gift of eternal life pass down to them? Or will we have to watch them grow old and die?" Tears filled her eyes. She couldn't stop the spiral of questions that stemmed from Sofyla's return.

"Stop worrying. We won't know until it happens."

"I can ask Gaia when She returns."

"But you don't know when She will, so enjoy what we have right now. Everything will be okay."

He was right. She would ruin their wonderful reality if she stressed over matters that were out of her control. It wasn't worth it, so she did her best to let it go.

"I have a new task," she informed him as she wrapped her arm around his waist and they walked toward the water.

"From the trees?"

"Yes. First, I should tell you that Jasper and I successfully grew a tree."

"He told me! That's amazing. I knew you could do it."

"Did he tell you what else happened?"

"He mentioned that you scared him. Something about you leaving your body for a little bit."

"I became one with the tree; I could see the world from its perspective. I looked down on myself and Jasper as we brought it to life."

"I can see why that frightened him." Roscoe offered, though his eyes revealed his fascination. "Maybe one day you'll be able to watch over the world through the trees."

"I hope so." Juniper smiled; she hadn't thought of that.

"So your new task?"

"Right. So now that I have figured out how to grow all variations of plant life, the trees want me to build the correct habitats for the animals seeking refuge here. They cannot reproduce without the proper conditions. They need me."

"That's an insanely large task."

"It will take a long time to complete, which is why I need to start now."

"Can I help?"

"Not with the growing, but you can help me stay organized and on track. I don't even know where to begin."

"I will do my best."

"I'll have to travel all over the continent, so I'd like to have you and the kids by my side."

"They can help you with some of the growing."

"Maybe. I don't want to put too much responsibility on them. They are little; I just want them close."

They reached the river and sat on the bank with their feet in the water. Juniper laid back on the grass and focused on the water lapping against her ankles.

Marisabel, she whispered in thought.

The cold water felt perfect in contrast to the hot air.

Can you feel this?

A moment later Marisabel arrived. She didn't say anything, she just quietly channeled the feeling of the river on Juniper's feet.

I miss home, she finally said. Juniper could feel the sorrow in Marisabel's mind.

You'll be able to join us soon. Have you been evolving?

I barely leave my room.

You must get outdoors! Do not let your depression win; you cannot fall behind. You have forever to return home, in the meantime, take advantage of this time to evolve.

Coral is evolving. She's stolen most of my people.

Stolen?

Yes, they follow her now.

Reemerge and join them. You can lead together.

It's too late. I've lost their loyalty. She has trained them to endure freezing temperatures and hold their breath for extended periods of time. I can't do any of those things. I'm no good for them.

You can catch up. I imagine they can't be too far into the process.

Coral and Zander are expecting a child.

That's wonderful news!

Marisabel made no comment.

I could be with child too, if I had Zaire with me.

Take care of yourself first. Time will reunite you with your Second.

I'm so far gone—I am cold, tired, and bitter. I snap at everyone who tries to talk to me. So severely that no one has bothered trying in weeks.

No one can help you but you. I will always be here for you, but you need to readjust your outlook. The moment you make a shift, I am certain the others will welcome you back with relief.

Perhaps.

Can you head to the White Room? I need to talk to everyone at the same time.

I'd rather head to Brazil.

I'm certain it won't be long before you're allowed to relocate.

Let's hope. Marisabel tuned into the sensation of fresh water on Juniper's skin one more time before departing for the White Room. Juniper hoped it was the motivation she needed to make a change.

She returned to the present reality, which was filled with squeals of joy and giggles. Everyone was okay, so she returned to her thoughts.

Aria, she said, summoning her sister of the air.

Juniper! Aria's voice arrived with a warm breeze. *I've been missing you.*

Has it been a year since our last meeting in the White Room?

I think so.

Think we can get everyone together now? I have fantastic news.

Sahira and I are available.

Great, Marisabel is on her way. I'll call out to the others on my way.

"I'll be absent for a little bit," Juniper warned Roscoe. "I need to tell my sisters about Sofyla."

"Got it."

He kissed her forehead as she slipped into the depths of her mind.

Chapter 34

The White Room

Juniper closed her eyes and traveled to the White Room, summoning Eshe and Coral on the way. Aria, Sahira, and Marisabel were already there when she arrived. Aria looked stunning in a white lace gown adorned with diamonds. The top half of her long, white hair was knotted into a braid that wrapped around the crown of her head, while the rest hung loose in long curls.

Sahira wore a metallic sari decorated with pale pink and purple patterns. Atop her head was a crown made of precious stones and gems.

Marisabel's appearance was a shock to them all. Her aura used to glow a bright, crystal blue before morphing into a dull, grayish blue upon losing her way in Antarctica. Juniper expected to see the monotone version of her aura today, but instead, was greeted by something unexpected. Though her energy remained dreary, her appearance was luminous. She wore a long sleeve, turtle neck dress made in a reflective white fabric that looked like snow. A white gold chain draped in crystals hung through her hair and over her forehead. Though her face remained stoic, her light blue eyes radiated like a frozen tundra in the sun. A frosty mist emanated off her skin and Sahira shivered as she took a step away from her.

"This is a new look," she said, half confused and half annoyed.

While Juniper and Aria showed Marisabel loving patience, Sahira, Eshe, and Coral had no tolerance for the martyrdom.

Marisabel looked down at herself in awe. She was just as shocked as the others.

"I guess I've changed."

"This is wonderful!" Aria exclaimed.

"Is it? She's an entirely different color," Sahira observed. "I don't think Gaia intended for her to turn into an ice queen."

"At least she's doesn't look like a sad puddle anymore."

"She still feels like one," Sahira murmured.

"This is my appearance here. I don't look like either of those things in the real world," Marisabel said. Her rising anger made her Brazilian accent heavier.

"What we see here are our auras," Sahira reminded her. "Our appearance here is our true selves. I have no idea what this look indicates for you, but I hope it's part of Gaia's plan."

"I'm sure it is," Aria said in defense of Marisabel, but Marisabel stayed quiet and Juniper suspected she knew more than what she was letting on.

Eshe arrived with Coral a few minutes later. They shared Sahira's skepticism upon seeing Marisabel's new look.

"What on earth have you been up to in your hideaway?" Coral asked.

"Perhaps you ought to check in on her more often," Aria replied on Marisabel's behalf.

"Guess so. Are you okay?"

"I'm fine." Marisabel's resentment covered the others with a chill.

"Lies," Eshe muttered under her breath.

"That's enough," Juniper cut in. "Picking on Marisabel won't help anyone. Show a little empathy." Eshe, Coral, and Sahira resigned to shameful silence and Juniper continued. She shifted her mood from aggravated to excited. "Sofyla is back."

"What?" Eshe blurted out. The White Room erupted with noise as all the Champions talked at once.

"Her spirit," Juniper explained. *"She came to me through the soil."*

"Why didn't she come to me?" Eshe asked in offense. They had spent a lot of time together and her feelings were hurt that she went to Juniper first.

"Riad is with me. If he wasn't, I'm sure she'd have found you before me," Juniper answered, irritated that they were more concerned about themselves than the miracle of her return.

Eshe fidgeted in her glowing fire gown. Her eyes were a redder shade of brown every time they saw her.

"Can she visit me now?" The tone of Eshe's voice was softer this time, more vulnerable. She didn't like to show weakness, but it was clear that she still missed Sofyla greatly.

"Yes. Absolutely."

"Can't she meet us here?" Sahira asked.

"I hadn't thought of that. Perhaps she can," Juniper said with consideration. *"Give me a second."*

She left the White Room, returned to the chaotic scene of her family in the river, and dug her fingers into the clay-like soil of the riverbank.

Sofyla, can you travel to the White Room?

I'm not sure, she replied a few seconds later.

Try. I just told our sisters the news and they are all eager to hear from you again.

Okay.

Juniper returned to the White Room. When she arrived, her sisters were waiting patiently.

"She's going to try."

No one replied. Instead, they held hands and waited with hopeful anticipation.

An hour passed in silence, but they never broke the circle. They remained steadfast with hands clasped. Their faith proved worthwhile when Sofyla eventually materialized in the middle of their circle.

She wasn't solid like the others, her silhouette was slightly transparent and colored in gold tones. She gleamed against the backdrop of the White Room.

Aria burst into tears and Eshe rushed toward her. She tried to embrace her, but her arms passed through the golden glow.

Sofyla smiled at her, appreciative of the attempt.

"Words can't express how grateful I am to see all of you again."

"We have missed you!" Aria said through the tears.

"In a strange way, this makes me less fearful of the afterlife," Sahira said. *"Even in death, we will never be apart."*

"You were able to talk to Riad?" Eshe asked.

"Through Juniper. He couldn't hear me without her."

"I don't understand."

"They needed to be touching so my voice could travel through her and into him," Sofyla explained.

"That's a rough twist," Coral commented.

"It's better than nothing," Aria countered.

"What took you so long to find us?" Eshe asked.

"It is dark and expansive on this side. Soil covers the entire earth and I can traverse through its entirety. I had no idea where I was for years. Took forever to determine up from down and left from right. I can only see upward from the soil's perspective and everything looks the same from that viewpoint, especially under the ash cloud. The soil spirits tried to help, but they've been speaking in riddles lately, so I was determined to figure it out on my own. I couldn't rely on the sky to pinpoint where I was, so I tuned in to the type of soil I was stuck in: wetland mineral soil. Once I understood how to feel through the soil, it

became easier to travel. Every place feels different; each has different identifiers. I can hear and see through all patches of soil, no matter where I am or how far away they are. So I started listening for Riad's voice. I eventually heard him, realized he was with Juniper, and headed toward the sound."

"It must have been hard to find one voice amidst all the others in the world," Sahira commented.

"Yes and no. It was hard to find him because there is so much ground to cover, not because of the excess noise. There's barely anyone out there."

"Did you hear the rebels?"

"I can't hear through the ash. Not well, at least. Sometimes I heard their muffled murmurings, but I could never decipher what they were saying. One time I thought I heard you through the ash," Sofyla said to Juniper.

"You probably did. We were traveling through it for a long time."

"I am so grateful to be reunited with all of you," Sofyla repeated.

"The feeling is more than mutual," Eshe proclaimed. All the Champions agreed. "I have to wonder out loud about the rebels though," Eshe continued, keeping the topic on their absence. "Their hatred for us was loud and apparent. Sofyla lost her life to it. Why did it stop? Where did they go? No one has seen or heard from them since Juniper passed their place of refuge during her travel to the Amazon. Did they give up? Shift their hatred onto something new?"

"Honestly, I've enjoyed forgetting about them," Coral stated. "I was happily imagining that they all died. That they couldn't survive and nature got the best of them."

"We are smart enough to know that's not the case," Sahira said with a scoff. "They were doing just fine nine years ago. I highly doubt there was a sudden shift that killed them all."

"I never said I believed *that happened, just that it was soothing to imagine.*"

"I doubt they're dead, but it's possible they are struggling," Juniper commented. "*It's awful out there. Life without sun is not only dangerous, but also depressing. And breathing all that ash has to be taking a toll on their bodies.*"

"It's too bad we can't spy on them through our elements," Aria said. "*The soil is covered in ash, the air spirits reside above the clouds, all the trees are dead, and the fresh water is poisoned by the volcanic residue.*"

"What about the mountain spirits?" Juniper suggested to Sahira.

"They've been with me since the purge. They sort of went dormant here and rarely leave. It never crossed my mind to ask them to spy on the rebels, but I suppose they could check in through the mountain ranges across the globe.*"

"Yes. It's important we keep an eye on what the rebels are up to," Eshe determined. "*Give it a try.*"

Everyone agreed, though they did not suspect there was much to worry about.

They said their farewells, focusing mainly on Sofyla's gleaming silhouette. It was tearful, but happy. Though their mortal lives were eternal with the capability to end, their souls were immortal. It gave the Champions comfort to know their work would not end upon their death. Even in the afterlife they would carry on as Champions of nature and their purpose would not cease. They were all morphing quite rapidly into their chosen element, evolving and becoming one with nature. Their developing identities were thoroughly intertwined with the responsibilities Gaia entrusted them with, and without their chosen element they'd lose all sense of purpose.

It suddenly made sense to Juniper why Marisabel struggled so ardently. While the others flourished in their elements, she was caged and separated from hers. It was time to take a stand on her sister's behalf. She would talk to the trees and lobby for her return to Brazil. Marisabel belonged with the river and it would hurt everyone if her departure from the ice-capped continent was refused. If the water spirits would not listen to her pleas, perhaps the trees would. Someone had to help her and Juniper planned to try.

Chapter 35

El Paso, Texas

Xavier and his crew crept behind the traitors down I-25. They kept a safe distance and were yet to be spotted. When the highway merged with I-10, his radio came alive with his father's voice. All the men turned, eager to hear from their leader, and Xavier waved them to keep moving forward while he fell behind.

"Where are you?" Sergei demanded again. Xavier lowered the volume so the men could not eavesdrop.

"Approaching El Paso."

"I told you to stay put." Xavier looked up to make sure none of the men had heard. They hadn't.

"I know you did, but this felt like the right thing to do."

"I want to be furious with you, but your intuition was correct. One of the traitors tried to kill your grandfather on their way out."

"What?" Xavier wasn't sure how the story took this turn, but he played along.

"Dante and your mother found him on the kitchen floor the morning the traitors left. He must have been onto them—maybe tried to stop them—so they tried to silence him. We won't know for sure until he wakes up. I want to know why they were in my house and what they stole."

"Supplies, maybe?" Xavier suggested. He'd let this lie continue if it meant he'd walk free.

"Regardless, they tried to kill my father, so now I will hunt them down and murder *them*. You did good following your gut. I'm proud of you."

"Thanks." Xavier felt less guilt than he should.

"We are leaving tomorrow. Gerald and Kelso will hold down the fort till Dante and I return. Give me your exact location."

"We are traveling down I-10 into El Paso, Texas. Looking at the map and the route we've traveled so far, they are avoiding crossing into Mexico. We're not sure why."

"Dante and I will be catching up in the Humvee. It should help us eliminate your lead."

"Okay, keep me posted on your progress."

"Keep up the good work, son."

The radio went silent. Xavier entered a brisk jog and caught up with the others.

"He and Dante are on their way."

"Finally," Gino said with relief. "I was starting to worry we were in this alone."

"I told you he'd come," Xavier protested.

"I didn't doubt you," Gino tried to explain, realizing that their young leader was offended. "I just felt like you were keeping us in the dark."

"You need to trust me."

"Sorry," he apologized. Though everyone there was significantly older than Xavier, they cowered beneath his anger. For now, it was because they feared his father, but one day they would fear him too.

They finally crossed the border into Mexico after spending two days in San Antonio, TX. The route confused Xavier and made everyone nervous that they still had a long way to go. To clear a path for the Humvee, they pushed all abandoned vehicles to the sides of the road in hopes this would help Sergei and Dante catch up faster.

Three weeks passed.

Sergei stayed in touch and was only a few hours behind them when they reached Mexico City.

"If we stay here over night it should give my dad time to catch up," Xavier explained to his men.

"Doesn't look like they plan to move again till tomorrow," Dennis observed through the walls of the broken building they hid behind. "Tents are going up and Ian is starting a bon fire."

"Good. We will keep a look out here, but set up camp much further back than usual. I don't want any of them hearing the Humvee as it approaches," Xavier explained. "Dennis and Oliver, you're on the first look out. Gino, Vincent, and Benny, follow me."

Xavier led them to a spot that was on the main road and a safe distance from the traitors. While the men took turns rotating lookout shifts, Xavier stayed put in eager anticipation of his father's arrival. At 3 a.m., he received the call.

"We are entering Mexico City. Where are you?" Dante asked over the radio.

His uncle's voice startled him awake.

"What road are you on?"

"The one you cleared for us. We've been following the path you left since El Paso."

"Okay, great. Continue down Boulevard Manuel Avila Camacho," Xavier instructed while reading the street sign he stood beneath, "but go slow. I'll be here to flag you down."

"Copy." Dante disconnected and Xavier walked into the middle of the road.

Within five minutes, the Humvee barreled toward him. He threw his hands up to make them stop and his father screeched to a halt a few feet from where he stood. The car spun and Sergei exited without turning the ignition off.

"Where are they?" he demanded.

Xavier was caught off guard. He expected a greeting, but his father was all business. He marched over and towered over him.

"The traitors. Where are they?" Sergei was livid. It appeared that he spent the entire journey hyping himself up and letting his fury build.

Xavier hadn't prepared for this.

"Why?" he asked cautiously. He knew the answer, but had to stall. He could not let his father ruin the greater purpose of this trip.

"Why?" Sergei seethed. "Have you forgotten everything I told you? One of them tried to kill your grandfather." He grabbed Xavier by the throat and pinned him against the side of the Humvee. "Where are they?"

"Calm down so we can talk," the 17-year-old said despite his struggle to breathe.

"Where is your family loyalty?" Sergei squeezed tighter. Xavier's eyes began to close as the air ran thin.

"You want another dead family member?" Dante stepped in, unable to let the madness continue. "Get off him. You're being irrational."

"The kid won't talk!"

"You didn't even give him a chance," Dante pushed his brother off his young nephew. Xavier keeled over and caught his breath.

"Killing me would have accomplished nothing," he eventually said in a pant.

"I wasn't going to kill you," Sergei scoffed.

Xavier rubbed the soreness from his neck.

"We're all on edge, understandably," Dante said to justify the tension. "But let's keep our anger focused on the correct targets."

"I need vengeance," Sergei stated through gritted teeth. "Tell me where they are."

"If you march in there tonight and massacre the lot of them, we'll never find the Champion," Xavier explained. "You need to remember the bigger picture, Dad."

"I need to know which of them did it and why."

"Even if you singled out the culprit and killed him, the others would never lead us to the Champion. And even if they thought we left, I doubt they'd continue. They know we want to kill her."

"I don't care about the damn Champion."

"Yes, you do! For years you cared about that more than anything else. Maybe your priorities have shifted, but I don't believe that your hatred for them is gone. I'm your son, I'm more like you than you know. We don't forgive and we don't forget. We get even. This is our chance to settle the score. We can take out another Champion if you can control your rage a little while longer."

"You didn't see him." Sergei's grief showed through his anger. "He was so weak, so fragile. They robbed him of his strength."

"When we kill the Champion, we can kill them too. You can have it all, you just need to be patient."

Sergei turned and began a slow pace. His energy was less toxic as he listened to his son's advice.

"Fine," he eventually conceded. "We will do it your way. You've gotten us this far, I'll let you maintain the lead on this mission." Xavier tried to hide his surprise. "But I will not go back until I've avenged my father."

"I suspect you will achieve much more than that."

His father let him enjoy ten seconds of leadership before reclaiming the role. "I brought a slew of backup weapons. When we get closer we will plan an ambush."

Xavier sighed. In the end all the shots called would come from Sergei. Xavier did not object. If he could keep his father focused and under control, the mission would stay on track and they'd conquer one more threat to their dominion.

Chapter 36

Sergei's presence shifted the entire dynamic of the group. The other men looked to him for direction moving forward, even though they had been following Xavier up to this point. Sergei reminded them on occasion that Xavier was in charge, but then he'd dole out orders right after saying so, which sent a clear and conflicting message. There was no stopping Sergei's commanding authority.

They followed the traitors through the Isthmus of Panama. The trip through Guatemala, Honduras, Nicaragua, and Costa Rica was long and exhausting. Everything flooded during the purge, so all that remained were the muddy ruins of the past.

There wasn't much ash through the southern tip of Mexico, and there was none along the isthmus. The dark clouds remained overhead but the air was easier to breathe. The struggle here was the sticky clay-like soil that plagued their path. Everything was still damp and soaked with moisture after years without sunshine. And unlike the smoky, sulfuric smell of the air northward, here the world reeked of mold. Still unhealthy to breathe, so they kept their masks fastened tightly, as did the traitors.

They maintained a safe distance, being cautious to stay quiet and out of sight. The traitors were leading them to a Champion and they had to let them complete their journey if they wished to reach the prize at the end. Sergei struggled to accept a postponed vengeance for his father during the first few weeks of travel, but was eventually able to recall the flame of his old hatred. The Champions were Satan reincarnated and he would act as mankind's savior. He would rid the world of these devils and all of their followers. His passionate hatred grew as they traveled south, as did that of his men. By the time they reached Panama, everyone was itching for the chance to slaughter a Champion.

"The reward at the end of this miserable trek will be so gratifying," Dennis said as he scraped the excess mud from the sole of his boot.

"Will we make it quick, or make her suffer?" Gino asked.

"What do you think?" Sergei asked his son. His redirection of the question aggravated Xavier—it was an insulting attempt to return ownership of this mission to him.

"You've been doing just fine on your own. I'm not sure why my thoughts on how we kill the Champion matter."

"Don't be sour. This is still your mission."

"I know it is." Xavier's tone was full of bitter resentment. All the men went quiet, trying to swallow the uncomfortable tension they helped cause.

"We wouldn't be here without you," Oliver offered after a moment of collective unease.

"I don't need your pity. I'm well aware of my own importance and what I contribute. I can't control your devout allegiance to my father, or how you all turn to putty in his presence. You don't worship me like you worship him, so let him lead. It's fine."

"It's not worship, it's respect," Vincent tried to correct the young boy, but his objections didn't change the facts.

Sergei intentionally cultivated a following of worshipers. He wanted fanatics, he wanted people who would die for him. Sergei observed the exchange with amusement. His son saw through his master plan, but his soldiers did not. Perhaps they were blind to it, or perhaps they denied it to salvage their pride. In either case, their lives belonged to him.

"I say we drag it out," Benny jumped in, eager to return to the previous subject. "Get as much information out of her before we end her life."

"Agreed," Sergei said. "I'd also like to make her watch us kill everyone she's worked so hard to protect. Rightful punishment, I think."

"That'll teach her," Benny approved with a smirk. The rest mumbled in agreement.

"They're moving," Dante shouted in a whisper to the group from his lookout nook. The men gathered their belongings, extinguished their fire, and prepared to travel.

The further west they journeyed along the Pan-American Highway, the more signs of life they began to see. They had prepped for the deadening cold of winter, but found that the weather grew warmer with each mile they completed. One hour out of Panama and they saw their first clean body of water. Three more hours and they came across the first set of living trees.

"Look at their branches," Vincent observed in awe. "They aren't rotted."

"They have leaves," Benny added.

Sergei's anger began to rise as he put the pieces of this puzzling development together, but he kept his suspicions to himself.

They continued onward, and though there were plenty of dead patches along the highway, there were also many signs of life. The earth here wasn't hopelessly dead. Its potential for rebirth showed promise.

"How are these plants alive?" Gino asked as he bent down to touch a fern that grew on the side of the road.

"It shouldn't be possible. There's no sun," Vincent contemplated in frustration.

"What's that?" Oliver asked, pointing straight ahead. All the men stopped to observe.

The highway appeared to end and so did the ash cloud. Light cast down upon the earth, creating drastic shadows and illuminating the world in the sun's glory.

"Is that sunlight?" Xavier asked, his voice a little higher than usual. The transition was far off in the distance, so it was hard to determine if what they saw was accurate.

"It can't be," Dante said in a whisper.

The traitors traveled steadily toward the light, their distant silhouettes perked with excitement as they got closer. When they crossed out of the dark and entered the light, their figures glowed beneath the sun and their celebratory reaction answered Xavier's question: The sun still existed in this part of the world.

"Has it been here all along?" Gino's voice was filled with desperation. "Did we waste all that time in the dark when we could have been here?"

"That was my entire childhood," Xavier said to himself, but loud enough so everyone heard.

"Why here?" Vincent asked, racking his brain for a logical explanation. None of his schooling in climatology helped. "Look at how the cloud ends. There is no movement; it's solid and still like a wall. That doesn't happen in nature."

"It's the Champion," Sergei spat. "She is here, in the sunlight, aware that we exist and choosing to let us rot in the dark."

The group went silent in introspective anger. It was impossible to argue his logic.

"We all survived the purge. We are all stuck on this dying planet together. What makes the traitors worthy enough to bring into the light, but not us?" Vincent contemplated out loud.

"Why not share the sunlight?" Gino asked. "Why not work together with us to survive? These Champions are not human, they are monsters."

"There is no justifiable reason for this behavior," Dante added.

"We did kill one of their own," Xavier commented, pointing out their obvious oversight. "And declare war against them years ago."

"Well, this has only confirmed that our fight against them is just." Sergei ignored his son's valid counterargument and continued his tirade. He would not let logic stand in the way of his hatred. "Our suspicions about them have been correct since the start. They would let us die when they have the resources to give us renewed life. They *want* us to die, and I suspect that if we continue to thrive as we are, they will one day take action against us. They will do whatever they can to end us. This is our time to prevent that fate. We can end *them*, here and now, and save ourselves from future battles."

They crossed into the sun an hour later, removing their facemasks and extra gear as they did so. The winter clothes they wore were unnecessary here; the sun was hot and carried with it high temperatures. It was summer again, a feeling none of the men had experienced in years. The earth was vibrant with color, the air was warm, and the sun provided them with rejuvenated energy. Though it could have transitioned their hate into understanding, the arrival of summer only intensified the rage that boiled within. The return of the sun would not deter them;

they would not lose sight of their mission. They had the entire human race to avenge.

Chapter 37

Panama-Colombia Border

Compass in hand, Brett led the group west toward the Amazon River. Ian and Cole took turns by his side with the map while Carine, Luke, and Misty remained at the rear of the group making sure no one fell behind. When they reached the end of the ash cloud in Panama the mood of the group lifted. Many had been struggling to stay positive, letting the exhaustion of the long journey take a toll on their moods, but a good dose of vitamin D lifted everyone's spirits. The continued sunshine meant continued happiness. After many months, they were on their way to a better life with Juniper and for the first time since they left Utah, it truly felt like each person of the group believed that.

Everyone was healthy and doing okay. They took breaks whenever needed, but the majority of the group was young and in shape. The youngest was Emeline Böhme, who was 14 and the oldest was Kurt and Olivia Courtland, who were 73 and 72 respectively.

A few miles into Colombia, they stopped to set up camp. Everyone was exhausted but content. They were almost at their end goal.

Carine started a fire with her sister Lara while the others constructed their tents. Little by little, everyone finished setting up their sleeping quarters and joined the gathering around the fire. By the time it got dark everyone was there, sitting and laughing together.

Misty began recalling stories from their nights working at the Dipper Dive.

"Remember when Frank's mistress stormed in and ripped him apart for not telling her he was married?"

"So uncomfortable, but so amazing," Brett laughed. "He tried to fire me the night before, but realized he had no one to replace me, so seeing him get his ass handed to him was perfection."

"Why was he trying to fire you?" Brynn asked her brother.

"Frank was always trying to fire Brett," Carine jumped in. "Understandably though. He and Teek showed up drunk most of the time."

"Maybe so, but we were damn good bartenders, sober or not."

"True," Carine agreed.

"How was Juniper as a bartender?" Valerie asked. She was fifteen when the purge happened and always looked up to Juniper from afar. Juniper, Teek, and Roscoe saved Cade back when the trees attacked and it felt wrong when they left her behind. Cade was her best friend and without him she'd be lost, so she was eager to see Juniper again and express the gratitude she wasn't able to articulate as a teenager.

"Juniper was an okay bartender. She wasn't much of a people person, but she did a good job faking it," Carine replied. "Even on her bad days, people still liked her. She could be in the worst mood ever and customers were still drawn to her. I guess her reserved nature gave off an air of mystery."

"All the guys loved her," Brett added. "Most weren't vocal about it because she was so intimidating and was known for her brutal bite. Most admired her from a distance. I found it fascinating. I don't think she ever realized how many people, men and women, took a quiet interest in her. She was so withdrawn it garnered great intrigue. Misty and Carine on the other hand were huge flirts. They kept the guys coming back while Juniper kept them wondering."

"And you and Teek were the party. We kept the ship afloat despite your many attempts to let it sink," Carine stated.

"Remember that time we lit the bar top on fire?" Brett laughed. "Doused it in vodka and set it aflame."

"Frank hated your pyro shows," Misty laughed.

"His reaction was the best part every time. He freaked out and screamed like a madman till we put it out."

"Remember that time you hid the fire extinguisher from him?"

"I thought he might murder me. Actually, I was certain he would. The fire was the only thing separating me from him, so I threw a little lighter fluid on it."

"Why didn't the whole place burn down?" Valerie asked, confused. She had never been to a bar and didn't understand that they did this for entertainment.

"The bar top was made of steel and we were careful. It's a common bar trick. The guests loved it, but Frank only cared about money and he was certain we'd eventually screw up and burn his building down."

"You almost did the one time I was there," Luke reminded him, then explained the occurrence to the group. "I brought this girl on our first date to the Dipper Dive, which was a horrible idea in the first place, but Misty promised me free drinks. When you two bozos found out I was on a date, you got all jacked up and wanted to impress her on my behalf. The flames on the bar nearly touched the ceiling and the fire department had to be called."

"In our defense," Brett interjected, "the place *didn't* burn down. No harm, no foul."

"If you say so, man," Luke laughed.

"Those were fun times," Brett reminisced with a sigh.

"Once we get to Juniper we will be safe and we will have time to make happy memories again," Misty reassured everyone.

"I will look back on this journey with fondness," Ian noted. "It's been stressful and a little scary at times, and maybe there haven't been too many funny moments, but I know I'll look back on this time with all of you and smile."

"I certainly think we made the right move leaving the Lamorte regime," Cole added to his brother's statement.

There was a collective agreement that they were all much safer away from Sergei. When they left Cedar City, he had thousands dependent on him for their continued survival. They flocked to him and worshiped him like a God. The cult he was creating was dangerous and the more distance they could place between themselves and the sinister world he was crafting, the better.

"Alright, Culver family, I'm off to bed," Dave said to his wife and kids. Not long after, the rest of the group did the same. They each retreated into their separate tents and the night became quiet.

A little after midnight, Misty rustled from beneath the blanket she shared with Brett and exited their tent to pee. She struggled with the zipper and tripped on her way out, but managed to do the whole thing with only one eye open. She stumbled behind their tent, where she would normally go to the bathroom, but the Culver's tent was right there with the mesh screen open.

She walked a little farther, past their tent till it was out of sight. She hadn't been to this part of the forest yet but took note of her path so she didn't get lost. She eventually found a good tree to lean against and the moment she finished, the sound of voices came from the distance. She hastily pulled up her shorts and looked for the source. It came from the opposite direction of camp.

She tip-toed toward the sound. It was a decent walk from where she was but when she got there, she found a tree to hide behind and observed.

"They are all asleep. We won't need a lookout again until dawn," a man said. Misty's heart contracted as he turned and she caught view of his face. It was Gino.

She repositioned herself so she could get a glimpse of the others. Gino spoke to Dante, who was the only other person awake. The rest slept out in the open on sleeping bags. Dennis and Oliver were near the front of their Humvee, which had an open trunk filled with guns. Vincent and Benny slept near Dante, and Xavier was by himself behind the truck. She searched for Sergei, praying he was not there. Gino and Dante continued talking, despite Benny's groans of aggravation and Vincent's pleas for them to be quiet. A minute later, Sergei's head popped out from the backseat of the Humvee where he had been sleeping.

"If you don't shut up I am leaving you both behind tomorrow."

Misty recoiled behind the tree at the sight of his face. It felt like a living nightmare. She pinched herself to make sure this wasn't in fact a terrible dream.

It wasn't.

Sergei and his crew were there in the flesh, stalking their journey toward Juniper. Their chance to join her safe haven was tarnished. They could not carry onward and lead them right to her. Misty raced back to camp as quietly as possible.

She woke up Brett, Carine, and her brothers.

"He's here," she expressed the moment they were all awake and together. "Sergei found us."

"How?" Ian asked.

"I don't know, but he's here. A mile or two that way," Misty pointed to the east. "I got up to pee and the Culver's tent was too close to ours, so I walked a little. Then I heard voices and investigated. They've been following us since the start. They've got a Humvee loaded with weapons."

"I can't believe we got this far without noticing them," Luke grumbled.

"This is really bad," Brett agreed. "What do we do?"

"Well, we can't lead them to Juniper. That's out of the question," Carine replied.

"But we also can't stop," Cole countered. "The moment we stop they will infiltrate, question us, and likely kill us. We have to assume they know we are on our way to reconnect with Juniper. Why else would they have followed us all this way?"

"What if they only followed us because we abandoned his lead? He's a bit nutty when it comes to loyalty," Luke offered. "Maybe that's all there is to it."

"No," Ian objected. "Sergei was onto bigger and better things. He's about to be leader of the new world. It would take much more than a few traitors to get him to disappear for this long and risk his title. He's just as obsessed with ruling the land as he is about killing Champions."

"Exactly," Cole confirmed. "There has to be more to this."

"But how could they possibly know we are heading toward Juniper?" Misty asked. "They certainly haven't gotten close enough to overhear our conversations."

"Who knows, but we have to act smart moving forward."

"We need to warn Juniper," she insisted. "If Brett and I leave tonight we will have half a day's lead on you."

"And we can start moving extra slow to lengthen your lead," Luke added.

"Do you think they'll notice we're missing two people?" Carine asked.

"Maybe, but it will take a while." Ian was deep in thought. "We outnumber them."

"But they have guns," Brett reminded him. "We don't stand a chance against them while they are armed."

"So we must unarm them," Ian continued his thought process. "If we can sneak up on them in the middle of the night and steal their weapons, or better yet the truck, then we'll steal their advantage."

"Sergei sleeps in the truck," Misty told her older brother.

"We will figure it out. In the meantime, you and Brett need to head out. In case our plan goes awry, you'll at least get the chance to warn the others."

"Should we start traveling in the wrong direction?" Carine asked the group.

"No, that would be unwise. We need shelter and safety. Juniper can provide that so we must continue toward her. If we cannot remedy this situation before we reach the Amazon River, then we will reroute to lead them away from her. Until then, we follow the course."

"Just give us enough time to get a solid lead," Brett requested. "If something goes wrong we need a few days between us."

"We will wait a week. We need the time to spy and scope out their situation anyway. Can't make a move until we are sure it will work," Ian said.

Brett and Misty packed up their tents and backpacks, then left with minimal goodbyes. They had to reach their friend; they had to warn Juniper that danger approached. Misty swallowed the guilt she felt for leading Juniper's greatest threat directly to her, but was determined to right this wrong by reaching her first.

It was a race they could not lose.

Chapter 38

Northeast Border of Colombia

"Something is amiss," Sergei announced upon waking up.

"What?" Dante asked with a yawn.

"I'm not sure, but I sense a shift. With us or the traitors, I'm not sure."

"Can't be us," Dennis replied. "We're solid."

"No changes here," Oliver agreed with his twin. No one wanted to witness the wrath of Sergei if he suspected internal betrayal.

"Perhaps not. Who watched over the traitors last night?"

"We took turns," Gino answered. "Vincent is there now, waiting for them to start moving again."

"My intuition is never wrong. We must keep an observant eye on them."

"Understood." Gino left the group to join his brother on watch. When they returned a half hour later, the group was packed up and prepared to move.

The world was bright and alive, a stark contrast from what they'd grown accustomed to. Xavier walked beside his father, pondering the possibilities.

"Knowing this part of the world has sun changes everything."

"It changes nothing," Sergei insisted.

"But we can be the ones who deliver sun to the masses. Imagine their gratitude. We'd be worshipped as gods."

"While that thought is brilliant, and one I've considered myself, you haven't thought it through. I am not the official leader yet. I haven't been elected and that won't happen until after the rebuild is complete. I need the keys to the warheads. I still need the codes to the nuclear weapon plants. They've given me access to everything else, in the name of rebuilding, but I've yet to receive full presidential access to all that remains."

"How do you know the bombs are still there?"

"Because they did not explode. The reactors did not collapse. I've spoken with the officials in DC, who still have access to satellite imagery, and like magic, all those spots were carefully preserved. It appears nature was smart enough to avoid destroying those locations when it attacked."

"When will you tell the others about the sun?" Xavier asked.

"When I'm certain they'll follow me to the edge of the world. The success of my leadership is dependent upon their desperation. They must continue to suffer so I can continue to alleviate their struggle little by little. It must be drawn out to magnify all that I do for them. Once I am president and certain that their loyalty is secure, I will share the gift of sunlight with them."

Xavier comprehended his father's rationale—it was genius.

Gino, Vincent, and Benny pushed the Humvee, which was left in neutral, while Dante steered it. The slow progression remained a few feet behind Sergei and Xavier. They could not use the truck for its speed because they had to keep pace with the slow-walking traitors ahead, so it did not make sense to waste the precious fuel. The truck crushed plants and flowers in its wake, leaving a trail of death behind the men.

"Do you hear that?" Oliver asked. He and his twin walked a few paces behind the Lamortes.

"What?" Sergei snapped his head toward the younger man.

"Listen," Oliver urged. Sergei raised an arm to halt the group's progression and paid closer attention. After a moment, he heard the sound. There was persistent buzz that filled the air.

"Insects?" Xavier asked once he heard it too.

"I think so," Oliver replied.

"Creatures exist beneath the sun," Sergei mumbled to himself, then lifted his head. "If there are bugs here, then there will surely be larger animals as well. Keep an eye out."

A mosquito landed on Xavier's bicep and he slapped it dead.

The following day the sight of hawks flying overhead appeared.

"I haven't seen a bird in years," Dennis professed. The long-lost sight was stunning and his voice was filled with wonderment.

Sergei zeroed in on the path ahead. While his men expressed their amazement, he was hesitant to see the return of the animals as a good thing. He was certain they'd come across larger, more dangerous beasts soon, so he kept his rifle at the ready. He was the only living creature allowed to induce fear in the hearts of others; no monster birthed in the wild would threaten his power.

A chorus of cicadas sang the group to sleep while Gino kept look out over the traitors. Xavier found it difficult to rest knowing there were likely larger animals stalking the area, so he joined Gino.

"Not tired?" Gino asked.

"No." He plopped down beside his older counterpart. For the first time in a while, he felt his age. He was 17-years-old and afraid. He had no control over the situation that once belonged to him and they were rapidly walking out of their former comfort zone. "More animals will come," he expressed to Gino.

"We have guns," the young man replied with a shrug.

This was true, and it gave Xavier some relief, but it didn't change the fact that out here, they were not in charge. Nature reigned supreme and they were unwelcome visitors. The feelings he experienced right after the purge crept back to the surface. They were not wanted on this planet; they were supposed to die years ago. If nature so chose, it could kill them off at any moment. He kept his worries to himself, but the fear was alive in his heart.

"There's a tent missing," Xavier said after a few minutes of silence. Gino squinted his eyes and tried to count, but Xavier was already peeved. "How did you miss this?"

"I never counted the tents before," Gino stammered, "I'm sorry."

Xavier stormed back to camp. He woke his father and uncle to inform them of his discovery.

"Since when?" Sergei demanded.

"Who knows when they went missing. I haven't been on watch since you arrived."

"Oliver and Dennis are our best bet," Dante offered. "They're the fastest here and should run ahead and see if they can find the missing traitors."

They woke up the twins and informed them of their new mission.

"Why did they leave their group?" Dennis asked.

"Do they know we are tailing them?" Oliver added with a yawn.

"There's no way to know without finding them." Sergei handed Oliver an extra radio pack. "When you find them, stay hidden and report back."

The twins nodded, prepped for the journey then took off in a light jog. It was dark and they were able to run right past the traitors' camp without detection.

"Good catch," Sergei complimented his son. Xavier nodded in acceptance of the praise. Sergei redirected his attention to the others. "Lookouts will now occur at all times. There will be no more skipped hours during the middle of the night. I don't care if they appear to be sleeping and if the watch bores you to tears, whoever is on watch during those hours will stay awake and alert. Missing the disappearance of a few of them is a grave mistake and I will not tolerate another slip-up."

He turned without waiting for a response and entered the back of the Humvee to rest. Everyone accepted his orders in silence.

The energy was tense and remained so when they woke the next morning. Sergei was in a foul mood and he did nothing to mask it as the day continued.

They marched forward only to stop an hour later when the traitors paused to rest. They were taking breaks more often, which heightened Sergei's suspicions.

The area they now resided was less wooded and more open. There were patches of condensed trees, but also tons of open fields, so it was harder to track the traitors in secrecy on this landscape. Instead of staying directly behind them, they added dimension to the space and remained a good distance north and west of the traitors.

Xavier walked to the opposite side of their small stretch of forest to observe the land. It was an expansive field with tall grass and prairie flowers. He inhaled a large dose of the fresh air. The moment he closed his eyes his senses heightened and he felt an unwelcome presence. His eyes shot open to the empty field. There was nothing there. He relocated behind the thick trunk of a Brazil nut tree and peered into the field with one eye. A few moments after taking cover, a small lion cub came out of its own hiding spot and continued its frolic through the tall grass. He could see its small head pop over the tall blades between adorable hops.

Xavier only saw a threat.

Surely its parents were nearby, ready to defend the slightest offense against their cub. While he feared this day since the insects returned, he found he wasn't frightened at its arrival. The sight of the little animal enticed a primal urge inside him; one that demanded he conquer the small beast.

Gino was patrolling the edges of their confinement and came across Xavier pressed against the tree trunk.

"What are you doing?"

Xavier hushed him and pointed into the field.

"Target practice," he whispered then knelt to steady his aim.

Gino watched with fervent anticipation as Xavier zeroed in on his target. The cub romped around the field with innocent glee, attacking the flowers with playful aggression and rolling on its back between sprints. It was happily oblivious to the threat aimed its way.

During a brief break in the cub's daylight prance, Xavier took the shot. The bullet came out quietly through the rifle's silencer and pierced the baby's front left shoulder. It cried a desperate whimper as it stumbled to the ground. Xavier cursed beneath his breath, angry that his first shot missed the heart, and without thinking, stood to enter the field. As he emerged from the shadows of the forest, prepared to march to the cub and finish it off, the mother lion appeared at her baby's side. It peered up at him with a murderous stare.

Xavier halted where he was, unable to breathe. She took two slow steps towards him before breaking into a sprint. He fumbled with his gun, trying to get it aimed to shoot, but his palms were sweaty and hands were shaky. She would reach him before he could pull the trigger.

A shot fired from over his shoulder, piercing the lioness in the head. She fell dead three feet from where Xavier stood. He turned around with wide, wet eyes. His breathing was a panicked gasp, one he could not regulate. Gino stood behind him, rifle with silencer attached at the ready in case another adult lion charged.

The tall grass swayed in the distance.

Gun still aimed, Gino grabbed Xavier by the collar of his shirt and pulled him into the shadows of the trees. A male lion emerged a minute later with his pride in tow. He assessed the scene before barreling toward the whimpering cub. While he licked the baby and examined the wound with his nose, the others in his pride ran to the mother's side. Upon seeing the bullet wound they roared into the sky. The ferocious sound filled the entire field.

The male lion stood over his cub, protecting it beneath his body, and roared so loud the ground rumbled. The magnitude of the lion's furious grief caused Xavier to tremble. The air remained eerily silent between the lion's bereaved howls that echoed through the sky.

"Should we kill the others?" Xavier whispered.

"No, there's too many now. We need to get out of here before they realize we are the culprits and hunt us down."

They walked back to the others and relayed the altercation. Xavier gloated as he bragged about his idea to use the animals as target practice and Sergei smiled at his son's savagery. The lions' thundering wails still echoed in the distance.

"We should relocate before they start their hunt for the killers," Dante advised.

"Let them come!" Sergei proclaimed. "I've been craving a good kill." His pent-up anger bubbled through.

"Think rationally, brother."

"You say they'll hunt us? Not if we hunt them first. We have guns, therefore we have the advantage. To kill such regal, malicious creatures for sport would be an enormous thrill. I've already got goose bumps from the thought." Sergei spoke like a young, enthusiastic child.

"So you'd rather stalk this herd of lions than follow the traitors to the Champion?" Dante rationalized with impatience. "You want to abandon the hunt for father's attacker?"

"Of course not, but we can do both," Sergei answered with his defenses raised. He was aware that his direction shifted with zeal often and without warning. "They are moving slow, why not have a little fun along the way? Xavier had the right idea when he saw the beast as target practice. While I doubt the Champion has any means to conquer us with our guns, it can't hurt to keep our skills up." No one argued.

They relocated to a different spot along the forest's edge, crossing the field on hands and knees so the tall grass hid them from the traitors, whose camp was in plain sight.

A chorus of mourning lions howled in grief. The sorrowful sound filled the men with a sense of triumph. Humans were the most powerful creatures on earth and the death of the majestic lion confirmed their authority. If they could conquer a wild beast, they could certainly conquer the female who claimed she was a Champion.

Chapter 39

Coast of Macapá, State of Amapá, Brazil

Juniper was dragged through her mind to a scene of gruesome murder. To her left was a dead lioness—a bullet between her eyes marked the spot of her barbaric demise. Beneath her was a lion cub convulsing in pain. She stood above the cub and roared a desperate cry of grief. Her howls were continuous and the heartbreak she felt was overwhelming. When she was given a moment to breathe between sobs, she saw that enormous paws replaced her feet.

She *was* the lion. Her heart ached so ferociously because she was witnessing this tragedy through the eyes of the cub's father.

::Who did this?:: she asked.

::Humans,:: The male lion replied. His solemn voice rang clear inside her mind.

::Not mine. They would never.::

::Others have arrived. They are hunting for sport. It won't be long before there is a trail of innocent carcasses in their wake.::

::I will take care of these invaders.::

::This was not part of the deal. Our treaty was to live off the land and only prey on the old and dying for meat. This promise has been broken. And though I will not take immediate action against you, I suspect animals with similar ranking to the lions won't be so kind. If this continues we will go back to our old and natural ways, and humans will return to their proper place in the food chain.::

::This wasn't me. It wasn't my people. Give me a chance to make it right.::

::You cannot bring my love back.::

::I am eternally sorry for that. I will enact retribution for your wife and son.::

::Yet she will still be dead.::

::I will not let you down.::

He paused, well aware that he could not survive without Juniper. She had yet to make their habitat and she was the only one able to do so.

::I strongly suggest you take care of this issue before these humans hunt and kill a species less patient than the lions.::

::I will. I promise.::

::I still believe in you, dear Champion.:: He looked down at his dying son and both their hearts swelled with anguish.

::Bring him to me,:: she insisted.

::You can help him?::

::I'm not sure, but I'd like to try.::

The lion breathed a sigh of relief and his sudden reemergence of hope filled Juniper with fear. She wasn't sure if there was anything she could do to help and she worried she was setting herself up for failure. Still, she focused on directing the lion pride to her location. A female lion picked up the cub with her mouth and placed him on the father's back with care. The lions were on their way to the coast and Juniper's abilities were about to be tested.

Juniper was doubled over in pain. The grief of an entire pride engulfed her senses and sent her to her knees. Tears poured from her eyes as her heart broke alongside theirs.

"Dad, it's happening again," five-year-old Landon said as his mother collapsed next to him. Fear filled his heart, but he placed his tiny hand on her back to offer comfort.

Roscoe raced over.

"What's wrong?" he demanded, but Juniper could barely breathe, let alone answer. She was crouched over with her forehead against the ground. Roscoe placed a gentle hand beneath her chin and lifted her head. Tears streaked her face and her eyes were a murky shade of vibrant green.

"She's left us," Jasper observed. "Those are the same eyes she had when the trees took her."

"Why is she crying?" Landon was frightened.

"She's never done that before," Jasper noted.

"Come back to me," Roscoe urged in a muted undertone. He did not want to scare his children.

Juniper mumbled incoherently, her eyes darting back and forth as she did so. A crowd was now gathered around her as Roscoe held her shaking body in his arms.

"This is a common occurrence?" Clark asked with alarm.

"Never like this. She said she could feel the plants dying on the other side of the continent, but those moments never took her away from us. Once, while we were sleeping, she was having a terrible nightmare and kept repeating the word 'mosquito'. I never asked her about that one because she gets very upset when she finds out that she frightened us with one of these spells. She can't control them."

"Well, you're going to have to tell her about this one," Clark expressed.

"I suspect she'll be very aware that this one occurred."

Irene stood next to her sister and mother with tears in her eyes. Jeb and Alice embraced and wore grave expressions of concern.

"It must be pretty bad," Aldon said, "Whatever she's seeing." He held his granddaughter Elodie in his arms.

Juniper gasped. Her eyes returned to their normal shade of green as she looked at the crowd that formed around her seizure-like disappearance.

"The lions are coming," she panted.

"In a bad way?" her Aunt Mallory asked.

"No, not in a bad way," Juniper explained with impatience, "it's more of a sad way. Humans have entered the jungle and are killing for sport. A lioness is dead and they are bringing an injured cub here to see if I can help heal it."

"Can you do something like that?" Clark asked in awe. He knew most of her abilities, but not this one.

"I'm not sure. I offered because I'm hoping I can do something to help."

"Bigger issue is, why are humans killing animals?" Roscoe stated with anger. "Who are they? Why are they here?"

"I am going to find out," Juniper answered. She did her best to control her temper, but could not hide her fury. "After we take care of the cub we will end this sudden spurt of human terror."

"Could it be the rebels?" Irene asked. Various heads within the group turned to her in confusion; only a select few knew about this threat.

"Rebels?" Russ Hazedelle asked.

"Yeah, the miscreants that murdered my Sofyla," Riad replied with anger. "They were hunting the Champions years ago and killed my love in the process. If they've returned to kill you, Juniper, I will gladly fight beside you to end their hunt for good."

"Whoa, whoa. No one ever told us we have enemies out there," Vance Hazedelle echoed his brother. "I thought we were more or less alone. Can someone please explain?"

"Other humans survived the purge. Buried beneath ash, hidden underground, etcetera," Roscoe divulged. "They weren't chosen by any Champion and their survival was luck. While we all could have united, they chose a route of hatred instead. Remember Phineas Devereaux?" Russ and Vance nodded. They recalled the pompous old man they met after they journeyed with Roscoe from Gold Bar to the Hall of Mosses. "Well, when he left with the others he found a group of survivors and spun our story to make us out to be devils. He convinced the others that we purposefully excluded them from our safe havens and that we wanted them to die out there alone. None of that is true. We barely had a handle on our own survival, let alone every single person in the world. We couldn't stop the purge, so we did the best we could. Anyway, the moment they found out who we were and what we stood for, they began to hunt for Champions. After Sofyla died we all lived in fear for a while, but the hunt went silent and we had to assume it ceased. We reached the Amazon and haven't heard a peep from the rebels since."

"Until now," Jeb said with disappointment.

"Possibly." Juniper hoped this suspicion was incorrect. She did not want to run anymore, she did not want to fight. They had lived so long in peace that this disruption of their harmony was devastating. She thought the battle was over, that the rebels had forgotten, lost interest, or could not pursue due to their own quest to survive. "Let's worry about the lions for now. The incident happened far away, a solid month's walk from here, which means we have time before they get close."

"When will the lions get here? Won't it take them just as long?" Jeb asked.

"No, they are moving fast and we will meet them halfway. Wolfe and Hazedelle brothers, please go charge the vehicles. We're taking them out."

"They should be fully charged," Dedrik informed, "I'll go check."

The group ran out of fuel years ago, but Dedrik and Wes never stopped tinkering and found a way to get the dirt bikes and 4-wheelers to run without gasoline. The brothers spent countless weeks scavenging the ruined towns throughout South America for parts and eventually built a design that worked. They installed four 12V 50Ah batteries onto each of the off-road vehicles, hoping to transform the old fuel motors into electric, and after a year of struggling to do so they revisited the plan and realized they could only get it running via solar power with an electric motor. It took two years to find six Perm PMG-132 electric motors, but once they had them they were ready to try again. Each of the dirt bikes and quads were stripped down dramatically to make the new parts fit, which altered the frames drastically. They used jumper cables and a solar panel they stole from a mansion in Minas Gerais to charge the bikes. It took four years, but the Wolfe brothers succeeded. They made off-road bikes and quads that ran without fuel. These newly designed vehicles could only travel so far and so fast without needing a recharge, but the quick and clean mode of transportation helped tremendously.

While Juniper spent the past nine years building her family and developing her supernatural gifts from Gaia, the Wolfe brothers spent that time converting their beloved dirt bikes into nature-friendly machines they could ride without guilt and memorizing every inch of the jungle, just like they had done within Olympic National Park.

Dedrik and Noah unplugged the dirt bikes and quads, which were fully charged, and rolled them one by one to the path along the river. Between crafting trails and traveling the entire continent to find parts for their eco-friendly dirt bikes, the Wolfe brothers were far better at navigating the landscape than Juniper. One day she'd be best acquainted with every corner of the jungle, but for now she'd let them take the lead.

"Who's coming?" Dedrik asked.

"We've got three dirt bikes and two quads. Me, you, and Roscoe will ride the bikes. Clark should be on a quad. He and Roscoe are the best at dealing with injuries. Laurel can be on the other. Her serene presence might calm the lions."

Dedrik ran to tell his mother, who was back at camp helping prepare dinner.

Elodie started wailing, which was odd because she rarely cried. Juniper took her from Aldon and held her close.

"What's wrong, my love?" Juniper cooed as she gently swayed with her daughter.

Elodie was still too young to form full sentences, but she relayed what she wanted quite clearly through her melodic, incoherent babbling. They were connected and Juniper could feel her baby's desires as if they were her own.

"She wants to come," Juniper said with a furrowed brow. Roscoe returned her confusion with defiant resolve.

"Absolutely not. She's an infant!"

"I agree, of course." Elodie fussed and wailed in Juniper's embrace, "but she is adamant. She thinks she can help."

"That's insane."

Noah stepped in. "The main trail is wide enough for the Jeep all the way to the end of the river. She'd be safer that way, since the car has walls. I could drive it. I'll be really careful, I swear," he said earnestly. It was clear he wanted to tag along.

"Perfect," she agreed to Noah's offer.

"This is absurd." Roscoe shook his head.

"I'll go with Elodie," Aldon spoke up. "There are no car seats. I'll hold her and keep her safe."

"Fine, Dad." Roscoe was agitated but let them have their way.

"What about us?" Jasper protested on behalf of himself and his brother. "How come she gets to go and we don't? That's not fair!"

"Lord, have mercy." Roscoe was exasperated. "You'll ride in the back seat and you will not unbuckle your seatbelts. Not even when we're there. You do not leave the car under any circumstance. Understood?" The boys nodded, their adventurous grins spanned ear to ear.

Dedrik returned with Laurel and everyone waited for Noah to return with the Jeep. Once he did, they got the children into the car and prepared to leave.

"Think of this as an opportunity for them to see the world; to get a life experience that will help them grow," Juniper said to Roscoe as they mounted their bikes.

"I get it, I just don't like it." He fastened his helmet and sped off. Dedrik was close behind and took the lead a mile down the path. Juniper stayed third in line with Clark and Laurel close behind on the quads. The Jeep trailed at the back, keeping up while maintaining a safe distance.

The dirt bikes were much quieter than they used to be. The electric motors were hushed and produced a small puttering noise. They did not stink of fuel, which allowed Juniper to appreciate the fresh air as they charged forward. She took in the trees and the lively colors, grateful for everything nature gave her. Without the trees, she wouldn't have this life. She wouldn't have Roscoe or her children. She wouldn't have the family of survivors she cared for so deeply. Without the trees, she'd have nothing.

I can never repay you, she said to the trees. They did not always reply when she called to them, but today they were present.

<<And we, you. Our bond is stronger than ever. You are flourishing, as we always knew you would.>>

I try not to question it too much, but sometimes I wonder how I got so lucky.

<<Love,>> the trees replied. *<<Your love for us was unconditional. You are worthy of all you've been given. Never question that, Little Blossom.>>*

Tears filled Juniper's eyes. Her father was still with her. She let the hum of the trees disappear with the wind, but held tight to their confidence in her. She could bring plants to life through sheer willpower, so maybe if she dug deep enough she could save the baby lion too.

When nightfall arrived, Juniper checked in on the lions.

::Where are you?::

::At the start of the river. We had to take the long route to avoid the humans. There are many.::

::We are traveling toward you along the north shore of the river. I wanted to save you some distance and get to your baby faster. We are on motorbikes, so don't be alarmed.::

::Understood. We've taken a break to rehydrate, but plan to run through the night. We can rest once we reach you.::

::I suspect we'll cross paths tomorrow afternoon.::

::We will keep an eye out.::

Juniper let the connection go and refocused on the path ahead. It was dark and their only light came from the moon and the Jeep's headlights. When the dirt bikes were converted, a lot of their smaller functions broke: no headlamps or blinkers. It took too much battery power away from the motor, so those lines were cut so the bikes could ride longer.

Their shadows were long and enormous from the bright lights of the Jeep, making the night feel like a surreal dream. It was dark, but they were on a mission, and the mood was reminiscent of when they raced to the Hall of Mosses and narrowly survived the purge. It was strange that this sudden nostalgia was welcoming, considering they had almost died and it brought back memories of when she thought she lost Roscoe forever. But time passed and they endured those days with bravery. Though it took time for all the pieces to fall back into place, they came out on the other side, intact and alive. They survived, so the scary memory had transformed into a fond one.

They took a break around midnight to rest. Juniper and Roscoe dismounted and headed straight for the Jeep. When they opened the doors, everyone except Noah was fast asleep.

"Good company here, huh?" Roscoe teased.

"Yeah, a real lively bunch," Noah laughed.

Elodie was nuzzled against Aldon's chest and the boys were sprawled across the back seat, buckles still fastened but their bodies bent into strange positions in an attempt to get comfortable.

"I think we can take their seat belts off for a few hours," Juniper playfully jested at Roscoe, who rolled his eyes with a smile.

The group took a five-hour nap to reenergize. It wasn't enough, but it helped, and they continued their trek as dawn broke. The sunrise illuminated their path and the rays gave them an extra boost of energy.

They passed through the devastated city of Manaus, which was significantly more overgrown than when they stopped there to rest during their initial journey nine years ago. Trees sprouted through the rubble and a few animals had made their homes amongst the blossoming wreckage. A group of monkeys hung from branches overhead as they drove beneath. Elodie shrieked with laughter through the open passenger window when she caught sight of them, and Juniper heard her amusement over the low-rumbling engines. She looked over her shoulder and saw her daughter's tiny hands outstretched through the window. Though Elodie wiggled and tried to get more of herself into the open air, Aldon held on tight.

The small village of Airão was visible across the river when a chorus of roars filled the early evening air. The lions were nearby.

Juniper sped forward to find the adult lions standing around the cub.

::*We couldn't travel any further. His suffering was too severe,*:: the father lion informed her as she approached.

::*Let me take a look.*:: Juniper crouched next to the cub and examined the wound. A bullet was lodged between its shoulder and front leg. She placed a hand on the cub's forehead to peer into its mind, only to be engulfed by pure agonizing pain.

"He is suffering a great deal," she announced to the others, who were a safe distance from where she knelt surrounded by grown lions.

Grab the med kit from the Jeep, she telepathically instructed Roscoe. He obliged, but hesitated to approach. He could not speak to the animals, so the scene of distraught lions was far more intimidating from his perspective.

They won't hurt you, Juniper assured him.

He walked slowly toward his wife and the moment he knelt next to Juniper beside the lion cub, Elodie began wailing from the safety of the Jeep. Aldon exited the car with her in his arms, hoping it would soothe her, but the moment they were out of the car her tantrum got worse. She reached for her parents, so he took a few steps closer to the lions to give her a better view. Still, she cried as loud as her little lungs would allow.

::Let the child see,:: a female lion advised. *::One cannot grow without suffering. Better she see tragedy through a stranger's perspective before experiencing her own.::*

"You can come closer," Juniper called out to Aldon. Roscoe's face shifted to object, but he swallowed his words before they exited his mouth. The situation was sensitive and fighting right now wouldn't do any good.

Aldon took slow, careful steps toward the lions and didn't stop until he was inches from them. Elodie calmed a little once she could see all that was happening.

Roscoe tenderly touched the spot of the wound, feeling for the location of the lodged bullet. When he located the shrapnel, he pressed lightly upon the lump. The cub shrieked a soul-piercing cry, which caused the other lions to snarl in defense. Roscoe took a deep breath, terrified that one wrong move would turn him into dinner, then continued with an even lighter touch. The cub squirmed with a growl and snapped its baby teeth at its human doctor.

Roscoe immediately retracted his hands. "Will he bite me?"

"I'll hold his head down. Keep working," Juniper assured him.

As the cub continued to fidget, so did Elodie. She could not express what was bothering her, but her actions made it clear she wasn't happy trapped in Aldon's arms.

The boys exited the car without Noah noticing. Jasper ran to the nearest set of shrubbery and Landon snuck up behind his grandfather as he tussled with the infant. Five-year-old Landon stared up at his baby sister, who was wailing uncontrollably again, then down at his grandfather's leg. He let out a heavy sigh before biting the old man's ankle.

Aldon howled in pain, surprised by the sudden attack. He tried to shake the boy off, but Landon had a firm grip. He placed Elodie down so he could pry his grandson from his leg, and the moment he did, Elodie crawled faster than she ever had before toward the lion cub.

"Look what you've done!" Aldon shouted at Landon, who finally let go.

"She asked me to do it!" the boy swore.

By the time he lunged to grab the infant she was already inside the pack. Roscoe glared up at his father in anger, but did not yell for fear of upsetting the lions.

What are you doing here? Juniper demanded.

Elodie ignored her and crawled to the cub's side. She cuddled next to the baby lion, who was just her size, and wrapped her arm around its torso. Humans and lions alike paused in bewilderment as the little girl lovingly held the cub and whispered a melody into its ear. The baby lion started to breathe a little slower and the rapid rise and fall of his chest found a calmer rhythm. Elodie stroked the cub's fur as she soothed its pain through her hypnotic song.

Juniper glanced with wide eyes at Roscoe, who returned the sentiment. Neither had expected this. As Roscoe was about to get back to work, Jasper squeezed his way into the circle.

"Not you too," Roscoe groaned.

"Let the lion chew on this." He handed a thick set of clear roots, still covered in dirt, to his father.

Roscoe exhaled deeply, aware he had lost all control of the situation, and waved his son forward. Jasper placed the roots into the cub's mouth.

::Chew,:: Jasper commanded via thought and the cub obeyed.

"Any surprise contributions from you?" Roscoe shouted sarcastically over the lions to Landon.

"Nope. I did my job." Aldon shot his grandson a nasty look and Landon returned his gaze to the ground.

Roscoe resumed without further interference. The roots numbed the cub's physical pain and Elodie's song erased its fear. The combination helped Roscoe remove the bullet and stitch up the wound without distraction. The cub was calm, so the lions were calm, which let Roscoe relax.

As soon as he weaved the last stitch, Juniper moved in and placed her hand over the bloody wound. She began focusing on the feeling she got when growing plants. She harnessed her connection to the surrounding trees and tethered it to the lion through physical contact. The organic energy of the trees filtered through her and into the wound. She could feel nature's vitality spreading into the lion's flesh and healing the injury. When the hole beneath her hand was as full of life as it would allow, she opened her eyes and broke the connection.

Elodie let go of the cub and sat up. She took the roots from its mouth and patted the side of its face to coax it awake.

The cub looked around, confused, as the numbness of the roots and the magic of the song wore off. He turned to look at Elodie, who grinned with love at the cub's confused expression. The lion nuzzled its head under her chin in appreciation. He then stood up with wobbly care and looked to Juniper. He took slow steps in her direction, afraid that the wound would still hurt, but it didn't. The pain was gone; the injury was completely healed. The moment he realized he'd be okay, the cub hopped in a quick sprint toward Juniper and landed on her chest. He licked her face and snuggled against her as she laughed with relief. The tension amongst the group eased. The lions approached their healed cub with joy and the energy directed at Juniper was of great gratitude.

::*I'm sorry I couldn't save his mother,*:: Juniper expressed to the father lion.

::*You did more than enough—more than I ever dreamed you could. Thank you.*::

::*I will find these humans and stop them. I promise.*::

::*If there is anything we can do to help, let me know. We are on the same side; this fight belongs to all of us.*::

::*Thank you.*::

Though this mission was complete, Juniper had a long fight ahead of her. There was an evil presence that lurked in her jungle and she'd stop at nothing to save every living creature under her care.

Chapter 40

Colombia-Brazil Border

"This was the town of Mitú," Ian announced while studying his map. The area was destroyed and overgrown, and they could barely see the remnants of human civilization. "This is the Vaupés River, which leads right into the Amazon River."

"We need to act soon," Cole said in an urgent whisper. They spoke carefully in case one of Sergei's men was eavesdropping.

Ian nodded in agreement, but said nothing. They were purposefully moving much slower than they would have previously and Brett and Misty were far ahead by now. He hoped it was enough time and distance to warn Juniper of their approach in case their attempt to seize control failed.

"Tonight?" Hanke asked at a low volume.

Ian nodded again. The group set up camp, aware that they could not cross the border into Brazil until they disarmed the rebels. They currently had the upper hand; Sergei and his men were not aware that the group knew they were being followed and they used this fact to their advantage. They moved at a painful speed, which caused their pursuers to move slowly as well. They should have reached the Amazon River over a week ago, but they dawdled and had yet to cross the border into Brazil.

"Let's get a bonfire going," Cole instructed after the tents were in place. Once the younger folks were good and drunk, they'd get loud and the others could have a conversation without being overheard.

By midnight, the Böhme sisters were happy off gin and conversing loudly between bouts of laughter. Hanke usually prohibited his 14-year-old from partaking in the drunken jollity with her older sisters, but tonight he let it slide. They needed the raucous distraction and Emeline was the loudest and silliest of them all. Valerie and Cade Culver participated, making the conversation even rowdier. The youthful group acted unknowingly as a shield for the strategic meeting that took place amidst their merriment.

"We raid tonight," Ian explained to those who were part of the plan.

"They can't realize we are following the river," Luke continued. "If we stop them tonight, they'll never know where we are headed."

"I understand we plan to steal their weapons, but what then?" Hanke asked in his thick German accent. "How do we stop them? How do we guarantee they'll stop following us? Are we going to kill them?"

Ian hesitated. "If they will not listen to reason, then perhaps. But I am hoping they'll cower without their rifles as shields and that they will turn around without any bloodshed. Luke, Cole, and I already plan to track their journey back if they agree to that course of action. We are healthy and well enough to make this trek a second time."

The group agreed with this course of action. They retreated to their tents a half hour later while the rowdy crowd stayed up until 2 a.m. When they finally went to bed, Ian reemerged from his tent first. Though many had been in on the conversation, only a handful were part of the action.

Carine and Lara were on lookout, while Cole, Ian, Luke, Hanke, and Dave infiltrated. If Sergei and his men woke up and fought back, they had enough strong men to defend themselves.

They circled the perimeter of the area slowly until they found the rebel's camp. Lara located them first and relayed her finding to the others through traveling whispers. Eventually, everyone was informed and met her near the trees surrounding the old airport. The rebels were set up along the landing strip.

"They're not even trying to hide," Hanke said in confusion. "There are a million spots with dense forestry all around, yet they chose a strip of old concrete that is out in the open?"

"This is a hike from our camp," Lara countered. "They probably thought it was far enough away."

Everyone agreed. The men spread out and on Cole's signal, approached from all sides. The moon was a sliver and the darkness of the wee hours was the perfect concealment. Ian reached the Humvee first. The arsenal was organized and all the weapons were arranged neatly. Most were stored in duffel bags, which were easy enough to transport. Ian grabbed two and Luke grabbed the third.

"Why'd they bring so many?" Luke asked in a low voice. "They have enough to start a war."

Ian hushed him and moved to glance through the car window. Sergei slept on the back seat with a rifle across his chest. He then looked down at the others, who also slept with weapons in their arms.

"We have to disarm all of them," he instructed the others. They were huddled around him, assessing the daunting task.

"What if they wake?" Dave asked.

"Punch them hard in the face before they shout," Luke advised.

The group of men took a collective breath before dispersing amongst the sleeping rebels.

Ian walked toward Dante, who slept the furthest from the others. As he bent down to carefully maneuver the semi-automatic rifle from Dante's grip, a piercing whistle emanated from the shadows of the forest.

Dante's eyes shot open and without delay, tore his arm from his sleeping bag and placed a knife to Ian's throat. His reaction was so quick and prepared, it felt rehearsed.

Ian backed away to run, but Dante grabbed his shirt before he could get away. He yanked him in closer, causing the blade to press against his skin and draw blood.

"Did you try to kill my father?" Dante demanded in a seething whisper.

"What? Of course not," Ian insisted. The question was absurd and unexpected. "Is that why you followed us all this way?"

"You don't get to ask questions."

"Fight back! Disarm them," Ian called to his men. They outnumbered the rebels and could overpower them if they acted fast, but the moment he declared this order, another voice shouted from the forest.

"I wouldn't do that if I were you," Gino hissed as he walked out of the shadows and into the dim moonlight with his arm locked around Carine's neck. Ian looked around for Lara, but she was nowhere to be seen.

"One quick snap and she's dead," Gino threatened as he got closer.

The men stopped their attack, which gave the rebels time to regain their senses and encircle the traitors with guns raised.

Sergei exited the back of the Humvee.

"I'm disappointed," Sergei hissed. "I thought you'd lead us all the way to her without a fight."

"To who?" Cole spat back in question.

"The Champion, of course."

"That's not where we are heading."

"No use lying to me. I'm aware of all that's going on."

"Guess you'll never get what you were after," Luke spat. "We'll never show you the way."

Sergei flashed a wicked grin before lifting the radio from his belt.

"I need an update on your status," he demanded. A few moments later, a voice replied. He directed the speaker of the radio at Luke.

"We are pretty far into Brazil. There's no way to determine our exact location, but Misty and Brett are maintaining a steady course along the north shore of Rio Negro. According to my map, we'll be reaching the diocese of São Gabriel da Cachoeira soon."

Sergei smiled and brought the receiver back to his mouth.

"Thanks, Oliver." He clipped the radio back to his belt. "We don't need you to lead us anywhere because we are already following the two you sent ahead."

"Why can't you just leave us alone and let us live in peace?" Hanke asked.

"Besides the fact that you are traitors?"

"What makes us traitors?" Cole demanded. "Our departure? The fact that we chose to leave?"

"You and your brothers were part of my core team. You were part of secret meetings and know my confidential plans."

"If your intent was harmless, why would it matter what we know?"

"After I took you in, adopted you as my own, and trusted you with confidential information, you left my side without warning to join one of my sworn enemies. It is the definition of treason."

"We have no ill-intent toward you or your mission," Ian promised. "We only wanted to live a different kind of life."

"Not once did any of you express dissatisfaction with my plan. You are spineless cowards. You should have told me."

"If we had, what then? We saw how you broke down Phineas. We saw how you locked your father away in the house once he started protesting your plans."

"Don't you dare speak of my father, you rotten bastards," Sergei growled. "Which one of you tried to take his life?" The group remained quiet.

"Tell us!" Dante roared.

"We did not see Oskar before we left."

"Do not lie to me! You stole supplies and he caught you. You didn't want us on your trail so you attempted to kill him in order to silence him."

"None of that is true," Luke stated. "We left from the center of town and have collected supplies along the way."

"You've traveled a long way for a falsely accused murderer," Cole advised. "Perhaps you ought to be looking among your own."

"Do not twist your guilt onto my men," Sergei threatened. "I will not be swayed."

"I suspect we still have a long journey ahead of us." Xavier stepped out from the shadows and into the conversation. "In time, they will confess."

"And if not, they will die with the weight of their sins," Sergei proclaimed.

"You really think you're a god," Ian scoffed. "It's unbelievable."

"We will kill the lot of you when we reach the Champion and the weight of your sins will drag you to the pits of hell with your chosen devil. You wanted to live with her? I will grant you that wish and see to it that you reside in eternal damnation by her side."

"Delusional, I swear," Luke muttered. Vincent smacked the side of his head with his rifle, causing the corner of his eye to bleed.

"Get these men in ropes," Sergei ordered.

Gino, Vincent, and Benny used a combination of chains and ropes to tie the men together. They were connected to the back of the Humvee and marched behind the truck as the rebels moved forward to find the rest of the traitors. It was their shared hope that Lara had gotten away and warned the others in time.

They arrived at the camp to find tents abandoned and a bonfire that still glowed.

"Looks like you're too late," Luke sneered with satisfaction.

"It's odd that you sound relieved," Sergei replied with feigned confusion as he climbed into the driver seat of the Humvee. "Men, load up."

His soldiers obeyed while the traitors tied to the back bumper scrambled.

"Let's hope we catch them soon," Sergei shouted to the back of the truck. He wore a sneer as he pressed upon the gas pedal.

The traitors were yanked to the ground as the truck moved forward. The pace started slow, and the less they screamed, the faster Sergei drove. They were dragged across the fractured pavement of the old landing strip, ripping their clothes and drawing blood, then into the forest where roots, branches, and rocks caused further damage. They were tied so close to one another that their bodies collided as they were hauled forward at unkind speeds.

"You're a monster!" Carine shouted and the young men sitting in the back of the truck laughed.

Ian maneuvered so that Carine could ride his back and avoid being crushed between the various bodies that were double her size. She cried into the back of his shoulder as the torture carried on. There was nothing they could do to stop the pain, nothing they could do to minimize the damage caused to their bodies. All they could do was endure the journey until it stopped and hope they were strong enough to survive.

Chapter 41

Coast of Macapá, State of Amapá, Brazil

The lions disembarked to the area of the jungle they now called home and Juniper led her people back to the coast.

They moved a little slower than they had on the trip out and when they reached their camp, Roscoe filled the others in on what happened.

"It was a family effort," he explained, hoping to leave out the details—they were still keeping Elodie's talents a secret. "The lion is healed."

"A family effort?" Mallory asked with an eyebrow raised. She glanced at her grandniece in Aldon's arms. Everyone suspected there was more to the child than what Juniper and Roscoe disclosed.

"Jasper grew some roots with medicinal properties, Roscoe stitched up the lesion, and Juniper did some nature voodoo to heal the wound beneath," Roscoe explained.

"Another gift?" Irene asked Juniper with wonderment. "And to think you thought you'd received them all."

"Yes, it appears I was wrong," Juniper replied to her cousin. "Though, it's really just an extension of a gift I already had. I channeled the life force of the trees into the flesh wound and nature's energy healed the lion cub."

"Juniper, the resurrector," Wes remarked playfully. "Good to have you on our side, you know, in case we ever die."

"The lion wasn't dead," she corrected him. "If the wound had been fatal, I don't think I could've done anything to reverse the damage."

"Dang, I thought we were granted immortality through you," the young man sighed.

"No such luck," she laughed, but a twinge of guilt passed through her. No one except Roscoe knew of their eternal lives, and not enough time had passed for them to figure out that they weren't aging. While her people wished for such a gift, she had it and was unable to share her extra years with them. Though the unfairness caused her grief, she could rest a little easier knowing that her healing powers could help some of them live a little longer. There was no doubt that severe injuries would occur as time passed and she hoped her skills would prove useful during those times.

"Was it the rebels?" Jeb asked.

"I'm not sure yet," Juniper replied. "I plan to figure that out so we can take action. If they keep harming the animals, the animals will turn on us."

"Are they here for the animals or for you?" Alice added to her husband's line of questioning.

"We won't know until I investigate, which I plan to start now. I'll keep the group updated." She turned and left, and Roscoe continued answering their questions.

Rooney dodged between the legs of the group to follow Juniper to her quiet place. Once she found a place to kneel, the fox sat with alert posture beside her. He would keep her safe no matter the cost.

Juniper dug her fingers into the dirt and focused. She never traveled through the trees before, but this was the only way to determine the source of the mayhem without physically traveling to confront it. It was the safest and smartest way to determine her next course of action.

She connected to the large kapok tree to her left and slowly felt her way around its spirit until she was able to latch onto its sight and see the world as it did. She was thirty feet tall and could see for miles in every direction. Her body sat directly below her, hands in the soil and face turned toward the sky. Her mouth was agape and her eyes burned neon green. She looked to the east and saw that her family was a safe distance away. Roscoe approached, but no one else followed.

She returned her focus to the west, unsure how to jump from this tree to the next. She stalled, afraid it might not work.

<<*You are limitless. You have no body to constrain you. Believe that and the transfer will be simple.*>>

Juniper listened to the trees and tried to forget her body. Her existence was boundless, but it was hard to imagine herself without ends.

She concentrated harder.

She had no feet, she stretched beyond the ground. She had no skull, her head filled the canopy. She extended what would have been her arms and finally felt the expansiveness of her being. She grabbed hold of the tree she wished to jump into and while her focus held onto her desired location, her consciousness rocketed through the roots of the tree she was in and into the neighboring one. She made the jump and it took less than a second to complete. Adrenaline coursed through her as her sight refocused from a new angle.

She continued to tree jump, traveling miles in mere seconds. Each jump left her blind for a millisecond, which caused the journey to have a strobe effect on her vision, but once in place everything was visible again. There was a fog around her periphery and every tree felt distinct from the others, but she was able to command the sight of each.

Her human body remained connected to her through an internal tether—the further she traveled, the stronger the tug became. Though it felt like she was stretching a rubber band that might snap, she continued forward, very aware of the body she left behind.

She still had yet to see the rebels.

Juniper journeyed all the way to Manaus before pausing. The process of tree jumping wasn't tiring physically, but mentally, it was exhausting. When she tuned into the tug of her body, she could feel herself back inside it. Rooney's soft fur was pressed up against her right arm and Roscoe had his hand on her left cheek. She had to hurry so she could get back to them.

She jumped through the trees that lined the north shoreline of the Amazon River, hoping she'd see signs of human life.

A few miles past the diocese of São Gabriel da Cachoeira she heard voices. She took root in her current tree and zeroed in on the sound. Once the voices were pinpointed, she grasped onto their location and jumped to a tree that was closer. To her horror, she saw Brett and Misty. They were kissing under the shade of her tree.

Her heart raced. Could they be the culprits of such horror? She struggled to understand, struggled to believe her old friends could kill innocent creatures for sport. She had told them to find her here years ago and when they finally obliged, they brought death with them. Her mind reeled. Her heart filled with betrayal. She lost focus on her connection with the trees and her consciousness ricocheted back into her body. Her eyes closed then reopened with a gasp.

"Misty and Brett," she panted. Her body was weak from her absence.

"That's who you saw?" Roscoe asked in shock.

"Yes. They are in the jungle."

"Alone? This doesn't make sense."

"They were near the start of Rio Negro."

"Did they have guns?"

Juniper hesitated. She was so distraught to find her friends during her hunt for the lion killers that she didn't even look for proof that they were guilty.

"I can't recall."

"You have to go back. They might be in danger," Roscoe warned.

Juniper collapsed onto her hands at the thought of going back.

"What hurts?" he asked.

"Everything." Juniper embodied nature and all she could feel was the death and betrayal of mankind.

"If I hold your body while you go, would it help?"

"I don't think so. It's a strange type of tired. It's not human."

::You ought to go back if you can find the strength,:: Rooney advised. ::We will protect your body while you're gone.::

She caressed the head of her small furry friend.

With a sigh, she placed her hands back into the soil. She tried to remember the feeling of the last tree she was in so that she could travel directly there. It was short with a thick trunk that had holes throughout. Not particularly sturdy, but solid in its perseverance. Its branches were light and extended from the body seamlessly.

The more she recalled the feeling, the easier it was to transport there. She remembered the sight through this particular tree, which had a fuzzy, mint-green peripheral, and her consciousness was ripped from her body and carried there.

Misty and Brett still sat beneath her, happy and unaware that she watched them. She searched for their guns but found none.

They weren't the culprits.

She listened beyond them and heard additional voices in the distance. She jumped from tree to tree until she found the source. It was a set of twins who were young, muscular, and armed with rifles. One sharpened a knife with another knife while the other spoke to someone over his walkie-talkie.

"Sergei," the boy addressed his commander. "We've got eyes on them."

"Keep up the good work, Dennis," Sergei replied. "We've got the other traitors in captivity."

"Should we capture these two?"

"No. They must not know you are following them. They are our guides to the Champion."

Juniper recoiled within herself at these words—the rebels were still hunting her. After all this time and false sense of safety, she realized her head remained their ultimate prize. She had heard enough. She let the pull of her body take her home.

"You were right, it wasn't them," she gasped as her soul refilled her body. "But they led the rebels to us."

"On purpose?" Roscoe said in disbelief.

"I don't think so. Seems they don't realize they are being followed. I found the rebels tailing them and overheard a radio conversation with others who were further behind. They said they imprisoned the other 'traitors'."

"Why were Misty and Brett ahead of the others?"

"I don't know, but if they aren't warned they'll lead them right to us. The rebels are here for me," she said, her voice low.

"We won't let them hurt you," Roscoe swore. "They're on our turf. *We* have the upper hand."

"They have guns," she reminded him.

"And we have you, which means nature is on our side. You are more powerful than you know."

"If we can keep them far away I can keep us safe, but I cannot beat their guns once they are in range."

"Then we keep them at bay."

::*Can you warn the animals?*:: Juniper asked Rooney.

::*Of course. Perhaps we can find a way for the animals to assist.*::

::*Once I know our plan I'll see if there is anything they can do. For now, tell all the animals to keep their distance. I do not want to provide these humans with living targets again.*::

::*As you wish, dear Champion.*:: Rooney ran off to begin his mission. He started with the birds who then carried the message overhead, singing the warning for all creatures to hear.

Juniper listened to the beautiful song of dire precaution. Its melodic eeriness echoed through the sky. The mood of the jungle shifted on a widespread scale and she sensed the heightened awareness of the other animals when they heard it too. One of her responsibilities was protected the best she could; now she had to worry about the humans in her care.

Chapter 42

Coast of Macapá, State of Amapá, Brazil

"If we somehow warn Misty and Brett to stop their journey toward us, Sergei will kill them," Roscoe offered. A week had passed since Juniper learned what was going on and they'd been strategizing how to take action ever since.

"And if they knew they were being followed, I'm certain they'd surrender," Teek added. "They'd never put us in harm's way."

"Have you learned anything new during your trips?" Clark asked Juniper.

"No. I have yet to find the rebel leader, but I plan to go back this evening. We are running out of time." She had no clue what she'd do once she found them, but hoped she'd overhear something that would inspire her next move. "What I need all of you to do is finish the work on the bunkers. I want everyone hidden in case they reach us before I can stop them. I might not stand a chance against them and their weapons, but that doesn't mean the rest of you have to die too."

"I'd prefer an offensive strategy, one that doesn't involve hiding like cowards," Jeb objected.

"Yeah, you're sorely mistaken if you think any of us will let them take you without a fight," Roscoe scoffed at his wife.

"He's right," Irene agreed. "We've come too far and accomplished too much to give up now. I think we ought to finish the bunkers for the sake of the children, but there's no way I'm laying down and giving up. You're my blood; I ride to the end with you."

The outpour of love and loyalty was overwhelming. Juniper smiled with wet eyes as she let their commitment sink in. It reinvigorated her spirit and gave her the motivation she needed to end this fight before it ever reached them. She'd do all she could to prevent those she loved from facing death on her behalf.

"It's time I got to work," she said with a look of appreciation. She took Roscoe's hand and called for Rooney to follow as she went to her quiet spot in the jungle.

Fingers deep into the soil and eyes closed, Juniper zipped from tree to tree until she found Misty and Brett. They still appeared to be blissfully unaware of those who trailed them. She focused on the surrounding noise until she heard the voices of the twins. She let her consciousness soar through the trees to their location.

"Oliver, wake up," Dennis said, shaking his brother.

"What?" he groaned.

"They just broke into a jog again. We have to go."

Dennis rubbed his eyes, strapped his knapsack and rifle over his shoulders, and then followed his brother in an athletic sprint to catch up with Misty and Brett.

Juniper let them leave and tuned back into the sounds of the jungle. She heard bugs and birds, buzzing in riddles and chirping nonsensical songs. She listened past their discord and heard the low grumbling of an engine. Her heart raced with fury as she sped through the trees toward the sound. There, she saw what she'd been dreading most: a Humvee trudged through the trees, mowing down plants and leaving a diesel-soaked odor in its wake. Its fumes saturated the air and she felt the tree she was in shrivel beneath the toxins. It didn't last long and the tree returned to normal a few moments after the air cleared, but the damage was done. If one truck could affect a patch of trees so intensely, no wonder Gaia fought back—millions of fueled vehicles had surely crippled the earth.

The poisonous fumes temporarily blinded Juniper, leaving her paralyzed inside the tree until they passed. When she regained her senses and found the truck driving away, sight from this new angle was horrifying. People she had known during their time at the Hall of Mosses were chained to the back of the truck and forced to run to keep up. Carine was one of them. They were tied so close together, they continually collided, making the trek even more challenging. Carine crashed into her sister Lara, which caused them both to trip. They stumbled and fell to the ground, but the truck did not stop; it merely dragged them along. The others did their best to avoid stepping on the women, and a few even tried to help them get back onto their feet without losing their own footing, but it quickly turned into a disaster. Luke almost had Lara up when he lost control and fell, taking himself, Lara, and Cole down. From there, it was like dominos. Everyone began to fall and within seconds, the entire group was on the ground being dragged at rough speeds along the rocky and course jungle floor.

Juniper followed this atrocious sight through the trees, occasionally jumping into one still reeling from the fumes. As her stalking continued and her friends suffering grew worse, her anger grew to a tremble. Each tree she jumped into quivered beneath her presence. Olivia sobbed in agony and Cole did what he could to maneuver so that he took the brunt of his mother's pain. The louder their cries, the more the rebels laughed. The youngest of them hung out of the back window and wore a smile as he watched the suffering.

"Faster, Dad," the adolescent instructed the rebel leader who drove the truck. Sergei picked up the speed per his son's request and the teenager cackled with laughter as his victims writhed in agony. His demented joy set Juniper's fury aflame.

Her flittering soul took firm hold of the tree she was in and rocketed through its roots. The spindling appendages tore through the ground toward the truck. They ripped up the dirt and latched onto the undercarriage of the Humvee. The body of the truck lurched forward while the engine and gears remained in place. The frame of the Humvee launched fifty feet down the trail before coming to a stop. Utterly broken, the rebels exited the crashed frame of their Humvee, ranting and raving at the damage. Before they could grab their beloved duffle bags filled with grenades, ammunition, and additional firearms, Juniper sent vines down from the trees, snatching the bags by their handles and lifting them into the air to prevent the rebels from salvaging their destructive toys.

"You've got to be kidding," Dante groaned with exasperation.

"And look at how our truck broke," Gino hollered as he ran backward toward the scattered parts.

"Impossible," Vincent said, crouching down to assess the damage better. He tried to pry the roots from the engine but they would not budge.

"The Champion is in our midst," Sergei said in a furious whisper. "Guns out!" he demanded.

"Let's get those duffle bags down. We need what's inside them," Xavier insisted.

The men obeyed and stood in a circle beneath where the bags hung. They began shooting, hoping to break the vines and release their bags, but the more they fired, the higher Juniper lifted their belongings.

"This is unnatural," Vincent gasped after lowering his gun in surrender. "We need to accept this loss or we'll waste all our ammo."

"Damnit!" Sergei howled into the sky. "I've never wanted to kill a Champion more."

Xavier looked around, then up at the trees. He turned in a slow circle looking for something he'd never find. "If she's here, we ought to make her pay for what she's done."

He walked to the group of prisoners, still tied together and huddled behind the engine. They were bloody and bruised from the abuse, and unable to run due to the constraints.

"Which one do you love the most?" Xavier shouted into the sky, then walked around the group poking each prisoner with the tip of his rifle.

Juniper jumped until she was in a tree closer to her friends and held her breath, praying the teenager did not follow through with this threat.

"How about this one?" The end of his gun pressed against Emeline's cheek. She was the youngest person there and a solid guess by someone who knew nothing of the group's dynamics.

Juniper remained still, afraid any outside indicator triggered by her emotions would get the young girl killed.

Xavier waited, felt no sign from his invisible enemy, and continued his slow assessment. Carine's face was covered in tears and her breathing was heavy.

"You seem nervous," he said as he placed his rifle to her forehead. "Is it her?" he shouted.

Juniper tried to mask her fear, but failed. Her soul shook with distress for her dear friend and a single leaf detached from her top branch and twirled with grace to the ground. It landed on Carine's knee.

Carine's expression filled with terror.

Xavier smirked. "Guess so."

He pulled the trigger and fired a bullet through Carine's skull. Her blood showered everyone around her and the evening air filled with screams of horror and rage. Brynn sobbed in pain on the opposite side of the group; the bullet passed through Carine and landed in her shoulder.

The earth began to rumble as Juniper's rage emanated through all the surrounding trees. She was prepared to kill the lot of rebels when Sergei stepped forward with his men in tow.

They quickly encircled their prisoners, despite the sudden instability of the world around them, and pointed their rifles inward.

"I'd be careful, Champion," Sergei warned. "You may have the power to kill us all, here and now, but you'll be killing your friends too. The moment one of your branches comes for us we will pull our triggers and everyone will die. Consider that before you strike in haste."

Sorrow filled Juniper's soul and the quaking ground was replaced by falling leaves. They cascaded over the tense scene as a mournful surrender.

Sergei's boastful grin widened.

He instructed his men to keep guns aimed at the prisoners at all times as they marched forward. Juniper sped back to Roscoe and Rooney with grief.

Many miles into her trip back, she heard Brett and Misty. They spoke of their loved ones so she paused to listen, wondering if there was a way to warn them through the trees.

"I miss my brothers and parents," Misty confessed. It was the first time Juniper heard them talk about something other than their excitement and wonderment revolving around joining the life Juniper had created in the jungle.

"We will be reunited soon," he assured her.

"Do you think we will reach Juniper before Sergei and his men catch up?"

"Your brothers are crafty. I am certain they are doing a good job stalling."

"I just hope the raid works. Those assholes need to be stripped of their guns."

"We just have to have faith that they'll succeed. For now, all we can focus on is getting to Juniper with enough time to warn her and prepare a defense."

Juniper panicked, aware that though their intentions were good, they were doomed to fail. They did not realize Sergei already captured the others, or that the raid was unsuccessful. Juniper had tried to assist, but failed. Her impulsive attack got one of her best friends murdered and she was distraught with guilt as she rebounded back into her body.

Juniper became reanimated with a sob.

"They killed her because of me." Her weak body fell into Roscoe's embrace. Rooney nuzzled against her with concern.

"Who?"

"Carine," she wept. "They are savages."

"It's not your fault," he reassured her as he held her close. Roscoe and Rooney waited with patient love until the worst of her sorrow passed. Her tears made her stronger and the grief she felt morphed into determination.

<<*Juniper*,>> a human voice called through the trees.

Carine?

346

<<Yes. I chose the trees. They say I'll lose recollection of my humanity soon, but I had to let you know that I chose you. I always did and I always will.>>

I'm sorry they killed you to get to me.

<<Don't be. Use their hatred as fuel. I believe in you and so does everyone else. You can save them all.>>

A leaf swirled from a tree above and landed on Juniper's knee. A final farewell from Carine.

She picked up the leaf, placed it in her hair, and turned to Roscoe.

"I have to save the others."

She wiped her eyes and regained her composure. This was war, and for the sake of all those she loved, she was determined to win.

Chapter 43

Diocese of São Gabriel da Cachoeira, Brazil

Xavier felt no remorse; he was not frightened by what he had done. It was his first human kill, yet it stirred no emotion in his heart—only adrenaline and a desire for more.

The almost-kill of his grandfather was a stepping stone for this achievement, and though that kill was incomplete, it stirred up the correct questions and strength to bring Xavier to where he was today: calloused and ruthless.

The week passed with no sign of the Champion's return. Their prisoners were more beat up than before and adding injury upon injury as they progressed. They hadn't been fed in days and were only given small rations of water to keep them alive. Sergei would let them die soon, but for now they were the only thing keeping his men alive. It was also Sergei's desire to have these prisoners killed in front of the Champion. Making her watch as he killed her loved ones was the ultimate punishment. Prefacing her death with theirs would prove his ultimate point: the Champion and her friends were not more worthy of life than he; she was not chosen and nature would not save her again.

While the plan felt foolproof and Juniper would surely turn herself over to save those she loved, learning of her powerful abilities instilled fear among Sergei and his men. Though this fear manifested as intensified hatred, there was no denying that they faced a force much greater than they originally anticipated. She was not a fragile woman they could overtake; she was more than human. She had evolved into a supernatural being with powers no human should possess.

"Maybe it wasn't her," Vincent tried to rationalize. Ever since the purge he'd been trying to apply learned science to events that defied logic. "Maybe it was the same force of power that caused the purge."

"It was her," Xavier insisted. "Nature has no emotion; it isn't human. She revealed herself when I killed her friend."

"I just don't like the idea of any human having that level of power. She could destroy everything we've rebuilt without breaking a sweat."

"That is why we must get to her first," Sergei reminded him.

"What if she lives on through death," Benny asked, having thought of all the wild possibilities. "What if she lives on through the trees as a ghost?"

"This journey has opened my eyes," Sergei said in contemplation. "When we return we must intensify the rebuild of America. My empire will be that of metal and cement. I want every morsel of land covered in concrete. I want every tree dug up from the roots. There will not be one square inch through which she can enter our territory. This is how I will keep us safe from the devils in the sun."

His men nodded, seeing this as a solid solution to the possibility of the Champion following them home and haunting their existence.

They agreed to skip a night's rest to catch up with Dennis and Oliver. They fed the prisoners for the first time in days so that they wouldn't slow them down and marched through the night.

Many of the prisoners were weak and unable to stand. The strongest of the group trudged forward while the weak fell and were dragged by the large chained group. Sergei and his men did not help those who struggled. As long as their progress was not slowed too much, they did not care how their prisoners suffered.

They alternated nights between sleeping and marching onward. In four days' time they reached the devastated city of Manaus and were only five hours behind the twins.

With motivation to move a little faster, the rebels made it to their counterparts the following afternoon.

"We've been following the river all this time," Oliver relayed. "The Champion must be somewhere along its shores."

"But if she's not, we need Misty and Brett to lead us to her. We will let them stay a few paces ahead," Dante stated. The men made a campfire and began prepping dinner, which consisted of the usual canned beans. The evening was quiet outside the lively buzz of insects.

"Misty!" Ian shouted unexpectedly from where the prisoners sat piled on top of one another. It was the dead of night and his voice echoed. "Run!"

Benny marched over to their hostages and slammed Ian across the face with the butt of his rifle.

"Next person to try that gets shot."

By the following week they reached the remnants of Monte Alegre. The town was overrun by forestry like all the others they passed through. Decorating the lush green jungle that swallowed the town were countless skeletons. They hung from the branches and remained trapped under tree roots. Similar sights spanned their entire trip through South America. There was no ash to smother the victims, but the aftermath from the attack of the trees and water remained visible. The purge occurred almost ten years ago, but every town they passed through still held remnants of the massacre. It fueled Sergei and his men; it reminded them why they were here and what they fought for: redemption for those who were lost and vengeance against the Champions.

"When we reach her, let me kill her," Sergei demanded. The more his thoughts roamed, the angrier he got. "I plan to make it slow."

The men grunted in understanding. They were exhausted. They'd been walking for months and though they found time to rest, the journey took its toll. They had traversed through countless states, countries, and into an entirely different continent. The magnitude of the distance covered began to sink in as they got closer to the coast.

"Has anyone thought of the journey back?" Xavier asked, pointing out a glaring reality none had the courage to chew on before.

Gino and Benny groaned simultaneously.

"Thanks for the reminder," Vincent retorted.

"I just hadn't thought much of it until now. And we don't have the truck."

"Focus on the task at hand," Sergei commanded. "The trip back might be grueling, but there's no point in dwelling on that while we are on the brink of reaching what we came here for."

The younger men grew quiet, but no one lost the dreaded feeling of the return trip.

Dennis and Oliver walked behind the slow moving group of prisoners with guns raised, and Benny and Gino did the same on both sides of the group. Sergei, Dante, and Xavier walked in front of the prisoners, rifles strapped around their backs, and Vincent led the group, ready to fire at the first sign of trouble. They hadn't seen Brett or Misty in a few hours, but there was only one visible path, so it was safe to assume it was the same one they had followed. The river moved with explosive currents to their right and the trees were so thick to their left it would be unwise to venture that way.

"Run ahead to check on the traitors," Sergei instructed Vincent. The young man nodded and darted ahead, losing his slow-moving group in seconds.

He returned fifteen minutes later, out of breath and panicked.

"We lost them," he panted.

"How?" Sergei shouted with a growl.

"They should've been about a five-minute jog ahead of us. They weren't, so I ran further. No sight of them anywhere."

"Could they have been running this whole time?" Dante speculated.

Before anyone could answer, a set of vines slithered with speed from the treetops and snatched Xavier by the neck. The teenage boy hung 15-feet in the air by his neck. His feet kicked futility as his oxygen ran thin.

Sergei and his men were in shock, unable to pick a course of action fast enough to prevent the ambush that came next.

With their stunned attention to the sky, Roscoe and his people infiltrated from all sides and disarmed the rebels while they were distracted.

Dedrik, Wes, and Roscoe tackled and disarmed Dante. The moment Dedrik and Roscoe had him restrained, Wes charged Sergei. The rebel leader was the last to be attacked and was able to catch on to the situation in time to react. He fired at Wes, clipping his left arm, and Sergei remained armed and free.

He turned his gun to the sky and fired his automatic repeatedly above Xavier's head until the vine-made noose broke. Everyone watched with quiet anticipation, unable to risk abandoning the rebels they constrained.

This fight came down to Juniper—it was her against Sergei.

The vine eventually snapped and Xavier fell to the ground in a heap.

The vines then zeroed in on Sergei, who kept his semi-automatic raised and blazing. Despite the unrelenting assault, the vines managed to snatch the gun out of his hands and break it in two. Within moments, Sergei was snatched by the neck and had taken his son's place in the vine-made noose.

Xavier rolled over, lying on the rifle still strapped to his back, to see his father suffering his former fate.

"Let him go!" he pleaded. The emotion he kept at bay for so many years flooded to the surface. He felt like he was eight-years-old again, fearful and on the brink of tears.

Make him take the oath, Juniper instructed Roscoe telepathically. She could feel Sergei's skin ripping and bleeding beneath the grip of her vines.

"We do not wish to kill any of you," Roscoe assured Xavier. "Human life is too precious and scarce to sacrifice. But you must promise to leave this place and never return."

"I promise," Xavier stammered. "We all promise."

Juniper sensed the urgency in the boy's voice and lowered Sergei to the ground. As the vines loosened from his neck, he gasped for air.

Relieved, Xavier's momentary bout of weakness faded and his anger returned. He bowed with a sweeping motion, grabbed the knife he kept in his boot, and charged at Roscoe, who held his uncle in captivity. The blade plunged into Roscoe's stomach and blood poured out the moment it was removed. Roscoe fell to the ground and Xavier turned his focus to Dedrik who had a gun pointed at Dante's head.

"Don't take another step," Dedrik warned. Before Xavier could decide if it was worth the risk, the vines returned and yanked Sergei back into the air by his neck. The motion was so quick it snapped his neck in the process. The crack was loud and final.

"No!" Xavier screamed, maneuvering his gun from his back so he could fire at the treetops.

As his bullets showered the trees, Juniper sent the vines down in droves. They swept the area, grabbing any rebel they could. Dante was lifted into the sky, but was able to saw himself free using the switchblade in his pocket.

When he landed back on his feet, he darted toward Xavier to stop the gunfire.

"You'll kill us all!" he shouted, smacking the gun to the ground. Dante dragged his nephew away from Juniper's inexorable fury and addressed those he could see.

"Please make her stop," he pleaded with the tree people who still held his men captive. "Let them go and we will leave and never return. I swear on my life."

"You're fate isn't up to us, it's up to her," Noah said, pointing at the vines that slithered toward them. "And considering you might've just murdered her husband, I suggest you run."

He let Benny go and the others followed his lead, releasing their prisoners.

Gino, Benny, Vincent, and Oliver needed no further convincing. They bolted away from the scene without hesitation.

"She killed my dad!" Xavier hollered at the fleeing Palladon brothers. The veins in his forehead bulged.

"You want her to kill the rest of us too?" Dante demanded, aware that they were running out of time. "Help me," he instructed Dennis, who stayed behind to assist.

The men grabbed Xavier by his shoulders and sprinted, dragging him behind.

"You will regret this day!" Xavier raged, his voice cracked beneath his fury. He continued shouting threats at the sky until his throat went raw.

No one chased after them, and eventually they could no longer hear his screaming.

Misty ran to the prisoners and released them from their constraints. She buried herself in a group hug with her parents and brothers.

Clark raced to Roscoe's side.

Not again, Juniper whimpered to Roscoe telepathically.

I'm not healing, Roscoe stated with confusion.

"It's deep," Clark announced as the others hovered over them. "He's in and out of consciousness, but breathing. Can't you do what you did with the lion?" he asked toward the sky.

Juniper could hear them, but could not reply.

I need to be there with you, she told Roscoe.

He was too weak to reply.

"The wound isn't fatal, but the blood loss will be," Clark determined.

"When she healed the lion, she was touching the wound," Aldon said, trying to hide the fear he felt for his son. "Should we carry him back to camp?"

"That's too far," Wes objected. "It's a three-day walk from here. He will die of blood loss by then."

"It's better than doing nothing," Noah countered.

Before they could continue their argument, Juniper intervened.

Though her mind resided in one tree, her grief filled the entire forest. The vines that were previously used to chase their enemies away now descended upon Roscoe with gentle care. Her friends took a step back as the vines cradled Roscoe's body and lifted him twenty feet into the air. Juniper's branched tentacles wrapped around him until he was safely inside her liana cocoon.

Sight of his body encased by vines let the others know that Juniper was taking care of the situation and there was nothing more they could do. They disembarked, leaving Juniper alone with Roscoe.

She wasn't sure how to help him, wasn't sure if she could. She could feel his aura fading, which meant his soul was fading too. His gift of eternal life was working, but not fast enough. The healing couldn't keep up with the blood loss. If she did not step in to save him, he would die.

Unsure how to proceed, she focused the bulk of her energy into a single vine and let its tip enter the lesion. She poured her energy into the wound, channeling strength from the entire forest and streaming it into him through the vine.

He gave no response.

Her heartbeat quickened as she lost control. Her body tugged at her to return, but her heart insisted she stay. If she left, he'd never survive; she could not get to this location in the forest fast enough to heal him before he bled out. The only way was to remain with him through the trees.

She tried again. She would leave her aching body vacant for as long as it took to save him. She would not abandon him here.

The energy of the jungle filtered through her and into him. Still, no response, but the blood began to spill a little slower. It was working, so she channeled another surge. Each rush of energy that passed through her was significant and took a toll on her spirit, but if it was helping him she'd continue, even it killed her.

The pull from her vacant body grew more intense with each bout of energy she expelled into Roscoe. It needed her to return. Though she hadn't pushed the limits this far before, she suspected her body could die without the strength of her soul inside, especially when she was tasking it to carry so much without her there to hold the weight.

Another rush of energy transported through her and all control was lost. She was torn from Roscoe's side and dragged back into her body. She screamed in defiance throughout the entire, blurry trip back, but she could not regain a grip on any of the trees she passed. The wrenching connection to her human body was too strong. The journey only took a few seconds, but those few seconds felt like a lifetime. Roscoe was gone. Out of sight and out of reach.

She wasn't strong enough to hold on, wasn't strong enough to save him. When she reentered her body, she immediately heaved and dispelled all she had eaten that day. The others weren't back yet, but Irene and Laurel sat by her side, waiting for her to finish so they could ask about the attack.

They were so shocked by the state of her reemergence that they kept their questions to themselves. They held her hair and rubbed her back while she vomited. When there was nothing left for her to expel, they tried to ask how it went but she could not tell them. She had to fix her error.

She was too weak to enter the trees again, so she stood to run, but the moment she tried, she collapsed to the ground.

"What on earth," Irene gasped at the sight of her extremely frail and sick cousin crawling in an attempt to run after all she just endured.

"I'll get the Jeep," Laurel insisted.

Mind over matter, Juniper mustered the energy to stay on her feet and began the painful walk toward Roscoe's vined cocoon.

Rooney darted through the trees and trotted beside her.

Juniper thought of how crippled she'd be without Roscoe, she thought of her children and how they needed their father. The entire group depended on *her*, but she depended on *him*. He kept her sane. He was her home. He was the foundation her life was built upon. Without him, her world and that of those she cared for would crumble.

::What are we after?:: the red fox asked.
::Everything I love.::

Thank you for reading *Field of Ashes* – I hope you enjoyed the story! If you have a moment, please consider leaving a review on Amazon. All feedback is very helpful and greatly appreciated!

Amazon Author Account:
www.amazon.com/author/nicolineevans

Instagram:
www.instagram.com/nicolinenovels

Facebook:
www.facebook.com/nicolinenovels

Twitter:
www.twitter.com/nicolinenovels

Goodreads:
www.goodreads.com/author/show/7814308.Nicoline_Evans

To learn more about my other novels, please visit my official author website:
www.nicolineevans.com

Made in the USA
Middletown, DE
30 October 2021